Other Books in The Vintage Library
of Contemporary World Literature

SOUR SWEET

SOUR SWEET

TIMOTHY MO

AVENTURA

The Vintage Library of Contemporary World Literature

VINTAGE BOOKS   A DIVISION OF RANDOM HOUSE   NEW YORK

An Aventura Original, March 1985
Copyright © 1985 by Timothy Mo
First American Edition
Library of Congress Cataloging in Publication Data
Mo, Timothy.
Sour sweet.
(Aventura)
Reprint. Originally published: London:
Sphere Books, 1982.
I. Title.
PR6063.017S6 1985   823'.914   84-40702
ISBN 0-394-73680-X
Manufactured in the United States of America

SOUR SWEET

ONE

The Chens had been living in the UK for four years, which was long enough to have lost their place in the society from which they had emigrated but not long enough to feel comfortable in the new. They were no longer missed; Lily had no living relatives anyway, apart from her sister Mui, and Chen had lost his claim to clan land in his ancestral village. He was remembered there in the shape of the money order he remitted to his father every month, and would truly have been remembered only if that order had failed to arrive.

But in the UK, land of promise, Chen was still an interloper. He regarded himself as such. True, he paid reasonable rent to Brent Council for warm and comfortable accommodation, quarters which were positively palatial compared to those which his wife Lily had known in Hong Kong. That English people had competed for the flat which he now occupied made Chen feel more rather than less of a foreigner; it made him feel like a gatecrasher who had stayed too long and been identified. He had no tangible reason to feel like this. No one had yet assaulted, insulted, so much as looked twice at him. But Chen knew, felt it in his bones, could sense it between his shoulder-blades as he walked past emptying public houses on his day off; in the shrinking of his scalp as he heard bottles rolling in the gutter; in a descending silence at a dark bus stop and its subsequent lifting; in an unspoken complicity between himself and others like him, not necessarily of his race. A huge West Indian bus conductor regularly undercharged him on his morning journey to work. He knew because the English one charged him threepence more. Chen was sure the black man's mistake was deliberate. He put the threepences for luck in an outgrown sock of his little son, Man Kee. Chen was not an especially superstitious man but there were times, he felt, when you needed all the luck you could lay your hands on.

Chen's week had a certain stark simplicity about it. He had once worked out the fractions on the back of his order-pad, dividing the hours of the week like a cake. He worked seventy-two hours at his restaurant, slept fifty-six, spent forty hours with his wife and child (more like thirty-two minus travelling time, and, of course, Man Kee was often asleep when he was awake). This was on a rotation of six days a week at the restaurant with one off (Thursday). That day was spent in recuperation on his back on the sofa, generally with open eyes, for his feet ached after the hours of standing. It was hard and the money came at a cost but he wasn't complaining: the wages were spectacularly good, even forgetting the tips.

Lily Chen always prepared an 'evening' snack for her husband to consume on his return at 1.15 a.m. This was not strictly necessary since Chen enjoyed at the unusually late hour of 11.45 p.m. what the boss boasted was the best employees' dinner in any restaurant. They sat, waiters, boss, boss's mother too, at a round table and ate soup, a huge fish, vegetables, shredded pork, and a tureen of steaming rice. Lily still went ahead and prepared broth, golden-yellow with floating oily rings, and put it before her husband when he returned. She felt she would have been failing in her wifely duties otherwise. Dutifully, Chen drank the soup he raised to his mouth in the patterned porcelain spoon while Lily watched him closely from the sofa. It was far too rich for him. Lily had the gas fire burning five minutes before her husband's footfall on the stone stairs and Chen would be perspiring heavily by the time he finished, abandoning the spoon and applying the bowl to his lips to drink the last awkward inches, the beads of moisture on his forehead as salty as the broth. He fancied they fell in and over-seasoned the last of the soup. Four years ago, at the beginning of their marriage, Chen had tried leaving just the last spoonful but Lily's reproachful eyes were intolerable. She was merciless now, watching him with sidelong glances from the sofa, her knees pressed closely together while she paired the baby's socks from the plastic basket on the floor. 'Did you enjoy that, Husband? Was it nice?' she would enquire brightly. Chen would grunt in his stolid way, not wishing to hurt her feelings but also careful not to let himself in for a bigger bowl in the future.

Although uncomfortably full, hot too, Chen would have liked a biscuit but Lily was unrelenting here as well. Sweet after salty was dangerous for the system, so she had been taught; it could upset the whole balance of the dualistic or female and male principles, *yin* and *yang*. Lily was full of annoying but incontrovertible pieces of lore like this which she had picked up from her father who had been a part-time bone-setter and Chinese boxer. For four years, therefore, Chen had been going to bed tortured with the last extremities of thirst but with his dualistic male and female principles in harmony. This was

2

more than could be said for Lily, Chen often thought, who concealed a steely will behind her demure exterior.

They had been living in the flat for three and a half years now. Before this they had lived in a room above the tiny restaurant Chen worked at in Liverpool. He got the job in London two months after they married. During their time in NW9 they had not added a single item of furniture (bar a gigantic television) to the stock purchased from the previous tenant: carpets and curtains in combinations of purple and orange, a hissing black plastic sofa and an armchair, siege perilous in which only Chen was allowed to sit. There were two bedrooms. In one of them slept Lily's older sister, Mui. Man Kee, their twenty-nine-month-old son, had his cot in the hallway.

Man Kee had a large, lop-sided head, amply covered with a soft black down. The size of his head was a favourite topic of his father's who, much to Lily's irritation, never lost an opportunity to point it out to visitors. 'As big as a football or water-melon,' he would exaggerate with a father's licence, prompting Lily to say crossly 'Bad talk!' and scoop her son up to kiss his sweet-smelling hair. He still spent many of his waking hours in a kind of moveable stockade on wheels which bolstered his strangely unsteady steps. He had been very late walking – eighteen months – and even now had frequent falls. Lily hoped he would soon grow out of this (only temporary) phase. She also fervently hoped he would stop dropping those periodic and dauntingly large packets in his pants. Against such eventualities his breeches were slashed at the rear – more, it had to be admitted, for convenience these days, although the intermittent emergencies were far from over. She *was* worried about his unsteady walking (surely her dear son wasn't, wasn't ... she didn't even like to use the words which might be unlucky, even the euphemism 'retarded'). But there was a light of intelligence in his eyes which, even though he didn't speak, much reassured her when she saw it. To exercise his feet, though, she made sure he wore no shoes in the house (Jumping Jacks for outside, no expense spared). Indoors he was provided with several pairs of striped red and white socks, the wool from which had a tendency to sabotage the plasticine balls which were his favourite toy. He was abominably spoiled by his aunt, a nervous young woman who had not left the house more than a dozen times – and then only to go across the road – since her arrival twenty-two months ago.

Lily did all the shopping at the big supermarket in Burnt Oak, more rarely going to the emporiums in Chinese Street in Central London. On these infrequent trips she never looked into the window of the big restaurant where Chen worked, nor did she consider asking him to bring the shopping home himself.

Her husband gave Lily £10 a week for housekeeping, in cash, from his total pay in hand of six £5 notes, on which the boss had paid a fraction of the tax due. Not bad for the early 1960s. Lily could have had more, and Chen sometimes offered, but though Lily always accepted, she never herself asked for the extra. Of the remaining £20, £2 went on clothing and gas, Chen kept £2 for his own amusements, paid £6 rent and remitted £10 to his parents.

What Chen didn't suspect was that Lily only spent around £6 of the housekeeping. She and Mui ate a frugal lunch of cabbage, rice, and a two-egg omelette, occasionally enlivened with four or five shrimps which Lily tossed in just after she had smashed the entire eggs in a lightly oiled *wok*. She then picked the fragments of shell out with large wooden chopsticks. After she removed the last sliver the omelette was ready. Shortly before Chen arrived home the girls might have a thick slice of bread each. Man Kee ate with his mother and aunt and fed well. His portions of chopped liver and fish were small but amounted to more than the total food bill of the two women. On Chen's day off Lily prepared something special at midday, duck or pork. Despite Chen's muffled exhortations, the girls only picked at the delicacies which he wolfed down from his upheld bowl, employing the chopsticks as levers rather than pincers.

By now Lily had saved £393 which she kept rolled in an old tea tin in her pantry. She had vague but strong plans as to the best way of using it, and had kept the existence of the fragrant hoard secret. As well as taking a sensuous pleasure in the growth of her savings, Lily liked the way the notes were impregnated with the odour of jasmine. Her own body was innocent of any perfume (apart from the rosy odour of the Camay soap she favoured) but she kept a spray-can of air-freshener in the kitchen to combat the sometimes powerful smells of Thursday's cooking. Once, in a moment of wild abandon, she had puffed some on to the underside of her wrist where her slow pulse throbbed and given herself a nasty rash.

She had been wearing a dab of 4711 cologne at the dance where she met Husband. This function had taken place in his home village of Tung San. It had been thrown for emigrant bachelors like himself in search of wives to take back to Europe. Lily was not a New Territories villager herself. She came from Kwangsi province, from a village by a major river town near the Kwangtung border. She was sitting on her own on a fold-up chair, away from where the girls of the neighbouring settlements were giggling together as they ate egg custard tarts and drank Coca-Cola and Green Spot from paper cups. Chen was then twenty-seven, an advanced age to have reached without acquiring a wife, not to say children, a fact which his father had strongly impressed on him. Old Mr Chen was a carpenter and lived in one of the small old houses at the back of the village, hard against the mountain, some way from the remittance-built concrete two-storey houses outside the old walls. The carpentry business had taken a down-turn in the early 1960s as rice production had shrivelled under competition from Thailand and, like other families in the village, Mother and Father Chen were now heavily dependent on their son's money from overseas. Whilst eager for more grandchildren, they couldn't help worrying that this would reduce the size of the allowance. When Chen took Lily home three days after the bachelors' dance his parents were pleased in a reserved way. The young couple had sat outside the hall and its loud music under the spinning lanterns hung in the village tree. The marriage took place three weeks later, a fortnight before the couple left for the UK.

Chen had thought Lily a sober kind of female, different from the talkative, excitable girls from the neighbouring villages. He thought she answered a certain stolidness in himself, later discovering her mercurial nature complemented his own bullish impassiveness. Lily wasn't a high-spirited character by any means but she was far from phlegmatic. Chen's female counterpart on the matchmaker's cosmic chart would have been listless and passive, which actually wouldn't have suited him at all. In any case marrying parentless Lily eliminated the need to pay bride-price.

Lily was twenty-three then. To marry Chen she had to break the contract she had made three years ago with the Tsuen Wan wig factory which employed her as a stitcher. Its salient clause prohibited her from marrying for the next five years. With the rest of the female work-force Lily lived in a barracks on the factory roof, as she had done previously in crocodile shoe, ornamental cigarette lighter, gramophone, and transistor radio factories. The dormitory was one hundred and thirty feet long and fifteen feet wide, accommodating a hundred and twenty workers in sixty bunk beds. She had gone to the dance where she met her future husband with five other factory girls. This had entailed breaking the works curfew of 9 p.m. In case they were stopped by the police, who would have returned them to the barracks, they had all clipped a ten dollar note to their identity cards. The factory wages were fair and the girls did not resent paying the police their tea-money. Certainly Lily earned more than she would have done as a servant in either a foreign or a Chinese household where the hours worked effectively amounted to a curfew anyway. The factory work was light in comparison with the unremitting demands a Chinese family would have put on a maid. Even after the supervisor had made his usual advances to Lily and received a blow on the ear that was stunningly forceful considering her sex and build, and he had given her coarser hair to work with, it was still quite tolerable.

All the same Lily did not trouble to give the management notice of her departure. She would simply have lost her job and the roof over her head at the same time, as had happened to other less astute girls in the past. She worked out her remaining time in the factory. On the day before departure she put her few things in a cardboard case and walked out of the building while the other girls were promenading on the roof. Escaping like this, she lost a little pay but it had to be accepted. Chen managed to get her on to his charter flight and they flew from Kai Tak on a Sunday. Chen buckled his wife's safety-belt for her, held his own clammy pad against her cool, dry palm during take-off and, whenever necessary, escorted her to the rear of the cabin, standing guard at the flimsy-looking door and eventually starting a large queue before the assembled eyes of which the Chens returned to their seats.

After the birth of their son, Lily had been unable to cope with all the housework. She allowed Chen to cable her sister Mui. Mui's full name was Moon Blossom, her younger sister's Moon Lily, 'Moon' to be repeated as a theme in the names of that female generation, had there been further issue. Mui was then working as a servant for a Cantonese-speaking English bachelor in government service. During her two years in this post she had acquired working English. In the light of this accomplishment Lily felt able to bring her over. Mui had small savings of her own; Lily sent her money from the tea-tin to make up the rest of the one-way ticket, telling her to say it was her own if Chen asked. Chen picked up Mui at the airport (recognising her from an old photograph), took her on the double-decker airport bus to Victoria, and they went by Underground to the flat. Mui had hardly left the house since then, behaviour which was beginning to disquiet not only Lily but her brother-in-law as well.

First the baby, then Mui, had temporarily dampened Lily's

superabundant energies. For some time now she had been trying to persuade Chen to start up his own business. Not to relinquish his job, necessarily, though that might be preferable. There was always the chance he could shoe-horn further hours into an already cramped working week. Lily was thinking in terms of a grocery store, specialising in tinned and dried delicacies, which she could run herself, although perhaps a take-away counter might be more sensible. It was for this that she was saving money. Stolid, unventuresome Husband had not been encouraging when she dropped little cues for him and finally blatant hints: 'I do so much cooking I ought to do it all the time!' – 'Who does business things better, Husband, Chinese man or Indian man?' She was not sure what she was going to throw her efforts behind but she did know there was money to be made somewhere: for Man Kee's education, for a motor-car, for a bigger television, maybe a colour set. Man Kee's own infancy was a necessary part in this building of an enhanced social existence, less the development of an individual than the settling in of a key brick in a planned and highly structured edifice. Discontent had begun to invade Lily's thoughts for the first time since she had been in England; for, perhaps, the first time in a life which had been spent for the most part since early childhood under circumstances of adversity and material hardship that might have crushed a lesser spirit. That had, judging by her irritating inertia, crushed Mui. Yet Lily had never once complained, surrendered, or felt a moment's twinge of self-pity.

Now, when at last luck seemed to be turning her way, with a kind (if uninspired) husband, a warm and comfortable home, help and companionship from Mui, and the various minor joys and tribulations of Man Kee's upbringing to fill her days, she wished to hazard all on what was nothing better than a gamble. The truth was that she was prepared to accept an existence for herself which she would not tolerate for Man Kee. Man Kee would have the opportunities from which she had been excluded herself because of her sex and ill-fortune. Rather than see him remain at her level she would risk all. This desperate resolve, an extreme measure from one trained to compromise in all things, small and large, was quietly adopted and nurtured undramatically. In her experience there was no stand-still in life. Families rose and fell. There was deadly rivalry between them. Their members were united against a hostile conspiring world. If one generation didn't climb, then the next declined, or the one after that; it wouldn't maintain the level. This was almost an axiom: look at her own life. She went to work on Chen with a seeming casualness which belied her determination.

Lily had been passed on from hospital to the practice of a Polish woman doctor in Mill Hill who provided her with means to 'plan' her family. Lily thought this a wonderful expression. Getting on the doctor's list was also a boon for Chen. Until then Lily had personally nursed him through several attacks of flu, almost willing him well again such was the intensity of her concern. As a supplement to this physical commitment to her husband's bedside, Lily concocted slimy herbal draughts for Chen, as vile-tasting as they were evil-smelling, which enveloped the whole flat in vapours that made the eyes smart and water. The formulas were improvised. Her father had given her the recipes. The trouble was the ingredients were not available in the UK, cornucopia of good things though the island was in respect of homelier merchandise. In a great improvising tradition, worthy of the host country, Lily stuck to the originals where she could and where this was not possible she included something she considered similar (i.e. carrot for rhinoceros horn). On the whole the effect of her spontaneous emendations and additions was to make her infusions seem more innocuous to the recipient, although the heavy grey-green suspensions of steaming, curdled liquid were still quite formidable to a reluctant Chen, eyeing them apprehensively from beneath the nylon bed-covers. Whether it was the draughts, fear of them, or the personal attention, Chen always recovered quickly.

Lily herself enjoyed good health; fortunately for both of them, she often thought. Until Man Kee had arrived neither had been to a doctor in their time in the UK. Some of the other restaurant employees went to a Cantonese-speaking Indian doctor in Southall if they were seriously ill. But Lily, even now, still felt it mildly disgraceful to take something for nothing. Chen was also puzzled by this business of registering and form-filling. He had once seen a medical card. The size of the number had been enough to intimidate him.

Lily had endured the pregnancy stoically, continuing to do her usual chores, climbing the stone staircase only a little more heavily with each passing month. On Sunday night she had still taken the dustbins down to the yard. Chen had offered his services but Lily turned him down. And so the neighbours had been regaled with the sight of a seven months pregnant woman dragging down the full grey bins one step at a time and scraping them up again, both distinctive sounds. Finally, a kindly neighbour had sent her married daughter, also expecting, and Lily had gone to the hospital with her. There had been no complications to the birth.

As Chen waited at the bus stop in the mid-morning he was conscious of accusing looks. Had he left the house earlier with other men going to work it wouldn't have been so bad; as it was he had to stand self-consciously in a line of women with shopping bags. Chen supposed the English wives stared at him because he was Chinese and he squinted obligingly at them while he shuffled his feet and waited for the bus. This staring no longer disconcerted, although he found the accusatory quality of the stares puzzling. There was a reassuring anonymity about his foreign-ness. Chen understood: a lot of Westerners looked the same to him too.

Lily had tried unsuccessfully to persuade Mui to go to the doctor. When she dosed her with her patent remedy, Mui swallowed the revolting mixture with an equanimity that was truly alarming. During her first week in the flat Mui had just sat in the kitchen with her back to the window and courtyard below. She was plumper than Lily with an ingenuous, round face that could easily deceive people into thinking her Lily's junior. It was joke of long standing between them and Lily would occasionally give the wrong tone when she said 'Ah Mui', which uttered in a different pitch meant 'Younger Sister'. Lily's energetic manner and Mui's natural diffidence helped give a wrong impression. But Mui's behaviour now went beyond anything before.

Only with difficulty would Lily persuade her to come to the sitting-room, when she deposited Mui on the sibilant black sofa and tried to draw her out. It wasn't easy to find out what was wrong with Mui. Mui herself didn't seem to know. She had worked for a foreigner before. Perhaps it was the concentration of them here she found so disturbing. Lily went to work on her gradually; took her to the window and pointed out the shops on the other side of the street. She had to propel Mui to the net drapes with a firm hand in the small of the back. From this point of vantage Mui clutched the curtains and peered round the edge in a fair approximation of the evasive behaviour of one threatened by a maniac sniper on the rooftops. Nevertheless, Lily persisted. She indicated the various premises on the shabby street: the Indian restaurant, the Hellenic provisions, the Jewish alterations tailor. Mui's reaction was not encouraging.

Television worked better. Suitable programmes began at six o'clock in the evening, starting with news (a long way from Lily's favourite programme). Mui watched avidly from the start. She developed preferences amongst the newscasters. There was a balding high-domed one with a flat, nasal voice she didn't like. Too much like her former master, she told Lily. Another's bushy eyebrows were 'eccentric', she said, using the pitchy Cantonese word. Her favourite was the jowly, snout-nosed one with the smudged, homely features of a Cantonese. Serials came an hour after the news. *Crossroads* (late afternoon broadcast) and *Coronation Street* were Mui's favourites. She watched with a fascinated interest that bordered on a special kind of horror. She was unable to catch more than a few scattered words of the dialogue, which was colloquial, compounded with regionalisms, and couched generally in a more demotic mode of the language than that which she had heard from her employer. The situations were universal enough, though, and not so far removed from the stock contexts of Cantonese drama as to be totally unintelligible; although the conventions could be very different. Mui was not able to retain the names of the leading characters but they were none the less real to her for that. She gave the characters names of her own devising; Boy, Hairnet, Drinker, Cripple, Crafty, Bad Girl. The composite picture she was able to glean of the British population was an alarming one. More than ever, Mui was reluctant to leave the flat.

It was a while before Lily realised her tactics were counterproductive. By now it was too late. By now Mui was an addict. She was even watching children's puppet-shows with Man Kee and giving every sign of enjoyment. She did not leave the sofa, with an appropriate faint sigh of compressed air escaping from the cushions as her weight was removed, until the last bars of the national anthem faded away into the high-pitched whine which denoted an end of transmissions. Even then she waited hopefully, as if it might be a temporary malfunction in the set or a ploy to weed out genuine enthusiasts from among the mass of viewers, for whose benefit broadcasting would resume at any moment. Barely controlling her irritation, Lily would have to switch the set off for Mui. Next morning Mui would be tuned in again to the schools programmes. It was a pernicious craving, Lily thought.

Perhaps the difference in the two sisters' characters was the product of upbringing rather than of any innate traits of the personality. Their father's attitude may have encouraged the growth of the aggressive side in Lily's character. If this was so, it was a sturdy shoot he nurtured. Four years Lily's senior, Mui had been brought up as a girl with the not unreasonable end in view that she should become a woman: uncomplaining, compliant, dutiful, considerate, unselfish, within her limits truthful and honourable; and, needless to say, utterly submissive to the slightest wishes of her superiors which included women older than herself and the entire male sex, including any brothers she might acquire in the future. This was the trouble. Their mother had not produced any sons, had died giving birth to her second daughter. Their father might have behaved in one of three ways. He could have had the girl-child smothered. He could have sold her and Mui to a brothel, which might have happened had he been not a less kind but a less wealthy man. Or he could pretend Lily was a boy, ignoring inconvenient and, in the nature of things, increasingly evident, physical indications to the contrary. He adopted the latter course, perhaps hoping that if he worked hard enough on his daughter in this life she might in her next incarnation enjoy the indescribable felicity of being a man. (He was a devout Buddhist.) So Lily had her hair cut short in a pudding bowl fringe and not only wore trousers (as did Mui and all other children on the Kwangsi-Kwangtung border then) but dressed in black as opposed to the floral stuff from which Mui's cotton suits were tailored. While Mui devoted herself to the study of flower arrangements, embroidery, and the arrangement of refreshments on lacquered trays, Lily was occupied with sterner pursuits.

At the age of five she began her instruction in Chinese boxing, under the tutelage of her father. He was a master in a notably severe system. No 'soft' or 'internal' style for Lily, with their passive, yielding techniques such as girls usually studied (there being nothing extraordinary about a female master, let alone a girl student). Lily was not to learn one of the suitable systems such as the eight-diagram palm, the supreme ultimate fist of *tai chi*, White Crane fighting, or the speedy, economical system invented by the Buddhist nun Yim Wing Chun in the late eighteenth century. Instead she was to be versed in all the pristine rigour and southern form of *siu lum* temple boxing. Her father, a stocky, shaven-skulled man with a bristling scalp that scratched Lily's cheeks whenever he bent to demonstrate a move to the child, was himself a student of the *Hung gar* style of *siu lum*, a hard-line sect which laid emphasis on brute power and savage gripping and gouging techniques. Her father made no concessions to his pupil. He had the child squatting in a low crouch for an hour at a time with legs apart as far as they could stretch, using two daggers stuck in the ground as markers. On her head he balanced a full earthenware wine-jar of the smaller type (a hard man, he was also a realist). At the same time he lightly rapped Lily's shins with a bamboo staff. Tears would be pouring down the girl's face half-way through her ordeal, her thigh muscles apparently on fire, the pain in her shins almost a welcome distraction from the major agony.

Training varied between hard days and light days. On light days Lily would be required to hold a pole at arm's length for an hour. Weapons-training, when her father swept at her legs with a tasselled blunt pole-axe which he had told her was sharp, was play by comparison. Lily's agility and timing were, as her father grudgingly conceded, excellent, better even than the best of nine-year-old Mui's friends; although, of course, in their games of keeping dyed-feather shuttlecocks in the air with their feet and jumping over a long rope of multi-coloured rubber bands they had considerably less incentive to keep the time of a human metronome than Lily, who regularly had nightmares involving amputated legs.

Failure had embittered her father. As a young man, he had been the best fighter in the province, the prize pupil of his *sifu*. The master had chosen him, rather than his own son, to carry on the *Hung gar* tradition in Kwangsi, had initiated him into the few tricks of combat that until now he had withheld from even his most favoured pupils – such as a short hook delivered with the right in a southpaw stance as opposed to the usual reverse punch, an ingenious combination leg strike and sweep, and a jamming kick to bridge distance.

Lily's father had never been the most stylish of practitioners. There were many flaws in his shadow-boxing sets which he executed mechanically and without an ounce of the panache of the other top pupils. But he was a redoubtable brawler: a powerful puncher who could also smash a man's shins or knee-caps with one low stamping kick. He could dislocate limbs, break a man's crown by smashing his own against it. Three years running he had been Two Provinces champion at the outlawed tournaments held outside Macao. In the last year he had rendered two opponents totally senseless for over fifteen minutes, and maimed a third. He hit the fourth and last with a rare, double-fisted technique simultaneously on each temple, causing blood to gush from the ears as well as the nostrils. Next year, to his great and ill-concealed chagrin, he was unopposed and had to content himself with a demonstration in which he uprooted a medium-sized tree, kicked a hole six inches above the ground through a mud wall, and in the culmination felled a diseased water buffalo with a single, crushing hammer-fisted blow on the skull. Shortly after, much to the relief of the tournament organiser who feared eventual murder proceedings, he left for Shantung, the coastal province in the North famed for its spicy food and tough boxers. Posing as a prospective student, he toured the various Northern schools; although his ignorance of dialect and the sneer on his face soon gave him away. The Shantung methods were

12

almost acrobatic, with their emphasis on speed and lightness and their reliance on kicking to the almost total exclusion of hand techniques other than for parrying counter-kicks. And what kicks! Not the stiff below-the-belt stamps of *Hung gar* but spinning, wheeling, pirouetting, flying attacks to the temple, neck, and ribs. More than ever, the southern visitor was convinced his power methods, based on his low horse-stance, would enable him to destroy the Northern gymnasts, even if he was giving height and weight away to the big men. He duly entered for the Province's major tournament. In the preliminary round he was matched with the grand champion of the previous year. What ensued – painful, humiliating, permanently shattering his confidence in his own abilites, for he did not think of blaming his limitations on the tradition he had been brought up in – was to haunt him for the rest of his life. Vainly he tried to cut his opponent off into the corners of the roped platform. He was out-manoeuvred, out-thought, out-reached, out-hit. His clawed hands grabbed at thin air; he was sent lurching against the ropes. His opponent's kicks thudded into his stomach, waist, kidneys, and thighs, and then began to crash against his head. Blood from his gashed eyebrows blinded him as the Shantung man darted in and out with his nimble attacks to the cheers and jeers of the partisan crowd. The Cantonese champion was strong and brave. He lasted the contracted distance but it was a fortnight before he had recovered sufficiently to start home.

He had always hoped to instruct a son to gain revenge for him, training the boy as soon as he began to walk. Surely such a son would be able to best the northern gadflies. But it was not to be. This bitterness, deepening over the years, made Lily's education more than usually arduous.

She performed her harder exercises in the privacy of the courtyard of their own house; weapons-instruction took place in the dusty space in front of the town's small dilapidated Taoist temple. While Mui and her friends watched from the shade of an old tree where there was a seller of sugar-cane, Lily played her two-pronged tiger-fork in the hot sun. (The last tiger in the district, wandering unwisely north from Thailand via Yunnan, had been tommy-gunned from a lorry in 1923 by a local bandit with aspirations to being a war-lord.) At these public showings Lily's father sometimes let her break thin-walled wine-jars with her head. He could sometimes be cajoled into giving a demonstration himself when he would shatter inch-and-a-half-thick vessels as big as a man with a single fearsome butt from his bristling head. There was always a small crowd gathered for this particular display of prowess. Afterwards the spectators would buy the boxer cup after cup of fiery rice wine which naturally had been emptied from the target vessel beforehand. Lily followed Mui home, trailing the prongs of her tiger-fork in the dust. She was charged with escorting Mui through the dark streets but once home the positions were reversed and Mui would help the amah put her to bed.

Lily's instruction continued until she reached the age of ten. She was spared no part of the initiation, however hard, apart from the progressive toughening and disfigurement of the hands, a tradition at the heart of the *Hung gar* style, involving in its stages callousing through plunging the fist into first sand, then loosely packed gravel, and finally charcoal before calcium deposits were built around two knuckles by hitting a plank wrapped in rough grasses. Lily's initiation stopped at the sand stage.

At ten she arrived at puberty. Her chest began to pout, her hips widened in proportion to her shoulders, and the end result of this structural rearranging of her body was that she no longer had the physique to punch, chop, or slash, although her kicking, balancing, and stretching abilities were enhanced. In disgust her father stopped teaching her. His decision was not brought about by any tardy recognition of his daughter's gender but by horror that her movements were becoming increasingly similar to those of the despised and feared northern stylists. As arbitrarily as it had begun, then, Lily's instruction terminated. Her hair grew, and she wore it tied into two pigtails in doubled-over red rubber bands. She fitted neatly into the flowered tunic suits Mui had worn two years ago. Even heavily handicapped, however, she was not allowed to join in the games of shuttlecock, hopscotch, and skipping.

By this time civil war was in its final stage. The girls' father had never been politically involved nor did he have a vested material interest in the *status quo* as a member of the landowning classes. But the communists were known to be hostile to men like himself. Many were retained as bodyguards or military instructors by high-ups in the Kuo Min Tang. Boxers had played a key part in the patriotic rising of 1900 but by the middle of the century they had been overtaken by an interpretation of history and were apparently no longer a progressive force. He joined the retinue of a prominent local landowner and three months later, while attacking fortified positions on high ground, was cut in half by shrapnel from a commandeered Japanese army pack-gun. Mui was fifteen then, Lily was almost eleven.

Soon after, the children put enough money together to take a ferry to

Canton and then Hong Kong. Their father's female cousin lived there. They had never seen this 'aunt'. They arrived to discover she had died during the Japanese Occupation. The money from the sale of their father's house never arrived. At this time there were no restrictions on immigration to the colony and the girls swelled a growing force of refugees from the mainland. Mui went into family service, keeping Lily with her for two years in the tiny amah's room. Then when she left to work for the Englishman, Lily went into the crocodile purse and shoe factory.

Lily's childhood initiation into the rigours of *siu lum* exercising had unlooked-for results in later life. Constant exercising and stretching had made her far taller but also slightly lighter and wirier than average for a Cantonese woman of her age. She also enjoyed good circulation and was rarely cold, even in damper and chiller zones than the south to which she had been bred; she had a supple pelvis and flexible limbs; a clear complexion, slept well, and gave birth to Man Kee without much pain. She was also an energetic, capable, and ingenious bed-companion for her husband: an initiator rather than the willing accomplice which was the most Chen had hoped for. He regarded the marital bed as less a point of communion than, from the female point of view, some kind of pneumatic degradation ground. Although the last of Lily's attributes – her physical boldness in this matter of the 'secret thing' – was not the direct legacy of childhood training in Chinese boxing (quite the opposite of the intended effects of that sublimating art of monks) it was the prime cause which made the rest of the well-kept machinery run. Chen, poor male, never suspected any of this. If Lily led it was by default and, even so, with such delicacy that Chen thought himself the dominator rather than the dominated. Towards Lily, later, Chen felt grateful, guilty, a little superior despite her odd accomplishments; proud of her in the way that a barbarian conqueror of a highly civilised people might draw an avuncular glow from the collective attainments of an apparently subjugated race, unaware all the time that the one who was being absorbed, subverted, changed, was himself. The pattern, in fact, of Chinese history repeated in microcosm. And, as there, the conqueror never knew it was he who was truly the conquered. Nor was it something Lily would admit to herself, at least not in rationalised form, although at the level of 'female intuition' she had an inkling, though it was severely repressed.

Chen was only a quarter of an inch taller than his wife and shorter when she dressed in shoes with slight heels. At home she wore flat Chinese slippers, thus physically exemplifying domestic inferiority. When they were out together Lily seemed more than the actual fraction taller, thanks to her long slim limbs and graceful carriage which contrasted to his disadvantage with Chen's stocky legs, long torso, and jerky strides; his wife floated beside him.

Chen had a pasty, bun-like face with squashed features which gave it a character it would otherwise have lacked. His skin was as smooth as a child's. Apart from some down on his cheeks near the ear he was free of facial hair; he had never shaved in his life. The only razor in the house, in fact, belonged to Lily. Since leaving his village and coming to the UK he had put on weight, particularly in the face, and there had formed under his cheeks and around the jowls a thin film of subcutaneous fat which while it did not entirely obliterate the planes of the bone beneath did have an effect of blurring them, so that there was an impression of wrong focus, fuzzy double images marginally unmerged as yet into one in the range-finder of the kind of sophisticated camera Chen's Japanese customers would carry. Working in the fields, Chen had once had a physique which had been lean, tanned, and sinewy; now it was almost impossible to see the outlines of his ribs for the plump flesh which clothed them. Not that he was chubby, just prosperous, as he was careful to explain to Lily. She teased him about it, pinching up the folds of adipose flesh between thumb and forefinger as they lay in bed.

'Fat boy!' she would say.

'Hakka girl!' he would retaliate, jokingly referring to the numbers of those immigrants in her home province (Lily was, of course, good Punti stock).

On Lily there were two opposing views. Chen did not think she was pretty. She had a long, thin, rather horsy face and a mouth that was too big for the rest of her features, and also a tiny mole just under the rim of her lower lip on the left side, which fell into a dimple when she smiled, which was frequently, too frequently to be consonant with Chen's passive ideal of female pulchritude. She was also rather busty and her hands and feet were a fraction too big to be wholly pleasing to her husband. It was her face, though, which really let her down (Chen had decided), being over-full of expression, particularly her bright black eyes which she had a habit of widening and narrowing when listening to something she found interesting. Probably there was too much character in her face, which perhaps explained the lack of Cantonese male interest better than any particular wrongness of an individual feature or their relationship to each other. Westerners found her attractive, though. Lily was unaware of this but Chen had noticed it with great surprise. That was if the second glances and turned heads on the street were anything to go by.

Chen wasn't disturbed. He knew what he liked and Lily didn't conform to the specifications. This he knew with a certainty as absolute as his knowledge that the food he served from the 'tourist' menu was rubbish, total *lupsup*, fit only for foreign devils. If they liked *that*, then in all likelihood they could be equally deluded about Lily. He did once attempt to see what exactly it was the English saw in her, trying to look with new eyes, starting at her well-shaped calves, and moving up in stages to her glossy but too short hair, but still couldn't detect the remotest hint of any sexuality, however exotic and alien it might be. Perhaps they could see from her general bearing what she was like in bed, in which case they might be more astute than he gave them credit for, because in all conscience he had no complaints on that score, none at all.

Man Kee's balance and posture had recently improved; not very much but still noticeably to an onlooker as anxious as his mother. Lily had been encouraging him to run into her outsretched arms, a smile on her face, scorning any other kind of incentive – sweets, for instance. He could be prevailed on to stumble over at a fast trot. On one of Chen's days off she kept him up far beyond his usual bed-time to show his progress off to his father (and also to check she wasn't prey to wishful thinking).

As Man Kee staggered over the purple carpet, his big head lolled alarmingly. Chen was rather matter of fact about his son's progress, further annoying Lily by repeating his usual comments about the disproportionate size of Man Kee's head compared to his body. 'I suppose you had a head the size of a peanut,' Lily commented acidly, carrying precious, maligned Son to his bed in the hallway.

While this had been going on, Mui had been watching television, with her chin cupped in her hands and her elbows on her knees. Lily turned the volume down decisively, then stood in front of Mui with her arms akimbo. Mui bent her neck to look round the obstacle. Lily sighed. She was looking after a household of irresponsibles of whom Man Kee, practically speaking, was the least trouble.

The next morning, Monday, Lily took one of the dust-bins, *scrape-bump, scrape-bump*, down to the courtyard. She could have carried it but although no longer pregnant she considered it unladylike. She put the bin in the corner of the yard and because it was a sunny day went to the white-painted posts and black chains that separated the flats from the street. An old man on a rag and bone cart was driving down the centre of the road, shouting his slurred refrain. Suddenly he reined in his horse and stood up on the seat. He pointed furiously above and behind Lily. She turned. On the window ledge, twenty feet up, Man Kee was crawling towards a large grey pigeon. As Lily watched, he lifted a hand and tried to catch the pigeon's head. It hopped huffily away. Man Kee laughed. As he reached out again, the pigeon flew off. Man Kee tried to snatch it as it went past, actually brushed its wing, over-reached, and fell into the courtyard.

Mui, suddenly, was beneath him, her arms held out to catch and break his fall. She was knocked to the ground by the impact and they both fell, raising puffs of dusty urban earth.

Lily's heart felt as if it had stopped beating in the seconds in which she took in all these events. Her knees trembled beneath her. She raced over the bald, dirty lawn to her child. Dead, crippled for life? Man Kee, crawling rapidly away from Mui who was gasping for breath, his enthusiasm for the chase quite unabated, was in hot pursuit of a second indignant pigeon which slipped out of his chubby fingers and flapped off to perch on the porcelain insulators of a telephone pole.

Lily hauled Mui to her feet, her relief beginning to turn into anger. 'Eldest sister, are you blind and deaf when you watch that television? Do you care if my son kills himself or not?' Mui, doubled over, still trying to get her breath, was unable to reply. Lily left her wheezing and hurried after Man Kee who seemed to be interested in crawling into the road. He turned a joyous face to his mother and gurgled cheerfully. Lily found herself quite unable to scold him. Mui joined them, nursing her stomach. Lily's anger began to dissipate; it was Mui who had broken his fall, not herself.

The rag and bone man, still staring at them, was at the end of the street. An ice-cream man had drawn up at the kerb by their flats. Man Kee recognised the van and tugged at Lily's sleeve. She handed him to Mui and went to the van. Lily served the ice-cream in rice bowls in the kitchen. Mui was unusually bright and talkative which Lily put down to gluttony. But from this point on she seemed to grow in confidence, though so slowly that Lily was never sure when it could be dated from, let alone the reason for it. Perhaps shock had jolted her out of her inertia. She eased her way into a new life inch by inch. Soon after Man Kee's fall Mui surprised her sister by accompanying her to the Burnt

Oak shops. The next evening she insisted on preparing her brother-in-law's soup herself. Lily didn't want this to be a precedent but let it pass for the moment. Unfortunately Chen, after a particularly hard day at the restaurant, didn't even notice that it was Mui bringing him his bowl of unwanted soup.

Lily who had been watching with a smile was now hurt. 'What long hours the boss makes you work!' she exclaimed. As Chen had arrived home seventy minutes earlier than usual, thanks to poor business and a connection with a delayed night bus, he was surprised. It was quite unlike Lily to be petulant. He was even more surprised when she produced her battered crocodile purse and stuck it under his nose. She sniffed: 'The wages he pays are an insult as well. It's really too bad.'

Chen put his hand in his pocket. 'If you want money there's no problem.' He pulled out some notes.

Lily changed the subject abruptly. 'Drink your soup,' she snapped, pushing the bowl towards him with such force that some slopped over on to the oilskin tablecloth and formed three puddles. Lily wiped them up and then used the same cloth to wipe Chen's hands. He shrugged at Mui as Lily clattered in the kitchen with untypical clumsiness. But Mui was watching the late news with great absorption.

TWO

Red Cudgel (426)

The first thing that might have struck any casual observer about Ma Lurk Hing would have been his extreme shortness, that and the scars of childhood smallpox which had endowed his pitted face with the colour and consistency of an amply aerated but half-cooked batter pudding. Had the casual observer spoken Cantonese he would have discerned in Ma's rasping voice – a voice so hoarse, so brutalised that surely the surface mutilations must point to some deeper penetration of the disease into the throat – the twang of a man used to another dialect. He sounded like a Swatownese; an emigrant from the poorer quarter of that teeming dock-town.

Ma had come on since those days. One glance at his clothes told you that. Winter or spring, the details of his under-suiting would be concealed by a long overcoat. This was an expensive garment: a navy blue which became black under street illumination, say on a corner. It was a soft cloth (pure cashmere by its sheen) that seemed poured around the contours of the stocky body which filled it. Brown alligator moccasins, another seasonal perennial, gleamed beneath the unfashionable cuffs of Ma's trousers. His hands were hidden in his overlong coat sleeves but when he consulted his watch (Patek Philippe, the strap again of alligator) it could be seen that the index and adjoining fingers of his right hand had been cleanly amputated from below the line of the second joint. Some industrial accident perhaps? A supposition to be encouraged by Ma's bow-legged longshoreman's stance and trick of carrying his hands curled into pudgy fists, the wrists cocked, facing outwards, as if he might be levering up a hatch by its bar in some atavistic reflex of labour. Giving the lie to this, the flesh of Ma's palms was soft and white, had long been so. But the first two knuckles of each hand were enlarged, protuberant as golf balls, functionally connected (it seemed) by a crinkled web of yellow callus. When Ma balled his fists, his hands, the mutilated and the whole, were indistinguishable; they looked like clubs.

As a Swatow man, Ma was somewhat unusual in the Street, coming neither from Hong Kong, the New Territories, nor even Canton, though the nosiest of his fellow provincials baulked at snooping here. Ma was clearly not a man to trifle with; at the same time there was also something slightly ludicrous about him – connected, perhaps, with a lack of proportion between personal appearance and social consequence. Ma acted on his own estimation of himself and others accepted it but there was nothing inherently prepossessing about the man. It was as if he derived authority from some source external to himself: great wealth, maybe, or the expectation of it ... but not wealth. But what?

He had no obvious means of support. No business, restaurant, teahouse, car-hire firm, supermarket or travel agency. Judging by the frequency with which he visited the Street's basement gambling houses he might have been a professional gambler, except he was never seen to wager; only to watch impassively with hands in his overcoat pockets. Family? None. Not even the hint of a mistress of whatever race. The groups of young men he was occasionally seen with might point to a proclivity of another kind. In someone else this could have provoked mirth and sarcasm, inspired hilarious witticisms, and the outrageous punning so dear to southern hearts, but not in Ma's case.

No one stared at him or at his companions when they took tea
back tables of restaurants or when Ma passed, in a black G
saloon, chauffeured by a single youth, or sometimes accompan...u by
another young man in the back. Tough-looking boys, these, with an
inclination towards pale corduroy or darker leather jackets, their long
hair brushing the collar in soft black spikes. They had a fashion for
wearing four heavy signet rings, two on each of the fingers that were
missing on Ma's right hand, in what might have been construed as a
tribute to the older man.

White Paper Fan (415)

Mao Sung, a man of mild and scholary aspect, was from Shanghai but
fluent in more than the Chinese dialect of that cosmopolitan city. In
addition to Mandarin which he spoke with a flawless Peking accent, he
had a pungent command of Cantonese and Fukienese, and a perfectly
grammatical but less idiomatic grasp of French and English which he
spoke with that well-known tendency of educated foreigners to
pedantry. The business letters he could compose in the last two
European languages were models of precision and elegance. This flair
for language was not surprising. It had been Mao's living. As a very
young man he had worked in Shanghai as an interpreter in the
international settlement, and later as a technical translator. With a
large number of fellow-Shanghainese, some of a less academic
disposition, he had come to Hong Kong as a refugee in the early 1950s
and settled in North Point. That mean district, with its pawnshops,
teahouses, and clanking green trams, soon acquired the nickname of
Little Shanghai. And the series of daring daylight armed robberies
which the old municipality's Green Gang organised rapidly ensured
that Little Shanghai rivalled its namesake in criminal enterprise.
While the Shanghainese fought their sanguinary territorial battles
with the established local gangs, Mao Sung, bespectacled, inseparable
from his brief-case, worked by day as a court interpreter and at
weekends as a tourist guide (mainly for Americans, with whom he had
a rapport). Finally the Shanghainese were contained, thanks to the
help their competitors gave the colonial authorities. During this
warfare, and also the fierce rioting of the Double Tenth in 1956, Mao
Sung continued to lead his quiet life.

In late 1956 some business associates of Mao Sung's had to leave
Hong Kong rather suddenly for Taiwan. The government of that
island, coincidentally, had no extradition treaty with the colony. Some

of these business acquaintances were recent associates of Mao's. They were from Canton. Mao Sung had become friendly with them at about the same time the Shanghainese had withdrawn defeated from their street fights with the locals. As these Cantonese didn't speak Mandarin (despite their history of friendship with some high-ranking Taiwanese generals), what more natural than for them to employ Mao Sung as an interpreter? Mao left the colony for the greater freedom of Taiwan. In time he left Taiwan for Vancouver, Canada, in the employ of a senior Nationalist general; and from there he came to London, England.

Grass Sandal (432)
To a hostile and superficial observer Miranda Lai's world might have seemed to orbit around the twin suns of fashion and money, in so far as those overwhelming gravitational forces could be considered as separate rather than as aspects of a single star. She had been born in Malaya, daughter of a wealthy merchant and currency speculator, was educated at an English private school, and 'finished' not in Switzerland (the unimaginative choice of her widowed father) but in Milan. Her mother had been drowned in rough water one windy day when Miranda was five. Shortly after losing his wife, her father moved to Singapore where he had obscure business interests, leaving the child in the care of servants in his up-country house.

If the manner of her mother's death suggested a certain head-strongness, then Miranda had inherited it. She was outrageously spoiled by her father during his short visits to the parkland mansion, and pampered for the rest of the time by her dead mother's Hakka maid-servant. For a child the mansion had been a wonderful place and Miranda had enjoyed the run of the house and grounds. The smooth lawns were fringed with rougher grass, left unkempt, and stunted trees and bushes, so that it was hard to tell where the mansion grounds ended and the jungle began. In 1948 the elderly Scots rubber-planter and his wife who were the mansion's closest neighbours were machine-gunned to death in their Buick by Communist terrorists hiding in undergrowth by the highway, who raked the crudely armoured vehicle with burst after superfluous burst of automatic fire. On his next visit Miranda's father took her back to the city. He did not take the Hakka maid, now effectively Miranda's nanny. The child did not cry as she left the house, nor did she take a backward look through the tinted window of her father's Mercedes saloon, but the maid wept every night for a long time after, holding Miranda's pillow which smelt with diminishing evocativeness of milk, talcum and urine.

In Singapore, in their rambling two-floored flat, Miranda saw more of her father than when she had been up-country. For the next six years, until her thirteenth birthday, she attended a convent school, delivered and collected by a chauffeur in a short-sleeved white shirt who bought popsicles from a bicycle seller for her to suck in the back of the car whence she descended with a stained mouth into the arms of a new, and younger, *amah*. At her birthday parties her father recorded the festivities for posterity with a ciné camera, the dark flat bright in the icy glare of film lights which glowed off the radiant faces of Miranda's schoolfriends and the gleaming blancmanges and jellies on a long table. Perhaps her father played the films to himself in his office. Miranda never saw any of them. At her last party, the one to which she wore her first nylons, Miranda's father took stills with a Leica, the bulbs popping and fusing with a faint crackle and smell of chemical singeing.

Her sixteenth birthday, which occurred at school in Cheltenham, was a different affair. There was no jelly, only cake: a pale blue Cupid's heart with an appropriate number of pink candles. Inside was yellow sponge with an apricot filling. Dundee fruit cake was what the other girls were sent, homely fare. Miranda took portions round on a plate to the prefects but had none herself. She was at school there two and a half years, during which she mastered grammatical but still heavily accented English and had the opportunity to become a proficient horsewoman.

Only the former was regarded as a voguish accomplishment at the young ladies' academy in the Via Buenos Aires, Milan, but Miranda soon familiarised herself with the new hierarchy and a set of aspirant values alien to the regime predicated by the founders of her old school around fresh air, the house system, and a diet massively over-balanced in its carbohydrate constituent. There was *pasta*, of course, in Milan, served in a charming panelled refectory in the green-louvred building that was Miranda's home for the duration of her minority, but there resemblance with England ended.

During this time she plunged whole-heartedly into a new world of blazered young men in sports cars, and fashion-shows organised by pupils of the finishing school. These were occasions on which Miranda came into her own, slinking squeakily down a makeshift cat-walk of shivering tables pushed together in the refectory, in cheongsams so tight she had to breathe, with great caution, from her abdomen. The silent flickering from the matt-black photo-flash units of the blazered young men which heliographed her progress down the tables reminded Miranda of home. She saw her father every six months and on the fourth of every calendar month a generous draft showed she had not been forgotten. Miranda's twenty-first which she gave for herself in a fountained restaurant in the centre of the city was a talking-point at the school for terms afterwards. Both students and selected members of the staff were invited to the celebration, the latter patronised by Miranda as they made conversation with glasses of pale vermouth in their hands.

Miranda spent the summer in Rapallo and Portofino. Using 'contacts' made at the school she worked as a freelance photographer and occasional model in Paris. She earned a pittance but still comfortably supported herself on her allowance. In the winter she was in Switzerland with a Belgian banker. In the spring she returned briefly to Singapore and rejected Mandarin cinema offers which would have earned her as little as her fashion work in Paris. In the autumn she arrived in London entrusted with work by her father, and there she met certain business connections with whom he had a long understanding.

Despite what the circumstances of her early adult life might have suggested, Miranda was fundamentally unadventurous. She was strong-willed, certainly; she was also prone to wager only on certainties. The various educational regimes she had come under had left little permanent influence on her. Primary realities of money, sex and power occupied most of what could be called Miranda's thoughts. She was incapable of abstraction. Her utter self-assurance was based on the solid foundation of a strictly limited view of the world and its workings. She might glance at a glossy fashion magazine but reading, even newspapers, was to her a sign of weakness, a flinching from what was really important. Not that she lived solely for the present: prudence was one of her prime qualities, developed to the point where it was an all-engrossing cunning. This extended to the most trivial details of her life. She stockpiled bars of soap, five deep, ten high in a cupboard in her St John's Wood flat. But for her to have made the imaginative projection into admitting at least the possibility of other points of view, different lives, other ambitions, would have been quite impossible. She had no idea what it was like to be anyone except herself.

This is not to say Miranda behaved overbearingly. She was self-effacing to the point where she seemed to go out of her way to please others. This was most obvious in pettier matters of etiquette or physical ease: in surrendering chairs to her father's associates, preparing tea, deferring in conversation (her bland contributions to dialogue never amounted to the critical mass sufficient to make up one half of an argument), or providing instant panaceas from the stock of expensive Chinese folk medicines she kept in a teak chest in her bathroom. All this was a mask for intense personal ambition. The solicitude was fake; as artificial as the fine stitching under the skin by her rounded eyes, and as delicately camouflaged. Only intermittently did a flash of will show through, a will that kept her modishly thin (despite a naturally enormous appetite) and which found regular scope for exercise in the piece of bacon-rind on a thread which she would dangle down her throat after indulgence in order to vomit up a too-calorific meal (in circumstances of great privacy, of course).

Night-brother (432)
Lam Wan Biu, known successively to his associates as Ah Biu, 'Lammie', or 'Ricky' Lam, had been at various times in his short life but long career, foundling, shoeshine boy, hawker, lottery-ticket vendor, debt collector, and labour organiser. Although he hadn't actually been a foreman of any kind it had lain in his power to get a stevedore's job on the wharf for anyone he wished. Despite his young years, Lam, in his narrow-bottomed trousers and Cuban-heeled boots, was a far more influential figure than any foreman. Twenty years ago at the probable age of six months he had been found abandoned in a Wanchai doorway by nuns of the waterfront's Catholic mission. Never at a loss for a witty remark, quick with his pleasant, open-faced smile, he was not unpopular with the older men on the dockside from whom he levied the commission on their coolie wages. He had presence, too, never mind the amiable exterior. When he went into the top man's cabin on the waterfront with his smart combination-lock case he always found what he had come for. In the door and out; just long enough for a quick jocular remark and time to snap the case shut and twirl the tumblers. Only once had he been kept waiting. No one outside had heard shouting. Lammie left still smiling pleasantly; had nodded at grinning labourers on the wharf, squatting over their meals of leaf-wrapped glutinous rice pyramids and sticky condensed milk on bread; so civilly it made you wonder whether, after all, that elegant case didn't contain something. Coming to his office quite a long time later with a taxi-dancer he had picked up, this particular foreman had

met with a nasty accident. He must have slipped and fallen into not-so-fragrant Hong Kong harbour, where he joined orange peel, dead dogs, and foam-encrusted ordure. On his drunken way in he must have caught the back of his head a wicked blow on the wharf's rusty iron ladder, for the coolies crowded round the trickling corpse had seen the hair there was thickly matted with blood. Lammie had seen there was a collection for the dead man's funeral expenses. Having no kin himself he was strict about family proprieties where a lesser man might have been lax. His general bearing, cheerfulness, confidence, were such that he might have been surrounded and supported not only by relatives of his own but by one of the most powerful and well-connected of the old-style Chinese families. Visiting the office of the deceased's successor, Ricky Lam was greeted with a thicker envelope than usual. The coolies noticed the boss actually bowed him out. Not a man for extravagant fuss on his own behalf, Lam rebuked the contributor.

A year later, Ricky Lam left the waterfront for good to pursue studies abroad in cold, foggy England, so it was said in whispers. Lack of education hadn't held him back up till now, the coolies joked. When the period of his stay expired, there was no trace of Ricky Lam in a foreign land and on the waterfront, where he had never seriously been expected back, he was now forgotten, regretted only by the shoeshine children who had loved him and fought for the right to clean his already shining boots, and not only for the huge tips he gave.

THREE

Chen's restaurant was in Soho, just off Gerrard Street and its complex of travel agencies, supermarkets, fortune tellers, quack acupuncturists and Chinese cinema clubs, in a quiet lane whose only establishments were restaurants. At the end of the row was a passage with a double bend, so that what seemed to strangers like a blind alley was in reality a concealed entrance, constructed on the same principle as a crude lobster trap. A sharp right turn after passing an iron bollard took the knowledgeable or intrepid into a gloomy canyon formed by the blind backs of two forty-feet high Georgian terraces. Rubbish filled the alley. At night rats scrabbled in the piles of rotting vegetable leaves and soggy cardboard boxes. There was a muffled silence in the enclosure. At the other end another series of baffles led, quite suddenly, into the brightness and sound of Leicester Square. This was Chen's habitual short-cut to the Underground station.

There were five Cantonese eating-houses, of which Chen's, the Ho Ho ('Excellence'), was the largest with three floors, each with room for twenty tables. Sandwiched between the Chinese restaurants was the Curry Mahal, run by a thin, dark-skinned Madrasi (the first to arrive in the lane in the early 1950s) who was now slowly being driven out of business by his Chinese rivals. He was considering selling out to a Greek who wanted to open a sauna and massage parlour. Each night he watched from behind his grubby net curtains as the restaurants of his competitors filled while a single tableful and a couple of Indian students munched gloomily through their chicken biryanis or rhogan ghoshts on opposite sides of the room in his long, dark corridor of a restaurant. It wasn't the Chinese fellows he disliked, but the Greek, who offered him larger sums of money every month.

The Ho Ho was an interesting blend of the modern and the dilapidated. Dirty stone steps connected the floors. When the owner, a wealthy New Territories entrepreneur, had taken over the property he had painted the walls brown (without troubling to strip the scuffed red flock wallpaper he had inherited) and laid a blue carpet on each floor. Neither walls nor carpet had been renewed in five years. The tables were lit by pointed bulbs on the walls which threw a dim undersea glow. Taken with the tendency of the carpet to accumulate static electricity and then fluff, this made the place look much dirtier than it really was.

The ultra-modern kitchens were spotless. The proximity of the doorless staff lavatory at the back worried no one. An old adage had it: the nearer the latrine, the tastier the food. Three extractor fans changed the air in the kitchen once a minute, so that the chefs and their elderly women helpers had to wear pullovers under their aprons in the winter instead of enduring more usual sauna-bath conditions. A boiler on the roof piped superheated steam for the lunch-time *dim sum*.

The chefs, respected men of uncertain temperament, masters of their craft, worked in efficient if uneasy harmony. Preparation chef, assembly chef, stir chef, they operated at high speed. They could produce beef and vegetables in oyster sauce in a total of fifty-five seconds from arrival of chit to materials steaming on a dish in the dumb-waiter.

Amongst the other employees there were two distinct groups: clansmen and outsiders. Chen was an outsider. Originally the boss had only employed men from his own village, preferably relatives. He had secured work permits for them, arranged flights, found housing. But four years ago there had been a strike when the assembly chef of the day had discovered from the books (carelessly left out) that the boss's under-payment of tax to the Inland Revenue had been treble the figure he told the employees. Although everyone was already getting a cut from this, any fool could realise the boss was making an unfair percentage out of it. The boss had refused to surrender a penny, had chartered part of a 707 to fly in strike-breakers. Other proprietors in the street had lent him employees or got him staff from outside London.

Chen was one of the new men taken on at this time, from Liverpool. Many of the recruits were from Kowloon City or Hong Kong island and there was reserve between them and the village employees. Chen fell between the two camps, being slightly younger than the other villagers. The new waiters tended to be taller and slender with long, *bouffant* hair-styles. They contrived to wear the white waiter's jacket with a touch of fashionable aplomb.

Chen had one particular friend, Lo, the barbecue chef, and also an enemy, Roman Fok. Lo worked by the window in a little glass-fronted booth under hooks of pterodactyl-like flattened duck carcasses pulled inside out, strips of pork loin, and glazed soyaed chicken. His main task was to prepare and chop the cold meats. His cleaver blurred in his hands, thwacking chunkily into the scarred wooden chopping-block when he encountered a boneless fragment. He often drew spectators. There was an element of the trapeze about the performance. It seemed quite possible he would chop off one of his own fingers, no doubt obliviously pushing it off the board and on to the plate with the back of his cleaver to join the other cubes of meat and slices of sausage where some shocked customer would find it under his garnishing. Lo's was an extrovert's job. But he was quiet, withdrawn to the point of moodiness. Some fifteen years older than Chen, he had been deserted by his wife six years ago. She had run away with the Fukienese distributor of a ventilation company, one of whose fans efficiently removed the savoury steam from the soup-noodle pot in Lo's own working-area.

The appalling Roman Fok should have been doing Lo's job; even Chen had to admit he had the flamboyant temperament to do it. But Roman was a kitchen-worker, labouring in the basement without a moment's contact with the customers.

28

Chen had different, but decided, feelings about their various patrons. The Japanese, for instance. Despite the lavish tips they left he was not entirely enthusiastic about them. Prejudices instilled since childhood died hard in Chen who, in general, subscribed to a stock Cantonese image of the race: sadistic, buck-toothed and myopic. The English, of course, provided the bulk of non-Chinese custom. Chen was affable enough to them. Some of his colleagues, Fatty Koo noticeably, gave short shrift. Chen could be prevailed on to make suggestions in his halting English. Koo either snorted, looked blank, inspected the ceiling, rolled his eyes, or simply walked off as the mood took him. The customers seemed to thrive on this abrupt treatment.

The waiters preferred to see Chinese customers, which gave them a good chance for chat about shortcomings in particular items on the special Chinese-language menu or the latest gossip from Hong Kong. The proprietor had an entirely different conception of the ideal customer. He preferred to see a preponderance of Westerners who consumed expensive and unsuitable wines as well as beer with their meal and did not share the irritating obsessions of the Chinese customers with their totally unreasonable insistence on a meal made up of fresh materials, authentically cooked, and presented at a highly competitive price.

The waiters often held impromptu discussions, when the boss was on another floor, about the various idiosyncracies of their hosts and patrons, the English. Among these eccentricities was the strange and widespread habit of not paying bills, a practice so prevalent as to arouse suspicions it was a national sport and which involved even the most respectable-looking of customers. Loud and rowdy behaviour was more comprehensible, including fencing with chopsticks and wearing inverted rice-bowls on the head like brittle skull-caps, writing odd things on the lavatory walls, and mixing the food on their plates in a disgusting way before putting soya sauce on everything. Fok had an explanation for the defaulting bill-payers whom he believed to be rival occidental restaurateurs or their hirelings out to sabotage the business of their more successful Chinese competitors. 'Just jealous,' he explained. Apart from possessing the intrinsic attractions of any conspiracy theory, this also flattered the boss where he was most susceptible: his ability to make money. And so the solution came to be orthodoxy; although why there were no absconding Indian customers, bearing in mind the business the Ho Ho had taken from the Curry Mahal, remained a mystery not even Fok could satisfactorily explain.

*

Relations between Chen and Roman Fok had only recently worsened, although there had never been sympathy between them. Chen's work did not bring him into close or frequent contact with Fok, so opportunities for friction had been rare. Fok was not popular even with the new, younger group of waiters, of whom he had been the last to arrive. The New Territories men disapproved of his lack of respect for them. His mocking, indefinably insulting manner made everyone uneasy. Had they been a closer-knit group he would not have been tolerated. Chen avoided him as much as he could.

Then one slack afternoon Fok had been bragging about his sexual exploits in front of a largely credulous group of New Territories men on the third floor. Although Fok had no business being there the general mood was one of appalled curiosity. 'Two American girls,' Fok boasted, 'blondes.' Despite themselves, the older men were visibly impressed. 'Wah!' said Fatty Koo, his eyes wide as oysters. 'How much money necessary, Ah Fok?'

Roman rinsed his mouth with tea, then spurted it into a half-empty bowl of rice. 'Tcha!' He shook his finger contemptuously at Fatty Koo.

Chen had kept his face expressionless through what he regarded as a disgusting recital. He had heard Fok's lies about other things: his wins at Big and Small in the basement dens, his ability to pick fast horses, his parts as extra in Mandarin-language sword films when his speciality had been that of wielder of a steel whip in multiple assault scenes. With that unusual weapon Fok had employed, he said, a flick of the wrist to snatch swords from the grasp of armoured men, crop ears, garrotte necks. Well, Chen had yet to see him in any of the productions at the cinema club they patronised in off-hours. Now he grimaced as he filled the tooth-pick sheaves with sticks. This was Fok's most blatant lie yet. It wasn't Chen's character to say anything out loud but Roman saw the face he pulled. He scowled at Chen who turned his back on him and walked away to put the toothpicks on the tables.

From then on Fok singled Chen out as a special target for his malice. This took the form of insulting innuendoes and, as Chen showed no signs of reacting, openly contemptuous remarks. Chen didn't care. His stolid face had only grown blanker. What surprised and disillusioned him was the way some of the others laughed at Fok's cheap witticisms. (Not Lo, of course.) In fact this focussing of general unpleasantness on the person of Chen resulted in Fok's becoming a great deal more popular. He had less bile to discharge on the others. And anyone who could raise a good laugh to hurry on the endless day was sure of some esteem. Chen's colleagues didn't expect him to take exception. They imagined he would be as amused as they were. Only Lo felt the pulsings of a dull resentment and clapped his friend sympathetically on the back.

While others liked to gamble in their off-duty periods, Lo and Chen amused themselves with an hour and a half at the cinema club. Lo had got his younger friend into the habit of going. Chen went mainly to please him. They both sat wooden-faced in the front row before the tiny screen. Yet it was Chen who made occasional interjections, grunted or, very rarely indeed, gave a snort of laughter. Lo gave no visible signs of enjoyment, never commented on what they had seen. Chen thought it offered poor Lo the chance to escape from an unhappy present. This particular club showed mostly modern Cantonese dramas: *The Legacy*, *The Unfaithful Servant*, *Ah Biu's Lucky Chance*, *The Kid*, *The Millionaire*, *The Lost Lottery Ticket*, *Old Woman Wong Finds a Husband*. Chen gathered Lo didn't like the old-time costume melodramas or sword extravaganzas because whenever one played he would fall asleep and begin to snore raucously, generally during the fight scenes; the loud buzzing he made in his nose and throat fortunately merged with the death rattles of the disembowelled and limbless on an anyway scratchy sound-track.

'There *was* one fellow who looked a bit like Fok,' Chen would volunteer sometimes as they came into a darkening street. Lo would not make the slightest acknowledgement. Sometimes he asked Chen: 'How's Son? He's well?'

'All right,' Chen would say cautiously, not wishing to upset Lo by talking about family matters. 'Head still big.'

Lo had once shared a taxi to Chen's flat during a public transport strike and Chen had made the mistake of pressing him into taking a glass of tea with the family before walking to Hendon at two in the morning. Chen had let him go, knowing it was the kindest thing, which Lily hadn't realised. Lily had thought her husband very heartless. 'Good,' Lo would nod, ignoring Chen's remark about the size of Man Kee's head. 'He's a handsome boy.'

'Not at all handsome,' Chen would say, as was obligatory.

Back at the Ho Ho they would go to their separate duties and probably not exchange a word for a couple of days. Occasionally, when the young waiters were indulging in a bit of horse-play around the lift system, Chen might catch Lo's glance. Then they would exchange the quietest of smiles.

FOUR

Red Cudgel had four aims. He wanted to maximise profits; eliminate competitors; recruit and train reliable subordinates to whom he might delegate with a free mind; and, so far as possible, he wanted to harmonise traditional aims, methods and organisation with the demands of the modern world. Personally, he would have preferred to sacrifice some efficiency if this was the cost of preserving old ways, but he was aware of a rising school of thought which took the opposite view.

More immediate matters had been on the agenda of the last sub-branch meeting, but if the four aims hadn't been obviously raised they were beneath the surface of discussion. It had been a lively meeting, by no means concerned with endorsing decisions which had already been taken at the top. As it had done for the last four years, as it had done previously in Amsterdam and before that in Mong Kok, Kowloon, and in the distant past in Swatow, Red Cudgel's authority had gone unchallenged – but his lieutenant had shown signs of independent, divergent thinking. Without getting excessively concerned Red Cudgel had noted this.

In the first instance the meeting concentrated on the rivalry with 14-K. Office and temperament combined to suggest to Red Cudgel a military solution. Street fighting prowess had taken him to the top; he was a legend in some towns. But so far these talents had lain dormant here. As society disciplinarian in Amsterdam, where the post of Leader was held by a White Paper Fan rank, he had once had to 'wash the face' of an errant member, liquidate him. In the UK reputation had sufficed, to date.

The meeting was held at the Wong Ho restaurant, in the fifth floor rear special banquet room behind a compound of screens. They had feasted on a superior shark's fin soup and, amongst other things, a homely dish ordered by Red Cudgel of chopped cow's lungs, sweetbreads and intestines, with coriander and parsley. Dessert was quail's eggs in lightly sugared water. Throughout Red Cudgel drank brandy and ice. White Paper Fan, the deputy leader, consumed tea and then a soft drink. After fruit, Red Cudgel said in his hoarse voice, which alcohol had made hoarser: 'See there are no serpents mixed with the dragons.' There was a grim jocularity about the way he gave the traditional instruction. Even before his favourite, Night-brother, returned from the perfunctory search, he began speaking. He worked on his own anger, wishing to transmit it to his audience, and, by the end of his speech, was genuinely enraged himself.

White Paper Fan said: 'They may have harassed our collectors. Is this important? It isn't. We must try to co-exist with them. Fighting can only be bad for business.'

Red Cudgel said: 'It isn't a question of "co-existence" or compromising. With anyone else, yes. But it is in the nature of 14-K to try to destroy all their rivals. The attacks are not isolated occurrences or accidental; they are part of a pattern, a plan. Their whole history, short as it is, shows this. They tried to destroy all the Wo groups in Hong Kong. In Shamshuipo they wiped out the Yuet Tong. That was less than seven years after they arrived in Hong Kong. They won't be satisfied until they are the only society over here. If they talk reasonably or ally, it's only to attack more effectively later.'

There was silence.

White Paper Fan said: 'From first-hand knowledge I can admit the truth of many of your arguments. But in the short-term should we not try to find a way of living with them? This would enable us to build our strength in the meantime.'

Red Cudgel said: 'Complicated. I prefer directness. Simplicity is most effective. Tangled policies trip you up.'

'Let me give recent accounts to you. This may change your thinking.' White Paper Fan, respected for his administrative and financial ability and also an expert on Hung ritual, had an abacus, a Parker ball-point pen, and a sheaf of thin paper in front of him. 'Protection money from restaurants remains unchanged: we have £1,000 after the various percentages have been deducted. We have lost a small amount because of the inroads made by 14-K. Our percentage from the two gambling basements affiliated to us represents the biggest part of our income: again £2,500.'

Red Cudgel said: 'We should raise the levy. £10,000 in a year from this is not sufficient.'

'Bad idea; they can turn to 14-K for protection.'

Red Cudgel let this pass.

'Sales of cinema tickets and protection: £300. Small pickings. Not a big operation here, unlike Hong Kong.' He took a deep breath. 'The big loss is to do with the white powder. During this period we made only £1,200.' He did not look directly at Red Cudgel. 'Gross total £5,000. After deduction of expenses of commissions, remittances to Wo headquarters, welfare, feasting for officials, the net profit is £4,444.' The beads of the abacus stopped clicking.

If anyone found the figures suspiciously neat coming from one steeped in the society's numerology, they said nothing.

Red Cudgel asked: 'What's the problem selling the powder? There should never be any problem with this.'

'There are three factors working against us: harassment from the official bandits, difficulty in distributing and peddling and smaller problems in importing the stuff.'

White Paper Fan gestured to Grass Sandal and Night-brother. 'Younger brother and younger sister are our intermediaries in the protection operation and also supervise most of the practical aspects of the drug sales. If I criticise them it is only because the protection money is so much more satisfactorily handled than the drug revenue.'

'Your criticism is more than justified. The stuff ought to be the biggest source of revenue we have.' Red Cudgel snapped the fingers of his left hand for more brandy and ice.

Night-brother spoke: 'I don't have the temerity to answer back but I ask my seniors to recognise that collecting restaurant money is relatively easy. We deal with Chinese after all. The business is discreetly done. A closed-doors business. Selling in the street, in the open, to foreigners is an entirely different affair.'

Red Cudgel nodded. 'Recognised. But you are still at fault. I am not interested in explanations and excuses, only results.'

Night-brother said: 'As Mr Mao, excuse my error, Second Brother, says, there are three constraints on us selling freely and making unlimited profit. Bringing No 3 heroin into the country is not particularly difficult at the moment. It's well handled from Brussels. We have large stocks in the godown flat and are amassing more all the time. Retailing and bandit harassment are the bigger nuisance. We become vulnerable on the street: a Chinese face is easy to see. Even the system where we get hold of a European addict our runners can use as a regular contact is not altogether free of risk. As you know, younger sister objected to the free dose the contact had for his reward – but what does this matter compared to the fact that he retails to six others of his kind for us? Since we have started working this system only four of our Chinese runners have been arrested – and these weren't members but the probationers I recruited.'

Grass Sandal said meekly: 'Outsiders will never be trustworthy as members. The system can lead to dangers. Nor should we be so ready to surrender our profits.'

Red Cudgel ignored her. 'It was a clever system you invented. So good I hear that 14-K are using it.'

Night-brother was modest. 'Only makeshift. The system is sound enough but the runners let us down. We have to deal with a certain type, flashy. They bring too much attention to themselves.'

White Paper Fan's lip curled. 'Common criminals. The kind who have destroyed the Hung family in Hong Kong. We need to keep this sort out at all costs. In Hong Kong and Singapore there are no more true societies. No central body. Only criminal gangs like the 14-K.'

Night-brother was familiar with the older man's prejudices; he steered matters to practical discussion again. 'It would be good if we had Chinese addicts to do this work for us. One always has control over a user. But then of course there's the problem of the different tastes. We don't market the barbitone Red Chicken mix here or the No 4 the Shanghainese like. I need hardly tell you Chinese prefer to smoke, and Westerners inject. Pure poison in the vein. At least the Americans use the No 4 grade – but over here there's no demand for the ninety-eight per cent stuff. A pity – the profit would be larger.'

'Definitely larger.' Red Cudgel smiled to himself.

White Paper Fan interrupted impatiently. 'This is a most important and lucrative business. The market grows every year. It is imperative we control it. It is not only the prize for dominance, it is what will ensure continued dominance. Never mind the fighters you can put on the street. Run this business efficiently and you will have no worries about 14-K. The funds from it are potentially enormous.'

'No.' Red Cudgel was vehement. 'What concerns me *is* the number of fighters I can put on the street, not who has most cash when it comes to be counted. What do you want us to do? Lay banknotes along the street and see who can go furthest?'

'Disagree. With respect. It is not just a question of meeting physical force with greater force. Money gives face and therefore power in the community. It enables us to perform services for our members which bind them closer to family Hung. It means we can undertake other things to gain sympathy at large. This was how the society flourished in the old days.'

The 415 officer was heard respectfully but he knew his arguments did not engage the minds of his audience. He began to speak more specifically.

'Proper organisation is as important as brute strength. It should be understood that the five sections of our sub-branch are like the five fingers of the hand. They work best together. General Affairs Section is my responsibility. If all else is well it reflects that state of affairs. Red Cudgel is in charge of fighting and discipline which are excellent. Our Recruiting section is in abeyance not so much because we don't have a Vanguard official as because we must proceed and select carefully here on foreign ground. Welfare section is important, as I have already insisted: we must take care of our own and be seen to do so. Recruiting and Welfare are closely linked. Liaison section is the responsibility of Grass Sandal and Night-brother. They have not done well. The different members of our family aren't aware of the others' problems. I admit that Grass Sandal has co-ordinated well with Singapore and Hong Kong for us. But in general we must work more as one.'

Grass Sandal bowed her head humbly. Looking at the soiled tablecloth. she said: 'My face cannot look at you. I will try to amend my ways.'

Smiling, Night-brother said: 'Little sister, I will help you amend your ways.'

Red Cudgel waved his strange fist. 'Enough. Whatever the different opinions as to the best way of acting, it seems there is agreement that we are at an important stage in the growth of the society here. It is not convenient for me to go into detail of my disagreement with White Fan's plans now. White *Paper* Fan, I should say in the Hong Kong style. But in general terms I believe that if we make a mistake now it will be increasingly difficult to rectify it in future years. One false step could be disastrous. We may not be able to recover.' He paused. 'From small grows large but if small does not become big, then it dies. Do you understand?'

Red Cudgel did not usually speak so obliquely: the junior officers were taken by surprise. He repeated himself, harshly. This time there were polite murmurs of assent. Red Cudgel correctly took this to mean they had not understood him. 'You,' he turned to Night-brother, 'do you understand?'

'Of course, Elder Brother. Quite obviously.'

'Good. This is not something which can be taught.' He gargled with tea and spat it into his empty brandy glass. 'Things are changing here. Our enemies have not been the official bandits as in Hong Kong. Here those sons of lepers can't harm us. How can you catch one fish out of all fish in the water? Chinese don't talk to the devils. They meet silence when they ask their foolish questions. This is good. Here too we could give tea to the bandits but it might be a little harder. In Hong Kong no need to give too much. Half police are Hung brothers!' There was sycophantic laughter. 'No Tang person talks to a devil official here. Even when he fears death very much he will not talk of our secrets. We are safe, although one day this may change. But there are other dangers. They seem small now. One day I promise you they will seem big.'

'May I speak?'

'Of course, younger brother. I should say, little sister.' There was more obsequious laughter for the worn sally.

'I believe both Leader and Deputy Leader are correct.' Night-brother smiled ironically at such blatant trimming but Grass Sandal ignored him. 'Elder Brother is correct to believe we must not trust false representations from 14-K. We must prepare and make ourselves strong. But I believe Second Brother is more correct as to the means of strengthening ourselves. We ought to put our activities on a more formal basis. We should also make every cent we can. Raise protection fees as Elder Brother suggests. We need not fear. 14-K will increase their fees in line with ours. If there is protest among the payers, Night-brother knows how to deal with this.'

Red Cudgel accepted the female 432 officer's mediation. 'Agreed. We have less variety of business here. No dancing-girls, hawkers, or dockers here.' He nodded at Night-brother who grinned broadly. 'So we must make the most of what outlets are available to us.'

White Paper Fan said: 'Speaking as society accountant, I ask that extra revenues be devoted to strengthening ourselves. I, too, am in favour of expanding to meet the threat from our rivals. I take it this is the meaning of our Leader's little proverb. However, I want this growth to be controlled – this is why we must have it done properly with a recruiting official from Wo headquarters in Hong Kong, armed with a warrant and recruiting flag.'

'As Leader I endorse this. Meeting terminates. Only 432-rank upwards remain.'

When the screens had been replaced Red Cudgel said: 'I did not wish to lower your prestige. Not for your own sakes' but the society's. Now I speak bluntly. I am dissatisfied with the conduct of all officers, White Paper Fan rank excluded.' He spoke less harshly now but was still able to intimidate his subordinates. All except White Paper Fan were his appointments; they owed their advancement, in some cases their very membership, to him. It was he who had come from Holland four years ago to reorganise the skeleton Wo structure in the UK; with such thoroughness and vigour that he might be said to have created it anew. Three or four of the 432 officers, including Night-brother, had been specially flown from Hong Kong at his request. They listened to him, even the most daring, with more than the respect a Leader could expect.

'Officers attend their duties without proper care. How is it that our 49s have been attacked when they make their collections at restaurants and cinemas? Why were they not protected? Failing that, why were they not more circumspect? We have lost a great deal of face. If we are treated with contempt here it will encourage our enemies to try to oust us from the bigger operations. This must be handled better. Improve this or suffer the consequences.'

'Easy to say, hard to do.' Night-brother showed more resentment than anyone else could have done.

Red Cudgel let it pass. He said: 'None of you is irreplaceable. Remember that. I want this society to be independent. In the past here orders have been taken from Holland and Belgium. I don't want to bring this about again but if necessary I will import members from Amsterdam, fighters not parasites.'

White Paper Fan said: 'I only recommend, I don't presume to command. But that seems unwise to me.'

'For the time being I take your advice.'

White Paper Fan acknowledged the concession, showing respect but without demeaning himself. 'Then let me draw the following formal resolutions from our discussion: resolved that 1) a careful check is kept on the activities of 14-K. 2) we run our operations in a more careful way, with attention to detail. 3) especial effort is made as regards the marketing and distribution of No 3 heroin, particularly street work. 4) the five sections co-ordinate better. 5) money should be set aside and other preparations made for a major initiation ceremony in the future. 6) we strengthen links with Hong Kong.' He paused from covering the paper with his rapid, elegant script. 'I believe that covers all we have discussed, at least in a general sense?'

Red Cudgel said nothing. In the prolonged silence White Paper Fan's thin sheafs of paper rustled; he squared them off complacently.

After a while Red Cudgel said: 'I have never believed in entrusting my thoughts to paper. Perhaps I have been wrong. Manipulated by educated men, words can come to mean the opposite of what was intended.' He held up his uninjured left hand to forestall White Paper Fan. 'I don't speak specifically of anyone here. I am a plain man. Add this, then, to the list: we arm and prepare ourselves for fighting.' He pushed his fist against his palm, *yin* to *yang*. 'There were how many other "resolutions"?'

'Six.'

Red Cudgel's grin showed metal bridge-work in the mouth. 'That makes it seven, doesn't it?'

White Paper Fan smiled thinly. 'Call it eight.'

'Let it be seven, it may be appropriate.'

FIVE

How she had filled her day before Man Kee's arrival, and later Mui's, was now no longer clear to Lily. She retained no oppressive memories of a boredom that might have been supposed intolerable; no sense of past loneliness to haunt her present or to make it seem much brighter by comparison. It was a blank, that past. She had stretched her chores to encompass the day, operating at automaton's pace: clearing the table of Chen's breakfast glass of milky, heavily sweetened tea, sponge-cake and sugar sandwich, the glittering grains from which still adhered to the margarine on the crust he always left. Then she would pile the washing-up in the sink, staring out into the courtyard as she ran the tap at a trickle, dreamily washing each article several times over before rinsing them laboriously under that thin thread of water, sometimes gripping the rim of the sink and staring at the tiled wall for half an hour before continuing. Then came the vacuum-cleaning and the dusting, followed by a slow walk to the shop, a trip she made daily because of the minute quantities in which she had bought her groceries. She was now twenty minutes on the round trip. In the old days she would have taken an hour and a half. After that there would have been the long wait for Chen. She had been a hunched, motionless figure in her kitchen, sitting in the dusk with only the glow of the gas fire in winter and in summer a slowly fading submarine twilight diffused through the tenement courtyard.

Those days had been short. They flowed over her. Their moments had hardly been perceptible. They had not contained demands. She would have been happy to drift along this way, her days expanding into a featureless but unthreatening future and receding into a past which was equally undifferentiated. She lost count of weeks, couldn't remember what she had been doing two days ago.

All this had changed. Days were full now. Full of incidents which, trivial and minor in themselves, threw the day into relief. They provided a guide, points of reference and recall. And the odd thing was that the days seemed twice as long, moving at this tempo. It seemed far longer between seeing Husband off in the morning and welcoming him home with soup at night. She still waited with a suppressed, unbearable excitement which was, if anything, stronger than her former anticipation of his footfall on the stairs. Lily's excitement would infect Mui; she would begin to tremble slightly, her breath coming fast and shallow. The girls sat close together opposite Chen at the table. Their sleeves just grazed; each could feel the warmth of the other's body through the gauzy material of her clothes. They giggled, rushing away every now and then to take a pan off the stove or put more meat and gravy into Chen's bowl of soup.

For his part Chen was ignorant of the effect he had on them. And though the girls in their combined anticipation incited each other to a far greater degree of excitement than Lily had ever known on her own, she was now actually less dependent on Chen. Then he had been the focus of her day, the point around which she organised herself and through which her activities took on meaning. Now she was using Chen. There was a subtle change. Her services had not changed nor had they deteriorated. But their point had altered. Unknown to Chen whole new outlooks were developing behind his back, potentially disruptive of family harmony and his hitherto unchallenged position as leader of that unit, except that both girls were far too loyal to let things get to that stage.

Lily started to experiment with a series of different addresses to the father of her child. 'Husband', her habitual usage, a simple descriptive term after all, implied respect as well as a salutary recognition of the *status quo* and all that it traditionally implied. Lily used the term as recipient of obligations which were bilateral. There was also 'Ah Chen', more familiar, used as a summons to ordinary household occasions, notably those through which Lily would be fulfilling a one-sided part of the marital contract. 'Ah Chen' was also a distancing term. Being Chen's family name, it also implied a reversion to the state of affairs prior to the marriage and separated Lily Tang from the Chens. To refer to her spouse by this alias was also suddenly to look upon him as an individual, whereas his importance really consisted in his role, his rank – if you like – of husband.

Thus: 'Ah Chen! Ready to eat now.'

But: 'Husband, the door is stuck!' when Chen would be expected to shift it from its stiff hinges, something Lily could do more easily than her husband.

The two girls' lives still centred around a male principal but there had been a major re-allocation of parts in the domestic drama, the lead now taken by a juvenile, Man Kee, whose persistent demands, irregular tantrums, and constant need for attention and physical reassurance from his supporting cast of adults far exceeded any ever made by the placid and equable Chen. Through no fault of Chen's, the transference of the centre of gravity in the household had resulted in a diminishing of his own stature in the eyes of the two females who, having a small and helpless child to succour during the day, had to make an effort to see Chen as an adult representative of his gender – had as it were to blink imaginatively before seeing him according to his true scale. Despite this, they still had a tendency to confuse his behaviour with Man Kee's, a hallucination which gained a subjective reality in time. Lily had to make a conscious effort not to burp Husband and, after Man Kee had passed beyond this stage, not to pat Husband on the back and stroke his stomach when he had finished soup. She still stood over him to make sure he drank it all, would dearly have liked to feed him herself a little faster. And perhaps, after all, that was just a diversion of the maternal instinct, as was the gentleness with which Lily washed Chen's greasy hair for him in the sink in the plastic washing-up bowl. Chen still sat unchallenged in his armchair and had the lion's share of food, but there was a novel layer to the girls' abstinence which had become self-aggrandising, an exercise in controlling and developing the self rather than the tribute of natural respect. Under these manipulations it was difficult not to think of Chen as a greedy little boy. Of course, the girls forgave him, never allowed themselves to see it in quite such terms, but there was no doubt Man Kee had undermined his father's authority in the most innocent way possible, by analogy.

Lily had never met the wives of Chen's colleagues; she knew of the staff only by report, having seen Lo just once for the time it took him to drink a glass of her scalding tea. She liked what Husband told her of Mr Lo and warmed to him at their first short meeting. At secondhand she conceived an intense dislike of Roman Fok; although when Husband complained about him, she tried to suggest extenuating circumstances or good aspects of Fok's character. She felt it was her duty to do this.

As Chen had no family of his own who might celebrate birthdays, lunar New Year, hold impromptu *mah jeuk* parties or christenings (there were a few Catholics and Baptists in the restaurant, the Baptists hilariously preponderant amongst the dishwashers), Lily moved in a restricted circle: herself, Mui, Man Kee. There were the English neighbours, the Polish doctor, but these were hardly more than nodding acquaintances. Husband, of course, didn't count.

It came, then, as a nice surprise when during a shopping expedition to the Brent supermarket she came across two Chinese women at the rice shelf, both a lot older than herself or Mui. One was plainly mistress, the other obviously *amah*. The latter was dressed in the maid-servant's classic uniform: black trousers, white tunic, her thin grey hair cut short and plastered close to the scalp, coming just below the ears, in the lobes of which she wore tiny earrings of jade. She had a bracelet of the same, flecked inferior stone around her bony wrist and was pushing the wire shopping trolley. It was crammed with food. At the moment when Lily came round the corner with her steel basket on her arm and Mui wheeling Man Kee in the rear, the *amah*'s employer was comparing two bags of rice. Lily squeezed past to pick up her own packet. The older woman politely made way for her, then noticed that Lily was an oriental. She nodded and smiled. Then Man Kee arrived, waving a rattle and banging his stockinged heels. Both the strange women melted. Man Kee closed his eye in a huge, lugubrious wink and kept it shut while Mui tried to lift his eyelid with her thumb and scolded him without much conviction. Man Kee hit her on the head with his toy and laughed at his appreciative audience.

'Handsome boy,' the strange woman complimented Lily in Cantonese. As Lily merely smiled without saying anything, she repeated her remark in English: 'The boy good-looking.'

'No. Not at all. He's a very plain child.'

'Ah, so you are Chinese. I thought you might be Filipino.' The woman used the idiom 'Person of Tang', a peculiar southern idiom. 'But not from Hong Kong. Singapore, maybe?'

'Kwangsi.' Lily smiled.

'I thought your accent was strange. Yes, you don't have the appearance of a Hong Kong person. Too independent-looking.' She laughed at her own joke. She was, Lily estimated, in her late forties and later discovered she had been over ten years out in her guess. Mrs Law was over sixty at their time of meeting. She was dressed in sober but expensive clothes and had a pleasant, homely face which was rather at variance with her elegant outfit.

'You must let me buy him something.'

'No, no. You will spoil him.'

They left together. At the check-out Lily finally allowed Mrs Law to present her son with a chocolate mouse bought at the rack of confectionery near the till. At this point Man Kee had an attack of shyness, burying his chin in his chest and moving his big head slowly from side to side, which further endeared him to his new admirers. He was persuaded to purse his lips and applied them in a kind of red trumpet to Mrs Law's cheek. Mrs Law insisted on taking their address and a fortnight later Lily received an invitation to 'drink tea', personally delivered by the servant Ah Jik who had brought a musical spinning-top for Man Kee.

Mrs Law was the widow of a wealthy ship-owner, twenty years older than his wife, who had died in Hong Kong. They had married in Swatow where he had been a lighterman and she the third daughter of a *yamen* clerk who had been forced to become a public letter-writer after the 1911 revolution. They had worked their way up in the world together until he had collected a fleet of fourteen rusty coastal tramps. At one point there had been eighteen but four, heavily insured, had foundered in mysterious circumstances. Greatly mourned by his wife but without children, Law had died in a private hospital of the nasopharyngeal cancer so prevalent on the southern coast, caused by a lifetime's inordinate consumption of the dried salt fish he had loved so much.

Bored and unhappy in Hong Kong, Mrs Law emigrated a year after her husband's death, starting a new life in England at the age of fifty-five. The country was her second choice: Canada had rejected her because of TB scars on the lungs.

Lily was over-awed on her first visit to the big flat. 'Tea drinking' turned out to be a sumptuous affair of delicacies she hadn't seen for years: sweet black gelatine rolls, formed of layers of transparent film thinner than tissue paper, which gleamed and shivered tantalisingly; cakes of crushed lotus seed paste with fiery, salty egg yolks inside; cold cuts of abalone, chicken, ham, smoked fish, fungus strips, mushrooms so thick and succulent they tasted like meat; English strawberry tarts and fragrant jasmine tea of the kind Lily adored. The girls seriously disappointed Mrs Law on their first visit when they were too shy to do more than pick at this magnificent buffet, but Man Kee more than compensated. He laid on a star's performance, turning somersaults on the carpet, playing hide-and-seek behind curtains and under furniture, turning on both taps in the bath, a thunderous cacophony heard in time in the sitting room so that disaster was averted. He fell asleep on the top deck of the bus on their way home but didn't cry when Lily woke him at their destination.

When Chen came home the girls didn't tell him about the visit; there was unspoken agreement on this.

The visit to Golders Green became a weekly event. Man Kee found a new present every time he went, which was added to the growing collection in Mrs Law's airing cupboard. The adults sat on Mrs Law's emerald silk sofas and were waited on by Ah Jik who watched from the kitchen door.

Mrs Law was a good listener. She even drew Mui out. Perched on the sofa with a cup of tea she became quite garrulous, much to Lily's surprise. Mrs Law found she had something in common with the girls' background, and she warmed to them. Her own father's fall hadn't been such a blow as the orphaning of the girls but she could sympathise.

'So father was a *sifu*, was he?' she said. 'How noble!'

The girls tittered, politely.

'Did he teach you or just Elder Brother?'

Mui answered her: 'We have no brother. But Father taught Lily as much as he could before he was killed. Quite unsuitable, really, for a girl.'

Hearing of their father's violent death, Mrs Law didn't make the jokes she had intended about them being a deadly pair. Instead she filled their cups for them in a respectful silence. Fearing Mrs Law's exterior of well-bred calm concealed embarrassment, Lily tried to put her at ease. 'If you look at my knuckles here you can still see how they are larger than the others although the callus went away years ago.' Mrs Law politely inspected the hand which seemed quite normal to her. 'And I'm still supple,' Lily kicked off her flat shoes and proceeded to do the splits on Mrs Law's fine carpet to the private alarm and consternation of the owner. Even with the last inches Lily needed no help.

'How truly remarkable,' Mrs Law complimented her, and for once the comment was not formulaic good manners. Then she changed the subject skilfully. Lily, only slightly abashed, felt old reflexes awaking. That night, in the locked bathroom, she went through some of the old suppling movements she remembered; did a half-hearted shadow set. For a few days she repeated the exercises, then grew bored and abandoned them.

*

A month after encountering Mrs Law at the supermarket, Lily met Mr Lo again. Lo had fallen ill. It was the first time in the three years Chen had known him; he was concerned for his friend. Still a strapping fellow, Lo was neither a shirker nor frail. This was what worried Chen. The illness must be serious. The boss, of course, had stopped his wages. Chen was sufficiently concerned to mention the matter to Lily and she, realising how rare it was for him to mention anything about work, was also disturbed. Her worry increased throughout the day (which would not have been the case had she anything of the most minor significance concerning her own family to occupy her quick mind) and she steered the evening's talk round to the sick Lo again. 'Perhaps I could take some medicine round to him?' she suggested, wondering why Husband grinned.

'That would get him out of bed – one way or the other.'

'Hah?'

After getting Lo's address from Chen, Lily did go a few days later. She took a thermos of soup, fruit, some flowers, plain sponge cakes, and some outdated Hong Kong newspapers. Thus provided with home comforts she set out for Hendon on her own.

Lo had one room in a house not too far from the bus routes. Lily walked slowly. She had acted impulsively. When she first put the idea to Husband she had been expecting resistance or at least an explanation why she shouldn't go. She had been using Husband as a safety net and his easy compliance was disappointing. He had failed, betrayed her by agreeing with her. It was his function to oppose, part of the natural order of things, the cycle of constant fruitful opposites. She felt this in her heart, and was hurt. If she fell, so to speak, if there was embarrassment, loss of face, it would be *his* fault. What faltering confidence she had fled as she stood in front of the grimy door. She almost went away. She went up worn linoleum stairs. There was no reply to her knock on Lo's door. Again she was on the point of going but some streak of obstinacy had her pushing the door half-open before she knew she had done it.

Lo was asleep in his narrow bed, hands outside the cover of a single grey blanket, stitched at the ends with pink thread. His face was waxy and pale and his chest was not noticeably rising or falling. Lily at once feared the worst. Should she get help, practise artificial respiration? Was there risk of infection? (A quick twinge of shame followed this.) She dropped her presents on the floor and pulled down the sash window with a loud clatter. When Lily turned, Lo was looking at her (without a great deal of curiosity, it had to be admitted).

'Oh, Mr Lo. Please excuse my rudeness and presumption.' Lily smiled prettily but in great confusion, revealing her dimple and also, unfortunately, through some trick of muscular contraction, emphasising the length of her face rather than widening it, as might have been expected. She found she was treading on the cut flowers she had brought and picked them up, trying to re-arrange the broken stems. All in all, Lo was taking the intrusion of a strange young woman into his bedroom very well (mainly because he was too ill to waste much energy on surprise and had at first assumed he must be hallucinating) but Lily was blushing deeper second by second in two furious spots of colour on her cheek-bones. These flamed further as she realised she had failed to introduce herself. 'Do you remember me? I am Lily Chen, Mrs Chen, I should say. Colleague Chen's wife. You took tea with us once. We are very worried about you. Can you forgive my presumption?'

Lo half-raised himself on his elbows. 'Mrs Chen, you are too kind ... ' He fell back again. Lily leapt forward and dragged the flattened pillow up behind Lo's head, trying unsuccessfully to plump the empty sack.

'But you are really very ill, Mr Lo.' Lily was dismayed. She hadn't been expecting to find a malingerer. From Husband's scattered references to Mr Lo this would have been most unlikely. On the other hand she had not anticipated finding him so spectacularly ill. Lo's face was a terrible grey; under his eyes and around the mouth, the skin had a purple tinge. When Lily touched the sheets they were damp with the sick man's sweat. Tears for this stranger which would not have welled for Mui, Chen, or even Man Kee, surprised her. She blinked them away and began efficiently bustling. There was not much for her to bustle efficiently with. Lo's room contained his iron bed and one chair, over which he had thrown his black trousers and a shirt. In a corner of the floor was a gas ring, a kettle and single glass. There was neither a carpet on the plank floor nor a vase into which Lily might put her snapped and bent chrysanthemums.

'Mrs Chen, I am ashamed of my humble home. You do me a very great honour.' Lo was now just beginning to grasp the situation and his agitation invested the conventionally self-belittling formula with real meaning. Perhaps he felt he had lost face? Lily did her best to calm Lo who was becoming feverish as the surprise and embarrassment of the situation came home to him.

For the time being Lily put her flowers in the few inches of water in the kettle. Lo refused the cakes but she cut the string around the cardboard box and left it invitingly open for after she had gone. She didn't administer the herbal draught she had brought. Chen would not have escaped so easily; Mui would have been forced to drink every last drop.

By the time she left, Lo had regained his composure and the stimulus of the visit seemed to have done him good. Lily promised to bring 'Uncle' Lo, as he had become, a radio, if he would drink the medicine she left.

'Poor man,' she thought, as she waited for her bus, 'so alone and such bad luck,' and she thought with warmth of her own little family, warmth that Chen's amusement over her visit could not dispel; nor Mui's intense observation of the television; nor reports that Man Kee had been throwing tantrums all day while she was gone. 'You spoil him,' she told his aunt, proceeding to do the same herself.

Mrs Law took from the start a keen vicarious interest in the plight of Lo. He struck some essential chord of her own experience (as did the girls), disparate though the external aspects of their lives had been. 'Poor man,' she exclaimed, unconsciously echoing Lily, and interrogated her exhaustively as her curiosity and sympathy for a fellow human being temporarily got the better of her old-fashioned good manners. Her kind, wrinkled face registered a variety of emotions that would have enhanced the repertoire of an actor. 'What mistfortune!' – 'Really!' – 'What a good person you are, Lily!' – 'No bathroom?' she ejaculated in rapid succession. Lily warmed to her account of the visit, which had been short enough in all conscience. Now she began to describe enthusiastically the journey, the stairs, the room, Lo's appearance. In retrospect a painful and also embarrassing experience took on a warm after-glow of achievement and sentiment. Lily didn't invent anything nor did she embroider her story but her tone changed as she began to enjoy talking about it, and this was the greater falsification.

Yet the fact remained: Lo was still ill; his circumstances hadn't changed. The fact that he was the central protagonist in a drama of absorbing human interest to others unknown to him did not by itself help him.

Three days later Lily visited him again with the promised radio and also Mui and Man Kee.

Lo was sitting up in bed this time, wearing a maroon V-neck pullover on top of his pyjama shirt. He was reading the out-of-date papers Lily had taken him with the aid of large, horn-rimmed spectacles. This time he was positively delighted with the wholesale invasion of his privacy. Mui, holding Man Kee's hand, had been correctly hesitant about following her impetuous younger sister in but, waved through by impatient Lily, was soon looking round the room. Far too inquisitively, Lily thought; though Uncle Lo didn't seem to mind a bit. While Lily tried to keep up a conversation with Uncle Lo who seemed much better, she coughed and stared meaningfully at Mui. Mui was poking around with the brown flowers in Lo's kettle and when she tired of that she looked under Mr Lo's bed, maybe for a chamber-pot.

'Uncle Lo, this is my elder sister, Mui. Ah Mui please meet Mr Lo.'

There was a mischievous look on Mui's face. Having tried with long lack of success to enliven lumpish Mui throughout the first months of her stay, when she had been nothing more than a tearful, silent bundle on the sofa, Lily found it quite intolerable that she should have chosen this particular moment to come out in her own right as a personality; an extremely tiresome personality, it was proving.

'Yes, Uncle Lo, my humble and worthless sister, Mui, and my son Man Kee.' Lily took pleasure in the traditional style of introduction. Mui tittered in a way Lily found exceptionally unbecoming in a woman of her advanced years, twenty-nine by western reckoning, thirty-*sui* Chinese-style, come next New Year. She did not answer Lo's kindly requests that they shouldn't stand on ceremony and must make themselves at home. Both superfluous injunctions: Mui was sitting on the edge of Lo's bed cockily tuning the transistor away from the selected frequency to one of her own choice. Music blared out now. Lily's mouth was pursed.

'Mrs Chen, would you be kind enough to make tea for all of us?' Lily's irritation dispelled bit by bit as she occupied herself with the chore of tea-making. Lo's kettle was a whistler, which intrigued Man Kee and he had to be restrained from burning himself. There was really no confining this boy's curiosity, Lily thought. Quite unlike the way she and Mui had grown up. Any signs of such undisciplined behaviour then would have been mercilessly dealt with. Poking fingers hadn't been in evidence for long in Father's household; perhaps a son might have escaped the full weight of a traditional upbringing. Somehow Lily doubted it. And yet here was the adult Mui setting a prodigiously bad example to her nephew. One might as well let the natural instincts of the young go uncorrected if they were only to surface again in strengthened form in later life. Poor Father! His whole life had been a battle which had been lost from the outset, if he had only known. There was a delinquent streak in Mui, Lily reflected, which would bear watching.

Lily had provided herself with glasses before they left home and they soaked the stale sponge-cakes from her last visit. Man Kee's mouth ended in a fine old mess. Lo was delighted with their company and, deciding that if Uncle was not offended by Mui there was no reason why she should be, Lily relaxed; although she kept looking reproachfully at Mui and once or twice reprimanded Man Kee on imaginary pretexts, using him as a scapegoat for his aunt (whom she could not very well smack on the bottom, much as she was tempted).

'How happy you all are together,' said Lo as he moistened a second piece of cake in his tea and dropped it into that gruesome orifice, Man Kee's willing mouth. He was silent for a while as he thought of his own wife and disastrous marriage. Then he smiled at his guests, for he had pride and saw them as visitors to whom he had obligations rather than as kind rescuers to whom he might be indebted. 'Mrs Chen, please don't stand on ceremony. Make us all some more of your excellent tea.' And the conversation turned to Lily's tins of fragrant jasmine, a topic near to her heart but not Mui's, with the result that as one sister became good-humoured, the other began to fidget. This time Lily's good-humour was proof against Mui.

They left rather later than they had intended, at seven o'clock when it was already pitch-dark; no lights were working in the street. Having emerged from a warm, bright oasis, they walked in silence to the station and did not recover their spirits until they were home again. There Lily turned on every light in the house and even raised the volume of the TV, so that from the dark courtyard their flat appeared as a glowing cube, throbbing with sound and diffusing rich odours of cooking.

Beyond his initial amusement Chen had not shown further interest in Lily's acquaintanceship with another man, even if it was only an older colleague of his own. That someone could be sexually interested in Lily, could find her even remotely appealing, would have been an enormity beyond his imagination. Nor did he find a visit with Mui and Man Kee remarkable. He had no idea what the girls usually did with their day.

Lo was back at work a week after Lily's second visit, as phlegmatic, silent, and handy with the cleaver as ever. Neither he nor Chen mentioned Lily or the visits to each other.

Mrs Law, though, couldn't hear enough. She let Lily do the talking again but halted her periodically to cross-check with Mui. 'Is that true, Mui?' – 'Ah Mui, did you hear that, too?' – 'Really, Mui?' Potentially insulting as indicative at best of doubt about Lily's powers of recall and evocation and, at worst, hinting she was a prevaricator, these interjections ha⁀ the ultimate effect of flattering Lily. They proclaimed he. a story-teller of flair since Mui (satisfactorily the old Mui again) corroborated all Lily said with smiling nods. Mrs Law's exclamations of disbelief become subtle compliments

There was for the moment no question of Mrs Law meeting Mr Lo. All three women operated on this as an assumption so basic it didn't even need to be mentioned. It wasn't so much a question of snobbery (although certainly the dilemma could have been expressed in similar terms) as of mutual embarrassment: for Lo, working in a menial job chopping meat, however skilfully; for Lily, whose husband was a humble waiter; for Mrs Law who did not wish to embarrass her young friends. All parties had the personal grace to surmount artificial social obstacles outside the immediate environment. But to meet in the restaurant was out of the question.

Then Lo was forced to find another job. During his short illness the proprietor had used one of his own kinsmen as barbecue chef. The boy had shown aptitude – he had not actually chopped any of his own fingers off – and, what was more, he hadn't tried to extract more than the very slight wage increase the boss had offered him. Lo found his position taken. A man of his skill had no trouble finding another place – in the window of a still larger restaurant on Shaftesbury Avenue.

This at once freed the girls of any embarrassment. Mrs Law had wanted to take them out to dinner for some time. Set in old ways, she looked on home entertaining as an inferior form of hospitality. Of course, the girls had persistently declined her invitations. But introducing Uncle Lo to Mrs Law changed everything. Not that they could have done it at the Ho Ho. Husband might have had to wait on them. Lily giggled when she thought about it.

But now they would be doing Mr Lo a favour by bringing business to his restaurant; it would help him with his new employers. Uncle, too, could welcome them as their 'friend' in the restaurant – a connection to be valued. Terms could be negotiated, discounts, fictitious but face-giving on all sides, be granted. How easy and delightful it had become!

Lily accompanied Mrs Law to Shaftesbury Avenue to talk money with the manager. Lo was already at work in the empty restaurant and Lily was about to rap playfully on the window when she thought better of it. What if there was an accident and he chopped off a finger?

They settled terms over the inevitable tea. The proprietor suggested some dishes: crabs were fresh and plentiful in the market at the moment, white vegetable was good, as were Holland beans. What about a baked crab with ginger and spring onion, roast pork and duck, a whole steamed sea bass, baked chicken or pigeon with potato puffs, and noodles and fried rice? Shark's fin soup to start, of course, and half-way through a sweet soup of almond or peanut. Fresh fruit and tiny sweet buns to end. Lily could smell it already. The manager could offer them this at £3 per head, with a discount of ten per cent because of special introduction. Had there been a bigger party he could have granted a more favourable tariff; the manager smiled.

Mrs Law smiled herself and suggested lower prices, while agreeing with the selection of dishes. She felt no false embarrassment about talking money in front of Lily. Why should she be embarrassed about money?

Lo was now summoned and introduced to Mrs Law, whom he pretended was an old friend. Everyone, manager included, was party to the little deception. Because of the unique introduction the manager offered a fifteen per cent discount. Mrs Law accepted and paid cash on the spot. She asked Lily to count the money for her. There was no discussion about the quantities served; there would be enough. Anything left over would be parcelled and taken home. Everyone was happy. And the meal itself turned out to be a culinary as well as social success. Even if it had been rotten, it would hardly have mattered.

Mrs Law took to eating there regularly. She didn't have elaborate meals such as the one Lily and Mui devoured, for once able to give free rein to their natural instincts, uninhibited by shyness of Mrs Law or by Chen's solid masculine presence (only to find that their shrunken stomachs were unable to accommodate quite as much as they wished and wistfully surveyed congealing on the dishes, for all Mrs Law's urgings). Mrs Law ate homelier stuff: the excellent cooking of the south, the unadorned barbecues in which Lo specialised and the crispest vegetables he could find for her.

It was unthinkable for a lady to eat alone, so Mrs Law took Ah Jik with her. Lo immediately re-seated them at the best table in the room and took extra care with the presentation of his cold meat collation. He welcomed Mrs Law respectfully when she came again.

Theirs grew into a warm and almost entirely sexless attachment, deftly maintained on both sides with equal tact and consideration. Both were lonely, unattached; both in their different ways disappointed with what their lives had become, although unable to change them. Social considerations made romance unthinkable. Personal temperament was also against it. Had the inclination been there perhaps the gulf in station might have been bridged with surprising ease. As it was, Lo's regard and respect for a widow a few years his senior was a contradictory mixture of the loyalty which an old family retainer might have given to the last of a patrician line, together with a sense of fellowship and sympathy springing from a common situation, and also – small but significant yeast to the leaven of mutual liking – a courtly, old-fashioned but still sprightly gallantry such as might legitimately be extended to members of the opposite sex (Lo being a man, after all).

Mrs Law was happy to be the recipient of such tribute. 'Poor man!' she thought again, yet without an ounce of patronage. 'Bad luck man,' was the phrase which most often came to mind and – though she had never thought of it that way – she would not have been offended but perhaps first surprised before she agreed with such an estimate of her own life. She did not see Lo as duped, pathetic or weak any more than she saw herself in those terms. She didn't feel sorry for herself; she didn't feel pity for Lo. All the same she was touched. As he was touched by her. The sorrow checked on one's own behalf was more easily tapped and flowed stronger because the plight of the other was so easy to envisage.

Their conversations derived an added poignancy from the interruptions caused by the periodic need for Lo to return to his chopping-board. This loaded the stock exchanges with a further burden of meaning. Lo always declined Mrs Law's invitation to sit. But she made a point of filling a cup of tea for him, which grew cold and remained undrunk, a libation to whatever tutelary deity it was that presided over their brand of friendship.

'Business is good tonight,' she would compliment him.

'Quite good,' he would agree, completing his half of the conventional exchange, his eyes conveying a quite different and tenderer sort of message, although naturally there was nothing Mrs Law could find impertinent or offensive in it.

'What delicious duck, Mr Lo!'

'Let me give you some roast crackling pork, Mrs Law. Try my special *hoi sin* sauce. Better than the usual. There are soya beans under the pork.'

And Mrs Law would partake with the appropriate exclamations of surprise and delight, unfeigned because Lo was really a very good barbecue chef. Then Lo might be signalled back to work by the manager, discreetly because the manager knew how to deal with a virtuoso and also because he wished to retain Mrs Law's patronage. What a little lady but what a lot she ate! When this happened Lo would disengage himself gracefully by pouring still more tea for Mrs Law, even if it was only a few drops into an already brimming cup, backing off apologetically, a look of infinite wistfulness in his eyes, before he proceeded to sliver the meat on his board with great ferocity. At such moments Mrs Law would be assailed by feelings of a delicious poignancy, quite disproportionate to the trifling and momentary nature of the inconvenience. Then Lo would be back for a while. Thus the friendship proceeded in fits and starts.

For these encounters Mrs Law dressed soberly, as if going to a Western-style funeral, in a black cashmere twin-set and long woollen skirt (despite the current heat-wave), leaving off the few diamond rings and the brooch she normally wore but lacquering her finger nails with a transparent varnish. Later she enamelled them a discreet, palest pink. Ah Jik was pleased to see her mistress cheerful. Wisely, though, she said nothing.

SIX

Late in the afternoon it had rained abruptly out of a clear sky. There was now a clamminess in the air which seemed to be fed by the puddles on the pavement and in the road. The brief shower had not cleared the atmosphere; it had turned the air moist and sullen. Sooty droplets ran down the ideographs of the restaurant and company signs. Off the street tributary rivulets ran out of the mouth of a narrow alley like black blood from the stump of some ruined tooth to feed the dark, rushing water in the gutter. In Dansey Place the water sliding down green, mossy walls had the viscous quality of beads of glycerine. As usual, the Place was crammed with motor-cars and tradesmen's vans. The sound of restaurants preparing for the evening hardly reached here: the scrape of tables and chairs, the clink of metal on glass or porcelain.

Three men in the back of a dormobile waited for one man. They crouched on the metal floor; the man by the back door watched through a tiny hole in the metal panel.

Late afternoon turned to early evening and then to dusk. The lights in restaurant windows came on, startling fish in the big tanks in the seafood restaurants.

One man came into Dansey Place. A bunch of car-keys jingled in his hand. As he inserted the correct key into the door of a Jaguar, three men emerged from the back of the dormobile. Two men went down the left side of the Jaguar, one down the right. The owner of the car was now trapped between the wall and the front bumper of the big car. His palms and the back of his head were against the damp wall. There was a murmur of subdued conversation; nothing loud, nothing angry. It was now quite dark. There were deep shadows in what had become a ravine.

The man talking to the car-owner was slighter than his two companions. He had a hand casually on the Jaguar's bonnet. A taller, thicker-set man stood behind him, arms folded. The slighter man appeared to be making placatory gestures. His low voice, inaudible three cars away except as a gentle, broken hum, had an earnest, apologetic tone. He stepped back. The man behind him seized the Jaguar owner by the hair and drove his head into the bonnet. There was a big boom. He pulled him up again still by the hair and slammed his face into the metal with greater force. He pinioned his arms behind his back. The man on the right-hand side of the Jaguar kneed its owner between the legs and again in the face as he fell. The slighter, quietly spoken man had picked up the keys; he opened the car-door, started the engine. He reversed slightly; then with the door partly open he drove over the fallen man's legs and back again. He got out, put the keys in the unconscious man's palm. He shovelled cabbage leaves and newspapers over him. Then he unzipped his trousers and urinated over the man's face. He and the man at his side left through the east exit, the third man through the west.

Grass Sandal took a deep breath. She had weighed out on tiny apothecary's scales 115 grams of the crude brown No 3 mixture stored under a floor board and placed it on a thick block of glass. To this she added ten grams of a base powder. She mixed it with the pyramid of

No 3. The result was not entirely satisfactory from the point of texture. There was a certain brand of fertiliser which bore a greater resemblance. Unfortunately it was also poisonous. Had it been a once-only operation Grass Sandal would not have hesitated. As it was, she was a good businesswoman. In the dark and in the small medicine-phials this would do. It would also leave her with a commission of ten per cent without defrauding the society (in her opinion). Probably the stuff was now only twenty per cent pure. Still, good enough for 'chasing the dragon' Hong Kong style with match, silver foil, and paper tube, and certainly good enough for the English to dissolve and heat in their tea-spoons and squirt into their veins. Once, in a cold-blooded experiment, Grass Sandal had shot the AA gun herself; embedded three grains of costly No 4 into the tip of an upwards pointed cigarette and sucked until the end had glowed brightly. She had never repeated the exercise, of course.

She turned her head away to sneeze delicately. She began to transfer the No 3 into forty-four glass phials. Four were her own to sell. When she had finished with scales and phials, she capped the containers securely and swept them into a large cellophane bag. This and the block of glass she took to the bathroom. She rinsed her working-surface carefully under the cold bath-tap before cleaning the tub with the hosed shower attachment. She flushed the apple-green lavatory cistern, took the lid off and slid a long metal fork under the ball-cock to prevent it filling again. She adhesive-taped the cellophane bag to the side of the cistern and replaced the lid. Then she drew back all the curtains and switched the light out. After locking the front door she pressed the lift-button and only then removed rubber surgical gloves, placing them in a brown paper bag. Outside, she put the bag in a rubbish bin and walked to her aubergine Mini. This was not her house but the 'godown' in which she stored merchandise. Occasionally it was used as a safe house, which Grass Sandal resented. She was prudent. Above all, she disliked other people putting her at risk, however minimally.

Night-brother stood respectfully as Red Cudgel entered the Nine Dragons Teahouse. The older man shook his head and turned back to the door. Night-brother found him in the back of his Mercedes. Red Cudgel opened the door for him, then pressed down the locking button. The driver took them away. Night-brother wondered why they couldn't have talked quietly or in Hung code at the back of the teahouse. As if reading his thoughts, Red Cudgel said: 'From now more care. With outsiders it is necessary to deal in public for all to see. Business between ourselves in secret.'

Night-brother found this excessively cautious; however, he gave an 'ah' of approval. 'Is it good for me to speak now, Elder Brother? Good. Both matters accomplished. I personally made an example of the man for others to learn. Done discreetly, according to your order. No one saw. The other matter of the drug is more difficult. Things move slowly here.'

Red Cudgel's face was impassive. He had been looking out of the smoked-glass window, apparently absent-mindedly. 'Good. You didn't cripple the man permanently?'

'According to your instruction.'

'I heard otherwise, Little Brother.'

'Enough to make an example.'

'Example is more effective when it suits the offence. Bad to punish indiscriminately. You should apply in measured doses, like medicine. Otherwise the recipients get used to it. How can you frighten others with a greater punishment when you need it? When you wish to give severe punishment you will have none to administer. You will have exceeded the measure already. Then you can only kill. When men know they face death, then they become brave and dangerous. What does he have to lose? You must learn these things, Little Brother.'

'You must teach me.'

'White Fan knows these things. He deserves respect from you which you do not give.'

Night-brother changed the subject. 'I knew this man last night. Owns two restaurants. He complained but like the others he paid more money in the end. Others still have their debt outstanding. Why was he chosen?'

Red Cudgel said: 'You should not try to aspire to the whole picture. However . . . I make an exception in your case. This man had the means to pay our levy and should not have argued with us. But this was not the reason I ordered an example to be made of him. He wants to open a casino in the Street. Legal. He has been to bandits and Gaming Board. I need not tell you how this would have affected us. I gather they are happy to give a licence to anyone who can put the gambling on an open basis, although we have been tolerated in the basements so far.'

'More than tolerated. Maybe this man was a nominee for 14-K?'

'The same had occurred to me. White Fan argues otherwise. He says they want as little to do with the bandits as ourselves.'

'I should still have killed him.'

'There will be killing, but when I say.'

The car was cruising beside the illuminated river, overtaking the rest of the light traffic. Red Cudgel said: 'Slower, idiot.'

Night-brother spoke again, in an apologetic tone: 'The problem with distributing the drug is still far from smoothed out. We badly need runners to meet the European contacts on the street. It has got suddenly worse since the meeting. Quite risky for them now. As I said, I don't like to use our 49s for peddling. There is always the chance one weak link might talk and implicate others. Last month we lost three probationaries who were runners. All caught by bandits. I have two 49s meeting Europeans in Earlham Street at the moment but I don't like it. Grass Sandal gives the phials to me and I pass them on. She won't supply directly. I cannot blame her.'

Red Cudgel nodded. Night-brother knew his unmoved exterior hid a quick brain, as incisive as White Paper Fan's but not as subtle, and he was at first disappointed in the senior officer's reply.

'I leave the business in your hands. There is a bigger business I am planning, bigger than your "brown sugar".'

He used the English term for No 3 ('Bah-lown Soo-gar', he said), surprising Night-brother who had thought he didn't speak the language at all (Elder Brother's Cantonese was not of the best either).

'No 3 brings a lot of money to the society,' he corrected the 426 officer.

'It does. It does.' Red Cudgel was known to look on Night-brother as a favourite nephew to be indulged rather than a younger brother to be chastised. He clapped him on the knee. 'We must not let our hold on the market slip or 14-K will gain a monopoly again. That's why I ask you and no one else to take charge of this business.'

'I'll do my best. Can I tell our 49s that they are to recruit runners? Not future members but expendables? Maybe some fools with big gambling debts?'

Red Cudgel's mind was clearly on other matters but he was not negligent. 'No. Bad thinking. If stupid enough to lose everything they are also too stupid to trust. That type has a big mouth. They could also try to cheat us. You want a quiet type whom no one suspects. But you must find a lever, fear or blackmail or gratitude. Or all three. They used to kidnap that type to join us in the old days.'

Night-brother said: 'I respect your need to concentrate on major matters. We juniors should look after day-to-day small things. But I respectfully ask you to involve yourself in looking at the problems of distribution on the Street. You will see at first hand my difficulties. Most runners, I have to emphasise, are bad: they drawn attention to themselves with cars and expensive clothes. If we can find more suitable types, then I ask you to inspect and impress them with the solemnity of our society. You must teach me the old ways and how to apply here.'

Red Cudgel said: 'Good. Agreed.' Night-brother saw he had pleased the older man. Red Cudgel considered a moment, then said to the driver: 'Park the car here. Leave and smoke two cigarettes.'

The car slid beside the pavement in a quiet street in Pimlico.

Red Cudgel said :'What I tell you goes no further or I *wash* this for you.' He sawed playfully at the younger man's ear with the edge of his hand, as if slicing it off with a sharp knife. Night-brother found the joke in bad taste.

Red Cudgel said: 'It's important to keep No 3 heroin circulating, of course. But I am planning to bring over a large quantity of No 4 grade, refined by our chemists in Hong Kong.'

'How much?'

'Twenty pounds.'

Night-brother sucked his breath in sharply. 'The street value is enormous! This is big money.'

'The stuff is still ninety-eight per cent pure. Of top quality. No one refines white powder better than our chemists in Hong Kong. But it is not for sale here. As you pointed out, the British market is set for No 3 heroin only. At the moment, at least. This is for America. We are intermediaries. Two couriers will bring it in separate consignments from Kai Tak to Brussels. From Brussels we bring here and store for a while. We sell from here to Toronto. This will not be repeated. Particular circumstances make it possible. The devious route makes it safe. Our profit will not be as large as you think but still sizeable. Only White Fan and myself know, and now you. I was foolish to make it three persons.'

Night-brother bowed his head. 'I am silent. Trust me.'

The chauffeur returned. Soon they were nearing the Chinese area. At a quiet corner Night-brother got out.

SEVEN

At this point for the first time in the marriage the question of money raised itself in a serious way for both of them. Until now Chen had earned far more than they needed; even the large remittances to Husband's parents hadn't made a big hole in Lily's family purse. Even with Mui to feed, clothe and keep warm she had managed to increase the margin of surplus on her housekeeping every week. But prosperity brought its own problems. Her nest egg had reached a critical size. She was growing impatient. If she had been filling her jar of plenty drop by drop she would have waited with the phlegmatism of an elephant. As the level of her savings was in fact rising rather swiftly she was eaten up with impatience. In another two or three years, given the present rate of growth, she would have enough to start (modestly) her cherished business. Had it been ten years she would have resigned herself. As it was, she wanted them out of the flat in the next twelve months. *They were wasting their lives!* She kept telling Husband this – no use of course.

But Chen had a bigger worry. He too had been faced with the need to get a capital sum, one far bigger than Lily's. His father's long lawsuit and feuding with neighbours had left the old man with a large bill. He had lost the case two months ago, after he had chosen to take it to court rather than settle according to the headman's arbitration. He had also been saddled with his opponent's costs. This was to the extent of HK$5,000. Worse was to come. A short fall from a ladder while painting gold leaf on to a tablet in the clan's ancestral hall had broken his pelvis and though he recovered from the fracture, he had contracted a lung infection while in bed, which, aggravated by the marshy air, had turned to pneumonia. He needed expensive convalescence away from the village in a private sanatorium. Cost: at least HK$2,000. Chen's younger brother had written to him for help.

He kept the trouble secret from Lily. He feared she would nag at him to open a business and make them all rich. He could hear her voice already: 'Husband, you will never have enough to look after your parents and ourselves while you work for others. They grow rich on your sweat. You must work for yourself.'

Chen was still as conscientious about sending money to his father as when he had been single. He was a dutiful son. Lily would have made sure he was anyway. She had no living parent herself. This made her more determined to respect filial ties. She personally mailed the remittances by registered post on the fourth of every month. With each draft she enclosed a note, which might be on a corner torn off the large brown paper bags the supermarket crazily gave away free. She always signed them with Husband's name; although this fiction was quite transparent since Chen had never bothered with personal enclosures. She put the white receipts the post office gave her in her tea-tin of one and five pound notes: snowdrifts on grass, she thought poetically.

The remittances gave the old couple a comfortable enough existence. The old man still earned a little from carpentry, even if the days of crates and barrels by the gross were gone. Chen was the most affluent of their five sons, who were all good boys. They never acknowledged his remittances. This didn't mean they were ungrateful (non-remitting sons were a favourite source of gossip amongst the crones at the water-pump). Correspondence would have trivialised what the old people felt. This was not to say Chen didn't acquire merit for what he did. Occasionally important news arrived: the birth of other grandsons, a photograph of the old pair, a request for a photograph of Man Kee (which delighted Lily).

It was now entirely up to Chen to raise the money to liquidate his father's debts and then to pay for the care which would nurse him back to a healthy and long old age. At the current rate of exchange Chen would have to find a little more than £500. Put as just figures, it didn't seem much; paltry even when you considered the human benefits involved. When Chen considered it was less than half his annual salary, it seemed insignificant. He would gladly have worked an eighteen instead of twelve hour day for the next year if he could have got the extra money that way. But this was fantasising. In any case you didn't make quick, big money through hard work. He wasn't naive enough to believe that. (Perhaps he might have been surprised to know how much Lily had managed to hoard simply through self-denial.) He needed the cash right now. Yet there was nothing he owned which could be pawned for a decent sum (not even the TV). Even raising a loan would be difficult, for his cash-in-hand wages were considerably higher than those on which he was officially taxed. And he knew better than to go to one of the Street's money-lenders. They were almost as bad as Indian loan-sharks!

As he waited absent-mindedly on his tables, Chen worried at the problem. Quite naturally his concentration on immediate matters slipped. He began to confuse orders (bringing lurid orange sweet and sour pork with pineapple chunks to outraged Chinese customers and white, bloody chicken and yellow duck's feet to appalled Westerners), bumped into his colleagues in the swing-doors, and stared vacantly into the customers' eyes as they indicated with diminishing degrees of subtlety that they wished to pay their bills and leave. Finally, as was inevitable, he collided with one of the boss's clansmen in a seemingly endless series of crashes and clatterings and sounds of soup splattering on tiles and wall. This was an accident heard by the customers upstairs, as was its aftermath, the beginnings of a tremendous row, halted by Roman Fok who had just finished his shift and was heading towards the nefarious gambling den at Number 1000 to ascertain the fate of his midday stake in the Chinese characters lottery.

Until now Chen had not considered gambling as a feasible means of getting the money he needed. He was not a fool. He had only gambled a few times (to be a good sort of fellow) in the basements. Roman Fok, of course, was a compulsive gambler. Little Wong had lost a whole month's wages in Number 1000; had come back with tears streaming down his face to be mocked, jeered at, and even jostled and pinched painfully on the arm by the unsympathetic audience he found – mostly habitual heavy losers.

Wong, like Chen, had been a non-gambler. He had hoped to win enough to pay for air-fares for his mother, father, and invalid sister to come to Europe and for the sister to be treated in Switzerland. He went back the next month to Number 1000 and lost everything. A week later he left the restaurant. He had lost face irretrievably.

If Chen needed an object lesson, and he was a prudent man, he already had a graphic caution. He only half-believed Fok's boasts about the fabulous sums he had won, lost, and re-won in all-night sessions at 1000. For weeks at a time, he noticed, Fok would be without his gold watch and glittering spread of Cross pens in his shirt-pocket. Then they would re-appear. At other times Fok would be carrying thick wads of cash, indiscreetly large sums bulging in his back and side trouser pockets or peeping over the top of his pens. Roman's solvency could be gauged at any moment with a tape-measure.

Sometimes Roman must have had £500 on him.

Chen was tempted.

Next afternoon Chen probed the odds discreetly.

'What's the matter, Chen, got a girl into trouble, hah?' Roman laughed at his own highly original witticism. He had his pens in his shirt-pocket but was without his gold watch.

Chen looked so embarrassed that Roman thought for a moment he might have stumbled on the truth. Who would have thought it of Chen, he thought with a twinge of envy; perhaps an English girl, a blonde? Lily Chen was reputedly the next thing to a *gwai lo* girl herself.

'No, Ah Fok, it's not that kind of thing at all. A family matter.'

'That's what I said, isn't it?' Roman laughed again in a high key. 'OK, come to 1000 with me tomorrow and you might learn something. What time is it now? Three? No time to waste on you now, Uncle. See you.' The last epithet was a new usage of Roman's; Chen wasn't sure whether he liked being called 'Uncle' in that ironic tone of voice. After all, he was only four or five years older than Fok.

Number 1000 was as Chen remembered it from his last few visits: a cramped basement, the size of the Ho Ho's kitchen, partitioned by a curtain, reached down steep steps and packed so solid that progress had to be made obliquely with sudden changes of direction like moving a peg in a board game. This mid-afternoon time was the most popular as people came off-duty after lunch and before dinner. Ginger was skewered on three tables by thin daggers to indicate play was in progress.

Chen had secured an advance on the next three weeks' wages from the boss after ritual grumblings and the payment of a five per cent deduction. Roman had also been able to lend him £100. Chen was deeply touched.

'No need to talk like that, Uncle,' Roman said. 'Just sign this piece of paper. *I* don't think you intend to forget a debt, you understand, but . . .'

Chen squeezed Roman's arm, his eyes rather moist. 'You don't have to say anything, Ah Fok. I understand. You are a good person. I thank you from the bottom of my heart.' He had signed on the back of his order book with his pencil. 'You don't mind pencil? I have no pen. Yours is gone too since yesterday?'

More than ever Chen was touched by Roman's generosity. He should have been pleasanter to him before.

In 1000 Chen fingered the sheaf of notes in his pocket, making sure no one would pick it in the press.

Roman guided him over to the other side of the room. 'Play at big bet table, Uncle. More chance you win. Many small bets are no good.'

Chen would have preferred small bets all the same. Now Lily, he thought, she would have put big bets ...

There were big sums on this table. Over the last New Year, it was rumoured the owners (whoever they were) had taken a quarter of a million pounds profit. Losers spoke of this huge sum almost affectionately, almost proprietorially. It gave the street face.

Roman began to play, slapping the giant dominoes down on the table with mighty cracks and a flamboyance which increased with each success. 'Greetings to your mother,' he shouted. 'I'll greet your grandma too!' he bellowed as he slapped down another domino.

Chen had told Roman he would watch him play, ease himself into the game rather than blundering straight in. Roman stopped as soon as he began losing seriously, which was unusual for him. Without counting his money, he thrust it carelessly into a back pocket. 'Try your luck, Uncle?'

Cautiously, Chen began. He won a few times with trifling stakes. 'See, Uncle, you should have been bolder.' Chen put down £50 this time. Won all the money on the table.

'Bad to count money, Uncle. Unlucky and wastes your time. Keep going.'

Chen won three more times. He couldn't help wondering how much he had. As if reading his mind, Roman said: 'Give your money to me for safe-keeping, Uncle. I can count it for you.'

Chen lost the next two games. Won the one after that. 'How much, Ah Roman?'

'£300. With what you have in your hand just now, maybe £350.'

Chen considered stopping. This was a good start anyway. He might be able to do something with this to get more cash. Roman again seemed to have a window into his thoughts. 'Bad to stop now, Uncle. Follow luck through. You are a lucky man tonight.'

Chen reluctantly put down another stake. Won. Yet again he won. He now won for the fourth time in succession. Perhaps he could win the entire sum tonight, *perhaps in the next ten minutes!* He felt dizzy with success and excitement. His normally stolid face was alive with emotion. He began to put down stakes of £100 at a time. In the next quarter of an hour he won £400, frighteningly lost £300, re-made his winnings to £400 and then in three sickening games lost all of it. His own advance on his wages was gone; worse, he had lost the £100 Roman had lent him. Chen's face was pasty and blank with shock.

Roman said: '£200 here for you to be brave with, Uncle. Take, take.' Chen shook his head. Roman thrust the soiled notes into his hand. In a dream Chen put them on the table. In a dream he lost them.

'You have a car, Uncle? Jewellery or watch?'

Chen shook his head.

'Don't have? No use then. We go now.' Roman nodded at a man who had been watching from another table. He pushed Chen through the crowd, which at half past four was a little thinner. Just before reaching street-level Roman flicked his steel comb quickly through his greased hair. He put his arm round Chen on the pavement. 'You can't win always, Uncle. Don't be down-hearted. Your luck will change.'

Chen shrugged. He remembered the example of Little Wong. With cheerfulness he did not feel, he said: 'Luck will be with me another time.'

Roman said: 'No need to pay me what you owe me. Not for a while. Wait a bit.'

'I will give you the £200 as soon as I can.'

'£300, Uncle.'

'£300.'

How would he be able to send even the usual remittance to his parents this month? Where would he get cash to give Lily for housekeeping money? And Roman – he had already hinted he wanted paying as soon as possible. Nor could Chen blame him. He had been a fool, the stupidest kind of fool.

That evening Chen took the orders and delivered the bills with a heavy heart. All that money going into the boss's cash-box! How he would have liked to take it and gamble it in one go at 1000.

At least Roman hadn't mentioned his big losses to anyone else. Next day Roman met him outside the kitchen and asked casually: 'What did you need money for anyway, Uncle?'

Chen hesitated, then said: 'My father is ill. Also needs to pay crooked lawyer.'

Roman offered him a cigarette and lit one himself as Chen declined. 'Stay out of the hands of lawyers, my friend! They take all you have. All they are is official bandits. Take my advice.' He threw the match on the floor. 'So it's a big bill then? That's bad.' He went off shaking his head to himself. Chen wished he hadn't told him. Too late now. He had his doubts about Fok once more.

When pay-day came the boss refused another advance, swearing angrily at Chen. The other employees nudged each other and grinned. Chen listened to their sarcastic remarks and choice witticisms. He forced himself to smile.

Roman beckoned to him from the bottom of the stairs. 'In here, Uncle.' Chen followed him into the men's lavatory. 'Uncle, if you need cash quickly, I know the people to see.'

'On our wages?' Chen grimaced.

'No problem, Uncle. How much do you need? Five thousand, ten thousand?' Roman was quite nonchalant about these sums. Chen assumed he must mean HK$ rather than sterling.

'Eight thousand,' he said to be on the safe side.

Roman considered. 'I see for you, Uncle.'

Chen was grateful for what he thought was just an attempt to keep his morale up. That was his mistake. As soon as two days later Fok beckoned to him again. 'Arranged, Uncle.'

'What is?'

'Money for you. My friend is arranging.'

Chen was dumbfounded. He licked his lips, rubbed his hands against the sides of his trousers.

'You pour tea and bring fruit, all that kind of old-fashioned stuff, OK, Uncle.'

Chen knew how to give face, of course. But to whom? 'This is money-lender, Roman?' Figures of compound interest flashed past his eyes.

Roman looked mortified. 'Of course not. Show respect to those bloodsuckers? These are good Chinese people who stick together to observe the old ways and are ready to help folk for the sake of it.'

Chen looked puzzled.

'Do you want the money for your father or not?'

'Thank you, Roman, *dojeh*.' An uncomfortable thought struck Chen: 'This isn't from the Communists, is it?' There was a club connected with the mainland further up the street and also a Communist news agency.

Roman laughed. 'No, from the other side, you could say. Now stop asking questions. I'll speak to you in a few days.'

Roman was as good as his word. The arrangements were these: Chen was to go to the Kowloon Teahouse at four o'clock on Thursday afternoon. He would find three men waiting for him at a rear table. They would recognise and approach him. 'How will they do that, Roman? You want me to wear a special sign?' But Roman ignored him. He also brushed aside Chen's remark that Thursday was his free day. In fact he became quite angry when Chen pointed this out. 'Can't it be in the morning, Roman? My wife will wonder about it if I go out halfway through the day.'

The conversation ended with Roman again instructing Chen to respect his benefactors.

Chen was quite prepared to make himself small if this was to honour the persons who were prepared to lend him so much money – but he didn't want Lily to know. She mustn't have the slightest cause to suspect anything was going on behind her back. He need not have worried. She unquestioningly accepted his explanation that there was a large booking from a Japanese tour on Thursday. The ease of his little deception pleased and surprised Chen. Together with the lifting of his anxiety about his father it put him in a mellow and superior mood so that he drank all of his bowl of soup, even complimented Lily on it, and that night made love to her for the first time in a fortnight. She was radiant.

As promised, three men were waiting for Chen at the back of the Kowloon Teahouse. There was no difficulty in identification on either side. With trepidation Chen immediately knew the people he was seeing, and the same mutual instinct of predator for prey, quarry for hunter, alerted his benefactors. Chen threaded his way through the close-packed tables, apologising as he bumped people. He was burdened with two heavy brown-paper carrier-bags of fruit: mangoes, pineapples, oranges, and apples which he now feared had been squashed in colliding. It was the mangoes, soft, staining fruit that they were, which gave him concern; he had packed them next to the spiky pineapples.

'Sirs.' He bowed his head, wondering if patches of damp were not already disgracefully widening round the sides of the bags. He should have put the mangoes and pineapples in separate bags.

One of the long-haired young men flanking the older, bald one took the bags out of Chen's hands. He shoved them under the table with the toe of his snakeskin boot. The other young man, who had a round, pleasant face without the cold eyes of Snake, waved to him to sit. He reeked of perfume. There were three empty tea cups on the table next to a pot. Chen poured, half-filling the thimble cups. The older man touched the sides of his cup with a misshapen hand in acknowledgement of Chen's tribute but did not drink. Chen took his eyes off the man's hand with an effort and kept them fixed on the table. The man began to speak hoarsely and in a strange accent, so that Chen raised his eyes to see if the man's face could help him understand what he was saying. And then he found himself looking helplessly into the Swatownese's pale brown eyes. There was a red flickering on the irises. The eyes seemed the only living part of that dead, gnarled walnut of a face. What did the man remind him of? His name 'Ma' meant horse, but that was not what he resembled.

Snake gestured to the older man's cup. Chen poured another few drops into it. The man grunted. What did he remind him of? Chen knew now. It was a crocodile, a very old, cold-blooded, waiting crocodile, floating with only his eyes and the highest part of his back showing like the rough bark of a log in black water.

Chen had not been listening properly. He was now further disadvantaged. He said 'Ah,' noncommittally, investing the breath of air with a respectful, agreeing sort of timbre. He obviously hadn't gone far wrong. As a safety-measure, he poured a few drops more into each of the three cups.

The kind-faced young man said: 'Uncle is being most generous.'

Chen realised he was being supplied with a cue. 'Ah, ah. You are too kind to your miserable servant, Uncle.' He almost choked on the 'Uncle', the presumption, the incongruity of it. However, this seemed to be what was expected.

'Our friendship association,' the man rasped from somewhere deep in his abused larynx, 'is always pleased to help those who know how to show respect. You do well to think of your father, Mr Chen. The younger generation are often forgetful of the old ways and need reminding of them. We like to think we play our part in maintaining them overseas.' The stilted sentiments sounded even more wooden in that grating, expressionless voice but still gave Chen as severe an attack of goose-pimples as if a knife had screeched down glass. 'Venerate your parents, be filial, be loyal to your friends and brothers. If your father does not recover, you must not stint money on the funeral you give him. We will be pleased to give money for that purpose.'

Chen had the strong impression that his benefactor would have been happier seeing cash spent on burying the old man splendidly rather than curing him unflamboyantly in a mundane Western way.

'About the repayment interest ... ' Chen began.

Kind Face held his ringed hand up. 'Not in front of Uncle.'

Chen was made to understand he had been unforgivably uncouth. He lifted the pot nervously again. By now the untouched cups were already brimming and he was able to add only a drop or two, so that the meniscus trembled above the lip.

The older man rose, pushing the table smoothly away from where he was sitting with his back to the wall, so smoothly that nothing was spilled from the cups. The young men followed. There was a faint squelch as Snake trod on what must have been a mango. Chen picked up the carrier-bags and tried to follow the men.

'Sirs!'

The older man was already waddling out of the door. Chen had knocked over the cups and spilled tea all over the table; some was running on to his shoes.

Kind Face held his hand up. 'Give the fruit to your children. Little ones like fruit.' He followed the others into a big black car. Chen remained motionless until they had driven off, then lowered the heavy bags. He noticed his best shoes had become quite sodden with tea. He exclaimed and moved away, seeing that the fruit in the bags had indeed been squashed and, as he had feared, there were greasy-looking patches on the brown paper. The bags were already starting to disintegrate. Perhaps this was why they had rejected his offering.

Lily, though, was delighted with the fruit which Chen told her was left over from the Japanese banquet. The bruised mangoes lent additional verisimilitude to this story as Lily imagined the uncouth, bespectacled Japanese rolling their unfortunate Chinese mangoes (in fact from the Middle East) down the table like hand-grenades, while others of the party, perhaps strategically perched on chairs, took photographs of these japes. She and Mui made purée out of the mango flesh, cutting the yellow meat away from the huge, hairy stones after they had sliced out the damaged black areas from the waxy, mottled skin in crescent-shaped gouges. Soon the flat was full of the heavenly perfume of crushed mangoes and the sound of ice-cubes being grated and tinkling into Lily's big red plastic bowl. Ah, those sounds and those smells! And she and Mui laughed and sang old children's songs as they prepared the dessert, remembering hot summers in Kwangsi long ago.

A week later Chen was hurrying to the Underground station, hoping he might catch the 00.06 train which would enable him to synchronise with the night bus and get home early to please Lily. Recently, she had been strangely resentful about the time he got in, showing him an angry face; yet he was certain he could hear her giggling and joking with Mui in the kitchen, whence she would come with a face of thunder and his soup.

He squeezed between two motor-cars to get to the zigzag alley which led to Leicester Square. Rounding the false ending he saw two cigarette ends glow half-way down, fade, intensify again. He hurried on.

'Little brother.'

Chen was determined not to miss those connections.

'Colleague Chen.'

He halted.

'Uncle wants you to know your honoured father is being taken care of in Hong Kong. Have no fear.' The speaker sent his bright butt spinning away end over end into the darkness. There was a strong smell of male perfume. He clapped Chen on the back. His companion watched from the shadows, motionless, his cigarette showing a long, lean face and hard, black eyes.

'This is for you, Little Brother.' The first man handed Chen a small packet. 'No need to thank.' He and his companion strolled back into the Chinese quarter.

Fine words, Chen thought bitterly. How was he to know what they had done for his father? Fok and his big talk. This was just the same. Chen went to the other end of the alley, checked there was no one around and opened the packet which contained £108, wrapped in newspaper. The sum was split into a wad of £72 and one of £36. Generous but not enough. Chen repacked it carefully and zipped it into his windcheater.

He got the train, just.

Then a fortnight later there was a letter from his youngest brother. It was quite an effusive letter. Father was now recovering from his illness in a private sanatorium. There were fruit and flowers in the room. The family had always expected their brother to do his filial duty but not to make the arrangements personally from overseas. The second rice crop had been good. The price of vegetables was up. The village football team had won three matches in a row. Chen May Ling was going to have an illegitimate child. Her brother-in-law was suspected. In the third ward was a new water-tap. Old man Hing, the drug addict, was dead. Third brother had piles. A wolf-cub group was being formed ...

EIGHT

White Paper Fan saw that it was now exactly eight o'clock, according to his battered but reliable Russian watch. He clapped his thin palms. Guards at the door of his prosperous travel-agency bolted the premises. There were forty-nine men seated in front of him in four rows of ten and one of nine. Their faces were expectant and respectful; some looked nervous.

'Have no fear,' he said, 'no harm comes if you are sincere.' He moistened his lips with tea. 'This evening is not the proper ritual of membership. That ceremony will be held next month under the auspices of a high-ranking officer from Hong Kong. In the meantime I intend to teach you something about the society you have the honour of joining.'

He sat perfectly upright in his office swivel chair, a small, meticulous man in a short-sleeved white shirt.

'Our society, the Wo, is an honourable and old one descended from the ancient family of the Hung sect. Hung family is over three hundred years old. It was founded to overthrow our foreign Ching conquerors and to restore our own Chinese dynasty, the Ming. Outsiders call us the Black Society, Heaven and Earth Association, or,' he spoke in English, '*Triad* society. But we call ourselves Hung family. Do not otherwise refer to it.'

White Paper Fan turned on his air-conditioner; heat from the bodies of these nervous lower-class men was making the room uncomfortably warm and rather odorous to his fastidious sense.

'Our founders were Buddhist monks from *siu lum* monastery in Fukien. Kang Hsi emperor,' (White Paper Fan used mandarin for the reign title), 'begged the monks to use their celebrated fighting skills on his behalf. This was when he was losing in his war against the barbarian tribes in the Western empire. After the monks defeated the barbarians, Kang Hsi emperor's advisers feared their power greatly and counselled him to destroy them. Imperial troops besieged their monastery. Using their martial skills, the monks successfully resisted.

Then one of their number betrayed his brethren and treacherously showed the Imperial troops a secret entrance. This was monk Ma,' (White Paper Fan permitted himself the thinnest of private smiles) 'who was seventh in the *siu lum* boxing rankings. Henceforwards, as the number of death, seven has been proscribed for us. All the monks were killed except eighteen, who fled under cover of a large yellow curtain Buddha sent. He turned a grass sandal into a boat to air their escape and sent them a fruit-seller to act as their guide. Only five of these monks survived the dangers of their travels; thirteen died. The survivors were our Five Foundling Ancestors. They were later helped by men whom we know and honour as the Five Tiger Generals. After leaving their final refuge in the City of Willows each monk founded one Lodge of the Hung society in a separate province of China. Each of the Five Tiger Generals founded a junior lodge in an adjacent province. There are, therefore, a total of five pairs of Lodges. In the south the senior Lodge is the Kwangtung Lodge, the junior the Kwangsi Lodge. They make up the Second of the Five Lodges.'

While speaking, White Paper Fan had been closely examining his audience for signs of incomprehension or boredom. He made a mental note of the fidgeters' faces.

'The Hong Kong societies are descended from the Canton Branch of the Second Lodge. Our Wo society is oldest of these. Famous men have been members of Hung family. Sun Yat Sen held 426-rank.' White Paper Fan also noted those who showed signs of recognising the historical name.

'You do well to remember our Wo origins. We represent the old and true way, a way which has all but vanished. No one living remembers the Five Lodges. In Hong Kong there used to be seven old societies. After the war was founded another: the organisation which calls itself 14-K.'

Again he examined the faces keenly, not for signs of recognition but to see who tried to suppress them.

'This gang calls itself a Hung society. They are nothing more than common criminals. Take the name: nothing mysterious about this invention worthy of a coolie's mind.' White Paper Fan's lip curled. '14 after the number of their Canton headquarters in Po Wah Road. K after they smashed a small Hong Kong society because Karat gold is harder than Hong Kong gold. Their founder was a Kuo Min Tang general who spent time in Hong Kong and Taiwan after the Communist victory in the Civil War. He was a first-rate man but the organisation ran out of control after his death.'

The guards grinned at each other. Persistent but wholly unsubstantiated rumour had it that White Paper Fan had been a 432 in 14-K at an earlier stage in his career.

'On becoming ordinary members after Initiation you will attain 49 rank. The codes, hand-signs, verses, and numerical system will be explained more fully to you then. You should know now that $4 \times 9 = 36$, the number of solemn oaths you will swear at that ceremony.'

White Paper Fan's gaze now ran down each man in the lines. His cold inspection took three minutes. Only two men met his gaze: a big, muscular fellow in the front row, who was a boxing instructor, and a young fellow at the back, gold watch and pens, who cockily stared back at him. White Paper Fan was familiar with this type: petty aspirant gangster, all show and big talk. Had it been up to him he would never have accepted that sort for membership. He knew this one had been a street-runner and vendor and had gained favour by recruiting several others for this risky and menial job. He had also specialised in blackmail of illegal immigrants. Night-brother had better keep him supervised. White Paper Fan made a note before dismissing the men.

'Understand: you will remain silent about this meeting, even though it is not an official ceremony. Leave now in small groups and avoid attention.'

He pulled out his abacus and began work on accounts.

Grass Sandal came from her kitchen with a tray of tea, dainties, and perfumed face flannels. It was an elegant refreshment; the tray was beautifully lacquered and inlaid with mother-of-pearl. She laid it on a glass table. 'Eat the things, gentlemen,' she urged them.

The men seemed completely unappreciative but Grass Sandal showed no signs of resentment, as if the act of hospitality was fulfilment itself.

Red Cudgel spoke to White Paper Fan: 'The travelling arrangements are in your hands, of course. Do you see any particular difficulties or risks?'

'None. Our couriers can meet our Hong Kong friends at the Brussels safe house in the city centre. There's no problem with regard to either Hong Kong or Belgium. Pay-offs have been made in Hong Kong. Brussels has no checks at all. Problems begin later. The best way of doing the second leg of the journey is to get three couriers to drive separately west and go to different French ports. From Holland is too risky, though we have more back-up there. "*Strong Wind*". Calais I don't like either.'

Red Cudgel said: 'Wind gets stronger all the time. A Chinese face is suspect. This means we have a problem with couriers. Who can we trust, if not Chinese? Younger brother's English sluts are OK for No 3 but I don't want to use them for something as big as this.'

Night-brother said: 'Too bad for me. No dancing and drinking with foreigner girls.' The men laughed.

Grass Sandal said: 'May I speak?'

'Of course.'

'I didn't presume to make suggestions at first. But I have contacts suitable for such work, a good class of girl, used to foreign travel and the customs officials. Good-looking girls. I can vouch for reliability if the fees paid are good enough.'

White Paper Fan said: 'It would be stupid to take a risk and stint when the eventual profit is so sizeable. That is just bad business sense.'

Red Cudgel said: 'The girls must be wholly dependable. It is more difficult for us to track or put pressure on foreigners.'

Grass Sandal reassured him: 'No worry on this. I vouch personally for them.'

Night-brother interrogated her: 'Hollowed-out suitcases? Or in a car's body-work?'

'Neither. We should make the most of the fact that the carriers are attractive young women. Of a certain class. They can wear thin bodybelts or put the stuff into culottes. But I would suggest sewing it into a coat. Fur would be best. This way they can carry over five pounds each quite easily.'

'Fur in *this* weather?' White Paper Fan was incredulous.

Grass Sandal smiled: 'Second Brother, you don't know women very well, do you?' All laughed at the joke. Grass Sandal went to her wardrobe to get a coat to show the other.

While she was gone, White Paper Fan said: 'Naturally, we'll adulterate. It should arrive at about ninety-eight per cent purity, so we can increase the profit quite substantially. My Toronto connections will pick it up from the ship at Boston.'

White Paper Fan weighed the heavy fur coat Grass Sandal gave him, dropping his arm in mock amazement. 'I congratulate you. Excellent idea.'

Grass Sandal took scissors and unpicked the satin lining. 'I shall sling pouches on a harness supported around the shoulders,' she said. 'Then I will put in a new lining. Using worn material, of course. There is no need for the girls to wear the coats; they could throw them over the car-seat.'

'Good.' White Paper Fan was satisfied. He had opposed Grass

Sandal's promotion from 49 to 432; not on grounds of sex since females had always been equals in family Hung. Now he had reason to reverse his opinion. He was a rational and open-minded man. 'This is the ideal way to conduct our business. There is no personal risk to us or our society. The execution is contracted to outsiders. The risk is purely one of capital investment. I have long maintained we should put some profit into straightforward ventures like launderettes or even restaurants.'

'Not travel agencies, Second Brother?' Night-brother ribbed him. 'I don't think you would welcome competition there.'

White Paper Fan's face remained expressionless but Red Cudgel said: 'Young fool, show more respect. White Fan is right.'

'I apologise if my ignorant remark caused offence.'

White Paper Fan nodded.

Red Cudgel said: 'We must remember this when we plan for the future. Now we must use the money from this operation to strengthen ourselves. The money was well spent on the man's sick father. Spend on recruiting, spend on face. As White Fan says, those two things are both linked. Everything is linked.'

White Paper Fan said: 'The Vanguard officer comes with a warrant flag for the Initiation. This will be quite expensive. He must be paid plenty of money.'

Red Cudgel said: 'I am also starting to stockpile weapons. I am increasingly of the opinion that knowing our enemy, attack is the best defence.'

A bureaucrat to the neat half-moons of his finger-nails, White Paper Fan surprised Grass Sandal and Night-brother by agreeing with Red Cudgel. 'Our leader is correct. There need be, though, as far as I am concerned, no contradiction between our traditional observances and the street-fighting we may have to resort to in the future. Personally, I recommend caution and patience for the time being. I saw at first hand the mistakes the Shanghainese made in North Point. Remember also the deportations of 14-K leaders in 1953 and 1956. But I defer to the Red Cudgel officer's superior knowledge of the martial strategy.'

At this point Grass Sandal reasserted herself as hostess. 'Gentlemen, I insist you drink and eat these trifling things.' She poured tea for Red Cudgel first, then waited on the other two. She knew the men felt more comfortable with her than with some of the hard-faced harridans who held office in Hong Kong. Such knowledge was power.

NINE

Chen's gloom, which had briefly lifted, thickened in the next few weeks; so that as his father regained his health his own spirits sank. He would never enjoy peace of mind again. But he didn't see himself as an innocent ensnared; he was too honest for that. He had, and this was a slow-acting corrosive, known all along about the kind of help he would get. He had known since Roman mentioned it to him and he had kept this knowledge from himself. He became increasingly on edge and abstracted. He didn't ignore his colleagues but he answered their questions and returned remarks in a flat and expressionless voice so that they drew a little apart from him. His naturally blurred features, the high cheekbones, fleshy jowls, and slanted eyes became even more wooden. The effect of wrong focus, as of looking at him through a fuzzy range-finder, was pronounced.

At the restaurant he took to standing on the third floor where there were fewer customers and sometimes none at all. It was turning into a rainy, grey winter and there weren't many people to be seen in the street. Chen preferred it like this. Later, when the neon came on in Leicester Square, the pinks, yellows, blues, green, and scarlets would shimmer on the filmy pavements and the glass-smooth puddles, charging the street with life. Chen preferred it grey and empty; he found the colours menacing. He would pull himself together, join the others. He must not seem to be shirking.

Previously he had preferred serving Chinese customers. Now he was decidedly less at ease with his fellow countrymen. Even family parties put a strain on him and groups of all-male diners could be a genuine ordeal. Worst of all, were the single diners, the young, fashionably dressed ones in particular. Chen's hands would tremble as he jotted their orders down on his pad. Depending on how depressed he was feeling, his manner veered between obsequiousness and defiance, the latter expressed in the form of dumb insolence, a flinty demeanour, general uncooperativeness, and sometimes a blatant, if elementary, rudeness ('This fish is undercooked,' 'Don't eat it then').

Only when he had succumbed to despair would Chen behave like this. Otherwise he fawned on the customers, giving a series of jerky half-bows as he took the orders with little breaths of surprise and approval, repeatedly pouring tea and making tiny adjustments to the crockery on the table.

Roman, whom Chen had been expecting to be egregious, lording it over him, was rather subdued. Chen had thought he might ask for a commission as his due as broker. Far from it; Fok went out of his way to avoid Chen. Chen was further depressed by this; he could not understand why. Had Roman seemed out of pocket Chen would at once have offered to lend him money. But these days Roman's watch and pens had become permanent fixtures about his person; in fact there seemed to have been reproduction amongst the colony of pens which now resembled a glittering stockade in front of Roman's heart.

Chen spent as much time near the kitchens as he could; it was his bolt-hole. When the dumb-waiter jammed, forcing the waiters to make frequent trips up and down the stairs, he was glad, although he pretended to grumble with the others. He was not able to look pleased when it was repaired. Perhaps he could transfer to the kitchens, he proposed to the boss. But why would he want to do this, the boss enquired. He was astounded that anyone in his right mind could wish to descend into that steaming troglodyte under-world (where there were moreover no tips) from the well-appointed if not exactly paradisal dining-rooms above. He felt almost insulted. In any case the other waiters would probably strike on Chen's behalf if he was demoted in this way. It was out of the question, he told Chen sharply and proceeded to his office (where Inland Revenue enquiries waited), wondering if the man was not after all slightly unbalanced. He had heard some stories about his treatment of the customers, come to think of it.

And at last came the approach Chen had been dreading. It came not from strangers; say, a group of three who would enter and ask for him on the first floor, while he hid in panic on the third; or trapped him in the short-cut in the early hours of a drizzly morning. (He had been taking the long way round recently and just missing the train, with inevitable repercussions from Lily.) The approach came from Roman.

'No one does a favour unless he expects a favour in return, Uncle. Don't you agree?'

'I agree, Ah Roman.'

Chen was secretly relieved. He had found Roman's altruistic behaviour very odd. He would be quite happy to give him a generous cash commission. He had already repaid his debt. He was now happy to give another £50 in stages from his salary.

This wasn't what Roman wanted.

'Money!' he said contemptuously. 'Who needs cash? I look a poor man, Uncle? I didn't help you to get money, Uncle. That was not my purpose. I need a *favour*, Uncle.'

For a moment, one ludicrous moment, Chen wondered whether he wanted Lily for a night.

'What's so funny, Uncle? You think this business funny, Uncle? Serious, Uncle. Very serious, Uncle.'

With every 'Uncle' Fok pushed him violently in the chest. The smile left Chen's face. He was confused, frightened. He was also full of hate for the first time in his life. He hated Roman, if not his 'benefactors'. None of this showed on Chen's currant-bun of a face. His voice shaking, he said: 'What do you want me to do?'

Fok, who was a bully, smiled contemptuously. He imagined Chen's voice shook with fear. 'I thought you would be sensible, Uncle. What I want is not difficult.'

He explained.

Chen passed his hand over his eyes.

'You see? Not difficult at all. Easy to do on Thursday. You can even slip out from here for an hour on another day. Any difficulty I can arrange for someone to work here for you.'

Fok was adept at a cheap kind of psychology and not wholly insensitive. He let matters rest there for a while. He wished to give Chen time to recover. Let him think about the situation and reconcile himself to it. Then he would press him hard; make threats, hint at blackmail, physically abuse him, or get others to do it. Then appeal to his better feelings. Alternate soft with hard. Chen owed a deep debt, after all. He owed more than if the favour had been done for himself. Working for his 'benefactors' could be presented as a continuing act of self-sacrifice for his own family. Fok knew his man. Another three weeks – and then he would really press hard.

TEN

By now, of course, Chen was thoroughly receptive to Lily's idea of starting a business of their own. The further away the better, as far as Chen was concerned; although he realised it might be better to stay in London where there were plenty of Chinese, rather than go somewhere more remote. A new restaurant or counter in a small town would attract interest. And these people had eyes and ears everywhere. He could be thankful that at least there wouldn't be the problem of persuading his obstinate wife to make the move. But he could not immediately fall in with a proposal to which he had previously been at best indifferent, on which he had poured volumes of masculine pragmatic cold water. Too respectful of Lily's cunning to execute such a sudden turn-around, Chen awaited an opportunity to be converted with a realistic amount of stubbornness and resistance. The stick once grasped again by Lily would come out of the mud with a satisfying feel of adhesive suction being overcome. But Chen had to wait. And wait. Lily was being infuriatingly uncooperative. If he hadn't known better, much better, Chen might have sworn it was deliberate.

A serene smile played around Lily's dimples as she did her housework around a Husband rendered almost apoplectic by the effort of enticing his wife into argument without betraying his motives and simultaneously keeping his own temper when she failed to rise to his lures.

'That idea of yours, you know, going into business by ourselves, it's absolutely ridiculous, of course. Absolutely ridiculous, Lily.'

Lily would keep polishing the table, smiling in a superior way, or most irritatingly switch on the vacuum cleaner and swirl the nozzle insolently between Chen's feet like some surrogate mechanical penis.

'Sometimes I wonder if you have any sense at all, Lily.' But Lily had not abandoned her long-cherished ambition. She, too, had decided on indirection as the best policy, although for different reasons. Chen had just happened to catch her in one of the passive phases of her campaign. The inactivity was calculated; she wished to concert her assaults on the bastion of Chen's male obstinacy in waves rather than commit herself to a once-and-for-all showdown. At the moment he seemed so set against the idea there wasn't much point in resisting him, thought Lily, following tactics evolved in people's war. Here, as in other things, she showed herself out of sympathy with the head-on *Hung gar* traditions so proudly espoused by her father, that perspicacious man whose decision to discontinue her teaching might not have been so arbitrary after all.

As both of them, husband and wife, worked in their separate ways to the same goal, each effectively frustrating the efforts of the other, they resembled miners, each driving a gallery to join the tunnel the other was projecting from the opposite direction, but approaching at a slant, so they would never meet. Things might have gone on in this thoroughly unsatisfactory way for a long time until one day their initiatives happened to coincide, had Mui not intervened. She provided, so to speak, the connecting branch between their workings.

'Brother-in-law, how much money do you earn?' she asked one evening.

'What business is that of yours?' Chen was sharp with her not because she was poking her snub Kwangsi nose where it didn't belong – after all, it was a question you asked perfect strangers – but because he was still edgy about his father's medical fees. (Perhaps Mui had read his brother's letter before he destroyed it?)

'Forgive me, Ah Chen,' said Mui meekly. 'I just saw on television how some Indian people started a shop and put the old grocery on the corner out of business. They must make a lot of money, I suppose. Even when they have to pay for broken window.'

Husband and wife eyed each other discreetly.

'Yes, they're good businessmen, those Indians,' Chen said cautiously.

'But you Cantonese are the best in the world, Husband,' Lily put in.

'Yes, look at all those little shops selling *lupsup* to the Westerners,' said Mui, thereby, if she only knew, endearing herself both to her brother-in-law and younger sister. 'The cooks in those places are no more trained cooks than you or me, Lily. Some of them were just cooks on ships and lots of them haven't even done that.'

'Yes, yes, Mui, you're quite right,' Chen agreed enthusiastically. 'Those people have had no practice at all. You and Lily could start up a counter tomorrow without any difficulty.'

'No difficulty,' Lily agreed.

'I don't know why you haven't suggested it to me before,' Chen concluded; then wondered whether he might not have gone too far. This could have knocked the breath for a reply right out of Lily. Chen hadn't, however, allowed for the degree of obtuseness of which his wife fully believed him capable; for her phlegmatic resignation to and acceptance of an extent of male insensitivity and plain stupidity would have deeply wounded him had he been aware of it. Not that there was anything *personal* about it. (Perhaps it was well he would never plumb it.) Lily just looked significantly at Mui before saying mildly: 'I think that's a very good idea. We should think seriously about it.' Then with equal pride in their part in stage-managing a satisfactory preliminary state of affairs, both decided to leave well alone for the time being.

Given this good start, the decision still took longer to reach than might have been expected. Lily was taken aback by the lack of resistance in Husband; she had been bargaining for a little more time. She did not want sole responsibility for taking such a momentous step. Lily's enthusiasm abated so much that Chen imagined she might have changed her mind. She remained convinced he was only humouring her. They did their best to mark time, while still worrying about losing momentum, secretly fearing the other would soon change his mind. Mui, whose imagination had been fired by the example of the television Indians, egged her sister and brother-in-law on to move far faster than either wanted.

Before they knew what was happening, Mui had copies of the evening newspapers covering the floor. Random triangles of purple and orange carpet showed through gaps in the pages.

Such and such a place looked promising, Mui would announce from her knees. Then Chen or Lily would do their best to find disadvantages: this place was too far out or the rent of that place was too high. This other place was a district of Indians who wouldn't eat their food (Chen knew quite well they would).

Finally, though, they had to do something. Chen arranged to see premises in south London, currently being converted to commercial use, which he had not been able to discredit from information in the newspaper.

They travelled in a family group, Man Kee in a cloth sling on his aunt's back. It was the first time Chen had been on public transport with Lily in over two years and the first time ever with his son. He had, of course, brought Mui from the airport to the flat. Remembering Mui's first difficulties in adjusting to her new life, he wondered whether the initial shock of descending into an Underground station and boarding one of the thundering, segmented, silver and red serpents might have been responsible for the dazed state of her first months. 'Perhaps I was miserly not to take a taxi?'

Looking at Mui now as she confidently pulled the bell cord of the 113 over her head and as she insouciantly (rather saucily, Chen thought) stared back at the burly West Indian bus conductor (it was a mandatory stop and fare stage, not a request, a distinction Mui had yet to learn and one unexplicated by the TV serial), Chen was unable to connect this young woman with the shrinking creature who had sat next to him all those months ago. As they congregated on the open platform of the bus, Mui pressed the red button causing the bell to ting again, more faintly. Just to make sure, she gave it three more rings. The conductor at the other end of the bus leant over a seat to shake a finger at them. Chen could see his black face contorting in the frame formed by the window. Getting in on the act, not to be outdone, Lily rang once as well, then lifted Man Kee in his sling on Mui's back and, holding his dimpled fist, helped *him* to ring lightly, four times in rapid succession. *Ping! Ping! Ping! Ping!* Chen shook his head vigorously at his wife.

The bus jerked to a halt, though fortunately Lily, who had an excellent sense of balance anyway, had been sensibly holding with her free hand the white pole bisecting the entrance to the bus. Chen bundled the women off into the empty road.

'Husband, the stop is a hundred yards away!'

'Do what I tell you!'

But he was not quick enough to be out of earshot of the conductor. As the vehicle moved off again the conductor was still on the platform looking back at them, no longer hurling abuse now he knew who the culprits were but shaking his capped head at the antics of the lunatic Chinese who smiled serenely, bafflingly, maddeningly at him as they disappeared into the specks far down the road.

And indeed there was an impression of invincible eccentricity about the little group now re-forming on the pavement for the next stage of its journey. Chen appeared unremarkable enough in his black trousers and brown padded jacket; although his trilby hat was a bit odd as accessory to these. The girls, however, having no uniform to provide them with an approximate sartorial guideline, nor a job to get them out of the house, had become rather disorganised about their clothing. One relaxation of convention had led to another. Both were wearing thin tunic suits in a tiny floral pattern (unfortunately no longer interchangeable as Mui was getting quite comfortable in her figure). Over these summery suits each was wearing a baggy cardigan of Chen's. Lily's was grey with walnut leather buttons, Mui's olive-green in a chunky knit with transparent plastic toggles. Mui almost filled her woollen but, having shorter arms than her brother-in-law, had been forced to roll the sleeves back several times. Lily, on the other hand, found Chen's sleeves too short, uncomfortably so, even with the cuffs rolled down, so that the top part of the garment acted as a strait-jacket, riding up under the armpits and exposing her wrists and a substantial length of her shapely forearm, while around her slender waist the cardigan's elasticated bottom had concertinaed in a thick roll rather like the domed edge of a toadstool. Lily's flat shoes – the ones she wore to the shops – were being repaired, which had left her with the choice of house-slippers or a pair of slightly longer than ankle-length wellington boots (in the vernacular 'larbah boot'), relic of typhoon seasons on the flooded barrack roof in Hong Kong, into which she had finally thrust her narrow, sockless feet. Mui had commandeered a pair of Chen's size 7 shoes, laceless unhappily, in which her own size 3 feet floundered like landed fish. She proceeded with a circular, scuffling motion, reminding Lily of the way Father had advanced on his opponents in order simultaneously to hook their leading leg and protect his own groin from counter flick-kicks. Despite the three pairs of her sister's socks she was wearing (which was why Lily's bare feet were now rapidly blistering) every now and then a shoe would detach itself from Mui's foot and Lily would fear for Man Kee in his sling on his aunt's back – though Lily had no doubts Mui would fall heroically *forward* on her face if the need arose.

Now they set off to the Underground station from which they would take a train to the railway station from which they would take a final bus to their destination. Man Kee dozed placidly in Mui's back, waking briefly as the train clattered through an eerie, spark-lit crossroad of tunnels and regarding his father with a large, incurious and unblinking eye before falling asleep again. Chen was grateful for this. The boy seemed quieter these days, or was it just that he was seeing him in the day?

On the BR train, where they had an entire compartment to themselves, Chen positioned himself near the window, ready to spring tiger-like on Mui should she succumb to temptation in the shape of the alarm cord. Irresponsible of the English authorities to put it so conveniently at hand; it was far too easy to pull. Also, it bore great resemblance to the bus cord which one might legitimately, under certain circumstances, pull. The red handle on the Underground was far less ambiguous, especially as this train kept stopping and starting at a variety of small stations in response to a pinging clearly audible in the compartment. But Mui, hunched forwards with Man Kee on her back, chin cupped in hands, was looking eagerly out of the streaky window. Chen began to relax. The girls woke him at the station. He pretended he had just closed his eyes.

The premises, directly opposite the bus stop, were being gutted. Shattered glass lay perilously on the pavement. Two windows had been knocked into one. The new front had been daubed with smears of white paint to prevent people accidentally sticking their arms through it. Though a clear square of glass they could see snakes of bunched electrical coils dropping from the ceiling.

Workmen came out, scraping their heavy boots on the plank floor. Chen was wary of this class of Englishman, crossing to the other side of the road on his way home from work as they spilled out of the pubs long after their statutory closing time, he used to think with fear and resentment. Mui and Lily stared at them with a blatant curiosity which, Chen knew, could offend. The English were peppery, often manufacturing pretexts for anger where none reasonably existed: a stare held too long, failure to meet their round eye at all. The girls' exposure to this kind of thing had not been as thoroughgoing as his, he thought protectively. He waved them away. 'Let's go.' The workmen seemed, fortunately, to be ignoring them so far. Mui had poked her head through the door and was inspecting the interior. Curls of wood-shavings covered the wood floor. There was a smell of fresh putty.

'Brother-in-law, this is too big for us. We are small people only.'

Chen, too, had been taken aback by the properness of the place, the presence of the workmen and the wholesale repairs they were making. This was not what he had been looking for. He wanted a more cautious, less obtrusive start. A place like this could be unlucky; it was arrogant, defying fate. This could be a large restaurant. Mui, although over-awed, was still curious. Chen took her by the arm and drew her outside. The workmen were brewing tea over a primus, stirring gobs of condensed milk into the pan which contained the boiling tea. When the Chens were twenty yards down the street the workmen began to whoop and stamp. Chen hurried his women on.

'What do the *gwai lo* sing, Brother-in-law?'

'They are singing songs, Mui.'

'What songs, Brother-in-law?'

'Their own songs, Mui.'

'Ah.'

'Don't look back, Lily.'

Lily, however, was not to be so easily denied. She turned round and with an arm through Mui's so she would not crash into a lamp post began to walk with short steps in the same direction as the others facing backwards (one of the exercises she had performed with Father in the courtyard).

'Lily!' Chen whirled round, scandalised. But now he was also able to see that the noise the workmen were making had nothing to do with them at all but involved one of their own number who had met with an accident (Chen thought it likely from his behaviour) involving the upsetting of hot liquid, in all likelihood tea, onto a sensitive part of his anatomy. Lily tittered. Chen found nothing amusing about the man's mishap, *faan gwai* or not. In fact he felt distinct masculine solidarity with him. Did the girls realise how painful this could be? Perhaps they knew and didn't care? Knew and gloated? Chen glanced at the nape of Lily's graceful neck, one of the few parts of her body that had up till now always pleased him. He must spend more time with Man Kee, he decided, staring into that infant's open, phlegmatic eye. He couldn't approve of all this female influence.

They had reached the end of the road. Chen did not want to retrace their steps and took them down a smaller street on the right. From here they reached the main road again which, on a whim, Chen crossed. Loyally, the girls followed, though Lily's feet were by now really quite painful in her wellingtons and Mui's back was aching from the weight of Man Kee's sling.

It became apparent that the main road formed an unofficial kind of boundary. The side they were now on was older, more dilapidated than the north side, a change which took place with startling swiftness. They had been walking for three minutes and already the houses were visibly decayed. They passed a derelict terrace, the doors and windows covered with corrugated tin sheets; through rusted holes in the crinkled metal they could see grass growing in the roofless rooms. There was still a sofa in one of the ruined houses and its springs had burst out of the rotten cloth like a robot's innards. This was more like it, Chen thought with satisfaction; they would start here. It was ideal. *Hardly anyone would come to the shop!* Stray business, that was. Obviously one needed a modicum of local custom to survive. He had a little money left. Lily had also surprised him by revealing the existence of a fragrant hoard in the tea tin. At first pleased, he had later been unsettled by this evidence of his wife's capacity to sacrifice immediate gratification and defer it for future providential uses, and even more upsetting, to carry it out secretly without his discovering. Not that there was anything sneaky or reprehensible about it. Nevertheless, he could hardly believe Lily had found a margin on the house-keeping. Whole new regions of the female psyche, not only unexplored but their existence hitherto unsuspected, opened before him. Chen did his best to put the whole thing out of his mind as quickly as possible. If there was more to Lily than he had ever imagined he did not, at this comparatively late stage of things, want to know. Could she, for instance, have manipulated *him* into directly raising the question of a move? When all along it had been she who wanted it? Had she known all the time and been laughing at him? Chen looked at her talking innocently with Mui (why were they both limping?) and frowned. What deceptions and secrets lay behind the childishly smooth skin of those faces? Chen decided to give Lily enough room to manoeuvre in future – for both their sakes.

They had now arrived at an open space, a demolition site, bounded by tall, braced buildings on two sides. In the middle there was an untended fire blazing. Chen led his party across the scattered bricks and tins. Lily deliberately walked through the large puddles, pleased with this chance to turn her boots to use. There had been, she now remembered, a small leak in the left boot at ankle height but time seemed to have plugged it. Fearing for Man Kee on such treacherous terrain, she took him from Mui and slung him on her own back. Mui, who was, indeed, experiencing some difficulties keeping her shoes on, fell behind the others. Lily and Chen approached the fire, which was much larger than appeared from a distance and was composed of rags, planks, straw packing, and half a car tyre which was giving off fumes and black smoke. There was no indication who had built it unless it was the English boys, throwing green bottles against the buttresses at the far end of the site. They had been hidden by smoke. But wouldn't they have been poking the fire with sticks? Lily turned to Mui to share a Kwangsi memory but she had vanished. A moment later Mui materialised through a pall of smoke, coughing and red-eyed. The wind had changed! 'It's not good to rub your eyes, Mui. Let them water.'

This piece of well-meant advice did not seem to be at all appreciated.

Mui scuffed resentfully after Chen, ploughing straight through a pile of beer tins and sending them clattering against fallen masonry and into puddles, just like a *gwai lo* hooligan. By the time she had rejoined Chen on the road her shoes were white with the ash from previous fires which lay thickly on this side of the site. As they turned the corner Lily took a last look at the fire, still burning in isolation, with nobody so much as throwing one extra plank on it or even enjoying its heat. How strange the English were, how indifferent, how careless of the consequences of their own deeds! And as for their attitude to their old people it was nothing less than shameful neglect, a national disgrace. With the image of the fire and the plight of the English aged now inextricably merged in her mind – both to do somehow with loneliness and a shirking of responsibilities as well as inevitable physical extinction – Lily wandered abstractedly down the road, barely listening to Chen. (Perhaps the fumes of the fire had poisoned her without her being aware of it.)

Each of the party was now locked into his or her own thoughts, no longer functioning as a single unit with a common purpose, the girls' sense of their own individuality reinforced by nagging little corporal pains: Lily vicariously indignant on behalf of others less fortunate than herself, dimly conscious of pinched, raw toes; Mui regretting having ever implanted the idea of a move into her sister's and brother-in-law's heads, sidling along like a crippled land-crab and wishing she was in front of her television. Only Chen was happy, walking on a cushion of air in this suburban wilderness where one street led into its twin, the whole area having the effect of a maze through its uniformity. Chen chattered excitedly to Lily. Here was where they should settle; this was perfect. Lily wasn't altogether happy but she didn't want to curb Husband's enthusiasm at this stage. 'You know best, Husband,' and she left the decision in his hands.

When they got home Lily levered her Wellingtons off with difficulty and – a stroke of inspiration – soaked her sore feet in what was left of the mixture she had bottled for Husband's flu. So eager to dose others, it was the first time she had tried her own medicine. Of course, it was the least objectionable way of taking it. As it turned out, the mixture, at first astringently refreshing on hot blistered skin, then warming and soothing, proved a panacea. Or (Lily pondered later) had her memory failed her? Had she been, in fact, administering to Husband not Father's patented internal draught but the liniment he had used to toughen the calluses on his already formidably armoured knuckles? At any rate her feet gave her no trouble the next day, while Mui was still limping. Rather ostentatiously, Lily thought.

Two days later Chen went to reconnoitre the area again. He insisted on going solo and was surprised at the lack of resistance from the girls, contradictory creatures that they were. The workmen were having another tea-break when he passed them. What incorrigible idlers! Crossing the main road into the ruined district but going in another direction this time, he found what he wanted. Within the week he was able to present the girls with the accomplished fact: premises vacant and ready for occupation in two weeks.

ELEVEN

The girls went quietly, with a sense of oppression hanging over them. Chen's obvious elation only depressed them further. On the verge of tears, a pale-faced Lily packed their belongings into cardboard cartons. Mui locked herself into the bathroom and wept as silently as she could. After a while she emerged and helped Lily pack the Sony rice cooker, bowls, spoons, and chopsticks. Her tears plopped into a spoon, hit the rice cooker, stained the cardboard with splashes that were startlingly wide. Anxious about rust, Lily dabbed at the rice cooker with a paper tissue. Mui, too, had the same fear and, as she attempted to wipe away the salty water with the back of her sleeve, her hand collided with her sister's and she wrung it. Lily squeezed back, harder than she knew, and Mui bit into her lower lip (from the pain of crushed fingers), heroically damming, as Lily thought, the flood-tides of extreme emotion. Man Kee, though, was having the time of his short, pampered life. He had now mastered running, small, staccato steps, not so much paces as a series of arrested topplings, and he blundered into the boxes, unpacking them with great energy when his custodians' backs were turned, crawling under the table with his trophies, re-emerging between the legs of the removal men. Expecting some kind of gentle chiding, he was confusingly hugged, the breath pressed right out of him. During the long ride in the dark back of the pantechnicon he found himself the object of much attention from his aunt and mother.

Chen gloomily observed them fondling Man Kee as he clutched an invisible protuberance on the side of the van for support. He was standing, rather insecurely, on the slippery metal floor while Lily and Mui squatted comfortably on their haunches. It was a long journey, full of sudden braking and starting, and surely there hadn't been so many corners before? Chen wondered whether the driver intended to take an extra-long route to cheat him. He slipped on the diabolically smooth floor several times, falling with a resounding crash on the same part of his rump every time, so that by journey's end he was quite severely bruised. Doggedly, he got up each time, only to be sent flying with the next sideways lurch or sudden halt. And were those disrespectful giggles the girls were stifling in the corner? When they got out he saw a surprisingly large amount of caked blood under the torn cuticle of his right little finger.

What the girls saw, blinking, cramped legs painfully twitching as they got out of the pantechnicon, was not calculated to inspire warmth or hope in the boldest heart. Not even Lily's, let alone Mui's. Like loyal troops presented with the appalling consequences of a loved commander's obstinacy, led perhaps into some deadly ambush, they felt if not actually betrayed at least substantially let down. It wasn't so much that the house was dirty or broken down; it was both those things. It was *where* it was situated. Lily and Mui at first imagined themselves presented for work at some heavy industrial plant. In fact Lily thought Chen had abandoned the original idea (on which, she reflected, he had never seemed very keen) and found some more remunerative occupation for them all. The high wages enjoyed by car-workers, for instance, were known to the family, thanks to Mui's familiarity with *Crossroads*. All around them the din was tremendous. Sparks flew in a corner. Men in grease-caked overalls lay prone under machinery or in concrete pits. Cars and parts of their insides lay everywhere. It was a garage! Above the hammering and screech of metal, the terrible hissing, Lily tried to call Chen but he, stocky, obstinate Husband, quite unconscious of the disastrous first impression made on his women, was already leading the removal men to the front door of their new house. Their new home, Lily thought inconsolably. Life in the UK had made her soft. Compared to the factory roof, to (in Mui's case) the cramped servant's back room, the grimy pebble-dash stucco building was more than adequate. Being merely human, though, Lily was unable to establish instant equilibrium.

Chen had vanished, taking the two removal men with him. Lily pushed at the iron gate which gave access to the flight of crumbling steps which led down to the tiny sunken lawn (balder than the flats' courtyard) and the concreted causeway to the peeling front door. Rusted solid. Lily shook the gate vigorously.

'Careful, younger sister, you don't know your own strength sometimes.'

Chen suddenly materialised in the gloom, as if through a secret trapdoor in the pavement. A moment later the driver of the van emerged through a hole in the hedge, presumably the one through which Husband had come. Lily helped the men carry their few belongings into the hallway of the house. They had sold the hissing furniture. The van was far bigger than necessary. If they had owned a small car themselves ... While Chen tipped the removal men with a flair they could not resent, Lily made a quick tour of inspection. As soon as she had started she wished she had left it until morning. Perhaps the most frightening room was the bathroom. Lily quickly shut the door before Mui could get in and shepherded her into the front room, which was upsetting enough. Had Mui known where the bathroom was she would have locked herself in and had her second secret cry of the day. Her face, and Lily's, had frozen into set, dead masks from which all trace of disappointment, dread and anxiety had been eradicated.

That night they camped on the bare planks of the front room, throwing down their mattresses without caring where they landed on the paint-stained floor. Lily pulled the light-cord on the single naked bulb, despite Chen's protests; she could not bear to see the room. She and Mui shared the double mattress with Man Kee protected between them, while Chen was relegated to a single mattress on his own. With uncharacteristic assertiveness, the girls had taken most of the blankets and although Chen wore his padded jacket over his windcheater he was still cold. Snug in a cocoon of assorted coverings, including the oilskin tablecloth, and cossetted by the warmth of each other's bodies, the rest of the family found oblivion while its titular head spent the hours of darkness on his bruised back, awake and painfully cold but happy for the first time in months.

TWELVE

Their shop, their home, could not pretend to have been anything other than an ordinary house up till then. Originally it had been the eastern wing of a terrace of three houses. The centre and western wing had been hit by a bomb in the war and subsequently demolished but a freak effect of the blast had left Chen's house unscathed. Two big braces, such as they had seen on the big demolition site, supported the western wall. The previous occupant, and Chen had no idea who he or she had been, had left over five years ago. No one had wanted the property. Being so near a garage hadn't helped either. Chen secured a five year lease at a ridiculously low price. He refused a mortgage offer from the estate agent. What a nuisance that would have been! He had even tried to get the lease on a six-monthly basis but failed. Why, he knew people who rented their restaurant premises by the week without a lease at all! He did have to get planning permission for the business. Hard for colleagues he had known in the past, this was quick and easy for him. He complied with health and fire regulations. The council was only too pleased to have someone move into the area. Perhaps others would follow suit, encouraged by their example. Chen hoped not.

Lily wasn't interested in any of these administrative details but she was to develop passionate curiosity about the previous owner(s) which she would never be able to satisfy. Had it been a family, like themselves? An old couple? Perhaps a widow or widower reluctant to leave the scene of former happiness and hanging on (poor old person) in increasing loneliness until the end came? Shocking as it might seem, Mui had told her how old people could lie unnoticed for weeks after they had died. What terrible callousness! What a society! Which room might the old person(s) have lain in (dead and shamefully alone), pondered Lily, thinking in Cantonese in which, conveniently for such musing, there was no distinction between plural and singular. In the front room; floating naked in the bath, nose just above water; in a bath, she couldn't help thinking, which must have been quite handsome then and was still as long and deep as a rich man's coffin; in the garden, pruning roses (typical English occupation), the corpse on its back like a dead insect, shears still clutched in hand like the mandible of some giant cockroach? She hoped the aged party or parties had passed away quietly in bed upstairs. At any rate Lily knew from the date of the house that it was probable there had only been one or two occupiers before them, perhaps a single aboriginal owner. She would have liked to know for certain. Twenty generations had elapsed since the founding of her own father's home village, she knew; twenty-five since the Founding Ancestor had established Husband's in the New Territories. A lineage should be traced, however much one might manipulate it afterwards. She annoyed Chen with her questions. 'Lily, leave me alone. I don't know,' he would say, and hunt for chores in another room.

There was plenty to do: cleaning, dusting, disinfecting. Lily might be oblivious to the aesthetic side of her environment but she certainly wanted it hygienic. She clouded countless buckets of water with a brown antiseptic which turned white in suspension. The house smelled like a hospital. 'Try some of Father's elixir. That would kill anything,' Chen felt like baiting her but lacked the nerve to say (winter, season of chills and flu was coming on, after all). Mui did not shirk either. A black and white bandana around her hair to indicate high seriousness of purpose, in the manner of a peasant rebeller or one of the Boxer bands, she assumed responsibility for the kitchen, mopping round the functioning TV which she had placed out of harm's, meaning Man Kee's, way in the sink. In the front room Lily's transistor put a certain rhythm behind her mop-strokes. Chen, bracketed on both sides by this aural depth-charging, worked at the staircase and wished he had his father's skill as a carpenter.

No one would ever be able to call the house elegant. Proud of it as she was to become, Lily herself would have hesitated to call it smart. Adjectives that sprang to mind were 'warm', 'happy', 'old' (in an entirely non-pejorative sense). They never got round, somehow, to putting the finishing buff on any of their efforts at home improvement. Chen, for instance, made the stairs safe, exercising what he liked to think of as dormant hereditary skills, but there was never to be a carpet or even paint on them. Lily daubed over the blisters on the bath but its monstrous length was never re-enamelled. They dissolved the dirt on the hallway linoleum but the newspapers they laid to protect it as it dried got marooned there, becoming brittle and yellow in a permanent indoor autumn. Lily felt it would be unlucky to remove them, as if they were some ancient clan warning of intruders about to enter the village clearing. So she tacked the papers into the edge of the skirting-board with small nails and did the same where the edges met in the centre of the floor.

There were three rooms upstairs, abutting on the tiny landing. Man Kee's was a virtual cupboard but was still a room with walls and door which, Lily supposed, was improvement on the flat's hallway if one was going to get technical. Encouraged by his success with the stairs, Chen made beds for them all, artefacts which bore a strong resemblance to capsized Yangtse rafts and which would presumably save all their lives in the eventuality of the Thames displaying an unruly, Yangtse-like tendency to spill over its southern bank.

All this was after they had converted the front room. Until then they slept on the floor. They would have to, Chen explained, sacrifice personal comfort in order to get the business started. That was Number One priority, or how would they support themselves? This appeal to close ranks, tighten belts, so far from causing mutinous mutters actually consolidated Chen's headship. When things were going well – during, for instance, the last months in the flat – the girls felt free to quibble, maybe even poke a little mild fun at Husband or Brother-in-law's stodginess, but in adversity their allegiance was absolute. Chen's call for them to rally round the fledgling business answered a strong inner need in both of them. For too long now their lives had been running on the same stable, unvarying course, without demand being made on them. Chen's wages came in; the bills were paid without difficulty. Neither had known such ease before and they had not been able to accept it as genuine security. Lily's scrimping on her diet, her steady accumulation of capital from this artificial margin on the budget, had been not only an attempt to insure against disaster or make a new future, but also a brave effort to create a challenge for herself. Even a self-imposed trial of the will was better than nothing. Like the fibre of the muscles, moral grain could slacken, wither, and finally vanish unless exercised, even infrequently. Superstition also encouraged the girls to fall in with Chen's plans. In Chinese Street Lily had bought a wonderful household god: red-skinned, pot bellied, with a fearsome scowl and curling black mustachios, nine squatting inches of concentrated energy which lit up with a baleful glow when the bulb in its interior was wired to the mains. Mui, Man Kee, even Chen were all in their different ways delighted with it. The little idol's somewhat minatory aspect alarmed none of them; it was quite endearing. The girls tittered over it.

'Ah Lily, don't you think it looks like Brother-in-law? Especially when he's taking medicine?'

'Yes, no mistake. But what about the moustache?'

'Yes, that's a shame.'

'Wait a bit.' Lily took her ornamental cigarette lighter and waved the smoky petroleum flame underneath a saucer. 'Husband!'

Chen, trusting male, was lured over. Assault was swift and ruthless.

'Eiyah, Lily! Have you gone mad?' Before Chen knew what had happened twin streaks of soot had appeared on each side of his upper lip. The resemblance to god was really quite startling; for a split-second as Chen looked very cross indeed, it was total. The girls were stunned. Lily recovered first. 'In the bathroom, Husband, quickly.'

'Wah!' Chen was not at all displeased with the moustache which gave him, he thought, a distinguished appearance as his face returned to its normal colour of old ivory. A pity he was unable to grow real whiskers of his own.

'You're the god of us all, Brother-in-law.'

'Hm. You two certainly don't behave as if I was a god.'

Lily had scrubbed the saucer under a tap and was now piling fruit on to it. 'We're going to make you an offering, Husband.' Mui plugged god into the socket in the front room and spread a clean *Ta Kung Pao* in front of him (a Communist newspaper, unfortunately, but still more suitable than the *Daily Telegraph* Mui was taking to reading). Lily placed the dish of fruit on the newspaper with a silver paring-knife and an additional plate of sesame-seed cakes; then she lit some sticks of incense. In the corner of the bare room, on the unvarnished planks, god acquired an authority and presence he would never have had in the flat. Now wreathed in pungent, stinging clouds of incense he gleamed like a phosphorus fire in a greenhouse. His diminutive, glowing form was charged with a tremendous energy. At any moment he might spring up. Lily would not have been surprised if he had exploded from the strain of containing all that quivering kinetic energy.

They ate their meal, their auspicious fifth in that house, squatting on their hunkers around the saucers on the floor with god as their only illumination. In front of that stern deity it would have been unthinkable to have worked for personal comforts first. That would have courted *extreme* bad luck. So under the bulging eye of their dwarf overseer, who seemed scarcely able to restrain himself from leaping up and joining or chastising them (for their own good), they put all their efforts into converting the one-time sitting-room into at least a facsimile of a shopfront.

Ideally, the front should have been all glass, an expanse of unimpeded visibility, like the premises they had first seen on the other side of the main road. But this would mean knocking down part of the wall between their two windows and then reglazing at prohibitive expense. Their windows were also unfortunately the leaded small-pane type, making it even more difficult for the passer-by to see in and be tempted. 'We shall just have to make the best of things,' Lily announced. 'We can put some profit by to get big windows later.'

Chen, who had accepted outrageous flattery for his carpentry without turning a hair, did not seem unduly disappointed. Lily had been nervous he would volunteer his services to reconstruct the windows single-handed. What a strange man Husband was some-times!

They would have to have a counter, though. No take-away business worth the name could function without one of those. Chen soon had one knocked together: twin surfaces making a 90 degree angle, top and side. Nothing could be simpler. Disappointed at first, standing with her feet in the dark cave of the counter, once she came to the customers' side, Lily had to admit it looked quite professional. So that's how it really seems to the owners, she thought: ramshackle and half-complete; and she fancied herself already part of the shop-owner's unstated conspiracy against the public. She and Mui covered the cheap wood with blue plastic sheeting and the deception was complete. There was already a serving-hatch in the wall between kitchen and front room and Chen took the little door off its hinges altogether. They put the flat's gas stove in the kitchen, together with a ring which ran off a huge, dented bottle they had acquired secondhand. On this they would heat their *wok*.

'Chairs,' Lily said suddenly. 'Where will they sit?' And of course, that was what take-aways had too, chairs. As important as the counter, really. You didn't want your trade walking off into the night because there was nowhere comfortable for them to sit. No good expecting the English to squat on their hunkers patiently reading the *Daily Mirror*. But then chairs, even secondhand ones, cost good money. Again Chen rose to the occasion. Proper chairs would have been too much to expect. His were rudimentary, very rudimentary, benches, looking like elongated packing cases. He made three, each accommodating at least four English backsides (broad-beamed luggers to neat Chinese sampans) in rows, facing the counter.

There was something particularly disturbing about this configuration.

Standing back to admire his handiwork, Chen felt vague unease. Nor were the girls happy. What was it? Not until they actually had customers sitting on the benches did they know. And it was Lily who realised first. She had been delegated to the face-to-face work at the counter. 'Husband, you have the experience,' she protested (here he was being peculiar, as he had been about the window) but Husband had consigned himself to kitchen-work. 'And you don't know how to cook, either.'

'That's not important, Lily.' Chen paused, then let Lily in on an observation: 'The Westerners like the look of you. I've noticed that before.'

Mui's English was now incomparably better than Lily's but she still lacked the self-confidence to do all the counter work. And so Lily, closely examining the surly or impassive English who came her way for evidence of impact of a personal charm she had never previously suspected she might possess, sat at the counter on a high, home-made stool and passed orders through the hatch. Poised up there, staring down at the waiting customers, she was struck by a sense of the absurd. What must she look like to the rows down there? An actress on the Chinese opera stage? No. Now she had it. *It was a church!* They had constructed the place along the lines of the interior of a *faan gwai* church and she was the preacher. No wonder the customers looked so subdued and on their best behaviour. She wondered whether the customers might find this offensive. Blasphemous? In the corner, half-way up the wall, on the triangular platform Chen had carved for him, god glared down through a palisade of smouldering joss-sticks at the half-empty pews in front of him.

As a distraction, Lily hung calendars on the walls, with pictures of the floating restaurants in Hong Kong and the grotesque statues of the Tiger Balm Gardens. That made it look more like a normal take-away. Entrance to the shop was had through the Chen's own front door, over the yellowing newspapers. Chen tacked a cardboard partition over the bannisters and hung a curtain of plastic beads over the mouth of this dark, interesting tunnel. PRIVATE, proclaimed a notice in Mui's best block capitals above the particle-fall of swaying beads. TRESPASSER WOULD BE PROSECUTED. Outside, under Lily's and Chen's bedroom window, they slung a six-foot white plank, five-inch red English letters, four-inch black Chinese ideograms: DAH LING RESTAURANT, after the girls' home village. Natural attrition saw it become the Darling restaurant, of course, and the girls the two Darlings. About three months after they had moved in, the reason for the customers' strange jollity and their obsession with languidly repeating the name of the restaurant out loud dawned on Mui. She didn't tell Lily.

THIRTEEN

Men had been going into the Truth Triple Loyalty Justice Hall of the Jing Yee Clansmen's Association in Covent Garden for three hours now. They arrived from separate directions, singly and in small groups, at irregular intervals and with little noise. They would knock at the thick door. This would open an inch. There would follow a terse exchange. Then the guard admitted them one at a time. Altogether almost fifty men must have entered between four and seven p.m.

In an ante-room three long-serving 49s marshalled the men and kept order. They enforced strict silence, making the men squat in rows in the small room. Night-brother remained at the door, permitting himself a cigarette and occasionally glancing through the spy-hole. New, shining bolts had been screwed into the seasoned oak.

Grass Sandal was in a second ante-room on the other side of the hall. The ceremonial Ming costumes hung neatly on its walls. The robes were crisply pressed but she smoothed out imaginary creases and pulled out a tiny thread from the *yin-yang* symbol stitched onto a senior officer's. She had cut, and removed the enamel from, her finger-nails. Laid on a table were nine long strips of red cloth which would later be knotted into headbands: three loops, dexter, sinister, central for Vanguard from a six-yard length; single central loop for Red Cudgel from nine feet six inches of material; single loop sinister of same proportions for White Paper Fan; single loop dexter, same specification, for herself and the other 432 officers. Old-fashioned grass sandals, all for the left foot, were in a neat line under the table. In a corner were Vanguard's yellow paper umbrella, pack of ashes of the monk martyrs, and whip. It was, in fact, a black umbrella from the big shop in King Street and Grass Sandal's own riding-crop. She was nervous and left the ante-chamber to make a final inspection of the ceremonial hall.

Filling the chamber was the ground-plan of the City of Willows, metaphor of that legendary matrix of Hung heroes. Its plan, in accordance with the design of the classical city, was rectangular with gates at four of the five cardinal points of the compass. Strips of red paper covered with black ideograms (in White Paper Fan's unmistakable, elegant calligraphy) represented walls and gates. Before the east entrance lay two tasselled swords crossed on the floor. After this two tables a yard apart, each covered with a large sheet of red paper, forming the Hung gate. After this, tables arranged in a square, forming the Hall of Loyalty and Trust. After this, Heaven and Earth Circle, a large bamboo hoop. Then in three lines: red paper representing the Fiery Pit; paper squares symbolic of the Magic Stepping Stones; and two white tapes, the Two-Planked Bridge. A long trestle table, flanked by memorial 'tablets' on the wall, did duty as the Altar. Finally, there was Red Flower Pavilion, a gauze canopy.

Grass Sandal had a check-list. She now began to itemise the offerings on the Altar: *1) Specimen of Ming calligraphy: Hung Family Expands Ten Thousand Cities. 2) Seven-stemmed brass lamp. 3) Pot of wine, seven bowls. 4) Pot of tea, three cups. 5) Pot of water, five bowls. 6) Incense pot for worshipping ancestral tablets of Five Tiger Generals. 7) Saucer of apples. 8) Saucer of mandarin oranges, stalks and green leaves still attached. 9) Saucer of nuts. 10) Saucer of red dates. 11) Three vegetable items: three pieces of beancurd, three betel nuts, three large mushrooms (hydrated). 12) Saucer of sugar and cinnabar covering empty bowl. 13) Strip of sacred yellow incense paper, bearing heads of thirty-six Hung oaths. 14) A needle, the Iron-headed Prince. 15) Peachwood sword. 16) Plum-wood sword. 17) Red tub filled with myriad grains of Hung rice and banners of Five Tiger Generals: Ng, Hung, Doh, Lee, Lam.*

Grass Sandal had seen White Paper Fan do the arranging before he left for the airport but she went through the items once more. She feared she might be blamed if there was anything wrong. Betel had come from an Indian restaurateur protected by the society. Red dates were unavailable; lychee stones substituted. Grass Sandal hoped this would pass unnoticed.

Vanguard, emaciated, dignified, sixty-nine *sui* of age, had been met, honoured, escorted to the limousine. Now, flanked by Red Cudgel and White Paper Fan, he was cruising at sixty miles an hour along the raised road into the western environs of the city: West Gate, traitor's gate. They had already joked about this. White Paper Fan handed Red Cudgel the small velvet box which Grass Sandal had collected that morning. Red Cudgel bowed and presented it to Vanguard. 'This was specially commissioned in Amsterdam. It is only a small and unworthy memento to show our appreciation of the honour.'

Vanguard smiled. He opened it with veiny hands. Inside, nestling on a satin bed, was a small solid-gold tortoise with jewelled eyes, symbolic animal of the 438-rank.

'Value £300,' White Paper Fan said. 'Give it to your daughter. This is apart from the recruiting fees, of course. I have ordered the recruits to pay £20 each, £15 over the official fee. Dispose of the surplus to the society's advantage as you see fit.'

Vanguard nodded. 'Good. Very satisfactory.'

Red Cudgel asked: 'Observing the rites now is not inconvenient after such a long journey?'

'Much safer, my friend, as you know well. Before there is loose talk. Here is safer than Hong Kong but even so official bandits and your enemies could hear.'

'*Strong wind* in Hong Kong at the moment?'

'Strong, but no major problems. The thirty-six branches of Wo still flourish. Co-ordination could be better. Some are slow to remit funds back to us. Unlike you. Things are not what they were before the war. An old man's life was easy then.'

'So no problem about *our* remittances and letters?' White Paper Fan wished to make the point to Red Cudgel rather than the old man.

'None. Wo group appreciates your contributions. I take it that the freighting of the No 4 heroin was accomplished?'

'There were no problems at all. I imagine it is already on the Canadian and American markets.'

Vanguard closed the jewel-box. 'We were fortunate there was a shortage from their Mexican and Middle Eastern suppliers. This was a difficult operation but the profits for all involved were substantial. I trust you spent yours in the most effective way?'

White Paper Fan changed the subject before Red Cudgel could speak. 'You didn't consider by-passing us and going through San Francisco or Seattle?'

Vanguard shook his head vehemently. 'It might have cut out the cost of some intermediaries but would have entailed risks. San Francisco is a bad place these days. The situation is totally out of hand. Society elders have no control. Young thugs form their own groups. There is a state of warfare on the street. Our different Wo branches may feud but at least there is some system of arbitration. But there, it's anarchy. One could not even consider doing business there.'

White Paper Fan said sententiously: 'Shocking. May it never happen here.'

Red Cudgel stared impassively out of the window. Now Vanguard turned to him: 'You, Ah Ma, I have always admired the way you respect Hung tradition. You were a famous fighter. Everyone knows how you led the Wo bands at the temple firework festivals. Armed or unarmed, no one dared challenge you on the street. Yet you always had respect for the 438 and 415 ranks. I find it hard to think of another enforcer of whom I could say the same.'

Red Cudgel said modestly: 'Because I am an uneducated man shouldn't I respect learning all the more? As to fighting, I closed my hands a long time ago.'

White Paper Fan said: 'Our honoured guest from Hong Kong speaks well. Mr Ma is a most unusual man.' Without betraying any impatience he asked the Vanguard officer: 'Which of the six initiation ceremonies of the Second Lodge do you intend using?'

'A three days initiation is out of the question, of course. I don't remember attending such a ceremony since the Occupation. On the other hand, bearing in mind your needs, we should not abridge as much as in Hong Kong. If you are going to recruit aggressively and widely, then it is important that the candidates should be suitably impressed. The ceremony must be imposing. I have written a scheme down here. I have also the Branch's warrant flag for a recruitment.'

White Paper Fan read in silence. Finally, he said: 'Good. You will enter with the recruits, of course, so I can ritually examine you in the responses on their behalf. Better for the "new horses" to enter in a body. It is my experience that repetition diminishes the awe of ignorant men. We have, of course, no Incense Master, so our Red Cudgel officer will be alone at the Altar. Our other officers will be in the usual flanking positions.' He coughed. 'May we rehearse the responses we intend using? My memory is poor.'

Red Cudgel understood White Paper Fan to be critical of the ceremony the Vanguard officer wished to enact and desirous of making tactful changes; also concerned about the old man's power to maintain a long dialogue, even if all the 333 ritual questions were not to be posed. He sat back and rubbed his knuckles while they passed down Cromwell Road.

The new horses were to be registered; fragrance of fresh incense blended with old. Vanguard prepared himself to conduct the Hung braves into the City of Willows. He gave the secret hand signals; the guard felt them under his robe. It was now the turn of the recruits to enter into the exchanges they had learned by rote.

The guards flung up their swords in a crosswise arch.

–Stranger, why come you here?

–We come to enlist in the army of the brothers of the Hung family.

–Then you will suffer many hardships. Your rations will consist of seven parts sand to three parts of rice.

–What our brothers can eat, that we can also eat.

The recruits passed under the Mountain of Knives. One by one the guards tapped them.

–Which is the harder, sword or neck?

–Neck.

They crawled under a low table, paid their lucky money at the recruiting desk and were given joss-sticks in return.

Elder Brother called: 'I see no strangers. Let the theatricals begin.'

At this signal the officers donned headbands and sandals, rolling up their left trouser legs under the monk robes.

White Paper Fan entered in the guise of the Hung fruit-seller, pannier baskets slung across his shoulders. He entered into his dialogue with Vanguard.

–State your business here.

–I am bringing you countless fresh soldiers, iron-hearted and valiant who wish to join the Hung Family.

–Why do they wish to join the Hung Family?

–To overthrow the house of Ching and restore the house of Ming.

White Paper Fan paused. When he spoke again it was with a question from far later in the catechism. Vanguard was confused but quickly regained his composure.

–How did you gain your knowledge of martial arts?

–These I studied at siu lum temple.

–What did you learn first?

–My first study was the art of boxing of the Hung brethren.

–How can you prove that?

–I can prove it by a verse.

–How does this verse run?

–The fists of the brave and valiant Hungs are known throughout the world. Since siu lum temple it has been passed on. Under the wide expanse of heaven we are called Hung. Afterwards we will assist the prince of the house of Ming.

White Paper Fan paused, again to let the 438-officer recover himself.

–Who do you worship?

–I worship Heaven as my father, Earth as my mother, the Sun as my elder

*brother, and the Moon as my sister. The name of heaven is **Sing**, earth*
*Wong, sun is **Sun** and the moon is surnamed **Tang**.*
–Where are your Hung brothers?
–They are far off over the horizon; they are near before my eyes. They
roam the world over. This is why I come alone.

Now White Paper Fan interrogated Vanguard on his knowledge of
the City of Willows, its plum tree with seventy-two fruits, peach tree
with thirty-six fruits, shops, markets, pagodas, temples, wells,
animals, pools, orchards, bridges, gardens, lakes and streets. The
senior officer's responses were crisp and confident.

Then White Paper Fan asked:
–What is considered most important in the city?
–Weapons.
–With what are cases decided?
–The Red Cudgel.
–As you claim to be the Hung Vanguard what are the classics you study?
–In civil affairs I follow Confucius. In military Yang.
–Where did you study?
–In the Red Flower Pavilion under the Hung master.

White Paper Fan paused again.
–What is your knowledge of the eighteen martial arts?

For a moment White Paper Fan thought he would have to prompt
the old man. But at last Vanguard said:
–I am skilled in the use of sword and chain. I handle the lance as well as Tse
Lung. My staff is like Hui-ying's. My single stick is better than the pair of
Wei chi kung's.

White Paper Fan said:
–I have examined you in everything and there is no doubt you are who you
say you are. Rise and prostrate yourself three times before our true lord. I
have a precious sword and a warrant to give you.

He led the senior officer and recruits forward to the Fiery Pit.
Vanguard was confused by the purpose of the twist given to the end of
the responses with the recitation of the verse from the middle of the
catechism.

But now a young woman who had been holding the tapes of the Two
Planked Bridge came forward with a coop in which was a white
cockerel. Her knotted headband denoted 432-rank.

Vanguard took a sheet of perfumed yellow paper from the Altar and
in a slow and solemn voice read out the thirty-six Hung oaths to the
recruits as they knelt with dry-wood candles in their hands, flanked by
the society officers.

Vanguard set fire to the paper and crumbled its ashes into a bowl of wine. The cockerel was quickly and neatly beheaded by a guard. Vanguard called:

–*Number 7 dies. Let all traitors share the fate of this treacherous fowl.*

Blood from the severed neck of the bird welled slowly into the bowl of wine; not a drop was spilled. Now the recruits each pricked their fingers with the Iron-headed Prince and added their blood to the mixture. Vanguard added sugar and cinnabar. All drank in turn, pledging:

–*We drink. To us it is sweet.*

Vanguard threw the bowl in the air and shattered it with the handle of a sword.

And now it was the time for the recruits to be taken to Red Flower Pavilion to wash their faces, don new robes, grass sandals, and receive the three Hung cash. Before White Paper Fan handed out the code books, certificates and diplomas, each new 49 crawled through the stocky, bowed legs of Elder Brother. Now they were truly reborn.

The feast, as prescribed, took place three days later but not as the culmination of continuous ritual over the period. The celebration was held at a restaurant in North London outside the usual networks on Night-brother's insistence. Red Cudgel commended his foresight, mentioning it to White Paper Fan, who had been rather morose since the initiation. He remembered it with distaste. A purist, he described it as a farrago of borrowings, improvisations, and pure invention. As a Chiu Chow Shanghainese to a Swatownese, he told the 426 officer: 'Typical of the Kwangchou school. A race of monkeys.'

Red Cudgel smiled. 'We must honour the office, if not the man.'

'Of course,' White Paper Fan said swiftly. 'We also need to send the man back happy if we are to preserve good relations with Hong Kong. The initiation fee is partly to thank them for using us instead of Amsterdam with the shipment of the No 4 heroin.'

'Younger sister is giving him hospitality at the moment, as is proper since she is our liaison officer.'

'What kind of hospitality?' White Paper Fan asked sarcastically.

Red Cudgel grinned, showing the steel pin in his mouth. 'He's too old for that now. Not that there aren't a few salty-wet old men I know.'

'She should give him some Snake and Tiger Bone Wine,' White Paper Fan said with uncharacteristic crudity. 'That would lift a dead worm. But seriously, I propose we give another feast for him as well as

102

the initiation banquet. Just for 432-rank upwards. We could give him Double Flower prefix. Send him home happy.'

'He's already a 438-officer.'

'Doesn't matter. Double Flower rank is purely honorific anyway. He would not be able to influence our policy but we would have a friend in Hong Kong.'

'Agreed. We need him. I anticipate trouble soon.'

FOURTEEN

At the beginning they were lucky. For a start they had a ready-made source of custom in the garage. What had seemed to Lily a symbol of disaster proved a fountain of modest prosperity. She had feared her savings would drain away before news of their business spread, and Husband had been against advertising in the local newspaper, as Mui suggested. It had been difficult enough getting him to agree to the sign under their bedroom window. But even before they had the kitchen properly organised there were people wanting food. These customers included garage-hands as well as motorists who had stopped for petrol. Word of mouth recommendation did the rest, especially amongst the heavy goods vehicle drivers on their way to the Channel ports, the aitchgevees, as the girls learned to call them.

One day Lily returned from the shops to find six monsters on each side of the road: a petrol tanker and a refrigerated lorry among them. They were reversing and advancing with a hiss of air-brakes. It was over fifteen minutes before the road was clear.

The garage owner came to complain.

Lily saw a large, balding man in clean overalls with extremely hairy arms come through the door. She smiled at him.

'No, don't smile at me, dear, because I'm not in a laughing mood.'

Chen looked up from where he was sand-papering one of his pews, lest a splinter should lodge in an English behind. Mui was stacking silver-foil containers on the counter.

'Are you the owner?'

'Owner, yes.'

'I'm Constantinides from the garage.'

Chen offered his hand in a manner calculated from experience to defuse *faan gwai* obstreperousness. 'Chen.'

Mr Constantinides wiped his clean, hairy paw before taking Chen's hand. 'I can't have you blocking my forecourt like that again, Mr Chen. You must understand my position – as a businessman yourself. Nothing personal, all right? I've got nothing against nobody.'

Without realising it, Mr Constantinides had flattered Chen by calling him a businessman, given him face.

'It wasn't our fault it happen, Mr Con ... Mr ... The driver just go and park their lorry and come in here. We didn't want it to be blocking your way.'

Mui had run out of containers to occupy her hands. She tittered. This was out of the nervousness, embarrassment, and excitement of seeing a flesh and blood Englishman, as opposed to a flickering one-dimensional image on the screen, in her house for the first time. You couldn't very well get a more flesh and blood specimen, redder and hairier, than the present example of an Englishman.

Mr Constantinides flushed even redder with anger.

Chen saw this and said quickly: 'Don't take notice please. Just stupid girl doing laughings. She didn't mean anything.'

Mr Constantinides took the point. He and Chen sat down together on a pew (Careful, Mr Big Man) and tried to work out a compromise, that admirable Chinese way. Tea was brought by Mui, simpering. She and Lily took Man Kee into the garden while the men talked.

'There is a way we could make this work out for both of us,' Mr Constantinides admitted. He came to what he had already had in mind when he stepped through the front door. Chen was receptive.

Mr Constantinides wished to attract business to his garage. So (theoretically) did Chen want more custom. Why not make their businesses mutually supporting? Mr Constantinides could have a menu posted prominently in the garage and have customers take orders from the forecourt. A five per cent commission might be appropriate. Even thinking the offer over quickly Chen could see the advantages of this scheme lay mostly with Mr Constantinides. Nevertheless, out of a desire not to antagonise the natives, Chen agreed to the plan. Mr Constantinides left in a good humour. He always knew the Chinese were sensible fellows, not like those West Indians, and his face darkened with blood as he thought of the youths who revved their cars noisily in his forecourt, lounging in their leopard skin seats with the radios on at full blast.

So now, at odd times of day and night, the telephone Mr Constantinides had installed for them double-quick, would ring. Whereupon Lily would pick up the receiver and out of habit say 'Wai?' or Mui would pedantically intone into the mouth-piece, 'Dah Ling restaurant,' followed by their number, just like the switchboard operator in *Crossroads* – both of which responses were equally irritating to Mr Constantinides. He would say: 'Two sweet and sour pork,' or 'One chicken with beansprouts, prawn crackers, and egg fried rice.'

Then Mui would climb the steps out of the garden, balancing the silver cartons on her chest. She would shuffle dangerously in her thin slippers. She would never wear anything more substantial on her feet, and she was always dressed in a thin tunic suit and holed cardigan, even when there was ice and slush on the ground. Punctiliously clicking the gate behind her, she would negotiate a way through the cans, hose, and iridescent oil pools on the slippery concrete of the forecourt and on tip-toe hand the little boxes to the driver high in his cab. Her tips were generous, sometimes amounting to a third or even half of the bill. 'That's all right, keep the change,' the drivers said, reluctant to send her to the shop and back again in such inadequate garments. (Mui isn't as stupid as she looks, Lily used to think.) Some of the long-distance drivers gave her a fistful of foreign coins or a wad of large, impressive-looking notes, so flamboyant and worth so much less than drab English money. Once home Mui added her gleanings to the now sadly diminished hoard in Lily's tea-tin. Chen had said they could keep their own tips. This was more an issue of principle than practical consequence since the girls had nothing to spend their money on. It was a reflection of an alteration in Chen's outlook: he was giving his women the status of colleagues in the new enterprise.

The food they sold, certainly wholesome, nutritious, colourful, even tasty in its way, had been researched by Chen. It bore no resemblance at all to Chinese cuisine. They served from a stereotyped menu, similar to those outside countless other establishments in the UK. The food was, if nothing else, thought Lily, provenly successful: English tastebuds must be as degraded as their care of their parents; it could, of course, be part of a scheme of cosmic repercussion. 'Sweet and sour pork' was their staple, naturally: batter musket balls encasing a tiny core of meat, laced with a scarlet sauce that had an interesting effect on the urine of the consumer the next day. Chen knew because he tried some and almost fainted with shock the morning after, fearing some frightful internal haemorrhaging (had Lily been making him overdo it

105

lately?) and going round with a slight limp until in the mid-afternoon the stream issued clear as ever. 'Spare-ribs' (whatever they were) also seemed popular. So were spring-rolls, basically a Northerner's snack, which Lily parsimoniously filled mostly with bean-sprouts. All to be packed in the rectangular silver boxes, food coffins, to be removed and consumed statutorily off-premises. The only authentic dish they served was rice, the boiled kind; the fried rice they sold with peas and ham bore no resemblance to the *chow faan* Lily cooked for themselves, although it was popular enough with their West Indian customers. The dishes were simple to cook; well within Chen's capabilities, which was hardly surprising since they had been invented by the Chinese seamen who had jumped ship or retired in East London a generation ago.

Mui threw herself into this work. Lily helped her in the morning when the counter was closed. They sang, as closely as she could in Lily's case, to the pop songs coming from the transistor, the fuzzy static from the tinny little set merging with the louder crackling of the batter musket balls in their pan of seething oil. The girls were happier then, had more purpose, than at any time in their adult lives. The effect of responsibility and joy was to throw them back to their earliest days and made them if not childish, child-like.

A rhythm established itself. They retired late and rose late. Customers came in bursts: between seven and nine in the evenings and from eleven o'clock at night until one a.m. Quite illegally, they were open until that hour. Between eleven and midnight things could become rather rowdy as the pubs closed. From midnight to one a.m. the phone would ring with drivers' orders.

They all ate together at noon and again at nine in the evening when trade slackened, with Lily posted at the counter and carrying on a conversation through the hatch while the others ate in the kitchen. They had never been together for so long at a time: twenty-four hours of the day instead of ten, eight hours of which Chen had spent unconscious though Lily had been able to divine a surprising amount from the relaxed, sleeping features of Husband which unblurred as he dreamed and twitched. Now, almost five years into their marriage, never having formed strong external friendships which might have acted as a diversion, Chen and Lily were still able to make fascinating, sometimes shaking discoveries about each other. For instance, Lily found out that Husband liked to blow his nose with his fingers in the middle of washing his face. After he had released this explosive snort with his eyes closed against the stinging lather, he would carry on rubbing soap and mucus into those smudged features: cheeks, nose, forehead, eye-sockets. He rinsed thoroughly, of course, with running water from the tap, and the reflex was probably a habit acquired quite legitimately under, say, a constant stream of water from a village pump cooperatively worked by a friend after a day's hard work in the fields and in an altogether more clement climate, both of weather and opinion, than that prevailing in the UK. Where, too, the discharge of the effluvia of colds and flu was likely to be that much heavier. Nevertheless, Lily couldn't help being put out. And that had been going on for five years while she lay in bed. And why did Husband have to do it in the kitchen sink when there was a perfectly good wash basin in the bathroom? Perhaps it was a substitute for shaving. At least Husband wasn't a spitter. Husband was, though, a tireless whistler of tuneless ditties through clenched teeth (an unconscious mannerism brought on by work); a compulsive starer out of the front window (could business really be that bad?) from which he would retreat rapidly into the kitchen as custom arrived; and, while he lavished unexpected attention on Man Kee, he rarely spoke to Mui. At least he had reduced his recent chain-smoking to the tolerable level of the years before the move.

But Lily couldn't help being scandalised when he told her to stop sending the remittances to his mother and father. This was quite extraordinary; it cut at the basis of everything she believed in, everything Husband ought to believe in, too. They hadn't moved so they could go back on their obligations. Even if they experienced hardships the remittances must continue to arrive regularly. She had assumed they might go without a meal or two, if necessary (adults anyway). How much more important to send the money when they were doing well in their modest way.

Lily didn't have to work hard to imagine the hardship Mr and Mrs Chen senior would suffer; she could all too easily see it happening to herself. One day she, too, might depend on a remittance from the family she had built up. In the end all obligations were reciprocal. But Husband was quite blind to this: 'Not yet, Lily. Not yet. We can make it up with more money later.'

'That is not the point, Husband,' she said primly.

Then he showed real anger: 'No. This is the end of it. Who is head in our family? You think wife tells Husband what to do?'

She cast her eyes down. There was something, though, stiff and obstinate in that slim, bowed neck. Chen thought: she intends to disobey me and continue to send the money. Lily looked up; her eyes met Chen's and there was mutual understanding.

Chen sighed. 'Do this for me at least, Man Kee's mother.'

'Yes, Husband?'

'Send money but make it cash, not money order.'

'Can be stolen; but,' she added, 'I will do it.'

'Good. One more thing, Lily. Don't give our address.'

She was puzzled. 'How can they write back? I don't understand.'

Chen thought. Then he said: 'They can write to a post-box.'

Lily looked even more puzzled. 'I thought they only collected letters from those things.'

Despite himself Chen smiled. 'This is something else. A numbered box at the post office. You have a key to collect your letters when you want.'

'All right, Husband, whatever you say.' Of course, she had no intention whatsoever of obeying him here. He'd never know; they only wrote once a year, if that.

She went off to pile foil-boxes. A little later she thought she had worked it out: 'You want to make the business big and surprise your mother and father, don't you? That's right, isn't it?'

Chen didn't reply but she had latched onto the explanation already.

Whatever her well-stifled misgivings, she intended to be a good wife to him. All these new characteristics she incorporated into a revised assessment of Husband – one which remained loyally high.

For his part Chen had made some discoveries as well. In his arrogance he had always assumed the girls spent the day in a kind of suspended animation, coming to life as his key turned in the lock at night. But this wasn't so. No, those two sisters were obviously rather good friends. Life had been going on behind his back; life of a gay, irresponsible, female kind. Little jokes, allusions, silent communication all attested a shared experience. Chen imagined them beaming telepathic messages to each other around the house. Holding a conversation with them could be unnerving, especially if it was an argument over their plans for the business. They always seemed two moves ahead of him, adept at anticipating any suggestion or objection he might make, for his ideas were increasingly at variance with those of the girls. He wanted a modest, unobtrusive living; they wanted to get on, expand, make as much money as they could. But how far was all this Lily and how far was Mui just her stooge? Chen would stand between them like poor piggy in the middle, tormented by older schoolgirls, as they batted ideas to and fro to each other, trying desperately to intercept his bundle – his business, after all – as it flew overhead and back again just out of his reach.

'We'll put a big sign at the end of the road telling people to come and buy our food,' Lily announced brightly.

'No, no, Lily. Bad idea. Really not good at all. We can't make enough food if everyone comes and then they'll get angry with us.'

'Oh, no, Brother-in-law, don't worry. We can *easily* do it. Just cook the food the night before and then heat it up again quickly when it's needed. We can buy another gas ring and bottle if we need it.'

Chen had been looking at Lily. Now he turned to Mui with some annoyance. She met his eye meekly but levelly.

'We could buy three or four gas-bottles, Husband.'

He turned his head.

'Brother-in-law, they would soon pay for themselves.'

Another turn.

'We'll stay up late to prepare the food, Husband. You can sleep. We don't mind, do we, Mui?'

'Of course not, younger sister.'

By now Chen was nervous, irritated, and also quite dizzy. He asserted himself. 'No, no sign. We must do things steadily,' and he went upstairs to take Man Kee into the garden, leaving Lily and Mui staring across the space he had lately occupied. They were singing to that infernal radio again as he went through the kitchen door, holding Man Kee's hand.

In general the effect on Chen of continual close proximity with his family had been to accelerate tendencies which were already working out more slowly. The move didn't alter his feelings towards them. There was just more opportunity for incidents to occur which would modify their outlooks on each other. This speeding up of the tempo of evolution had a physical as well as an emotional aspect.

For every year he had been in England Chen had put on four pounds in weight. But now, deprived of the constant exercise at the restaurant, not to mention the calorific expenditure of travel, he was getting heavier at an alarming rate. His features were no longer occasionally blurred; he was becoming positively moon-faced. And this was without eating more. In fact he asked Lily not to give him so much. He had been shocked to discover just how little the girls really ate; he had always assumed they must have their big meal during the day. Even so, th girls had doubled their food intake since leaving the flat. Yet how, Chen wondered, was it that Mui remained so plump on what amounted to starvation rations? She and Lily ate exactly the same portions but they looked so different. How did they distribute their fat store so idiosyncratically? There wasn't an excess ounce on Lily's delicate-boned tough gadfly's frame but Mui was a little saffron marshmallow. Could it be possible that some people just burnt their food stores up more quickly than others? Doubtless Lily could quote one of her father's crank theories on the subject. Not wanting to end up like an Englishman, however, Chen had resolved to take more exercise, and the most convenient way of doing this had been to take charge of Man Kee. He didn't want his son to be subjected to all this female influence either. It couldn't be good for the boy. Let *yang* balance *yin*.

Together they explored the back garden which labourers hired by the estate agent had trimmed into some sort of order. The flower beds and vegetable patches were still choked with weeds but the six-foot waving grasses were no more. Now you could plainly see the allotments at the end of their fence and beyond that the wire preventing access to the railway line.

Man Kee poked about in the earth, uprooted handfuls of weeds and piled them at his father's feet. Soon they had turned over most of the soil in the beds; they had also uncovered a host of worms wriggling here and there amongst the clods which Man Kee appeared to mistake for *chow mein* noodles. Chen intercepted his son's grubby hand as it went to his mouth. 'No, no, bad to eat. Bad.' He drilled a hole in the earth with his finger and dropped the worm into it by its tail (head). Let the poor creature hide itself in the earth and escape. They were good for the soil too, he knew.

Chen gathered up an armful of weeds and Man Kee followed his father's example, tottering after him to scatter his armful on the compost heap. At the end of the week there were no more weeds and a large pile of mouldering grass at the garden's end. Chen felt he had benefited from the open-air work and the girls (he felt he had better face the truth) certainly seemed happier to get on with their work in their own way. His turn to labour in the kitchen came later in the day.

Lily was both pleased and touched by Husband's new interest in Son. 'You are a good father,' she told him, playfully pulling the roll of surplus flesh above his hip-bone.

Encouraged, Chen took Man Kee further afield. They discovered a small park near by with swings, two slides and a roundabout. Man Kee rapidly became bored with the swing and developed a preference for being placed on the seat, twisted round and round until the chains were coiled into a tight black knot, and then released into a ferocious spin. At first Chen was worried Man Kee might be sick, throw up all that delicious, sustaining liver and fish the girls stuffed him with, but he actually seemed to enjoy being giddy and disorientated, staggering and falling to the grass repeatedly, chuckling all the time as his great round face grew redder and redder.

Lily, perhaps, would have been less amused by this game than either father or son; although the difference between what Man Kee willingly played in the park and the complicated disciplines his mother had been forced through as a child could be described as purely academic, the lack of a defining purpose behind the activity. And, of course, Chen had neither expertise nor a sense of his own failure to impart to his son at a precocious age. Man Kee, happy child, was getting a fresh start. He had no history, no heritage to live up to, no goal to fulfil, no ancient burden to carry. Not one his father imposed, anyway.

FIFTEEN

-Husband, I heard you coughing in the night.
-Just a dry throat, Lily. The house is dusty. Fill my glass with tea, it's cold this morning.
-But Mui helped me clean upstairs yesterday morning when you took son to the park.
-There must have been some dust hanging in the air after you cleaned. It's an old house.
-No, you did a wet cough, Husband.
-I'm all right, Lily.
-All the people of your village suffer from TB, it's the wet air.
-But we live in England.
-Not important. You bring it with you. Father always said ...
-If I have, it's too late anyway.
-No, Husband. Tomorrow I shall make you more medicine.
-No need, Lily. No need. 1 don't work those long hours away any more.
-It's no trouble, Husband.
-Absolutely not, Lily. On no account.

-Brother-in-law?
-What is it, Mui?
-Not important, Brother-in-law.

-Husband, are you awake?

-I am now.

-You should talk more to Mui, Husband.

-What things do I have to say to her?

-You must talk to her, Husband. She feels she is in our way.

-How can she be in our way? She lived with us in the flat, didn't she?

-You hardly ever saw her then.

-She was welcome in our household then and she is welcome now. She isn't a guest; she's part of our family. She does more work than I do.

-Speak to her, Husband.

-What do I say? Good morning, young mistress? Have you eaten evening rice yet, Miss Tang?

-Speak to her, Husband.

-Husband!

-What is it now, Lily? I'm busy with these extra benches.

-A treat. Close your eyes.

-Sweet red-bean stew!

-Mui, bring the best bowls and spoons, the finest one for Husband.

-Girls, you must eat some too.

-We have eaten ours already, Brother-in-law.

-Get a bowl, Mui. I don't start until I see you eat yours.

-Brother-in-law, you give me so much!

-Not another word, Mui. And you, Lily, give me your bowl. Right, all together now. Wonderful! Nice and thick! What are you laughing at, Mui?

-Nothing, Brother-in-law.

-Come on, what is it?

-I hope you won't be offended, Brother-in-law, but you make such a loud noise, like a dragon putting his fire out in a big lake.

-That must show I'm enjoying it anyway. The red water shows it's good for the blood. I should take this for colds instead of that bitter medicine, Lily.

-That's not a bad idea, Husband. The beans are easy to get here. They come from Japan.

-From Japan! But they taste just like Chinese red-beans!

-Of course, Husband. Beans are beans. What a loud belch, Husband!

-Younger sister, where do you think Brother-in-law and Man Kee go?

-I don't know, Mui. It's their little secret. I know they enjoy themselves.

-No mistake. It's good for Nephew to have man's company, especially at the age he is now. Look what happened when Father had you to himself.

–What happened to me, elder sister? What on earth are you talking about?

–Never mind, younger sister. It's not important. Please, don't take offence. Ah, I think the 'sweet and sour pork' is cooked now.

–Give it another five minutes, the harder the coating the better they like it.

–Son spoke to me this morning, Mui.

–Yes, he's getting quite talkative really. I was a bit worried for a while, he was such a silent little boy.

–Yes, but Mui, he spoke in *English*!

–Eiyah! In English! But where would he learn that?

–It's as mysterious to me as it is to you.

–What did he say, Lily?

–He said: 'Hello, Dah Ling.' But that's just nonsense; it's only the name of our village. Mui, why are you laughing?

–I'm not, I'm not.

–Husband where do you and Son go to play?

–In a park near the railway station. There are swings and slides. But of course I don't twist him on the swing. It might make him sick.

–What are you talking about? How can you twist someone on a swing?

–Ah ... it's not important, Lily. I don't do it anyway.

–You two enjoy yourselves the way you want. I was just worried you might go to the waste-ground where the fire was. You could cut yourselves on glass.

–No need to concern yourself about that, Lily.

–They go to a park where there are swings and slides and a 'twister', whatever that is, and Husband 'twists' Man Kee.

–How charming!

–Yes. I like them to be together. Too much mixing with members of the opposite sex is bad for children. Father spent too much time teaching me *siu lum*.

–I wouldn't say that, Lily. You do yourself an injustice.

–Lily, the ground has turned quite white! Look out of the window!

–Of course, this must be the first snow you have seen, sister. Apart from on television.

–How beautiful it is!

–But then it gets dirty and melts and gets in your shoes. Yes, it's beautiful now, all right.

–Ah, but like this it seems beautiful. And when the trains go by the blue flash lights up the whole horizon.

You should write poetry, Mui.

–Eiyah! What was that?

–Stay where you are, Mui.

–It must be hooligans. Have they broken the window? Please put that cleaver down, Lily.

–Ah! It was only Husband throwing a ball of snow. Come to the window, Mui, they've built a white man.

–How clever!

–Phone is ringing! My hands are full!

–All right, Mui, I'll answer it. You take the silver boxes out.

–What's wrong, Lily?

–That's very odd. I'm sure there was someone at the other end. I could *feel* them.

–Didn't say anything?

–Said nothing. Just hung up. How strange.

–It happened to me the other day, too. I picked it up and answered. Then a click and 'burr'.

–Maybe Mr Constantinides forgot the order and didn't want to look silly. Their ways are odd.

–Maybe. Shall we tell Brother-in-law?

–No, no. Certainly not. What for? Bad to bother him with silly little things. Anyway he can't hear a thing in the kitchen.

–You're right, of course. Lily?

–Yes?

–We're lucky people, aren't we? To have our own place and be able to build it up, I mean. It's like a second chance in our lives.

–We *are* lucky, Mui. And I'm especially lucky to have you and Husband.

–And Son, Lily.

–And Son.

–Business is down this week, Lily.

–Little-little. Husband says it will only be temporary; then it will be bigger than usual for a few days before going back to normal.

–That's right. Their holiday is only a week. We can relax a little but it's a shame to lose business as we've been doing so well.

–One must adapt to circumstances. Anyway, the aitchgevees have been generous with their tips to you since the snow fell – perhaps they get extra pay at this time of year.

–That *is* customary. Still it will be nice to have the house to ourselves, I suppose.

–Yes, I'm happy. The house is well-aspected. *Fung shui* must be good. Maybe we should have guests of our own at New Year next month. It will be ...

–Year of the Cock, but perhaps I'm wrong. Can you really persuade Brother-in-law?

–I'll do my best.

–Poor man!

SIXTEEN

The men stood in ten files across the length of the hall, each file six deep. There was a gap of seven feet between each man in the files. Red Cudgel, his rolling swagger more pronounced than usual, critically inspected his sixty fighters. The church hall in New Cross was used as a boxing school by a burly instructor, newly recruited and given immediate 432-rank, despite society regulations stipulating at least ten months wait. Red Cudgel had personally trained the front man in each file; the ten were his personal bodyguard. He knew their abilities. He had reservations about the potential of the fifty others, selected from the newly swollen membership. He would have to make the most of imperfect material. By his side was the new 432-officer, Iron Plank. He was a good eight inches taller than Red Cudgel and thirty pounds heavier, with the long, unknotted musculature one would look for in a fighter. Despite White Paper Fan's strictures, Red Cudgel knew that he needed this man and that he deserved his rank. He said to him: 'This is going to be hard.'

The younger man asked: 'How long do we have?'

'Two months at most. I want them effective and hardened street-fighters at the end.'

'Then we don't teach Chinese boxing.'

Red Cudgel shared the joke. He knew only a real fighter could have made it. It was a remark of some sophistication, in context. He, too, knew the classical teaching method of blind repetition and stereotyped drilling was ineffective and time-consuming. It produced weak, predictable boxers. Fighting couldn't be planned. Moves were improvised on the moment; it was pure instinct translated into movement.

'None of that ten punches, ten kicks stuff by rote,' he said. 'We'll just teach them how to win. You teach *choi li fut*, don't you? A good *sui lum* style like *hung gar*. In fact we're so close you can almost call me Uncle.'

'I teach *Choi* but naturally I've studied others: *Wing Chun* intensively, Southern Mantis, and White Crane until I saw it was practically useless.'

'Quite useless,' the older man agreed. 'We have a common basis, then. Not much fundamental difference between the application of *Choi* and *Hung*. Only *Hung* apprenticeship is different. In this case it doesn't matter – we don't have time for the Two Hour Horse Stance.'

'No mistake!'

'Younger brother, I'm a fighter pure and simple. You have experience of teaching. Do you recommend we teach weapons first, then fist and foot? Or do we follow tradition and teach empty hand first? Bear in mind, we have mostly novices here and we fight armed when it's for real.'

Iron Plank said: 'Well spoken. I know there are modern *sifu* who teach staff or sword first. But I believe we should initially teach them balance and control of their own body. In any case practice in giving punches and kicks leads to a better appreciation of distance. Giving the limb a weapon and extension to start with destroys this understanding. My experience is that it also leads to a tendency to strike with only the arm or leg rather than the whole body.'

'Agreed! Agreed!' Red Cudgel was delighted. 'Understanding of distance, balance, and a commitment of the whole body – that's the secret of real fighting. We proceed from that then.' In a curt tone quite different from the familiarity he would employ with another serious student of the way of the fist, he began to give orders. The bodyguards were each assigned five men to instruct in the cardinal principles. Red Cudgel and Iron Plank toured each of the groups.

'As little as possible on stance and blocks,' Iron Plank recommended. 'You can try to teach too much. You teach a shadow-boxer. A fighter is born. You mustn't confuse the instinct of a natural fighter.

You don't mould him – you help him find himself.'

'Agreed.' Red Cudgel was really warming to this 432-officer. 'Attack is the best defence on the street.'

Iron Plank put both hands on a student's shoulders. 'Lower.'

Red Cudgel said: 'You heard.' He kicked the man's feet wider apart.

'Train low,' Iron Plank explained. 'Fight higher if you feel comfortable that way, but practising like this will give you speed in attack.'

'*Hung* stance is particularly suited to weapons,' Red Cudgel told the group. 'We used to wear a small buckler on the left arm and a short-sword in the right. We go low because this is the best way to come under a long weapon and stab upwards. Remember and understand.'

'More from the hip,' Iron Plank exhorted a second group who were punching on the move. 'Good boxing comes up through your feet and hips and only then through the arm and into the fist. Lead with your left fist for range and follow with your right. Practise in a right foot forward stance as well. You must be versatile.'

Red Cudgel had finished his tour of inspection of the ten groups. He was exasperated by the inept and clumsy movements going on around him. His face was blank but his eyes were small and hard and a muscle twitched in his ravaged cheek.

Iron Plank said: 'Your own ten fighters are a credit to you. Six of the new recruits are already fair, another fourteen could be good with practice. The rest will never learn.'

Red Cudgel said: 'At least I have you, you are ten men.'

Iron Plank grinned. 'How many do we face?'

'About twenty properly trained men. Maybe fifty have knowledge of the thing. Their enforcer is a White Eyebrow man.'

'Jackie Fung?'

'Correct.' Red Cudgel was surprised. 'You know him?'

'By reputation. He's the only teacher of White Eyebrow in this country. Had a school in Glasgow. Very strong. I know he crippled four western devils single-handed when they left his Uncle's place without paying what they owed.'

'That's a well-known story. Also true.'

'But I didn't know he was 14-K. How can a White Eyebrow exponent be *Hung* family when the founder of the style killed one of the *siu lum* patriarchs? I thought the style was outlawed for us?'

'Correct again. But anything goes with 14-K. Fung has his uses for them.'

'He is really very fast indeed. I must tell you that at once. If it is at all possible he must be caught on his own, unarmed and unprepared. Incidentally, do you plan to take them in small groups where we have numerical superiority at that moment?'

'Impossible, unfortunately. I agree this is the best way to weaken a strong enemy. But if we do this we alert them and they still have strength to defeat us. It has to be one big hit which permanently destroys their command.'

'In that case I suggest we plan around their weaknesses. White Eyebrow is an excellent close-range style, not as effective as *wing chun* but still good. I should add their weapons ability is strictly limited. But Chen is a good kicker and likes to try sweeps as well.'

'Well spoken. We plan with these things in mind.'

Red Cudgel clapped his hands. 'Enough. You make me despair. Watch now and try to learn, if you can.'

The men gathered in a large circle. He nodded to a sturdy 49 who had been leading one of the groups. The man stood a short distance in front of the stocky Swatownese.

'What you learn in conventional *goong foo* bears no relation to real street fighting. Forget all you have learned in the past. In combat will and courage mean more than technique. Strength and guile prevail over style. Your movements must be simple and efficient – what suits you best, not what you have been taught. It is *you* who lives or dies, not your teacher. Take your enemy by surprise whenever possible – from behind or in the dark. Make sure you outnumber him at least two to one, three is preferable. Make sure you are armed and he is unarmed. An untrained man with a sharp weapon will kill a trained man. A trained woman can never hope to beat a strong man. With a weapon she can kill him. However, we begin now with unarmed combat.'

He pushed the student away from him. 'The body is divided into four main target areas.' Red Cudgel's voice was crisp and confident; even the habitual hoarseness seemed to have been soothed. 'Head, trunk, groin, and legs. Imagine a line drawn vertically down the centre of the body between the eyes, linking the bridge of the nose, navel, and groin. Then draw a line horizontally across the hips to quarter the body. These sections are the four gates through which you launch your attack. Usually left hand attacks through enemy's top right gateway, right hand through his left. Some variation is possible. Art of fighting is to get in range to deliver a blow and also to manoeuvre so that the gate is open when you are in position to deliver it. To have a clear path you can feint, beat by speed, or batter it down. You, on guard.'

The 49 came into the sideways-on low stance typical of *Hung gar*.

'Note, this is trained man. He leaves only three gateways open for me: his left-upper, mid-section, and leg. For practical purposes, only two, as his arm and elbow protect the flank. A good man always keeps his elbow down, even when hurt or striking. Now: speed is not my asset. He can stop a simple, direct attack.'

Red Cudgel threw a short, curving left to the point of the 49's chin, which the man caught in his cupped right palm with a loud smack.

'Note: this was an unorthodox blow with the leading hand to a point normally unassailable. It was a blow made famous by a Kwangsi boxer who used it in the right foot forward stance. Most men would throw a reverse right at the side of the head. My partner still blocked me. Observe now.'

The Swatownese leaned forward, then swung his body back as he delivered a powerful kick to the 49's knee with the inside of his right foot; he feinted a short left to the head and then delivered a blow to the lower ribs of the 49's left side with his open right palm. The man gasped but stayed on his feet.

Red Cudgel said: 'Feint attack. Alternatively, grasp his left hand, pull it across his body, and strike with your right. This kind of complex compound attack is best suited to untrained or half-trained men like yourselves. The hand-pull and kick to leg enable you to traverse distance as well as distract your opponent. The two moves can be combined. A young, trained man,' he indicated Iron Plank, 'can land with sheer speed using a simple attack. Simplicity is the height of technique.' He gestured again to the 49. 'Stand square on. Have no fear.' He touched the man's hip. 'From here to the head – only use hand attacks. Never kick above the waist – you leave yourself vulnerable. I advise you never to kick above the knee-cap. Shin-hack is best. Untrained man's instinct is to kick this – Golden Target,' he indicated the 49's groin. 'Very difficult to do. In fighting one is always conscious of the need to protect this spot. It is best to attack the groin with your hand – either Dragon fist,' – he raised the proximal phalangeal joints of his left hand above the knuckles like two horns and executed a short uppercut just short of the 49's testicles – 'or grab them and pull. Incapacitates totally. If you must kick, always execute a preliminary technique to distract. Never use this kick.' He raised his knee to his chest and thrust out, stopping the toe of his shoe just short again of the target; on neither occasion had the student flinched. 'This is the classical kick. Popular with Japanese. Its only advantage is its length. Very dangerous to execute. Your foot is easily caught. Nor is it necessarily decisive. Note: your opponent's penis lies in front of and

protects his testicles. His *yang* can save him. Deliver the kick like this.'
He tapped the instep of his foot just above the buckle of the crocodile
shoe. 'Drive upward, not forward. Short-range kick. It squashes a
man's testicles against the pubis. No protection. Even better to use
knee-ram instead of foot.'

Iron Plank said: 'Listen carefully. You hear secrets of a master.'
There was admiration in his voice.

The Swatownese continued: 'Open hand is also best for untrained
man to use.' He held his left fist up. 'In serious fighting it's very easy to
break your hand. Not knuckles but these.' He rubbed the back of his
pudgy hand. 'Bones run here which can break like twigs. Even long
hand-conditioning cannot entirely protect. You may punch to a man's
body with your fist. When you attack the head, use your elbow or curl
your fingers and use the palm. This is a good blow: you can burst his
ear-drums or dislocate his jaw without risk to your hand. If you
misconnect, keep your palm on his face, slide it around until you find
his eye-socket, then gouge with your thumb but not your fingers. For
serious combat: kick to shins, gouge eyes, attack the testicles.'

Iron Plank said: 'This is all correct. I add this: when you attack his
eyes don't poke forwards with your fingers. This is untrained man's
attack. To block, you hold your hand in front of your face. Attack to the
eyes is a tiger's slash – sideways and across. This way you will not risk
damage to the fingers.'

Red Cudgel nodded. 'Eye attack is *yin* attack. *Hung gar* is *yang* style
but even a hard style must have its soft aspect, as a soft style has its hard
aspect. Eight-diagram, Sing Yee, they have a *yang* aspect too.'

Iron Plank grinned broadly: '*Yin* more vicious than *yang*. I have
great fear of *yin*.' Red Cudgel gave a short laugh.

Iron Plank said: 'You have heard your *sifu*. Let's see if you
understood. In pairs: not the same height – tall with short. No gouges
but don't pull your blows. Then we'll go on to multiple attack and
defence.'

He watched them critically, occasionally calling out: 'You, too much
weight on the front leg. You know what will happen.'

Red Cudgel shouted angrily as one of his own bodyguard dropped
his hands to block a kick: 'Fool. You should know better. Haven't I
told you the way to block a kick is with another kick? Don't drop your
hands. Time your counter-kick: break his leg when it comes up.'

He swore as the man repeated his error. The Swatownese simmered.
The younger man smiled at the novice's efforts but there was contempt
in his eyes. He knew the older man was not so much irritated by the

120

incompetence he saw around him as filled with the sympathetic urge to do violence. He felt the same himself.

There was a head-sized canvas bag nailed to the wall, splattered with brown stains. Iron Plank caressed it with the bottom three knuckles of his right hand, then fired a short, rising left at it with a 'standing' fist, from the centre of the chest, elbow down. The bag burst, scattering a flood of tiny red beans which bounced and rattled over the floorboards.

Red Cudgel smiled at this youthful exuberance. 'Not bad,' he said. 'You're left-handed?' Iron Plank shook his head. 'I've worked heavily on it, that's all. You can learn from western boxing. And that reminds me Fung *is* a southpaw.'

'Good. An important point to remember.'

Iron Plank asked: 'What weapons are we using?'

'Depends where we take them. On the street, nine foot six inch poles, swords, some spears, iron bars, seven-sectional flail. Indoors, cleavers, axes, long knives, a spear for the door guard. I intend to carry my usual arms: cleaver and flail – long and short.'

Iron Plank considered: 'Good. I will use my pair of butterfly knives.'

'You mean the *Wing Chun* short swords? Without compare. Superb weapons. I could wish my cleaver twenty years ago had a guard like the butterfly knives.'

Iron Plank smiled sympathetically. 'No weapons-training for these incompetents yet. It encourages them to stand away.' He clapped his hands. 'I see a lot of cowards in front of me. Little commitment. You don't understand: attack is your best defence. It keeps your enemy off-balance; it means he is unable to think or develop his own rhythm. Don't let him force you back with your feet coming close together. That's when you are most vulnerable. Stay low, feet wide. When you punch, punch in sequence. At least three blows, maybe five. Always an odd number, so you are ready to start another combination with the leading hand again. I want to see more spirit. Remember: when we fight you may be wounded. You may be in pain or faint. You must keep fighting then or die. Begin again.'

The two men watched now with intense concentration. As a man fell or grunted or gasped, they would smile grimly without looking at the other, aware of a sardonic sensibility in their companion which matched their own. They were more satisfied now.

SEVENTEEN

Glowing furiously on his platform, god presided over a festive scene which did him full honours as a deity in exile. Lily had turned the counter into an altar, covering it with a finely embroidered tablecloth. The centrepiece was a large goldfish in a round bowl, flanked by the usual plates of fruit, and savoury and sweetmeat snacks. After long persistence she and Mui had bought from a cooperative greengrocer festive tangerines, with the all-important green leaves and stalks still attached. Salted melon seeds, sugared pumpkin and red dates had been unavailable – Husband had forbidden them to go to Chinese Street. Instead, their greengrocer had sold them monkey nuts. The girls had taken great trouble with their preparations; they had been a work of love and pride. In previous years Chen had taken Lily to see the communal celebrations in Soho, the lion dance and the rest of it. Once there had been a boxing demonstration. Lily had been critical of the performers' technical attainments: their balance was single-weighted on the leading foot, cardinal error which could lead to broken legs in combat; the shadow boxing sets left out moves, and so on. Chen had been irritated by this casual assumption of superiority; she was only a woman. Next time he went by himself. Last year, the girls stayed in the flat without making special celebrations, while Chen worked in the restaurant without a break.

But this year it was different, an auspicious occasion to mark the founding of their own business. The festival, after all, was closely linked with money: the distribution of the cash in the lucky red envelopes, the symbolic goldfish and lettuces representing bullion and bank-notes.

'It's fortunate we haven't been going long enough to run up debts or we'd have to pay them at New Year,' Chen joked.

'Don't worry, Husband, Mui and I have saved up a hoard,' Lily rejoined.

The *wok* sizzled; the pots on the gas ring bubbled merrily, releasing aromas quite new to the kitchen. 'What would happen if we sold this?'

Mui reflected, stir-frying a village dish of liver, dried squid, spring onion and salt ham.

'We would be out of business next week, that's your answer, Mui,' Chen said. 'Stick to what has been tried and don't adopt new ways just for the sake of them.'

'Just speculating, Brother-in-law.'

After argument, the girls had invited Mrs Law and Lo to celebrate the festival with them. Chen was quite happy about Mrs Law but objected to Lo, surprising Lily who expected the reverse. 'But he was your colleague, Husband.'

Chen was silent.

'Do you wish to invite Roman Fok?' (she had been dreading he might).

'Don't be so stupid, Lily. Of course I don't,' Chen said angrily. It was the tone which was new and hurtful, not the words: the same or similar had conveyed mild exasperation in the past. Fortunately, Lily was too startled for her feelings to be seriously hurt; also too relieved.

'It would be a kind gesture if you invited colleague Lo, Husband,' she persisted (courageously). 'He must be lonely in his new restaurant. After all, you were his only true friend even before.'

Chen reflected, visibly reassessing a situation unknown to Lily. The workings of Husband's mind could be mysterious. One pulled levers and hoped the right combination would click somewhere in there. There was a jackpot this time, as at length Chen relented. 'All right, but I still don't think it's a very good idea.'

When Lily told Mui the good news, she clapped her hands for joy.

Lo and Mrs Law, chaperoned by Ah Jik, arrived in the same radio cab shortly before midday, mildly scandalising Lily. Was there a romantic association going on that she was unaware of? Fancy coming in the *same taxi*. Had Lo gone to Mrs Law's *house*? How very unconventional! Husband put them right, though. It simply saved money; why take two cars? Of course, of course; how foolish of her. Lily thought: I have a long way to go as a businesswoman.

'But this is charming!' Mrs Law complimented them as soon as she entered. 'Do you really carry on business in this delightful room? I can hardly believe it.'

The girls were beside themselves with glee and excitement.

'This is our cash till, Mrs Law. It rings when you total the cash and the drawer slides out. We bought it secondhand from a sweet shop.

You have to push the drawer back yourself.' Mui gave a demonstration, ringing up twopence and meticulously adding that sum to the till's contents.

'How confidently you work the machine, Miss Tang! So young and already to have such a head for business! I wish you "smooth sailing".'

The girls were reminded that Mrs Law's manners were formed in the old school. She presumed on nothing. It wasn't so much the courtesies themselves which were excessive, fulsome as they were, as the social distance which had to be covered again at every meeting. Mrs Law might have been encountering strangers for the first time instead of the acquaintances of relatively long standing that they were. Naturally Mrs Law made up the ground quickly but the basic steps had to be observed. The girls were familiar with this little peculiarity and waited patiently for her to catch them up in what was very much like a staggered handicap race. But Chen, whose social grounding had been rudimentary, and who besides lacked the instinctive tact and subtlety of the sisters, was highly confused. Was this the older woman friend? Surely not. Had Lo married again? But then the girls wouldn't have been surprised to see him sharing a taxi with her.

'Mrs Law, please meet my unworthy husband.'

'Ah! Mrs Law, please don't stand on ceremony.'

Lily was surprised at the genuine warmth of recognition in Husband's voice. She mustn't misjudge him in future. Chen nodded at Lo. The two men hesitated, then shook hands. Lo had to transfer a paper carrier-bag to his other hand.

'Mrs Chen, we have brought a few trifling things you might like to eat.'

'You embarrass us, Mr Lo.'

The carrier-bag, and the one Ah Jik was carrying, contained a bottle of Remy Martin brandy, two bricks of New Year pudding (one beige, consisting of sweetened rice flour and millet, studded with those rare red dates; the other transparent, moulded from water-chestnut paste), yet more fruit, coconut candy and orange jelly sweets from Hong Kong, sour plums, preserved lemon peel, a porcelain jar of root ginger in syrup, hard bitter Chinese biscuits, and (Uncle Lo's gift) cuts of marinaded pork loin, roast suckling pig, duck, and chicken with soya beans. These reposed in the same silver boxes as the Chens gave their customers. Lily entertained uncontrollable misgivings about the contents until she peeled the cardboard lids away to reveal the wonderful treasures inside.

'Just to stimulate our appetites before your delicious meal, Mrs Chen.'

'From your chopping board, Mr Lo?'

'From my board, Mrs Chen.'

And the lacquered duck, glazed tablets of baby pig, plump white chicken slices nestling on their beds of glutinous rice or yellow beans, beans that looked like tiny hen's eggs, had an air of perfect contentment with their fate, having assisted as materials in the creation of such culinary masterpieces.

'How handsome Son has grown! How tall, how big!' Mrs Law *was* genuinely pleased and surprised at the transformation in Man Kee after six months.

'Yes, Big Head.'

Lily darted a furious look at Husband. Traitorous, flippant Husband. She gathered Man Kee in her arms and kissed the top of his head, which was no longer downy but a thick black poll. 'He has a beautiful head. Nothing wrong with its proportions.'

Wondering why Lily was always so touchy about this particular subject of Man Kee's head (no doubt about it; he was the boy's father and it *was* a big head) Chen went to help Lo open the brandy. Did Lily feel he was blaming her for getting the proportions wrong? He must make it plain that this was not the case at all.

'Remy Martin, hah? That's a first-class brandy, Ah Lo.'

'No need to tell me, Colleague. Have you glasses? Now then: *Yum Sing!*'

'*Yum Sing!*'

As obliged, both men emptied their glasses without setting them down again. 'Wah!'

'French brandy is it, Ah Lo?'

'French.'

'They know their business.'

'No mistake. You've got to get it down quickly to do it justice. *Yum Sing!*'

'*Yum Sing!*'

Used to *Yum Sing*-ing with cruder, less forgiving rice spirits (if at all) Chen found the Remy Martin slipped down easily enough but from the pit of his breakfastless stomach fumes seemed to be rising through his gullet to settle in his brain in a swirling cloud. This couldn't be anatomically feasible; Lily would know.

The expert in question was providing their guests with tea at the counter. She and Mui had made a gallon early in the morning which they had put into three large thermos flasks so that they wouldn't have to be in and out of the kitchen. Chen walked steadily to the other side of the room. How steadily he could walk!

'That's threepence please, sir!'

Chen grinned, rather a slow, fixed grin. He put his glass down on the counter next to the steaming tea glasses.

'Are you all right, Husband?'

'Of course I am.'

Chen decided to get some hot tea into his stomach and perhaps steaming up the gullet and into the head (if possible). He took another glass for Lo.

Lily put Man Kee down on the counter. He took advantage of her inattention to crawl down within inches of the tempting pile of shiny red apples. She pulled him back by the seat of his dungarees, his hands still outstretched. 'Son, those are not for us.' She held him in the crook of one arm while she filled the remaining glasses and then kissed his crown again. All this knocking back of spirits and talk of heads reminded her of Father, she knew not why. Ah yes, he had liked to butt those big wine jars in the town square, hadn't he; smash them to smithereens with that bristling head of his after which the onlookers would treat him to the contents, all *Yum Sing*-ing away into the night, while she and Mui found their way home. Strange how she had to act as Mui's bodyguard in the street, yet once home had been fussed into bed by her older sister. Times changed: now she did the equivalent of escorting *and* fussing. And what had happened to her tiger fork? It was a shame in a way that she had never met one of the tawny beasts and put her drill to the ultimate test, that of practice.

'Are you all quite warm enough?' This was Mui. 'I can turn the oil heater on.'

'Quite warm, Miss Tang.' Nevertheless, Lily saw, Mrs Law had kept her fur coat on. She turned the knob to maximum; they had all, perhaps, got tougher than they knew since leaving the home comforts of the flat.

'Please to taste these nuts, Uncle Lo. I will fry your puddings in the meantime.' And these turned out to be delicious: the little rectangular slabs Lily sliced off the main blocks were crisp on the outside, hot and glutinous inside, and perfectly complemented the fragrant tea that was Mrs Law's personal present to her. There was more. Mrs Law wanted to give them all *lai see*. So did Lo.

'Oh, no, we can't possibly accept,' Lily protested. 'It's not right for us to accept. Only married people can give lucky money. Isn't that right, Mui?' But Mui was having a coughing fit and was unable to back up her younger sister, even had she wished to refuse a cash present. Lily was not being excessively punctilious (what were customs made for except to be broken in special cases, after all?). She would have accepted from anyone else. It was just that she suspected Mrs Law's envelopes would turn out to contain rather enormous sums of money. Lily might have been able to accept the red envelopes Lo held in his hand with a clear conscience but it was both of them or nothing.

'Why don't we pretend Mrs Law and Uncle Lo are married just for today?' Mui suggested slyly. 'It would be quite in order for them to give *lai see* then.'

Lo blushed. His sallow face was already inflamed by the unaccustomed intake of spirits so that it seemed his heavily greased hair might soon catch fire through sympathetic combustion. Mui's face was also flushed and her eyes bright, the convivial effect again of brandy – in this case Chen's second glass of Remy Martin left amongst the tea glasses which Mui had unsuspectingly drained at a swig. Really, she had gone too far this time, thought Lily crossly. Insulting our guests like that! What a gross suggestion! Mrs Law, though, was tittering and Mui's proposal had sent Ah Jik into coarse cackles.

'Do you mean a *marriage of convenience*, Mui?' enquired Mrs Law, using the English expression and generally relaxing and entering into the spirit of things for the first time. 'Mr Lo would have to be agreeable to it first, though, wouldn't he? It takes two, you know.'

Lo, inarticulate with mortification and an embarrassment that was also wholly pleasurable, made a strangulated noise of assent, grinning now through his blushes. 'Well, then, there is no obstacle. Here you are, Mui.'

'Ah. Ah. *Gung hei faat choi*, Mrs Law.'

'Say *Gung hei*, Lily.'

'Thank you, Mrs Law. Congratulations and make money in the New Year.'

They were thick packets. They all had one, including Man Kee, whose envelope was thicker than anyone else's. 'Say *Gung hei* to Auntie, Son.' Man Kee who had already eaten two packets of coconut candy could not be coaxed into speaking.

'He's too young, poor little boy. Don't bother him, Lily.'

Lily put his envelope under god. On behalf of the Chens Lily presented their own envelopes to their guests.

After lunch, a remarkably happy and companionable meal, 'hot and noisy', and with Mui only a little more boisterous than Lily would have thought entirely becoming, Chen suggested a 'tour' of the premises. This was just what the girls had been waiting for. 'Our bedrooms, Mrs Law, you must see them. Lily's is big, mine is small.'

Through the draughty corridor, over the rustling newspapers they went, abandoning the originator of the idea.

Mui parted the bead waterfall for Mrs Law.

'Is that notice your idea, Lily?'

'No, Mui's.'

Lily took Mrs Law's hand and led her up the tunnel of the stairs. They reached the landing which was cluttered with wood Chen had yet to convert into useful household articles; although it remained an article of family faith he would.

'Please be careful of your stockings, Mrs Law.'

Lily threw open the door of Mui's room.

'Charming,' Mrs Law pronounced, politeness proving a stronger force again than sincerity. 'But a little damp, I would imagine, from the duck-boards on the floor.'

'No, that's my bed.'

'Ah.'

Not at all put out, Mui brought Mrs Law to the curtainless window through which an icy draught was infiltrating. 'Look, you can actually see the railway track from here. The blue flashes light the snow at night. The black line is the canal they didn't finish and the big white tower is the gas tank. It's green but the snow is covering it, isn't it beautiful.'

Did Mui fearfully resent living in this chilly cubb-hole, Mrs Law wondered? Was she being ironic? But no, here was Mui pointing out her Ho Yeh Oyster Sauce calendar on the wall, her loudly ticking brass alarm clock, her steel-frame mirror on its little stand, her comb. Mrs Law rubbed her eyes. 'The cold makes them rheumy, Mui. I thank you for your kind concern.'

'Husband and myself have the room overlooking the front, Mrs Law.'

'Ah, this is better . . . that's to say . . . I mean better even than the charming room downstairs which is so pretty,' Mrs Law hastily amended herself. 'Shall we join the menfolk, girls?' She picked her way carefully down the tunnel, which made one uneasy, looking as if it should be a chute rather than steps.

Lo and Chen were in the snowbound garden with Man Kee. Fortified by the brandy they had been drinking steadily, neither had put on extra clothing. Man Kee was sitting on his father's shoulders while Chen pointed out the allotments to Lo.

'Have you thought of applying for one, Colleague? You could extend your land that way.'

Before Chen could disclaim any such conventional householder's ambitions, Lily rapped insistently on the kitchen window, the sound carrying crisply over the snow to the bottom of the garden.

'In at once!' Chen could see her mouthing. He considered ignoring her. He didn't want to lose face in front of Lo. On the other hand Lily still held the ultimate deterrent of a heavy, undiluted dose of medicine which could be appropriately applied in this case. (It's for your own protection, Husband. Do you want to see me a widow in this strange country?')

Lo was already turning back. They trod carefully in their own footprints; Chen reflected that Lo might have been nagged into total submission before his own wife left him. Maybe that's why she deserted him, he thought, resolving to be more vertebrate in his handling of Lily. There was no time like the present. Half-way up the garden, he halted at the low, rectangular white mound that was the flower-bed he and Son had weeded. It was already quite dark and from the gunmetal sky big, fresh flakes were starting to fall. Our footprints will soon be covered, he thought, shivering. In its way the mound was quite sinister. Had you not known it was a flower-bed, you would have thought it was something quite different. He said to Lo: 'You should have seen the worms that came out of that, Colleague.'

'Don't they say they are good for the soil, Ah Chen? Let the air in?'

Man Kee seemed to remember their afternoon of happy labour or at least those strange, wriggling noodles, for he now became restive on his father's shoulders, trying to swing his short leg over Chen's head but succeeding only in knocking the snow-flakes off his father's hair and into his eyes, and remaining forked around his neck.

'Stay still, Son, you mustn't disturb them. They are all warm, hidden underground. You don't want the bad birds to catch them, do you?'

Feeling he had satisfactorily compromised on the issue of who ran the household, Chen led the way back. As they kicked the snow off their shoes, Chen asked Lo casually: 'You don't see any of the others, I suppose? Fok or anyone else? Koo maybe?'

Lo shook his head, dislodging a flurry of flakes.

Lily was waiting inside with hot tea. She scolded them thoroughly but there was no mention of medicine which Chen attributed to his display of masculine firmness in the garden.

The front room had become extremely hot. Mrs Law had rolled up her *cheongsam* to an inch above the knees, revealing a pair of surprisingly shapely calves. Was Lo deeper than he appeared, Chen wondered? Should he ask him to keep this visit confidential? Better not; it might offend or make him suspicious. Lo had always been reticent, he remembered.

While he was turning things over, Chen eyed Lo with a shiftiness that was all the more noticeable for being utterly uncharacteristic. He had really looked very furtive indeed, and his suspicious behaviour had not escaped Mrs Law's notice.

In the radio cab home, after she had dropped Lo a tactful hundred yards from his restaurant in what was fast becoming a blizzard, she thought of Mui and Lily with concern. 'That man has something on his conscience,' she said to herself. 'I hope it is not because he is maltreating my girls.' She rather feared it might be.

EIGHTEEN

There were three cars parked opposite the Yuet Hop Peking Restaurant, Twickenham: a pair of Ford Cortinas and a Citroën. All were four-door models; all had been removed from a car park off Shaftesbury Avenue that morning and the number plates changed.

Red Cudgel was in the Citroën, the middle car; Iron Plank in the rear Cortina; Night-brother commanded the front vehicle. It was 9.30 p.m. The raid was staged for 10 p.m. – to give the enemy time to *Yum Sing* their way to maximum befuddlement. Drunk men were easy prey, Night-brother had pointed out, his only major contribution to the planning of the attack. The two fighters had wanted to attack earlier but had then seen the advantages of Night-brother's timing. Otherwise Red Cudgel and Iron Plank had been the sole strategists.

There were only four men in each vehicle. One would remain at the wheel, engine running, while the others entered. This left an attacking force of nine. Too few, Night-brother feared. There would be at least twenty men feasting. He didn't like the odds, even with sober, armed attackers against men who were drunk and weaponless. Red Cudgel had explained that under the circumstances more than nine men would be a handicap in the confined space; they would fall over the tables and chairs, even strike each other on the back-swing.

'Even in the open you cannot use more than three men to attack one simultaneously. The angle of approach is strictly defined.'

There was also the question of a quick get-away. The cars had to be warm, ready, and running, and the drivers watchful for official bandits.

Red Cudgel calculated that in the first ten seconds of combat they would be able to kill or cripple a minimum of six or seven men. This left the remainder at the mercy of ruthless, armed fighters with blood-lust on them. The seven fighters would slaughter indiscriminately. Iron Plank and Red Cudgel would seek, engage, and kill the enemy enforcer. Red Cudgel's Patek showed 9.45 p.m. He got out of the Citroën and signalled the others to follow. He had always intended to attack fifteen minutes earlier than stated in order to minimise the physical effects of nervous tension on his men.

They did not trouble to conceal their weapons. Darkness covered them, the road was empty, and the enemy banqueted at two tables in the centre of the ground floor. The axeman was through the door first, a yard clear of the choppermen, weapon low. He arced it high and buried the blade between the shoulders of a man drinking beer. The two diners on either side veered away, left and right, and were on their feet before the axeman could lift the heavy weapon again. But in a rush and whirl of falling chairs the other raiders were there now. By the time the axeman had swung again and caught a seated man on the head with the crack of a coconut split on a frosty morning, the choppermen had cut six or seven times with their light weapons. There was blood on the tablecloth; the cries of the injured mixed with the yells of the attackers.

In these first ten seconds eight men had been put out of the fray.

The second table was still intact, the diners seated in shock. Ignoring the carnage behind him, Red Cudgel swung left-handed with his long flail. He hit two men in the face and knocked them off their chairs. He shortened his grip a hitch and was among the scattering men with his cleaver. He went low, stabbed upwards with short hooking blows to groin and abdomen and dropped two more. The flailed men had gone over without a sound; these screamed. Steel glinted in Red Cudgel's mouth. One of the flailed men was on his knees. There were red and white beads on the carpet in front of him. His hands were over his shattered jaw. Red Cudgel pulled his hair from behind and slashed his throat. He cut two men off into a corner with long sweeps of his flail. Out of the side of his eye he was looking for the enemy enforcer. Iron Plank commanded the centre of the floor with the same intention. He had not struck yet. His two square-bladed short swords were at his side, clean. A man ran for the door. Iron Plank stepped into his path, put his blades left to right across his body in an X and then sliced outwards into the fugitive's stomach. They were relaxed, contemptuous cuts, made without hurry. As the man fell, he chopped down into his neck, so that the blades had described a broad circle with the sequence of blows. He stepped over the body to the first table. He had identified his man.

Jackie Fung, a tall and deceptively slim young man, had been at the back of the first table, his head against the wall. The men on his left and right had dived under the table to join the wounded man already there. Jackie Fung remained in his chair and waited calmly. A chopperman struck awkwardly at him across the table. Jackie Fung swayed six inches to the right. He threw the neat brandy in his neighbour's glass into his assailant's face. The misdirected blow smashed a rice bowl. He seized the man's wrist, broke the glass and scraped the jagged edge over his nose and eyes. He grabbed the man's testicles savagely and then disarmed him. Armed now with the cleaver, he pushed the table over. As he did so, a swordsman struck at his head. Fung parried late with the chopper which was jarred out of his hand but just caught his attacker's sword-arm as it went back. The man went for the knife in his belt. Jackie Fung threw his palm over the swordsman's face, found the socket with his long thumb, and gouged into the eyeball. The man fell back with a cry, covering his face. Jackie Fung now had a sword. He came into the open and a man slashed at him with a cleaver. He parried, again slightly awkwardly. Then in a short, hopping action he brought his rear right heel to the left heel and, having made the necessary ground with the half-step, simultaneously high-kicked and punched to the face with the left side as smoothly and easily as a pair of scissors opening. The crack of the clean head-shots cut over all the other sounds in the room. He stepped over the body and stabbed in the back a man who had an axe poised at the top of its swing. He thrust badly; the sword jarred on bone. Jackie Fung swore, dropped the tasselled sword, put his weight on the rear leg and smashed a left-handed reverse punch to the axeman's kidneys. The man dropped without a sound.

The other banqueters were now trying to fight back and had massed between the up-turned tables, defending themselves as best they could with a variety of improvised weapons: broken bottles, chairs, a heavy ladle. There were eight left standing. Men groaned quietly on the floor or were still. Five of the raiding party were out of the action, including the four dropped by Jackie Fung.

The spearman, who had been guarding the door, moved in on Jackie Fung. He made short, stabbing feints with the six-foot weapon. Jackie Fung surprised the man by taking the offensive. He moved in swiftly. As he anticipated, the spearman withdrew his weapon before thrusting instead of stabbing at once with the weapon uncocked. The spear came out again. Jackie Fung broke the rhythm of his rush, stepped sideways and seized the shaft six inches below the metal tip. He pulled sharply, swept the man's legs, and impaled him on the ground. He stabbed him three more times, the last in the neck.

Fifty-five seconds had elapsed since the men had come through the door.

Iron Plank went to Jackie Fung. Red Cudgel followed, swinging his flail slowly. Jackie Fung hesitated, dropped the spear, and picked up the axe. His two opponents could see his balance was wrong for the weapons, his feet too close to each other. Red Cudgel said: 'Give.' The two younger men were breathing hard. Red Cudgel was still in control of the heaving of his diaphragm. He knew his ability to relax would offset the younger men's superior strength and speed. Behind them were shouts, scufflings, and the clang of metal. Occasionally there was a cry.

Iron Plank moved in fast, describing a shuffling in-and-out circular movement with his feet, twirling the pair of short swords so that they resembled the wings of a butterfly. Jackie swung his axe clumsily and Iron Plank trapped it with both blades. But the telegraphed blow was a feint. Iron Plank found himself sprawled on the carpet from a neat ankle-tap. He still held his swords. Jackie Fung ran through the gap in the encirclement and then leaped in the air, knees tucked to chest, and Red Cudgel swept at his knees with the seven-sectional flail. The unaccustomed weight of the axe caused Fung to land off-balance and the older man was able to stab him in the side of the thigh. Jackie Fung stumbled forwards, regained his balance, and hit a chopperman on the back of the head with the blunt axe-head. Another man swung at him. The cleaver-tip sliced across Jackie Fung's forehead, causing a flap of skin to drop forwards and blind him with the rush of blood. The man struck again, the blade twisting in mid-air in his excitement. The flat crashed against the side of Jackie Fung's head. A third assailant tried to stab him in the side but the blade buried itself in his biceps. Jackie Fung, in pain, dizzy, vomit rising in his throat from the concussive head-blow, forced himself to widen his stance. He swept crudely with the axe. The man gave ground. Jackie Fung could no longer see him.

Three car-horns sounded in unison.

Iron Plank went forward to finish Jackie Fung, who was now supported by two allies.

Red Cudgel said: 'Finish. It's finished.'

Iron Plank regained his control.

Red Cudgel called: 'Get our wounded out.' The enemy made no attempt to stop them as they half-dragged, half-carried, their casualties out and into the waiting cars. A man slipped in the frozen slush. There was a flashing blue light far up the road.

Within three minutes of the first blows being struck the Citroën was leading the other cars up the street.

NINETEEN

Lily was throwing open the windows, every single one the house had. She wanted to shout, sing, such was her exuberance. Opening them was just a way of expressing her feelings. The house was more than adequately ventilated; in a word, it was draughty. They certainly knew that after the winter. Even now Husband muttered and complained, buttoning up his jacket ostentatiously. But the thaw had come; the birds sang; there were tiny, tiny buds on the trees and the earth, humped up like an animal, gave off a raw smell that was disturbingly like a glandular secretion. Bandana-ed now in the manner of charladies rather than insurgent peasants, Lily and Mui dusted and mopped for the second time in under twelve months. What, Chen wondered, had got into Lily's head this time? The house was quite clean enough; anyway the innocent grime they had collected gave the place a homely feel. It made it seem more like a proper Chinese restaurant. 'Look, they expect the place to be a *bit* dirty,' he argued with Lily. She was deaf; showed no sign of having heard him. Even the famous unfocussed serene smile and flickering dimples with which she usually favoured him during cleaning had vanished. Now it was just scrub, scrub. The gas rings and *wok* had given off a lot of smoke and stained the walls and ceiling. Not much could be done about that. But Lily set about removing the grime on the skirting boards, using a knife to scrape the last layer, dusted god, wiped the streaky windows.

'You don't want people looking in on our private business, do you?' Chen remonstrated. It was like talking to a machine; she was relentless. Finally, even Chen was affected. The smells, wafting in through the wide-flung windows, were so evocative of the locale, so *English*, so indescribably alien, they set his nerves tingling, quickened his pulse: aroma compounded of creosote, wood-smoke, pipe tobacco, grass and mud. Mud lay deep in the garden with a few green blades here and there; it was like a paddy field but for the heaps of dirty snow and the alien smell. Chen felt at home and yet not at home. He had been more comfortable rootless.

During the winter trade had continued to increase. Neighbourhood custom now equalled that from the garage. There were often long queues on the benches. On Friday nights after eleven o'clock there were often no spaces left and their customers, mostly young people, lounged against the wall. This explained the uneven line of grease smudges at head height along the three walls. Taking down and calling out the orders ('One egg fu yung ready,' or 'You giving three shilling sixpence, please'), Lily felt like asking them to stand up straight. How would you like it if I leant on *your* wall with *my* head, Mr Pink Face Young Devil? Husband's motto, though, was please the customer and Lily kept back the sharp words which rose to the tip of her tongue. She lacked not the vocabulary but the inflection which might request or admonish without causing offence. Her voice, so expressive and alive in her native Cantonese, became shrill, peremptory, and strangely lifeless in its level pitching when she spoke English. She would have sounded hostile and nervous; a cross between a petulant child and a nagging old shrew, neither of which descriptions adequately fitted the mature and outward-going young woman who was Lily Chen. She and the customers ignored each other; they couldn't even look one another in the eye. Each regarded the other as a non-person. There was no hostility involved; how could there be when the transaction was totally impersonal? They might have been machines. The silver boxes came through the hatch and Lily distributed them into the waiting hands as if she were on a conveyor belt at the transistor factory, while the customers, for all the animation they showed, might have been putting money into a cigarette machine.

When there was a lull, everything paid for but yet to materialise through the hatch, Lily sat on her high stool behind the counter and gazed out over the heads on the pews, through the straggling hedge Husband was trying to train and thicken, and into the main road. From her angle, looking up from the house's sunken situation, she could see the passengers in the cars only as busts, heads and shoulders gliding smoothly along without a clue as to locomotive happenings lower down. Sometimes they looked as if they were all pedalling furiously but trying not to give the fact away. When she tired of counting first cars and then occupants (and the activity was strangely soporific, Lily's industrial equivalent of insomniac sheep-counting) she would discreetly examine the customers. She would have quite liked to be friendly with some of them. She *was* frightened of the rowdies who came in the worse for drink after the public houses shut. Only once – thank god – had a group run out without paying. Terrible, shocking. How could they have such a degraded sense of their responsibilities? All right to cheat the government of tax – like at Husband's old place of work – but not to do it to the person whose face you saw. She served this sort quickly and with what she thought of as her 'closed' face. But she could have felt quite maternal towards the young girls of thirteen or fifteen, not that she was so much older herself. They had life, at least, giggling and smoking on the pews, but also a terrible coldness. Once she had smiled at a young girl whom she thought particularly ill-favoured and pig-like, and yet who was at the centre of her little group, all curly blonde hair, pink face, big blue eyes, empty like the sky was shining through them, ludicrously big-breasted for her age. And yet this girl towards whom she felt only kindness and pity had snubbed her; had stared insolently and rudely at Lily until she had been forced to drop her eyes. There had been louder, renewed giggling. Well, that would teach her to feel sorry for people. It was only a form of arrogance. She had taken the incident, if it could be called that, as a warning. Later, she tried to make allowances for the girl's age. Young people were bold and unthinking. Yet surely not to that extent? At that age Lily had been fulfilling her original three year indenture at the first factory in Tsuen Wan. No extra money for take-away meals from the stalls or for nail varnish, she thought censoriously and with just a trace of smugness. What possible sense of decency and family honour could those reckless girls have? All running round together until a scandalous hour. It was after ten o'clock when they came in. No wonder they were always getting themselves pregnant. And she thought complacently of her own little family. Really, there was no question how superior Chinese people were to the foreign devils.

There were also young women who must have been her own age. They came in mostly with men (their husbands?) or with just one other female friend. At some stage there was obviously contraction of the social orbit. Perhaps she could have established contact, even communication here: a smile, recognition. It was not to be. In the first place, Lily found it difficult except in certain obvious cases to distinguish between those bland, roseate occidental faces. They all looked the same to her. And how quickly their pink skins aged. How few types of face there were compared to the almost infinite variety of interesting Cantonese physiognomies: rascally, venerable, pretty, raffish, bumpkin, scholarly.

She confided her little difficulty to Mui and Husband. Surprisingly, it was Husband who was more sympathetic.

'It *is* hard to tell the difference,' he agreed. 'It was often embarrassing at the restaurant. Just pretend you recognise them, Lily.'

But Mui affected to be able to tell even similar-looking individuals apart. 'Sometimes I don't understand you, Lily. Of course I can tell them apart. We have quite a few regular customers by now.'

Lily's mouth opened.

'I suggest you look at the English people on the television a bit harder, younger sister,' Mui continued in a thoroughly odious and superior manner. 'People show their character in their faces. Westerners just show their feelings in a different way. How would you like it if someone called you a pig?'

Lily looked instinctively to the Ho Yeh Oyster Sauce calendar, performing rapid surreptitious feats of subtraction against her palm with her finger-tips. Could it be *that* time of month for Mui? No, it wasn't. 'You mean you can tell your big bear lorry-drivers apart?' (Mui had been earning tips in all kinds of weather.)

'Naturally I can. And don't call them bears.'

Somewhat staggered by this display of sisterly truculence, Lily closely scrutinised all who entered. It was no use. Was Mui bluffing? She brought her to the counter. 'Go on then. Which ones?'

'Don't be so obvious, Lily. You'll drive our customers away. In fact there are several regulars on Brother-in-law's benches at this very moment.'

Lily was not at all convinced. However, she did have their TV set installed on a bracket opposite god's corner (Husband was only too pleased to use some of his store of planks) and kept it on during business hours as much for the customers' benefit as her own education. They certainly appreciated it (all that endless football!) but it didn't do Lily much good. If it could safely be assumed that Mui was not telling outrageous lies after all, Lily suspected financial incentives lay behind her sister's new skill. She probably got bigger tips if she could greet the drivers by name. Lily was just about certain she did it by memorising the number plates.

The connection with the transport trade paid an extra dividend that summer, gratuities apart. (And Mui had already started a third tea tin just for foreign money.) The kitchen was now operating at maximum capacity. In other words poor Chen was working his fingers to the bone. He had four *wok* going simultaneously, not forgetting the four pans on the gas stove. A moment too long on the flame and all would be spoiled. The recipes were unforgiving. The thin slivers of meat, mushroom, bamboo shoot, and sprouts which Mui prepared could be frazzled on the *wok*-side within ten seconds. The cornflour staple in the sauces thickened and congealed disastrously in the pans if left unstirred or too fiercely heated. Chen would willingly have discarded the last elements of authenticity about the dishes, fried thick tombstone slabs of meat or entire splinters of bamboo, used clear sauces of pure Knorr stock or thickened with Bisto. But the recipes, alas, were constructed along cynical economic lines. The meat-shavings went further; the thick sauce camouflaged, gave the illusion of substance. So sweat-soaked, chronically thirsty, perpetually harassed, sometimes reduced to utter despair by the consequences of momentary neglect of a saucepan's contents, Chen orchestrated his instruments to the best of his abilities. There were times when a pot's contents refused even to simmer, only a huge bubble painfully forming and bursting with a resentful *phut*! before subsiding into a crater, rather like the mud geysers of Tientsin which had been featured for June on the Ho Yeh calendar. Then there would be a terrible sizzling, reminiscent of steam trains, followed by a signal cloud of white smoke rising from one or more *wok*. As soon as his back was turned, of course, all four bewitched sauce pots began to hubble-bubble simultaneously. There were times when it seemed more like an alchemist's magic laboratory than a kitchen.

Chen had to cope with all this by himself. The pace of work and the space taken up by new equipment meant only one person could work and yet they were now doing double the volume of business two had catered. Mui and Lily wished to relieve Chen of the work or at least do their share in shifts. But he refused. So now the girls watched TV together from the counter or took it in turns to amuse Man Kee upstairs. The atmosphere in the front room was less like a church now; it had become more of a cinema. It was definitely less of a strain on all parties concerned. No more of those excruciating face-to-face intervals of waiting, with Lily and the customers scrupulously avoiding each others' eyes. Now the customers had done an about turn, as it were; Lily had turned the pews round to the TV, so that she and Mui looked over the back of their heads. Could Mui recognise the *gwai lo* from a posterior aspect? Most certainly she could. And now, too, they could point at the head in question without the smallest constraint. It was all wonderfully liberating. Occasionally, muffled swear-words or clattering, the sound of fierce scorching (although oddly not the smell), or of a tap suddenly run at full force would come through the hatch (which Chen insisted they keep closed). Then the girls would grin; even if these little accidents cut into the profit-margin, a term with which they were now all too familiar. Mui suggested they put up a new notice:

MANAGEMENT NOT RESPONSIBLE FOR COOK'S COOKING

There was not a big return on food. The materials, even eked out, thickened and disguised, were not cheap. Chen had told Lily that the wholesalers would not deal with a business as small as theirs, especially not those dealing in Chinese groceries. She didn't believe him but gave in without argument. There was also the price of gas, oil, and foil boxes to take into account. In addition, they had to keep the tariff competitive; there were several fish and chip shops and a new kebab counter in the neighbourhood. Jointly, they earned as much as Chen had taken away from the Ho Ho for three times the man- (woman-) hours. This was not the target Lily had in mind when they abandoned the comforts of the flat for a new future. And now the ceiling of expansion was set: the largest amount they could get out of the cramped kitchen in the shortest time. Lily would have worked further hours for increased profits at the same meagre ratio. But to know one could go no further, even when the will was there, that was too galling.

One morning Mui went out to deliver a lunch to the forecourt. She was swiftly back – some of her trips lasted half an hour and only god knew what she did (Lily used to think crossly).

'Come with me, Lily.'

'What do you mean "Come with me", just like that? Who will take the money? Prepare cuts for Husband?' (as if Mui didn't know these things already).

'Don't argue, Lily. This is important.'

Bundling Man Kee up in her arms (he had unsuccessfully been trying to pick fluff out of his plasticine ball) Lily went, blinking at the bright sunlight, into the garage forecourt. Parked away from the petrol pumps was a big lorry stacked with crates of lemonade. The driver and his mate were on the step of the cab, eating out of the foil boxes Mui had brought them. They were drinking a large bottle of their freight.

'Ah,' said Lily, 'Whore Lock!' (or a close phonetic representation to that effect), identifying one of the products in question by its Cantonese name.

'Eh?' said the driver, considerably startled.

Lily smiled her charming (for Westerners) smile. 'You like Whore Lock all the time, too, hah? *It's the real thing*!' she quoted enthusiastically. Mui averted what might have turned into major embarrassment all around. 'My sister not understand English too much,' she explained. 'You please excuse.' Her own command of the language it turned out, its colloquialisms, ambiguities, if not all the inconsistencies of its grammar, was well advanced. Too advanced for Lily to stay abreast of the conversation. She wandered down the lorry, raising Man Kee so he could touch the bottles. 'Did you ever see so much to drink, Son? Not even you could drink it all up.'

The lorry was starting now, making the bottles shake in their crates; they didn't look too secure. 'Wave goodbye to the men, Son. That's nice.'

Mui had money for the lunch, a shilling tip, and a big bottle of drink.

'Thank you, Mui, for showing us the lorry. Very interesting for Son.'

'Yes, all right, Lily. Here you are, Nephew.'

'How kind of the men!'

'It's all arranged, Lily.'

'Excellent, Mui, excellent.' What was arranged?

Husband was waiting for them, cross because the day's rice had not been put on yet. Lily had to work quickly to wash it and then get the counter cleaned up and ready; by which time they were already serving and she had completely forgotten about the Whore Lock men.

A week later there was a rap on the window. Chen immediately slammed the hatch cover down, narrowly missing Lily's slim fingers as she was receiving some foil boxes.

'Down here all right?' It was one of the lorrymen with a crate of bottles. Mui came out of the kitchen with her tea tin of English money: 'We say 25s, hah?' Money changed hands.

'Wah! So cheap, Mui.'

Mui translated for the driver. He winked at Lily: 'Fell off the back of the lorry, didn't they, darling.'

Lily's face clouded. Bargains were one thing, ruined merchandise quite another. She inspected each of the bottles. No, none of them were cracked or leaking. What excellent packaging to survive such a drop at speed!

'We'll be around next week. Shouldn't have no trouble selling it but don't drink the stuff. Rots the teeth something terrible.'

How did the man know in advance that a crate would fall off his lorry in seven days' time? Why didn't he tie it on more securely? Mui was trying to lift the crate without much success. Lily carried it through the hallway into the kitchen.

'Lily, we can sell the drink by the glass while they wait or to take away for three times what we paid. Even wholesale it costs you almost £2 for a crate. I'm talking to the man who drives the ice-cream lorry as well.'

'Ah, that should be much safer, Mui.'

'What do you mean? No one can find out. They allow for two boxes to break whatever happens.'

'Well, the ice-cream can't break like bottles, can it?'

'Are you mad, Lily?'

'When it falls off the back of the lorry, I mean.'

Mui put her tea tin away. 'No, no, Lily. "Falling off the back of the lorry" doesn't mean what you think.' She explained.

When she had finished, Lily said: 'So you mean we're stealing from the big company?'

Mui was a little taken aback: 'Well, Lily, I suppose you could put it like that ... '

'Of course it's stealing from the company.' Lily looked pleased and reassured now that she understood. 'That's *quite* all right then. Just like the way I got my radio and crocodile purse from the factory.'

Much easier in her mind now, Lily put seven bottles to cool in the refrigerator. By next morning they were sold out, and had made a profit, not of 75s as predicted by Mui, but of almost 85s (Lily had watered it). And this wasn't taking into account the half-bottle Husband, soaked in perspiration in the summer inferno of a kitchen, had drunk. He hadn't had it at a swig which might have been easier on his conscience but a few sips every so often, suffering a twinge of guilt on each occasion. The girls said nothing but Chen knew as well as they that he had enjoyed almost 5s worth of profits. Nevertheless, the fact remained that they had made their biggest profit margin on a single commodity to date without capital risk or extra labour. It was almost indecent it was so easy – like gambling or ... well, Lily wasn't sure what else.

The men could only let them have the two crates a week but the ice-cream brought in another £3. They could have sold more of this, in fact, but there was no way of storing larger quantities, especially in the hot weather they were enjoying. Lily didn't mind serving *lupsup* food but she drew the line at mass-poisoning their customers (a question, after all, of a contracting market). Mui's other brainwave was chips (potato, not bamboo) with sweet and sour sauce. Not quite the money-spinner, chips, that Whore Lock and ice-cream were but still outselling anything else they cooked. They were easy to fry in large quantities. They developed a taste for chips themselves, minus sauce, of course.

TWENTY

'Not exactly a resounding victory,' White Paper Fan said drily. 'But then not a defeat either. Statistically, it was a success. We now know you damaged the enemy in a ratio of 3:1 which is acceptable. But *who* did you eliminate?'

Red Cudgel said: 'Luck was not with us. You can plan. You need luck as well. This is true of all military undertakings, small or large.' His face was blank but in the eyes there was a gleam of anger.

White Paper Fan said: 'We had only one fatality but the injuries were all severe: fractured skull, broken spine, one man has lost sight in one eye, another needed twenty stitches in the face. This is against four enemy dead whom we know with certainty were killed, another two who may have died of their injuries, and about ten severely wounded. Against this we have to set the aroused interest of the bandit authorities and prospect of retaliation from 14-K. The fact that there has been no retaliation in the last three months is no cause for congratulation. If we have destroyed their leadership this will all have been worthwhile. If we merely eliminated low ranks then it is bad.'

Red Cudgel said: 'Who knows? A man stands up and I kill him. Difficult to say. I wish we had killed their enforcer. Given time we could have killed him. He knew how to fight well. At liberty and hurt he is dangerous. A wounded animal.'

White Paper Fan said with asperity: 'I'm not concerned with the half-formulated schemes for revenge of some young thug. I am worried about the long-term plans of the 14-K leadership to re-establish themselves and oust us. I note their leader is a 415-officer. The Red Cudgel you mention, Fung, is not even Deputy Leader.'

The two men's eyes met before White Paper Fan continued: 'There is now a state of open warfare between us. This can only be bad for business. Both societies' business. Bandits will be curious.'

Red Cudgel said: 'This was the original reason why we left matters half-finished. Luck was not with us. We couldn't plan for bandits nearby. My aim was to get my fighters out intact. Better let some enemies escape rather than risk capture by bandits. That would be disaster.'

'Agreed. I don't criticise your execution or leadership. As society planner, I merely indicate the situation before us. Seems to me that we don't immediately fear physical retaliation. They must reorganise first. If they want to catch us off-guard it may be a year or more. Correct or not?'

'Correct.'

'Then I suggest that while you keep your fighters watchful, I work to strengthen you again in other respects. Our injured fighters naturally received the best medical treatment money could buy. I kept my promise to you. There was no stinting. I paid over £2,000 for medical care. Major surgery was required in one case. We paid for total discretion as well as first-class work.'

'This was not the male nurse you used before?'

'Certainly not. A western surgeon. Money talks in all languages.' White Paper Fan rubbed his thumb and forefinger together. 'We look after our members when sick in the normal course of events. All the more need when they have been hurt in the service of the society.'

'This should be made widely known. It is most important for

morale. Especially the new fighters. Not the details, of course.'

'I think you can now appreciate my point that all our activities affect each other. They are all linked in a chain of causes and effects. The work of the educational and welfare sections overlaps the work of the recruiting and fighting and discipline sections. I intend to double welfare spending in the next months. Our own injured fighters will receive extra cash compensation. The dead man's family will be supported. I also intend to undertake more open community work. Any objection?'

'None.'

'I want close liaisons between the different sections. This is most important. No secrets or misunderstandings between separate sections. There must, for instance, be no fighting while I am doing my work.'

'Good. Personally, I don't think there will be any more minor harassment. Molesting our street-runners is also bad for their business. It may come to a battle in the next year but that's a different matter altogether.'

'Any violence, large or small, would be against our best interests. For the first time in twelve months revenue from street sales of No 3 heroin has exceeded our gambling commissions. I want the balance to stay that way.'

'This is excellent!'

'It is. Grass Sandal is now hard pressed to supply the needs of the runners. A complete reversal of the earlier state of affairs. I am beginning a campaign to recruit more runners of a satisfactory nature.'

'Linked with welfare spending?'

White Paper Fan smiled. 'You've got the idea now. Correct. The best runner we have is the waiter whose sick father we put in hospital in Hong Kong.'

Red Cudgel groped for this piece of trivia beneath more important memories and current preoccupations. His grasp of the detail of society activity was as good as White Paper Fan's ability to perceive a pattern in the total. 'He still works at the Excellence?'

'Still. Liaison through the new 49 who works in its kitchens. We have nothing to do with the runner and it is best he never sees us again. The less he knows the better. I have forbidden the contact 49 to peddle himself any more. A typical Hong Kong street type. His style was such that he would inevitably have been caught. He now loses money but will have to come to terms with it. The new runner shifted thirty bottles in Earlham Street on New Year's day.'

'He must have repaid our expenditure on the sick father.'

'We are never the losers! The sum we spent was an investment. Now we see its interest. In this particular instance I was going to take twenty-five per cent of the runner's commission and remit to his father through Wo headquarters, as before. I believe it to be a more acceptable mode of commission and one which gains additional influence over him. But the 49 said the runner had objected.'

Red Cudgel said: 'I remember him. That seems rather out of character.'

'Money is a potent force when you deal with ignorant men. In any case I instructed the 49 to remit it direct. I gave him the father's whereabouts. He seemed happy with the arrangement. Perhaps too happy. I think this one bears watching.'

'A job for Night-brother. But I congratulate you on the work. A real piece of old-time society work.'

'We have carried seed overseas. Let it flourish.'

TWENTY-ONE

Chen and Man Kee had raked up all the brown and red leaves from the grass. The smoky bonfire they had made hid the allotments and railway line from sight. Man Kee was walking steadily down the garden with a great armful of leaves almost as big as himself. Even through the closed kitchen window Lily could hear the pleasant crackling and smell the fragrant smoke. When Husband came in, a Husband so much more relaxed than he had been even a few months ago, she judged it a good opportunity to speak what had been on her mind for some weeks now.

'Husband,' she began, alerting Chen by her tone at once. 'Don't you feel we ought to reward ourselves a little after all our hard work this year?'

Chen hoped she wasn't trying to suggest a Sunday excursion for 'drinking tea' in Chinese Street, and particularly not at the Ho Ho. He remembered all those provincial restaurateurs and counter-owners with their noisy families, creating seven different kinds of pandemonium on Sunday afternoons as they wolfed through basket after basket of steamed snacks.

'Husband,' (there she went again), 'Husband, don't you feel a little isolated here sometimes? Don't you feel hidden away from the rest of the world? Husband?'

'What is it you want, Lily?'

'Husband!'

She went to the stove (how delightfully warm the kitchen was! Quite the nicest room in the house now!) and poured a treacly black fluid into a glass, adding a sliver of lemon. 'Here, Husband, boiled Whore Lock, just like they do it in your village tea shop. Drink up.'

After the last customers had been served that night, Lily returned to the attack. She discarded preliminary feints. 'Husband, have you ever thought how useful it would be to have a car?'

Chen was stunned. Some of the things that went on in Lily's head. She went on in a persuasive tone. 'How useful it would be! We have enough money now from the drinks and ice-cream and Mui's tips as well. In fact it wouldn't be expensive at all. Mr Constantinides has several secondhand cars at the back of the garage.'

'Lily, I don't know how to drive a motor-car.'

'You can learn, Husband. Mui knows the driving instructors.'

'I don't see the need.'

Lily persisted. 'It's very necessary. What if one of us becomes ill? What if a gas bottle blows up and starts a fire? And Son will have to start school. How will I take him there?'

'I'll give it thought, Lily.'

But her final arguments had convinced him. Under certain circumstances, rapid departure for instance, a car could be useful.

'Some people say that Whore Lock is a great remedy for colds,' he hinted next morning.

'I have heard so, Husband. Maybe I won't need to mix more medicine stocks.'

Mr Constantinides had four cars at the rear of the garage. 'This is a Volkswagen Beetle,' he said, putting his huge, hairy paws on the bonnet and leaving its imprint in the dust. 'Nice seats and very reliable, too. This is a Mini – too small for you. That's an Escort. The other's a Prefect. Forget about it,' he added, noticing that Mui was peering in through the driver's window, 'it's years old. I doubt if it would run.'

'How much you want, Mr Constantinides?'

Mr Constantinides, who had been noting the number of trips Mui made to the forecourt, wanted £300 for the Escort or Volkswagen. This was £200 more than the Chens were prepared to offer. Lop £50 off Mr C's asking price to get the true figure and it was still too much. 'Think about it, then,' Mr Constantinides enjoined the backs of a disconsolate little group.

'Really, those foreign devils just try to exploit us all the time,' said Lily, on the verge of angry tears back in the kitchen.

'Don't you think we do the same to them?'

Lily could hardly believe this. Mui had just gone too far this time. What a traitor she was to her family! As if they were responsible for anyone but their little group. She was so annoyed she slammed the door of the the bath-room behind her and sat on the lavatory, with her fists clenched on her knees. It was the first really cold day of autumn and Chen had not started kitchen work yet. Consequently his bladder was full of purified hot Whore Lock. He pushed open the door and from Lily's whitened knuckles and posture of strain made the wrong assumption.

'Sorry, Lily. Face turned away.' He had an idea: 'Try some of Father's medicine. Very loosening.'

Lily emerged with expedition, omitting, Chen couldn't help noticing, to pull the chain. She must be very constipated. Lily began to vent her ill-humour on the pots and pans, proving that the body's toxins could speedily poison the sweetest system in the world, which Lily's wasn't anyway.

At the counter Lily was frosty to Mui until 9 p.m., while Mui watched the TV happily enough. But it was Lily who capitulated first and spoke to Mui. She surprised herself.

And it was Mui who got them the old Ford van. £50 from one of the aitchgevees, driven to their front door. Cash on the nail from Mui and 'There's a tank full of petrol in there for you,' said the driver.

Lily almost struck her when she saw it, so close to her irritation of the week before. 'It's filthy,' Lily said. 'There are dents all over it, there is rust in the fenders, that door is held on by string, the holes in the body have been filled in with . . . with *cement*! and it's not even been painted over. So much for your big-bear drivers. They've swindled you, Mui. All our money gone!'

'My money,' said Mui quietly. 'And it only cost £50.'

'You have still been robbed,' said Lily, rather relieved.

'You go by externals, younger sister. Which of Mr Constantinides' cars was the best? I will tell you: the little old one with the window so dirty you couldn't even look inside. It had a stout heart. Do you remember the story Father used to tell us about the blind sage and how he could tell which of the Duke of Chou's race-horses was the fastest?'

Lily smiled pityingly at Mui.

But Mui was right. The motor ran sweetly when an obliging mechanic tuned it for them. When Lily kicked the tyres (secretly hoping to bring the van down in a heap of folding, groaning metal) the tyres were hard and springy. 'Huh – so you think the brakes are safe, Mui?'

'Naturally.'

'What makes you so sure? You know nothing of these things.'

'No. But I know the man who sold it to me.'

Pathetic trust, Lily thought to herself, but with the beginnings of doubt. Again Mui was right, as she discovered later.

Who was going to drive it?

Now here was an embarrassing problem. On learning none of them could drive, the man who had sold them the van had kindly offered to give a few lessons. Chen was the obvious recipient. The girls did not wish to trespass on what was so obviously a male prerogative. Chen himself was keen to learn. The trouble was he had no aptitude, none at all. That much was made plain within fifteen minutes of the first lesson.

The family had gathered on top of the steps behind the front gate as if to watch a champion joust. Chen had mounted side-saddle, back first through the front passenger door, swinging his leg over the gear-stick and into the front seat. The driver's door was firmly lashed with rope around the central window-pillar. This meant that the back door on the driver's side was also jammed. The windows on the right-hand side, it transpired later, had to be kept permanently open for the same reason, so that while it was not easy to fall out of the van at high speed it was possible to become wet and extremely cold. Back-seat passengers had all the protection of a pillion rider.

At some stage of its career it was obvious the van had been converted from commercial to private use: extra doors let into the side, windows cut, net curtains hung on little rails, a sunshine roof opened, while the owner had omitted to paint out the italic legend on the side: *Hardiman's for Hardware*. Like some mythological creature, a unicorn, or the Shang beast – part tiger, part dragon, part ox, part who knew what else – the van was many things at the same time. It hadn't quite made up its mind what it was.

But these were minor details, hardly noticeable at the time. What was immediately noticeable was that Chen had almost disappeared from sight. He was looking through the spokes of the steering wheel, having slid so far down the (jammed) seat to reach the pedals with his short legs that his snout of a nose appeared like a snorkel.

The instructor hopped in agilely after Chen. Lily and Mui watched with proud expectation, holding Man Kee between them on the gate.

'That's your father in the car, Son,' Lily informed him. Man Kee was every bit as full of anticipation as his mother and aunt but in a different way. To date, his associations of his father with machinery were confined to the swing, implying violent, unconventional corkscrew movement and falling over in a dizzy and breathless state. The coiled ropes around the central window-pillar of the van encouraged him in the belief that this was some form of adult recreation similar to the swing. Certainly his guardians were filled with the same kind of expectation he had when being wound up by obliging Father. Perhaps he would get a go later. Man Kee's expectations were only briefly postponed as Chen, after receiving instructions as to position of accelerator, brake, and clutch, fired the ignition to no immediate effect.

'Choke out,' advised the aitchgevee, pulling out the stop as Chen looked blankly at him. (Was the man threatening to strangle him if he failed again?)

'Gear in neutral? We're away then.' This time the engine spluttered healthily before settling into a steady ticking; the whole van was quivering like a blancmange model. Suddenly it stopped. Chen had taken his foot off the clutch too quickly.

'A little slower the next time, mate,' the aitchgevee advised in a kind voice. Again the scratching of the ignition, followed by the shaking. The van inched slowly forwards. As Chen took his foot off the clutch and 'gave it more gas' as urged, it leaped on in a series of jerky bounds.

'Hand-brake off,' said the aitchgevee phlegmatically.

Next Chen had trouble with the steering. The van crept slowly towards the white lines on the middle of the road, then over into the other lane. As Chen desperately over-compensated, the van veered back over the camber and down onto the pavement, straight for the gate where the spectators were standing. Lily and Mui had as their first inclinations a healthy desire to retreat down the steps, instantly suppressed in the interests of preserving Chen's face. But was she justified in risking Son's life, Lily asked herself at the last moment? The van came to rest against a lamp post, cutting short this quandary. The aitchgevee had stamped on Chen's foot over the brake-pedal which was why he was now wincing. Lily imagined it was because

Husband was terribly humiliated, and her heart softened for him. Man Kee on the other hand was laughing, clapping his mittened hands together. It had been exactly what he expected.

The van reversed into the centre of the road and executed a neat three-point turn, the aitchgevee turning the wheel for Chen with one hand. He had a cigarette in the other. They now proceeded by fits and starts up the road with an execrable grinding of gears and roaring from the revved motor. The engine cut out several times as Chen failed to find the correct balance between the pedals but the van still glided along now while he turned the ignition key desperately until it coughed and he could give full throttle again. The van turned the corner by the garage but the girls could still hear the engine as Chen did a lap of the allotments. It sounded as if Husband was going at quite a reckless pace; at length, at long length, the van appeared at the other end of the road, still making an enormous roaring but travelling at a sedate six miles an hour. At a distance it seemed to be out of control, driverless, before Chen's nose and eyes came into view between the spokes of the steering wheel.

'That's enough for today,' the aitchgevee said swiftly as the van drew up at the gate with a final roar and Chen released the clutch, halting the machine with a sudden shaking.

The episode might have been put down to inexperience. But Chen got more and more dangerous as he lost confidence.

'It's no use,' the aitchgevee told Mui after Chen's third lesson a week later. 'If you're not mechanical, you're not mechanical.'

Lily was puzzled by the precise terms of this tautology but accepted the basic verdict. (*Plenty* of other things Husband could do that you could bet the aitchgevee couldn't.)

She and Mui went out to the van together. 'I'm sure it can't be that difficult,' Lily reflected. She opened the left-hand door with caution and slipped gracefully into the driving seat. She could reach the pedals easily enough with those legs that belonged on a Northerner.

'That handle between the seats, Lily, is the *gear-stick* ... ' Mui identified all the controls for her sister by their English names. 'Then you release the *hand-brake*,' Mui concluded. 'I know how a car is started but not how it's driven or stopped.'

Lily ignored the warning in Mui's last words. 'Shall I turn the key, Mui?' Before Mui could recommend caution the motor came to life. What fecund fingers Lily had! She had manipulated all the controls in a twinkling of the eye even before she, Mui, had finished speaking. To get a reaction out of all that complicated-looking machinery under the bonnet! Lily obviously was 'mechanical'.

'What's that smell, Mui? It's like the glue Husband used on the benches.'

Mui sniffed. Like Brother-in-law's glue? Petrol! Surely not from the car? No, it was welling out from the garage pump Lily had knocked as the van inched forward. 'Out of the car, younger sister. Quick!' Mui had visions of her younger sister incinerated to a crisp. Sparks – that was what you had to look out for. Mui quickly corrected herself: 'Slowly, Lily, slowly and carefully.'

Lily had lost one of her house slippers under the accelerator. As she bent to retrieve it, with one hand on the clutch pedal, her slim, flowered rump in the air, one pink foot simultaneously beeped the horn and activated the side indicator before, dropped hastily, it pushed the gear-lever from neutral into first. A slight touch on the accelerator as she retrieved her slipper was enough to send the van three feet forwards with a growl. As it slid back to the pump, Lily, as physically self-possessed as always, pulled up the hand-brake without fuss or obvious hurry but in time to avert a second collision against the pump. The van came to rest against it with the gentlest of bumps. The petrol now stopped coming out either because the tank was almost empty or because a valve had been clicked back into place (Lily thought the latter). The pool on the concrete was already evaporating before their eyes. In another two minutes it would be gone. Mui's relief was tinged with annoyance at Lily's seeming casualness. It appeared to her that Lily had only just pulled the handbrake in time. Lily sensed what Mui was thinking.

'It's not hurry which makes speed, elder sister, but coolness.'

This precept impressed on Lily a hundred times in childhood, sometimes painfully, meant nothing to Mui. Lily had been quick enough starting the van with those mischievous fingers, hadn't she? Mui was even more irritated when Lily suggested moving the van outside their house not by pushing but by driving it. As if they hadn't had the narrowest of escapes already. Daring and reckless hardly described Lily adequately these days.

When the aitchgevee, an honourable man, came to give Chen his fourth lesson, Lily was waiting for him a little beyond the gate. He was reluctant to give her the lesson. But: 'You're a natural, Mrs Chen,' he told her afterwards. 'A few weeks' practice and you'll be ready to go anywhere.' She was pleased, flushed with success. She was unable to show her pleasure in front of this affable *faan gwai*; she bit her lip with her bright eyes modestly downcast and two spots of colour in her sallow cheeks. At home, though, it was all she could do to stop herself leaping up from behind the counter, switching the TV off, and turning somersaults and handstands in front of the customers. (What effect would *that* have had on business?) As it was, she positively vibrated on her high stool next to Mui. Waves of suppressed triumph emanated from her disciplined, straight backed body. Mui kept glancing at her with concern.

Of course, she didn't intend to take anything so mundane as a driving test. And pay all those exorbitant taxes? Not to mention insurance. Mui wasn't happy about this. She reminded Lily of the large fines, the possibility, even, of prison. Lily scoffed. 'I shall put a little tea money in a plastic folder. That'll be my licence, Mui.'

Mui's jaws dropped at the enormity of this. 'Bad, Lily, bad. You can't get away with that sort of thing here. The English police-force is the finest in the world,' she said, thinking of Dixon of Dock Green, one of her favourite programmes. ('Evening all,' Mui would say, beating the avuncular policeman to the words as he tipped the brim of his helmet every week.) Wicked Lily just smiled in a superior way: 'Believe me, Mui, you have a lot to learn. Life is not a TV programme.'

Only her fear that the car would fail its M.O.T. kept Mui from applying for a provisional licence on Lily's behalf. (For all their good qualities the English had a tendency to go on appearances rather than more fundamental judgements.)

'We won't be using it much anyway,' Lily reassured her. 'Just for Son's schooling when he's older. Maybe for shopping and a little trip or two. Don't worry, elder sister. We are little people.' Presented with the van in its new light, as necessary adjunct to Nephew's education, shibboleth of coming days, Mui could hardly object. The shopping bags were getting heavier, too, as they did more business. Mui had a ridge of callus on both palms and she carried only half of what Lily managed. Mui tried to present her surrender as in the interests of Lily's palms rather than her own but still felt quite bribed and corrupted as they sped to the shops and back in a fraction of the previous time. And Lily, too, couldn't help comparing their business-like weekly excursions with her daily trek to the shops when she and Husband had lived alone in the flat. Truly, the individual found real fulfilment and happiness only in his family. Impossible on your own, she reflected as she deftly hill-started the van without a single jerk.

They kept Lily's driving a secret from Chen, sneaking out to the back of the garage where they kept the van parked. This was until some acceptable, face-saving formula had been devised for his future passenger status. They blundered on the first trip when they returned in preposterous time. 'We got a lift from an aitchegevee,' Lily lied quickly. Next time she drove them around the allotments and the railway line and gasworks, shooting the tiny hump-backed bridge with all four wheels in the air and a tremendous bump (Lily's only misjudgement to date), before completing the journey by the gasworks in an odour of sulphur and brimstone.

Imagine Mui's dismay when she discovered Lily had only been practising for longer journeys, wider, irresponsible roving. A month later, instead of turning left at the gasworks as usual, Lily went straight on to the main road all the way to the major roundabout.

'What are you doing?' Mui exclaimed as, hemmed in on all sides by thick, rapidly moving traffic, Lily described half a circle and shot off at a tangent onto the approach road to the dual carriageway. Her lips were pressed tight against each other, her gleaming eyes were fixed on the fast traffic, gauging a moment to slip into the mainstream.

'Eiyah! Lily!' Mui wailed in dismay.

Lily accelerated. The van shook. The needle of the speedometer (not that Mui was looking) fluttered at 60 m.p.h. Mui shut her eyes as Lily edged them onto the dual carriageway. Mui expected an impact and the sound of breaking glass at any moment. Then they were cruising along at a smooth 50 miles an hour in their own little box of black road. Mui slowly opened her eyes. 'Are you all right?' vivacious Lily enquired, thoroughly enjoying herself. The big lorries thundered past them in the fast lane. 'Look, there's one of ours!' Lily sounded the horn. 'I've made him angry. No, he's seen it's us now, he's waving. Look, elder sister!' But Mui, eyes shut, shrinking into her seat, didn't reply.

A week later there was a worse shock.

'Not the sea-side, Lily! You can't be serious.'

She was.

Mui hoped Chen might make a stand. That unpredictable man, however, was actually amused by what had been going on behind his back. 'So you can really drive it then, Lily? Well done! That will be useful in the future.'

Men were strange creatures, Mui thought. Brother-in-law should have been upset about this. Yet here he was enthusiastically planning a jaunt to the sea with Lily and obviously revelling in her mastery of this new skill.

Lily touched Mui lightly on the arm: 'Please don't worry. Everything will be all right. Unless there is fog the big road is much safer than the little road.'

Did Lily think she was a complete fool? Obviously the faster you went, the more you put yourself at risk. Lily seemed to have completely deceived Brother-in-law.

'The sea air will be good for us, Lily,' he said. 'I wouldn't be happy about driving into the city.'

'That's a difficult road, Husband,' Lily agreed.

They fixed on a Monday at the beginning of next month. This was the slackest day of the week; they planned to leave early in the morning and return by midday. That way they need lose no customers. In the meantime Lily would practise around the allotments, have a few final (advanced) lessons with the aitchgevee. Resolved to go along with the majority despite her personal misgivings (better for them all to be caught red-handed together as a mutual responsibility group), Mui had been to buy one of Mr Constantinides' road-maps. She had been able to get a ten per cent discount, which impressed Chen, though Lily felt a bit insulted by Mui's lack of faith in her navigating abilities.

Within an hour of stepping over the newspapers and out of the front door, they were looking at the English Channel. Lily had driven impeccably. Even Mui, sitting in the back with the map spread over her knees, one hand on the cross-braces of Man Kee's rompers as he pressed his nose against the window, had to grant this. On the road Lily had actually overtaken a couple of laggard vehicles with immense verve and such timing that Mui had pressed her lips closely together against her own protest. Chen went as far as applauding.

Now, after coming through the gasworks of this seaside town (reassuring, familiar sight), past the lagoon and its miniature motor boats, they were moving smoothly along the empty promenade.

It was eight o'clock on a November morning.

Lily parked in a small street off the sea front which was full of empty bays. She was unclear about the meanings of the various road-markings and preferred to pay a fee rather than risk being towed away. Or even being served with a summons. Might this evidence of basic prudence set Mui's mind at rest? On the way down Lily had several times observed her elder sister's taut face in the driving mirror, which she used with great frequency in accordance with the aitchgevee's advice. Perhaps it would be best not to put worries in Mui's mind which would not have occurred to her in the first place. Lily personally locked all the van doors and meticulously tested each in turn.

'Don't worry,' Chen joked. 'No one will want that heap of tin.'

Both girls bristled. 'What do you mean by that, Husband? "The old heap", as you call it, brought us here and it will take us back. Don't be so ungrateful.'

'Brother-in-law, don't be so proud,' Mui rebuked him in her turn, 'you should never be deceived by appearances.'

Taken aback by this concerted attack, Chen took Man Kee ahead of the two sisters to look at the grey barbarian sea. He perched Son on the top railing and put his arms around his stomach. Man Kee was a soft, warm, and what was more, these days an increasingly responsive bundle. He reacted by putting his hand, a tiny replica of the shape of Chen's, with its broad palm and stubby fingers, on his father's sleeve. Chen resolved to bring Son up *his* way. He would have an education in figures (Chen's own weak point) and grow up to own many restaurants, gaining experience in all aspects of the trade on the way. The sombre sea put Chen in a pleasing melancholy as he planned Man Kee's career.

There was a trail of smoke just before the horizon met the sea in a thin line and then, suddenly shimmering in the glitter of the rising morning sun on the metal waves, a hull.

In a small curve of the railings was a grey telescope. The sparkle of the water instantly altered Chen's mood. He put a coin in the slot and trained the glass on the ship. He was unable to find it at first, although he had aimed off carefully with the gun-sight on top of the barrel. Chen swung the tube in wide circles. There it was! Gone again. Chen swivelled the telescope more carefully. Now he had it in the centre of the circle, surprisingly large, red, and very rusty with a small bow wave: tramp steamer. Chen lifted Man Kee to the eyepiece. 'Do you see the ship, Son?' he asked softly. 'It is a special little ship for people like us, Son. It is very little and very old but that is only what strangers see. We know better, don't we, Son, because it is the ship that will take us all back home when we are finished here. It will take you to your homeland, Son, which you have never seen.' Chen kissed the top of Man Kee's head. Behind him now were Lily and Mui. Lily put her arm round Husband's shoulders. 'The little old ship,' Chen repeated. 'Let your mother see, Son.' But Man Kee would not be parted from the telescope and when he had been persuaded to relinquish his grip the whirring inside the mounting had stopped and all Lily could see was a quivering opaque circle of white light with a scratched surface and one jumping hair. By the time Chen had found a second coin the ship was over the horizon and Lily was left with a view of seagulls scavenging gash in the wake. 'Very pretty, Husband.'

'Could you see the ship, Lily?'

'Of course, Husband.'

Chen would have carried Man Kee down the stairs to the sea shore except the child scrambled into his aunt's arms. Instead Chen went down to the beach with Lily. Beach, he supposed was what it was and what it, therefore, had to be called. The undulating stretch of rattling, oil-streaked grey and brown pebbles, with its hollows and slopes, like a chain-mail shirt moulded around the torso of a sleeping giant, hardly evoked the fine white-pepper sands of a thousand miles of South China coast. Chen remembered the sun and crystal water of the eastern side of the New Territories. This grey water broke with a phlegmatic regularity, characteristic of the English, pulling the rattling stones back into the sea. Or was it throwing them on the beach – one step backward and two forward, as Chairman Mao said? Above them the gulls swooped, dived, and quarrelled over their gleanings. There was a flock of them to the left on a long, barnacled breakwater which ran half-submerged fifty yards out to sea and, to the right, more perched on the cross-struts between the pillars of the big pier. The water under the planks was startlingly different from the open sea: calm and icy emerald green.

'Shall we go on the board bridge, Husband?'

But it was closed.

They walked further along the promenade, past the Lido. It was now, according to the ornamental clock, quarter to nine. An amusement arcade, built into the cliff, had just rolled back its front. They stared at the rows of fruit machines, the gauntlet of pin-ball tables. Chen was fumbling in his pocket when Lily gave him a coin. 'You do it, Husband, you have our good luck.' They waited around the machine for some time after it had stopped spinning as if it might relent and give them a prize after all. A bit disappointed, Mui bought Man Kee a toffee apple but not the pink fluff on a stick he wanted. It looked like the fibre-glass Brother-in-law had packed between the rafters above her room, certain to do him no good at all. Anyway Man Kee was hot enough already in his woollen clothes.

The manager of the arcade had activated the small shooting gallery at the end of the hall. Dented metal ducks jerked along a conveyor belt, ping-pong balls played on jets of water. As the family passed by without interest, the manager turned the switch off and the ducks halted, the balls dropped from vanished fountains. Neither Chen, Mui, nor particularly Lily had the slightest desire to let off firearms, let alone pay good money for the privilege of doing so. Lily remembered Father impressing on her how no serious boxer could ever use guns in a private affair. One would have to be a traitor to the entire tradition. (He remembered the patriots of 1900, whose spells had not been proof against foreign lead.)

But Lily did stop at the coconut shy. Both she and Mui had liked these as children. The pickle vendor in the town square had sold delicious white strips transfixed to a leaf and a sliver of ginger by toothpicks. Perhaps Son would enjoy some; it would certainly be healthier for him than the gruesome red and brown sweetmeat on a stick (the flesh of the ancient apple had discoloured rapidly on exposure) which Mui had so irresponsibly bought for him.

Chen paid the man for five wooden balls which he indicated should be handed to his wife and in an awkward-looking, disjoined overarm motion, emphasised by her left-handedness, she hurled these in rapid succession and with immense precision at the hairy nuts. Four bounced on the floor and the fifth wobbled in its cup, for although Lily's aim had been unerring she had not thrown with much force. Even Mui, who remembered barring her younger sister from the childhood games of hopscotch and skipping, was surprised. Chen produced another sixpence. 'You must be joking, mate,' the man said. He gave Lily the four nuts she had won, fairly and squarely, and the Chens left.

On the way out they passed a strange mirror, a set of mirrors, in fact, arranged to reflect into each other; perfectly normal mirrors, glittering, empty, from a distance, but when you came close up to them, what a fright! Lily had never seen anything like it. She was quite alarmed as the whole group of them sprang into view. Them being a family of compressed dwarfs and elongated giants, repeated into infinity in a series of diminishing, mutually reproducing images. Mui had come out long and thin, Lily-like, with a lugubrious rectangular face very much like her younger sister's, while Lily was squashed into a toddling midget three feet wide and two high, an unkind caricature of the real-life Mui. Chen was pleasantly surprised, though, by this trick of revelation, which gave him a freak insight into the shared physical inheritance of the girls, seemingly so different. Now he knew they really were sisters. He smiled, and a fiendish grin came over the face of the thick-set, bandy-legged simian in the mirror. Lily turned away from the nasty family of grotesques, insulting specimens of humanity. (She was sure westerners didn't come out like that!) Man Kee was staggering over the bare wood floor, chuckling richly. It seemed that the mirrors had disturbed his anyway precarious sense of balance and he was now as disorientated as if, coiled upside-down, all the blood had been spun into his head on the swing. He appeared in the mirror as a mantis-legged giant, looming tall over the rest of them. Lily moved to take him in her arms but Mui swept him up first.

As they were emerging into the morning, the amusements man caught them up. He had a coconut for Lily: 'Nothing personal. If everyone was like you I'd be out of business tomorrow.'

A nice gesture, Lily thought, recovering her composure now; it was business-like but polite. She resolved to emulate it in her own dealings with their customers; if, say, unlikely though it sounded, some of them took it upon themselves to criticise the food as inauthentic.

'You're quite right,' she would say, forcing extra white rice on them. 'I congratulate you on your acumen and advise you not to return. We have a living to make, too, you know.'

A crack as one of the coconuts slipped from her cold fingers to the pavement brought Lily back to the present. While she had been acquitting herself rationally but honourably before her customers in her daydreams, Chen had brought them to the edge of the commercial sea front. There was a tiny platform and a small-gauge, single-track railway running out under the cliffs beside the endless pebble strand. Despite the cold wind Lily would have enjoyed a ride along the sea in one of the open carriages but the ten shilling return fare (no concessionary half for Man Kee either) was too much. Regretfully, they walked back into the town. They had skimped breakfast and were now hungry. Mui, in particular, looked wistfully at the cockles and winkles on one hardy entrepreneur's stall. No good even thinking of sampling a saucer with Lily as monitor; if one was ill subsequently she was capable of being very callous. Mui was becoming quite faint with hunger and her stomach gurgled. Chen, less accustomed to fasting than the girls, was also famished. On their way through the narrow, winding streets, which looked older than the other parts of town and reminded Chen of his home village, they saw several unsuitable-looking shops selling cakes and coffee. Then at the sea front again, they passed a fish and chips shop with an enviably wide all-glass front window. It was the window which attracted Lily's attention first. How clear it was and thick; presumably both vandal- and wave-resistant. It was clever, too, of the owner to paint prices onto his glass.

Mui had her nose against the window, though for different reasons from her cold-blooded younger sister, since a wonderful aroma of vinegar, chicken, fish, and newly frying potatoes was seeping through to the pavement.

The clock showed quarter to twelve.

'Shall we try?' Chen asked.

Mui was already half-way through the door.

And the food was quite good, really not bad at all. Even Lily, depressed at spending two shillings and sixpence a head, had to concede it was good stuff as she bit a long finger of potato in half. She now exchanged coconuts for Son, the former awkward, the latter heavy.

It was midday after they had finished their meal on a promenade bench and quarter past before the cold engine started.

Lily warmed it gently, the old motor sighing like an animal, its metal flanks trembling and creaking as they heated up. Clouds of condensation (not fumes, for it was a healthy piece of machinery) swirled from the exhaust and enveloped the van in mist. The dials on the dashboard glowed, the white needles flickered restlessly. Through a hole in the cloud Chen saw them reflected in a shop window; the indicator winking like a bright eye. They were some devilish armed chariot or harnessed war animal, maybe a giant tortoise; they were an infernal carapace. Having nursed the elderly machinery to life, Lily engaged gear and eased it out of the bay between the two cars which had sandwiched it. The revs took on a less anguished note. The mist cleared – to reveal a policeman, young, with notebook in hand, who made no attempt to tip the brim of his helmet. Mui, only just recovered from her alarm at the car's failure to start, was filled with dread. She repented of her earlier decision to come. Who would look after Man Kee if they were all imprisoned?

The policeman rapped on the driver's window. 'Licence please.' Lily unwound the window briskly and passed out her plastic folder. The policeman examined it beneath the level of the window and handed the empty folder back. 'Get that exhaust seen to.' He was making a note as Lily eased the Infernal Carapace into the line of traffic on the sea front. Gripped by emotions she could not name, almost wishing they had been arrested, Mui sat numbed in the back. Not until they had been moving for fifteen minutes did she notice they were taking a different route. On the right hand was the sea, grey and mournful, and surely that wasn't right? 'Lily ... '

'On the way back we are going to visit a different town,' their driver announced cheerfully. Mui was far too demoralised even to try to object.

In a few moments they were passing along another promenade, with less shops than the other front but by the same inhospitable sea and 'beach'. There were, however, a lot more people around, unless it was merely a question of the hour.

'Don't go so fast, Lily,' Mui called out. She wasn't worried about speeding, just keen to get a good look. They seemed to be flashing past the promenaders.

'We go slower, motor stalls,' Lily replied.

The dancing needle showed she was holding the van's speed down to just under 5 m.p.h. Mui looked at the kerb for reference; they were crawling along. *It was the promenaders who were moving at snail's pace!* Everything in the world is relative, Mui reflected sententiously. Some of the promenaders, in fact, so far from moving at all were so inert as to be giving no discernible signs of life. And how old all of them were!

Lily swung the van round in the opposite direction so they were actually alongside the promenade. Never had she seen such a formidable concentration of *gwai lo* old. There they were in their wheelchairs, drawn up in regular rows, as if cavalry about to charge and repel invaders coming up the pebbly hill. In front of the ranks three or four chairborne individuals were being wheeled briskly up and down, commanders reviewing the massed lines behind them. The plaid blankets all wore neatly tucked round their stick legs and knees (how emaciated this big race could become in age!) only made them look horsier. What an odd choice of place for families to send their parents and grandparents, Lily thought. The damp and cold air must be cruel on old bones. Chen, too, was reminded of his own father's suffering in their marshy village.

'Just look at them, Mui,' said Lily with a mixture of pity and jubilation in her voice. She decided to do something to lighten the old folk's day, foreigners or not. 'Everyone wave and smile, come on,' she urged. She gave the horn (nothing decrepit about that part of the van's equipment!) a lady-like toot or two and also flashed the headlamps, rather waterily, despite the gloomy day, since they were still proceeding at a sedate four miles an hour. 'Wave, Man Kee, smile!' Still crawling along the kerb, indicator lights now jovially twinkling as well, the plastic side-signals stiffly out at the salute, the Chens grinned, not too fixedly they hoped, and waved out of the window that opened. The old folks seemed mostly too far gone to notice, let alone respond, but, yes, there was one elderly warrior in a tweed cap shaking his stick at them and shouting, though unfortunately the wind snatched his words away. Not that Lily was looking for thanks. As Lily gave him a special toot of his own on the horn in acknowledgement, he was wiping his eyes with a large handkerchief. Probably overcome with gratitude, Lily thought, or maybe they were just rheumy in cold weather like Mrs Law's. He looked like one of the old colonial types and the weather must be particularly hard on them.

'Lily, there is a police-car behind us.'

She checked in the driving-mirror. Mui was right. She speeded up gently, switched off headlights and indicators, and turned right at the next opportunity. Soon they were proceeding smoothly along the dual carriageway and, despite increased traffic, were home again within the hour – only slightly late.

TWENTY-TWO

Two events briefly disrupted the new life they had made for themselves before it settled down again. They had an encounter with the tax-man which was annoying but short-lived in its consequences and they had to settle the question of Man Kee's schooling, which was less immediately unpleasant but remained a source of great worry in the long term.

It was Lily who had been keeping track of business. No more formal description could be applied to the casual methods she used; they certainly weren't accounts. Although scrupulous about keeping the till money intact during the day, none of them made a note of the monthly takings. At the end of the day Lily would carefully count the money, setting aside exactly one-fifth to go in remittance to Husband's parents and putting it in the satin lid-pocket of the Great Wall tartan suitcase in their bedroom. The rest went between an old shirt of Chen's and Lily's second-best tunic suit. At the end of the week, reckoned as shopping day (Friday), Lily would use the cash to stock up on supplies, both for the business and themselves. The residue was, she supposed, profit, remembering, though, that rates, heating, and lighting, as well as telephone rental still had to be paid three-monthly. She was conscientious about honouring these in cash at the town hall and show rooms within a day of receiving the bills. She knew that after all outgoings they had roughly £50 more spending money a quarter than when Husband had been at the restaurant.

What Lily didn't keep were the utility bills themselves, receipts for foodstuffs, cleaning requisites, foil packages, or gas bottles. She knew yesterday's takings to the last halfpenny. What the month's gross was, still less the net figure, were mysteries beyond her comprehension. It was impossible to turn in a balance sheet. Lily wasn't even sure how tax was calculated. Were tips taxed? Was it worked out on the numbers in the family? On the windows you had? She remembered the heavy taxes in Kwangsi and Father dressing them in their poorest clothes when officials visited. It could hardly be the same here. And did the collector take a squeeze? Husband was no help. Innumerate Chen had just decided to ignore the whole problem; then it might go away. It could be years before they were found out. The boss used to get away with murder. Chen decided to live for the day.

Fortunately for Lily and Mui they were found out before things got completely out of control.

There had already been unwelcome visitors. A woman had called to put them on the electoral register. As if they were entitled to vote! Lily thought, scornfully seeing through the woman's shoddy pretext. She had come in during business hours: iron-grey hair, tweed suit, and board with dangling pencil. This last piece of apparatus should have alerted Lily at once. (One thing about the flat: if you didn't like the look of anyone through the spy-hole, you could sit tight and not answer.) Probably the woman hadn't intended to masquerade as a customer; she had just considerately waited so as not to interrupt business. But the first impression Lily had was that it was a trick. Her face set into a dead mask; her bright eyes dulled. She shook her head.

'Not understand.'

'But I heard you talking in English to that girl just now.'

'No, not understand these thing. Only small people.'

'Perhaps your husband can supply me with information. I only wish to know who lives here.'

'No, no husband here.'

'But surely that's your little boy?'

'No. My friend son.' Lily's grip around Man Kee's stomach involuntarily tightened. Fortunately the hatch had been shut when the woman came in. But now Mui entered.

'Are *you* the mother of this child?'

Man Kee stretched his arms out to his aunt (good boy, you would have thought he knew what was going on).

'Does she live here or is she your employee?'

'Not understand.'

'Well, can you tell me how many people live here?'

'Not understand. Small people only.'

162

At length the woman had left. 'We'll find out in the end, you know.'

Lily would dearly have liked to stick her pink, unfurred tongue out at this snooper. This sort of person preyed on ordinary people; it was almost licensed brigandry.

Then the tax man came. This followed a series of brown envelopes which Chen, inhabiting his fool's paradise, promptly binned. Mui would not have been so imprudent. They paid the price when an official descended on them. From the start Lily sensed he would not be put off as easily as the register woman. (Were the two visits possibly linked?) He wanted their 'books', whatever they were, bills, receipts, bank statements, cheque stubs, till rolls. Lily didn't know where to begin. No use pretending she didn't understand the language: the man just talked through her protestations and it was all figures anyway. A week later, as promised, he was back. For the occasion Lily dressed Man Kee in rags, purpose-made, for naturally Man Kee's clothes were the softest and warmest money could buy. She devoted care and flair to fabricating his ragamuffin outfit: tearing seams, rubbing woollen elbows and cotton knees against the concrete pathway, soiling them with (clean) earth. His Jumping Jacks were already well scuffed. Lily gave instructions to Mui to bring him in and feed him white rice at a pre-arranged signal. She devoted her remaining efforts to mustering as much information for the tax man as she could, in the shape of bills discovered at the bottom of her shopping bags, brown cardboard tags still tied to the gas bottles, plus a formal record of that week's shopping at least. Before spending the week's cash she also counted it. She got Mui to help her in these chores.

They did it on the floor of Lily's bedroom, their breath smoking. But it's so easy, Mui thought to herself as she counted out the cash and made some simple subtractions in her head. For the first time she had serious misgivings about Brother-in-law's ability to fend for them all.

The tax man spread the assortment of papers on the counter in an intimidating silence. He had already asserted himself by refusing to allow customers in, not one, and making Mui turn the TV off. Otherwise they would have to come to the tax office with him, way up in another part of the country.

That would have been terrible; they preferred to confront authority on home ground. For some reason this seemed to have won them favour with this official. This good start was quickly lost. The tax man, who had been given Lily's stool, held a gas bottle's creased tag by its string with the same distaste as one might convey a dead rat to the dust bin by the tip of its scaly tail (always assuming the necessity). He poked the pile of papers – a heap of rubbish, the gesture implied – with the butt of his Bic biro.

'Are you seriously telling me that this is all you have to show the Inland Revenue?'

Lily nodded. She and Husband were on the customer side of the counter. How humiliating! Would their business be taken away from them? At least Husband had never sunk to drawing unemployment benefit, a disgraceful surrender which instantly and forever disqualified you from running a business of your own.

The tax man had not taken off his fawn trenchcoat nor had he accepted a cup of rapidly cooling tea (Lily's little litmus test of his amenability) but now he took off his wire-framed spectacles and wiped his bald head with a handkerchief. He sighed. 'Do you realise you have a legal obligation to keep a record for Sales Tax and Purchase Tax? You do? Where is your till roll then? A cash book, a day book, your invoices in order? Would it be impertinent of me to enquire why you bother with a cash till at all when you have no record of your business?'

Lily smiled serenely but was inwardly frightened and, forgetting herself, nervously depressed one of the keys of the said till (which *all* lucky and well-run businesses had to have). She wished to assert her right to it in case this brigand in a raincoat tried to confiscate it. By an unfortunate coincidence the ringing of the bell was the signal she had agreed on with Mui. The drawer slid out with a *ting!* and, on cue, Mui entered with a small apparition. Not content with the beggar's fancy-dress contrived by Lily, Mui had also smeared her nephew's face and hands with soot.

This is going too far, Lily thought.

But incredulity was not among the things registered on the tax man's surprisingly expressive currant-bun of a face. He watched Man Kee run in his peculiar way over to his father before putting on his spectacles again.

'How many children do you have, Mrs ..., Mrs Chen?'

'This son only.'

'Well, you can claim child allowance for him.'

'Hah?'

Mui came over. She said to Lily: 'Because you have children you pay less tax.'

'Ah!'

'Any aged dependents?'

Chen shook his head vigorously and the girls, puzzled but quick-thinking as well as obedient, kept blank faces.

The tax man produced a form from his tattered black plastic briefcase. 'This is a tax return, like the ones we sent you. Do you know how to fill it in? No.' He took his spectacles off again. His eyes looked tired to Mui. 'All right. Now listen closely.'

Mui crossed to the owner's side of the counter, while Lily took Man Kee away from Chen.

'You must put a roll in your till and keep it. You must also keep receipts for purchases. Do you have a wholesaler?'

'Buy from Co-op.'

'Well, it's not for me to tell you but you would get a much more advantageous price from a wholesaler. Never mind. Just keep all your bills in order in a file, or even a box would do. No bank account? No. Now let me explain about a cash book, you won't need a day book . . . '

Mui's earlier suspicion about the simplicity of the procedures was officially confirmed. She felt she had a natural, untutored flair for these things. Finally, the taxman said: 'The inspector of taxes will have to make an assessment on what I recommend, which you will pay in two parts in the next twelve months. We can make some estimate from similar businesses in your area. It may be higher than if you had kept a record but that will be your own fault.'

'You do our tax from Kebab House tax?' Lily asked hopefully, remembering how empty that establishment always was.

'I can't speak for the inspector, I'm afraid.'

Mui saw him personally to the door. It was a pity he was too upright to reward for his kindness, though his probity made her feel warm. A real mother and father official. She felt she had proved a point to Lily. Mui explained the situation to her. Lily was jubilant, and Mui was aghast when she shouted: 'Husband! We can cheat almost all the tax!' She passed on Mui's good news and her own analysis of it: tips need not be declared, ice-cream and drinks were invisible earnings, they could keep a separate box for, say, a quarter of the earnings and not put it on the till roll. And the cost of heating and provisions could actually be deducted from the tax liability! Idiots!

Chen was not at all interested, although he had suffered one worrying moment. He was sponging Man Kee's face and hands in the kitchen. The boy was filthy. The girls really ought to look after him better. That kind of thing wasn't his responsibility at all.

A little later Lily had to deal with the social worker whom the tax man, kindly grandfather of three- and four-year-old boys respectively, had exceeded his brief in notifying about Man Kee.

'Yes?' said Lily warily, fast developing a technique for this kind of visitor, the old stone-walling front of incomprehension having been so obviously outmoded.

She produced Man Kee readily enough, plump and somnolent as he had only recent eaten. He was wearing a bright red woollen jersey with Donald Duck (*Toh No Ngaap*) on the front, purple dungarees, and a leather cap with chinstraps and earmuffs, a sort of peaked flying ace's helmet, which had been left on after play in the garden.

She was the mother and he was her only child, Lily told the young woman, who was surely some years her junior. He was just three, she lied for no reason other than to be mendacious. *Of course he wasn't ill!* Just sleepy (as you would be if you were lucky enough to enjoy food as rich as his, Lily thought. She was quite annoyed). Yes, her husband was out; Lily managed to leave the exact numbers of the household vague. No, the woman could certainly not look at her son's room. What an interesting old van it was outside? (Their visitor now grasping at straws.) No, it wasn't theirs.

Satisfied that at least the child was well-cared for – if only all cases were false alarms! – the social worker gave Lily a card before she left. Lily thanked her, smiling falsely, and threw it away when the Englishwoman had left. She was quite obviously a spy from the Ministry of Transport. Lily didn't suspect this; she *knew* it.

Man Kee was no longer just an unamenable, living lump to be fed, kept clean, hugged or insincerely scolded. He was a personality, with all the problems that implied for others; had been for some time, not that Lily wanted to notice.

His education would have to be settled soon. In fact it would be legally taken out of their hands. They had a bare period of grace before the state took their decision for them. Both Lily and Chen had their ambitions for Man Kee. Dissimilar in their means – Lily wanted him to be a professional man, perhaps an accountant (a calling which seemed increasingly honourable and lucrative to her these days), while Chen wanted him to follow in an expanded restaurant business – they had a similar interested end in view. Man Kee should honour and respect his parents in their old age and have the substance to make that honour and respect worth having. Son was the most valuable long-term investment they possessed. On maturity the realisation of this asset could be worth far more than the business would ever return. Assuming they could run it in an enfeebled old age. He was the last piece to be laid in the edifice of their new life and yet he was also its foundation stone.

But what sort of schooling should he have? This was vital. Should he be sent back to Hong Kong? This would ensure he was imbued with correct Chinese qualities, veneration for parents, for instance. His grandfather and grandmother would certainly be pleased to have him. Many young grandchildren lived in the village while their parents worked overseas. In fact the grandparents were frequently reluctant to surrender their charges, who were a certain guarantee of regular remittances; not that Chen's parents needed such a mini-hostage while their son was married to Lily.

'I don't think it would be a good idea to send Son to your parents,' Lily said to Chen, determined to make a real fight of it if anybody tried to take her child from her. Fortunately, Husband was similarly inclined.

'It would be a big nuisance for them and us,' he said. 'A lot of trouble with letters going back and forth. Anyway they'd find out about everything here. What they don't know already from you.'

This was not what influenced Lily but it made agreement possible. She was, though, unable to persuade Husband to send Son to one of the Chinese schools near the Street. Chen couldn't find it in him to deny his son his heritage. He would have made any financial sacrifice for this; had that been the sacrifice required. 'Let's wait until he's a little older,' he argued plausibly. 'He couldn't understand such things now.'

'First lessons stick firmest,' Lily argued in her turn, but she had already compromised. Perhaps Husband was right. And she wouldn't really have liked to surrender Man Kee at this stage, even for a few hours.

Son, providentially, had not displayed any further disturbing tendency to speak English as well as Cantonese. It was now possible to hold quite complicated exchanges with him. He had an unusual vocabulary. This included: cash till, foil container, the names of all the dishes on the menu, refrigerated truck, articulated lorry, and compost heap. This last, and other words relating to garden, were uppermost in his thoughts. He had lost his taste for slides and swings, even for being twisted until he hung above his father's head like a bat. Father and son had gone garden-mad, as far as Lily was concerned.

No longer was the landing cluttered with planks to the ruin of the girls' cardigans and flowered trousers: Chen had made a little red wheelbarrow for Son (invented by the Chinese a myriad of years before the West, even if they'd only exploded an A-bomb a few years back now). He'd also made a hutch to go at the bottom of the garden by the fence. Chen wasn't sure what kind of animal was going inside; probably rabbits. Meanwhile rows of cabbages, spinach, onions, broccoli (Chinese and English), and winter greens had flourished in their due seasons, showing Chen's skills as a farmer were not lost. He planned carrots and beans for summer. At home in the New Territories vegetable growing was an ignominious mode of agriculture, practised by refugees and immigrants. It was fitting he should grow them here in alien soil.

Son was very useful in the garden. He trundled respectable loads up and down in his toy wheelbarrow. Lily had bought him wellington boots at Woolworth's in the same violent pillar-box red as his barrow (black Taiwanese sneakers, laces too, for herself and Mui). She spied on the gardeners from Mui's window. There was not a hint of play about the proceedings which father and son conducted with great earnestness. Man Kee never made any detours, trotting behind his barrow, head lolling. Lily supposed that dear head *was* rather big when you looked at it objectively, in a non-maternal spirit, not that she would ever admit it to strangers, let alone Husband. She was beginning to think though, that love and concern lay behind Chen's apparent flippancy. A recent display of sentiment in another area had deepened her understanding of Husband.

At first Lily had wanted to cook and sell their home-grown produce to the customers but Chen had surprised her with an unusual show of whimsicality. They had been grown for their own nourishment; no one else was to have a single onion or leaf of spinach. Lily humoured him. Really they did taste better than greengrocer's vegetables, apart from the inestimable advantage of having Husband and Son under her eye instead of in the park. And if Husband could get worked up like that about his onions and cabbages (whatever they were), what must his real feelings for Son be? He must love him almost as much as she did.

Lily resolved not to be a mere passive onlooker. To encourage Man Kee and show her interest, she gave him an old mango stone. This was more in the way of a nature study lesson than serious horticulture. She was explaining the basic facts of life to Son. From seed came the plant which bore fruit which in turn ripened and fell, causing the cycle to be repeated. Human life was like this, too, not that she could expect Son to comprehend these profound and peculiarly Chinese realities yet. Son had held the big nut, bigger than his fist by far, gazing at it with a face wiped of all expression. (Sometimes you might think he was very backward if you didn't know him much better.) Anyway, he had trotted off to the wheelbarrow and probably thrown the stone away. There was, naturally, no way you could expect tropical fruit to grow in the land of ice, snow, and benevolent tax collectors who showed you how to defraud the authorities. Still, he might have let me keep it on the windowsill for him, thought Lily, rather hurt. But what a surprise when little green shoots pushed their way between the finger-nail sized lumps of broken earth on the edge of the compost heap. It was Chen who saw Son bending over it. Man Kee was patting protective wisps of hay over the shoots. It didn't look like weeds. Chen wondered if Lily had put something down: it was a nut of some kind, cracked now by the life bursting from it. Lily was delighted.

'Clever Son! You planted it, didn't you?'

No answer but the big head lolled.

'Son, did you maybe just throw it away here? You can tell me.'

The big head lolled again. Man Kee was rubbing his chin against his chest and sucking his thumb. How frustrating! No amount of questioning could elicit a definite answer from him and in the end Mui had to rescue him from his mother, who had always been obstinate, even as a little girl.

The separate shoots united into a single, thicker root. The plant was nurtured by the rotting matter around it. (Husband claimed fires could start spontaneously in the heart of such heaps, not that Lily was naive enough to believe him.) Later, Chen took it indoors to the kitchen (where he had been displaced by Mui while he worked outdoors). This was until there was a more clement environment outside. The plant pushed through the compost in its bucket, aided by liberal doses from Lily's medicine bottle which Chen administered surreptitiously.

They celebrated New Year quietly on their own. Spring and summer came and went. Chen's bean-rows produced abundantly. He even succeeded with aubergines and peppers under glass. Now the mango sapling was twenty-one inches high, twelve shorter than its planter and, by any reckoning, including the state's, it was high time Man Kee's formal education began.

TWENTY-THREE

School, five miles south-east as the black, rapacious crow flew, was a gaunt and sooty red-brick edifice, built, Lily could see from the foundation-stone when she delivered Son by Infernal Carapace, in the year of cession of Hong Kong island, 1841. It bore a remarkable resemblance to Castle Dracula (the Count's escapades had been showing as a series of late night films on TV, making them all glad they had god to protect them). So far from being oppressed by the school's appearance, Lily was encouraged. This was what school ought to look like. How severe, how forbidding it was! Lily was quite elated for Son. He, too, was now starting on the great adventure of life but, luckier than she, was experiencing its thrills and delights right from the start. Lily thought back to her own boring, utterly unexceptional childhood (all that monotonous boxing practice!) and, comparing it with the glamorous, fulfilling life she now led of running her own business in a strange country (her own business!) thought she ought to be thankful for remission, however late. It made her appreciate her good fortune all the more, not that she was ungrateful to Father or unafflicted by nostalgia for little things.

'You should be grateful, Son,' she told Man Kee, who was sitting beside her in the front seat with his new satchel and inside it his new pencil-box, new crayons, and new ruler. All the same she felt a few motherly pricklings in the eye as he went through the gate, a miniature, equally stolid version of his father. He had not said a word on the fifteen minute drive. Lily had been bright and vivacious, although her stomach felt hollow (surely she had eaten enough tea and bread?). She had forbidden red-eyed Mui to accompany them. 'Really, eldest sister, you must pull yourself together or you will upset Son. Do you think he is leaving us for ever?'

When she went to pick up Son four hours later he was on the pavement outside the iron gate, holding a young woman's hand. Young and kindly faced, she was not Lily's idea of a teacher.

Apparently other mothers had met the school staff that morning (what for? Lily asked herself), and the teacher was sorry she hadn't been able to meet Man Kee's mother then. She was glad to be doing so now. Lily smiled her insincere smile. She had read the invitation the school had sent them late in the summer after Mui had been to the local authority. She had decided it would be politer not to accept; you shouldn't make trouble and she didn't want to incur odium on Son's behalf with her own impertinence. Interfering Mui had wanted to go, of course.

Before Lily could warn her, the teacher opened the door of the Infernal Carapace and it fell off, inevitably, held on only by the ropes attaching it to the window-column, from which it dangled like a ripped toe-nail. In the ensuing mutual embarrassment the teacher forgot to ask if Man Kee was merely shy or spoke no English.

He might have spoken no language known to man for all the good he was to Lily on the way back. Not a word did he utter in reply to her bright questioning. She longed to shake him, sitting there so lumpishly just like his father at his most exasperating, but fortunately for Man Kee his mother had her hands and feet occupied with the controls of the van and (in the back for safety now) he was beyond her long reach. Serious interrogation began at home. Mui joined in. They tried everything: coaxing, bribes of ice-cream, gentle threats (no TV for awkward boys). All they could extract from him was a cryptic: *'Ho Wan!'*, 'Good playing!' or perhaps: 'I enjoyed myself.'

Ho wan! Lily could hardly believe her ears.

Mui placed a hand on her sleeve. 'Nephew, are you hungry? Would you like a biscuit?' He had already eaten.

'Son, what did they give you?' *Mince, jam tart, and custard*, he told them in English.

Then he opened the kitchen door for himself with great self-possession, removed two trowels from his barrow and wheeled it down the garden to join his father.

The girls watched him leave the room and followed him with their eyes down the garden. Their mouths were very slightly open. They could think of nothing to say to each other. There was something new happening; something which Lily realised was beyond her experience and from which she was forever excluded; something she could give no name to; something which separated her from Son. She didn't like it at all.

The two trips to school and back became a routine, to be assimilated into what Lily realised was really a very flexible, eclectic day; a Chinese day. Son's morning absence and early afternoon return came to be a part of the cycle, as inevitable and natural as the rising and setting of the sun. (For Mui, that first day, it had been a little death.) Try as they might, though, the girls could not draw any more information from Man Kee. Every day, it seemed, the fare was mince, jam tart, and custard. Quite wholesome, of course, now that they had found out from the Bowyers van-driver what these staples were, but rather monotonous every day, Lily would have thought. 'Son, are you telling the truth?' she asked gently. She could think of no reason why he should lie, other than paucity of vocabulary. Maybe *'mince, jam tart, and custard'* was simply a generic term for food – as one said 'eat rice' instead of simply 'eat' in the traditional evening greeting of the south? Surely Son wouldn't be so disloyal as not to wish Mar-mar to know what was digesting in his stomach? Now, instead of asking Man Kee what he had eaten, Lily would ask cunning leading questions: 'Did they put sauce on the pie today, Son?' – 'Was the chicken cold?' But the answer was always the same, repeated as if it were a ritual chant.

She and Mui gave up. Man Kee just dropped his satchel now and went straight into the garden. Strangest thing: his pencils and crayons never seemed to need sharpening or even to dwindle in length, for Lily would ferret eagerly in his satchel for clues to his other life, the one from which she was forever excluded. Perhaps the state supplied free pencils, too. She couldn't believe what Son dropped in an aside: that they played with plasticine and flour and water in class-time. He had been doing that at home for years.

'Bad to tell lies, Son,' she admonished him gently, dandling him on her knee. These days he couldn't wait to get off his mother's rather bony knees and into the garden with that stupid barrow Husband had knocked together for him. Only Mui was allowed to squeeze and cuddle him as much as she wanted. Lily was jealous.

Down by the compost heap Man Kee's sapling was still growing at more or less the same rate as its tender. It was now twenty-three inches high to Man Kee's two feet nine inches, tall for a mango sapling in an inclement environment, small for a five-and-a-half-year old boy. The plant was sturdy but showed no signs of flowering, still less of bearing fragrant yellow fruit which Lily might crush with ice next summer. She had remarked on this to Husband.

'No, no. Fruit doesn't come from stone or pips,' he said. 'Not possible. In any case the plant is far too young.'

'So from where does fruit come?' Lily enquired sarcastically. 'It falls from heaven? Hah? I'm asking you, Mr Farmer.'

Chen said seriously: 'To make a tree which produces fruit you must cut a piece from the mature fruit tree itself and graft it. Its seed will not produce fruit.'

She noted that Husband rarely touched the plant. Man Kee alone watered it. Father and son toiled at their plots in happy, silent sympathy. Observing from her spy-point in Mui's room, Lily never saw them speak to each other, yet Man Kee seemed to know just when to bring a trowel or rake for his father, or when to fill a watering can at the outside tap. Sometimes Lily would see them in the sunset at the wire fence, gazing down over the allotments and railway line to nowhere in particular, Chen leaning his chin on his rake, Man Kee in between the shafts of his wheelbarrow, seeming to aim it at some distant mark in the east behind the sun's bloody yolk as it disappeared under the green dome of the gasworks. Bearing in mind their oriental origins it would be a splendid time for an impromptu geography lesson, Lily thought. Husband's love for Son was evident in the hand he occasionally put on Man Kee's shoulder but he was remiss to neglect such a golden opportunity to instruct the next generation. She remembered being shown the full moon through a telescope when she was a child: so smooth and silver to the naked eye, a perfect disc; so scarred, broken and rough when you saw it properly for the first time. And now, watching in the wings, Lily felt the same twinges of jealousy as when she saw Mui receiving the tokens of Son's affection that should have been a mother's right.

Sooner than Lily would have expected Man Kee's school holidays arrived. They were also somewhat longer than seemed right. Perhaps the pupils had a lot of lessons to prepare. 'Son, no homework?' she enquired, only to be silenced by Mui.

'Not yet at his age, Lily. Don't be ridiculous.'

Lily pouted in disapproval of Mui's laxity. She was only trying to curry favour with Son. Secretly, though, she was glad to have Son for an entire day again, even if he was only fleetingly glimpsed from the window as a miniature coolie.

She wondered whether she should keep him with Mui in the kitchen or as a companion on her forecourt trips. The earlier he learned the fundamentals of the business the better. Father had started teaching her *Hung gar* when she was younger. On the other hand she would hope to bring her own child up rather more leniently. She must avoid

Mui influencing him with some of the increasingly peculiar ideas she had.

Already disturbing evidence was beginning to accumulate. On the first day of the vacation she had prepared for Son a special dish of bitter winter greens, melon, and beef, and a nice shrimp omelette (taking care to pincer all the shell out with her wooden chopsticks). Son had picked at the delicious items, unenthusiastically chewed a shrimp and actually spat out the leaf of winter green as a colourless little ball of fibrous matter. Lily was hurt; offended, she realised, by the behaviour of a five-year-old. And Mui had abetted, no, encouraged him in this unfilial behaviour.

'You don't like it, Nephew? What would be good to eat then?'

Man Kee moodily mashed the ball of winter greens with his spoon.

'Nephew, I know what you'd like,' cooed Mui in a tone Lily found amazingly obsequious from a grown woman.

Man Kee's porcelain spoon hovered above the cow's pat of winter greens.

'You'd like *"mince, jam tart, and custard"* wouldn't you, Nephew?'

Man Kee put his spoon down and nodded with his big head.

'Tomorrow you shall have it. Now is too late.'

Lily's fingers itched to box she wasn't quite sure whose ears.

These were rather tendentiously known as the 'Christmas' holidays, so Lily was informed. Apart from being a bit of an insult to god, the timing was also highly inconvenient. It was all very well for the adult members of the family to have Man Kee to dote on uninterruptedly over the *faan gwai* festival, but what about lunar New Year? Man Kee would be at school then, and his absence fell during the morning, the nicest part of the festival. This ruined Lily's hopes of a car trip into Soho, though Husband didn't seem at all upset. It was ages since she had tasted a piping hot steamed pork bun. She was also hoping to make enquiries about Chinese classes for Man Kee. High time this young man was having them. Now it would have to wait. There was, of course, no question of keeping Man Kee at home and thus depriving him of an entire day of his schooling. How irresponsible that would have been! He might never have caught up again. But Lily was still disappointed. Where was the joy of New Year if Man Kee was not there to stuff with nuts and candy? (He wouldn't spit those out, that was for sure). They had enjoyed such a lovely time together, too, last year.

'Younger sister, why don't we have a little celebration of our own? Why don't we have a holiday at Christmas when English people do? Man Kee would be here then.'

Mui's suggestion was one of the first sensible things she had said to Lily in a long time. It wouldn't actually be ante-dating New Year for their own convenience, just *pretending* to; a workable distinction for Lily. It was only really doing on a larger scale what they had already been doing with their elastic day. And such flexibility, Lily told herself, was typically Chinese. Look, she had already talked herself into it. They could have a small party on actual lunar New Year, just for the adults.

A few days before Christmas one of the livestock lorry-drivers presented them with a turkey, not conveniently bald, pimply, and trussed, but a great indignant, living bird. He was taking them to a new farm in Kent, the driver told Mui. They were difficult creatures to transport, capable of sulking and dying just to spite you, which was why they were normally slaughtered on the farm.

'Put its neck across a broom-stick and then do the business,' he advised.

Mr Constantinides, who bore the Chens no ill-will on the Infernal Carapace's account, helped Mui carry the coop into the front room. From there Lily took it into the garden. The bird smelt high, as if it had spitefully died already. What were they to do with it? Serve it as one might chicken, with peas and cashew nuts? Eat it themselves? Sell it? Mince it? (Son might have some.) Then turn it into dumpling stuffing? Keeping it alive was uneconomical. It had already presumably been fattened up for market and would be losing weight with every hour, unless they fed it which was not particularly good business. Already, from her upstairs spy-point, Lily had seen Son scattering uncooked rice grain on the grass in front of the coop for the turkey to peck. It stuck its neck out between the bars in a condescending way. She had taken the tiny fistful of grain from him, holding out the flat of one palm and prising his obstinate little hand open with the other. Then she had put the rice grains in the bin again. The sooner Son learned these business things the better. Mui admitted opening the bin for Man Kee. Lily pursed her lips angrily. How were children meant to learn from adult example under these circumstances? It would be convenient to eat the bird soon. Perhaps it would live up to its reputation and die in the night of exposure.

Late next morning, a frosty morning without snow, the white rime still stretching unbroken from the garden all the way over the allotments, Lily took the kitchen chopper and a saucer into the garden. Chen and Mui followed her, bearing respectively Uncle Lo's two-year-old, quarter-full bottle of Remy Martin and the methylated spirits for cleaning the gas rings. It was Chen's idea to incapacitate the turkey with drink before opening the door. The bird was standing in the coop, rather ruffled, but still very much alive. Lily filled a saucer with purple spirit and set it in front of the turkey. It looked haughtily at the libation, put its beak in it, then turned its back. There was nothing for it. Lily flicked the point of the cleaver into the frozen earth and opened the door. The turkey hopped out. It shook itself and took a few steps sideways, its crop working. It really was, Lily thought, a big, formidable-looking bird. She stepped forwards and the turkey gave ground. Then it moved towards the house. Lily chased and cornered the bird at the back door and it gobbled pompously at her. It was going to be difficult.

Lily called to Mui: 'Go inside and bring me a string and two pieces of plasticine.'

Mui went warily past the turkey which had somehow an angry look about it.

In the meantime, having tried speed and found it a failure, Lily decided to employ more cunning tactics of feint and indirection. Staring backwards in the direction of the gas dome, she sauntered absent-mindedly towards the bird which moved briskly off into the other corner. She took tiny shuffling steps of a few inches at a time. Repeat result. Stupid bird! Didn't it realise it was doomed! Didn't it know there was no way it could escape its fate? It was just postponing things for everyone.

She was bound to catch up with it eventually.

Mui returned.

Lily quickly moulded a heavy lump of plasticine around each end of the string and then swung it round her head in a slow, wide arc, releasing it in the direction of the turkey's legs. As the bird fell, only partially snagged around one foot, Lily jumped on it and seized its neck.

'The chopper, where is it?'

Chen looked vainly.

'Husband, near the bird cage!'

He set off at a run.

Mui came over with the bottle of brandy and jammed its neck into the turkey's beak, tipping the contents down.

'What do you think you're doing, Mui?'

'Sister, I don't want it to feel pain.'

Occupied with holding the bird down, Lily was unable to prevent

Mui pouring away the expensive brandy, most of it on the concrete. She was cross about the waste – on a bird!

Chen handed Lily the cleaver and she rose. 'Hold its legs together!' But she was too late. The turkey was up and lurching from side to side. Lily, angry and excited, missed with her first blow and the second caught the turkey on the wind-pipe and bounced off. The bird dropped on one leg but was immediately up. Lily rubbed the chopper blade briskly against the kitchen windowsill, melting the frost on her make-shift whetstone. The turkey was now against the wall and Lily measured her blow, levering her entire body weight from the waist and channelling it into her long arm. The turkey's head flew off and a surprisingly small amount of blood came from the neck. The headless bird began running in small circles which widened. Lily watched in amazement; there was no killing this bird. Its great feet scratched the ground. She gave a short snort of laughter at its ludicrous appearance. The back door opened and Man Kee emerged. The decapitated bird was now running in a big circle and it went straight for Man Kee who had stepped into its orbit. The bird showed no sign of flagging. Man Kee screamed and ran for his father with the turkey apparently in pursuit. Looking over his shoulder, Man Kee saw the turkey's path would take it to his father before he could reach him and he turned to Mui instead.

Lily was laughing helplessly at the comic sight. How alarmed Son looked over nothing! As Mui gathered Man Kee into the sanctuary of her arms, Lily stepped into the bird's path and tripped it neatly. It fell on its back, legs and claws still stubbornly pedalling. Chopper dripping, Lily went over to Mui. Man Kee was crying and would not look at his mother. Mui took him indoors while Lily brought the twitching turkey into the kitchen.

An hour later she was still plucking and cleaning it. Even without the feathers it was a huge bird. How did you cook it? It would take ages to braise, dismembered, as one cooked duck. Boiling in the huge washing-cauldron would destroy flavour and reduce nutritional value. The oven was too tiny to accommodate the bird, even had Lily been confident enough to attempt this alien cooking.

It was Chen who had the idea.

'Beggar's Chicken!' he suggested.

As Kwangsi-born Lily looked at him blankly, he explained. 'Like the northerners. When poor people stole a chicken they had no pans to cook in, so they put leaves and mud round the chicken and cooked it in ashes.'

What things Husband knew! It was worth trying, though. Lily cut thin strips of salty pork and plastered them on the side of the turkey, glazed it with peanut oil and soya sauce and stuck fennel, garlic, and spring onions on the breast. Then she wrapped the big bird in five layers of the broadest blades of winter greens Husband could find in his patch. Finally, on went the mud. Lily was timid with the first application. It seemed such a barbarous, not to say unhygienic thing to do. There were tiny water-snails in the wet earth Husband brought, and once an actual worm. But the soil was the right sticky, claylike consistency and once the leaves were smeared, Lily packed on the rest of the mud with reckless gusto until she had a crust three inches thick. Chen lit a fire near the compost-heap and when it settled into embers Lily rolled in the big ball that was the turkey and raked hot ash over it.

After some hours, during which they drank tea and ate premature New Year sweetmeats in front of the TV, Lily and Chen went to inspect the clay ball. There was only a rosy glow from the dying fire but when Lily tried to touch the ball she burnt her hand. Chen pushed it up the frozen grass with his hoe, the frost crackling and melting in contact with the hot clay, while Lily sucked her fingers. She marvelled how Father could have immersed his fists in hot charcoal for what must have been agonising three second intervals. The hot ball had left a watery trail that was faintly phosphorescent in the dusk and Lily yearned to cool her scorched hand in it. It was only just four o'clock and it was as if the short day had never been. Indoors she ran an icy tap over her prickling fingers; then she cracked the baked grey clay with a sharp tap from the back of the cleaver. It fell open, as if hinged, into two neat halves. A savoury smell arose and grew richer as Lily cut the string around the leaves to reveal *a green turkey*! Well, not emerald green but definitely a nasty, pale veridian hue, as if it was in the early stages of decomposition. The colour seemed to have got *under* the skin. Slightly disconcerted, to say the least, Lily put the cleaver down and ran the tap again. After a rinse and a rub with a damp cloth, the turkey's flesh grew much paler but unfortunately the tone-down green, a kind of undetectable blue, luminescence rather than colour, was even more unappetising. And when Lily carved deeply into the breast she could see the bird was only half-cooked. The meat was pink and around the joints there were caked flecks of red. It had been in the ashes long enough. Maybe she'd made the crust too thick. Bloody chopped chicken with green ginger sauce might be delicious when prepared by Uncle Lo but a giant half-raw turkey was something other. The meat tasted vile, too, bitter and tough as if the bird's spirit still lingered in its cells.

It was not surprising, then, that Man Kee rejected his portion, even diced as finely as Lily could manage without imperilling her temporarily desensitised fingers. And when he ate all his winter greens she put it down to hunger. Yet next day he spurned the beef mince made for him by the loving hands of his aunt. There was a part of Lily which was gratified to see Mui rebuffed; there was another part which was concerned about Son. Again Man Kee devoured the greens. The pattern was repeated in the evening. Next day Lily gave him a Buddhist dish of textured soya curd, the yellow beans themselves, shaped carrot, Chinese dried fungus, bamboo shoot, tinned mushrooms, Chinese dried mushrooms, and white rice. He ate it all, to the last bean. 'My little monk,' said Lily, and hugged him, but quite why Son had a taste for Mar-mar's cooking again was a mystery. Perhaps it was the lashings of monosodium glutamate.

And there was another mystery which Lily was less happy to leave unsolved. Mui had been starting to find discrepancies when she went through the accounts. Nothing very large at first but there was definitely something amiss. When she calculated the profits they should have been making and set it against the cash she could count, there was a short-fall of £10 per month. This had been going on for three months. Not around £10, not a figure which fluctuated but exactly £10 every month. This was despite the fact that the profit was never a round figure but included shillings and pence. Mui could work it out from the amount of food they bought and the regular sum they set aside for quarterly bills. Then it became a monthly shortfall of £15.

What was going on?

At first Lily wouldn't believe her sister. 'You must have done your sums wrong,' she said carelessly. Or: 'Sure you haven't been eating the food yourself, Mui? That explains less money if we have less to sell. You're a real fatty these days.' But, no, Mui showed her the figures – far too much for anyone to eat.

Then (really disturbing) money started to disappear from the tea tins. This was too much – that money was untaxable. You could add at least a third to the amounts that went missing from there. What was it? A junior kleptomaniac at large in the household? Could Man Kee be stealing? To buy sweets? Surely not. He couldn't reach the tin even if he stood on a chair.

Husband? Lily smiled. Poor, dear Husband. What would he want money for? To keep a concubine perhaps? To pay someone to keep quiet about a concubine in case she went for him with a chopper, wretched man. What a ridiculous thought! She laughed. Poor Husband had no secrets.

Anyway, they were doing so well now they could spare a little money, she supposed. Sacrificial money was the way to think of it. Maybe Mui had got her sums wrong in some mysterious way after all. After that moderate but encouraging first year and the growing pains of the second with Husband sweating in the kitchen, things were getting organised nicely now. Husband's decision to plant them in the wilderness, as it were, had been a brilliant stroke of strategy. She could see that now. The Chinese businesses in more promising-looking areas simply cut each other out of business. Husband had the grace not to gloat; indeed he seemed singularly indifferent to business success, perhaps not wishing to court divine jealousy. As a personal counter-measure, though, Lily burnt a whole series of prophylactic incense sticks in front of god (no need for counterfeit money under prevailing circumstances). God was quite black with smoke now but as ferocious as ever and the mantle of soot surely was appropriate, bearing in mind he was an adoptive Londoner.

TWENTY-FOUR

Surrounded by flowers and baskets of fruit, White Paper Fan held audience in the filthy basement of Number 1000. Two teapots and a dozen or so cups stood on the table, those filled corresponding to the number of clients he had received. He had found jobs – in one case made a note to pressure a powerful New Territories clan into giving a job to an outsider in a seafood restaurant. He had also given money to a sick man and a widow; paid for a parent's funeral. Upstairs in the disused coffee bar with its dusty Gaggia more clients waited patiently, their fruit or flowers by their knees. Night-brother and two guards sat with the Deputy Leader in the basement. Others were stationed unobtrusively in the street and by the basement railings.

White Paper Fan was now receiving two widows who ran a chop-suey counter in Portsmouth. They were vexed by drunken sailors. This was not something White Paper Fan could handle. Night-brother knew he would have to disappoint the women. Self-help was the only remedy here: the iron bar wrapped in newspaper, resorted to after intolerable provocation. Night-brother, a critical spectator of the senior officer's performance, watched with interest.

The 415 officer shook his head in dismay as he listened to the widow's tale. 'Terrible! How terrible!' he interjected. 'But what can I do for you?' He was adopting a pithy, official manner of speaking. 'If I sent men to protect you the hooligans might revenge themselves on you later. Best to make little trouble. Endure. If matters get really serious, then come to me again.'

To Night-brother's surprise, a sympathetic and courteous hearing seemed enough for the two women. White Paper Fan indicated a present of money should be given to them.

The only man whose plea he rejected had requested that his boss should be compelled to give him a tax rebate. Even this man, after a sharp lecture, had received a small cash present.

As the last petitioner was led away, Night-brother commented: 'Very generous.'

White Paper Fan looked at him quickly; there was no trace of irony in the younger man's expression. Nevertheless, the senior officer was curt: 'This is not aimless philanthropy. It has a purpose. We have no responsibility to outsiders. Our only concern is with building our own power.'

Night-brother said: 'Now that you have taught me, I understand.'

'What do you understand?'

'That dominance is not necessarily won and held at the point of the knife.'

White Paper Fan ushered his junior into the car first. As the vehicle turned into Shaftesbury Avenue he said: 'You have shown genuine understanding. No situation ever remains the same. What is appropriate under one set of circumstances becomes inappropriate under another. For a time in Hong Kong crude street-fighting ability became the qualification for high rank and the main criterion of usefulness. That was right for the time and place. Those qualities were most correct for the society then. In another place and another time one would perhaps be justified in looking for other qualities in a leader.'

Night-brother said nothing. But he didn't shift away from the 415 officer. They sat close together in the wide-bodied limousine in a communicative silence.

'I see that there are no serpents mixed with the dragons. Then let the fair begin. Accounts first.' Red Cudgel and the other officers listened to White Paper Fan's accounting. The beads of the abacus clicked. At the end Red Cudgel said: 'Satisfactory. The balance between gambling and white powder has remained the same, although both have increased revenue over the last nine months. Excellent state of affairs.'

White Paper Fan said: 'Excuse my opinion.'

Red Cudgel looked at him with what, on that dead, cratered face, passed for a large degree of surprise.

White Paper Fan said: 'Expansion is good. But it must be strictly controlled. Increase in quantity does not mean increase in quality. Often the reverse. A small family is easy to control. Members of a large family may become undisciplined. At this stage that could be fatal for us.'

'You talk in riddles. Talk plainly to me if you wish to be understood.'

The quality of silence in the room had altered.

White Paper Fan said quietly: 'I mean to say that although we can be satisfied with an increased turn-over we should closely monitor it as well. It may be even bigger than it seems. The reliability of new members is not the same as the oldest servants of family Hung. There are opportunities for self-enrichment in a bigger operation that do not exist in small. They can put squeeze of their own on those we protect. To take an illicit commission from ten thousand pounds is easy, from one thousand hard. I speak figuratively, of course. Also the increased number of members at large can be dangerous as well as a source of strength.'

Red Cudgel said: 'Do you think I am not aware of this? What do you want me to do? Stand on every street corner with all the little brother street peddlers and runners we have and count the cash in their pockets?'

White Paper Fan looked at his abacus.

Red Cudgel said: 'Let it be known. It goes hard with any found cheating his brethren. You did not swear thirty-six solemn oaths lightly who received grass sandals in the Red Flower Pavilion. You swore to be slain under ten thousand thousand knives, annihilated from all points by thunder, perish in a tiger's maw, be struck with 108, 36, and 72 blows. Believe me, little friends, my anger is far worse than any of those things. Let this be known.'

TWENTY-FIVE

Mui had become very plump; had put on so much weight you couldn't really call her plump any more. She was . . . fat. On a man it would have been quite acceptable; could be taken as evidence of prosperity and the ability to maintain an assortment of wives and concubines. On a woman, Lily knew, it was merely gross. Of course. And it was not something she personally liked on a man either. Her views on the male physique had been modelled in childhood around Father. For instance, she much preferred the new slim-line Husband who had evolved out of many hours' toil in the garden, even though the convenient handles of flesh around the hip-bone she had gripped and teased him about had recently melted away. Poor pear-shaped Mui waddled around on her size three feet, carrying piles of foil boxes, looking like a giant spinning-top in her new striped cardigan. A musical one, when she hummed to the transistor. Lily could hear her panting and wheezing when she climbed the stairs to bed, sometimes stopping for a rest half-way up.

She wasn't eating more, so Lily supposed her weight gain was the result of diminished activity, probably motoring to the shops instead of walking, even though she was making more and longer trips to the forecourt. Lily couldn't keep track of her sister's comings and goings any more. Perhaps she should encourage her to take more exercise; though forcing her to walk to the shops again would be too unkind, even in her new, laced Taiwanese sneakers.

'Ah Mui, I think fresh air could be good.'

This subtlest of hints fell on wilful, unhearing ears. So did: 'Really, Husband and Son enjoy gardening so much.' Lily thought her last suggestion particularly generous as it would have left Mui alone with the men in the family while she did all the work. If ungrateful Mui appreciated this, she showed no sign. She ought to have made some acknowledgement. Just because they were sisters didn't mean there was no need for courtesy between them.

Now that Lily had noticed, Mui seemed to be getting fatter by the day. Husband's cardigan was straining at the buttons round her stomach. Her new one no longer fitted her. The thin cloth of her flowered trousers threatened to tear like paper when she bent. Her bottom was like the full autumn moon. Lily didn't think she was being spiteful about this. More often than not, Mui watched TV from the ampler customers' benches instead of the high stool behind the counter.

And, at last, studying Mui's contours and the angle of her spine from the rear, Lily realised what had happened. Was happening. Surely it couldn't be true. Something told Lily it was. Mui was pregnant! Her first instinct was not to rush over and shake her vigorously by the shoulders from behind with a terrible creaking of the bench. No, she wanted to go away, lock herself in the bathroom, and laugh which (she knew) was an appallingly irresponsible reaction. How many weeks, months, gone was Mui? Very difficult to say. Her own experience did not offer a good parallel. She had stayed abnormally slim until late on, though there had been an awful third month of sickness.

But Mui, Lily was certain, hadn't been paying surreptitious dawn trips to the bathroom. She also looked far too weighty, even for her, to be in the first months. So where did that make her? From these speculations Lily naturally began to wonder about other things: you didn't get pregnant without doing something with a man first. She was almost overlooking that rather basic preliminary in her surprise at the *fact* of Mui being pregnant. It was something she associated with young English girls, not her own sister. She couldn't imagine Mui performing the act. Lily laughed, not in a very pleasant way.

Husband now came in, forcing Lily to postpone the questioning she planned. She didn't want him to know yet. She would look a fool if she was wrong. She was positive she wasn't.

Next morning she intercepted Mui as she was returning from the garage. She had just delivered lunch boxes.

'Mui, you are pregnant.' (Lily had decided one could only be blunt.)

Mui kept walking (waddling).

'Eldest sister!'

Mui opened the gate.

'Ah Mui!'

Mui stopped but kept her back to Lily.

'Did you hear what I said?'

'Heard.'

'Hah?' No confirmation or elaboration was about to come from Mui. 'Are you pregnant or not?'

'Don't know.'

'*You don't know!*' Lily's eyes turned to angry slits. She pressed her fists against the sides of her thighs. After ten seconds of silence she stamped her foot angrily. Mui still had her back turned to her. An aitchgevee passing by gave them a friendly toot. Lily realised she shouldn't make a scene in public. She took Mui's arm roughly and brought her, unresisting, to the Infernal Carapace. She bundled Mui in first in case she should resort to slow, undignified flight. But this meant that Mui sat behind the steering wheel in the driver's seat, because of the roped right-hand door, while Lily herself had to take a drop in rank and occupy the front passenger seat. As an afterthought, Lily locked the door-handle from inside.

Now she was able to start on Mui in earnest. 'You don't know? You don't know how children are made either? You want me to tell you?'

Mui stayed silent, annoying Lily more. She hadn't intended to strike conventional outraged attitudes. She had been ready to offer sympathy, humour even. She was being forced into scolding Mui when she had never felt indignant to start with.

'When did you have your last period? Do you remember that?'

'Six months.'

Six months! Lily digested this. Not a clue had Mui given. It was too late to do anything about her pregnancy at this stage. Mui was staring defiantly through the front window and had still not met Lily's eye. In case anyone might see the expressions on their faces Lily switched on the windscreen wipers which worked, just. Not an impermeable screen by any means, but it would have to do. Mui's face had turned a shocked, pasty colour. Lily began to feel sorry for her. Perhaps she had kept her condition secret in order not to worry her family.

'Eldest sister, how did you think you could keep all this to yourself?'

Mui shrugged.

Lily's curiosity took a prurient turn. 'Ah Mui, when did you do it? Where did you do it?'

Colour came into Mui's cheeks again. 'You don't ask *who*, Lily, only where? And when?'

Lily was taken aback. Who did Mui think she was, getting offended all of a sudden? Taking umbrage, under the circumstances, was her own prerogative. A terrible thought struck Lily: had Mui been selling herself? Were those generous tips for services over and above delivering foil boxes? Perhaps Mui had been running a one-woman peripatetic brothel, a lorry-driver's home comforts consolation service. An even more dreadful possibility: surely not Husband? That kind of thing did happen. Something, accurate generalisation from past performance, told her no, and made her smile to herself.

'Mui, how many men did it?'

Mui's amazing answer was to assault her in a flurry of puny fists. Lily seized her sister's arms and pinned the wrists together with her own left hand. Already Mui was out of breath.

'Have you gone mad, Mui?' It would be an awkward possibility if she really had.

Mr Constantinides, coming out of the forecourt, had seen them in the stationary van and was looking at them curiously. Was it hairy Mr Constantinides who had put Mui in the family way? All the more need for secrecy if it was. Lily dropped her sister's wrists and the circulation began to return to Mui's numbed hands.

Lily started to pat Mui's palms with her own, crossing alternate hands, left to right, right to left, in one of the Kwangsi children's games.

'Come on, Mui. Mr Constantinides is looking.'

Mechanically Mui pushed back with her own hands and Lily worked up a rhythm. 'Mui, does the father know?'

(Pat, pat.)

'Doesn't know.'

(Pat, pat.)

'Do you want to tell me who?'

'Don't want to.'

'As you please.'

Lily didn't want to upset her and precipitate another attack at this moment.

'All right, Mui, he has gone back.'

Mui's hands flopped to her chubby thighs. Whatever it was that had inspired her little assault had been discharged. She sat there listlessly. Again Lily felt sorry for her. After all, she was a grown woman. It would have been unnatural, really, for her not to feel certain needs; although Lily could not condone her satisfying them, for then what was the difference between Mui and those shameless English girls? At the same time Lily's pragmatic side strongly reasserted itself without her feeling the least inconsistency. How annoying that Mui could not have taken her into her confidence! She could have given her essential advice which might have averted all this big nuisance; even presented her with a supply of what Lily thought of as her anti-Husband tablets. It was no good regretting these things now. Lily said in a kindly tone: 'Don't fear, Mui. It's not important.' She opened the van door and helped Mui out. Now, she knew, she must make sure eldest sister did not strain or have an accident. Down the garden steps she guided her and placed her in front of the TV. 'I do the running and carrying from now on, Ah Mui.'

An hour later Lily jumped up and raced out of the front door, startling the two or three customers. Eiyah! The windscreen wipers! Too late – the battery was already flat.

As she was coming back she met Mr Constantinides. She dropped her eyes politely as usual. Apart from the fact that Mr C. was so hairy it was quite embarrassing, she didn't at this particular moment want him to ask potentially prying questions about Mui. He did, of course.

'Oy-oy,' he said, a strange greeting Lily could never understand and which seemed peculiar to Mr Constantinides. 'Oy-oy,' she and Mui had said to each other in less stressful times, breaking down into helpless giggles. Occasionally Mr Constantinides gave it such a pitch that he appeared to be saying 'I love you' in a perfect Kwangsi accent. It was already hysterical enough as greeting from a man who looked like a friendly bear. 'Oy-oy,' cheeky Lily would have said straight back to him at almost any other time (had been awaiting the chance for a few weeks). But now she merely twisted her cheek muscles in a watery sort of smile and then looked down quickly to her right; all this without breaking step.

'How's Mui, then? Everything all right with the Darlings, is it?'

Could he be the father brazening it out? No.

'How's your brother, then?'

'Brother?'

'Yes, your brother. The young chap your old man sees every month. He told me he was your brother. Always fills his car up at the garage. He's got a gold Jag. Wealthy young fellow with a big Rolex. Looks like he should be the one doing the hand-out, not your old man.'

'Ah, my brother,' Lily said, determined that if Mr Constantinides was mistaken and confused, he should remain confused and mistaken. He knew a good deal too much about them for her liking already. Going up a few false trails would serve him right. The less people knew about her family the better. These things should be secret.

'My brother very rich. Big man in Hong Kong already.'

She went into the shop feeling a little better.

By now she had decided it would be best not to tell Husband. What he didn't know couldn't trouble him. He was a kind man and she could not for one moment imagine him throwing Mui out of the house but sometimes he was unpredictable. And Lily knew she would have to take her sister's side, disapprove as she might. With luck and good management she and Mui could keep it a secret between themselves, the women of the family. But Mui would have to cooperate or be bullied into obedience.

She proved surprisingly cooperative.

'You have to go to Mrs Law's house,' Lily told her – and the sooner the better. Even Husband's obtuseness couldn't be relied on indefinitely. There was the chance he might guess the truth even before Mui went into labour. Nor, if Lily knew her sister, could Mui be relied on to start at the correct time, always assuming she had given the month of conception accurately. Working from the dates Mui had given her, Lily could see her sister would have to be away between three and four months at least. And then there would be the problem of the baby. Would it be best to part Mui from it at once? Then give her a month to adjust before returning? Bring her straight back? Send the baby to an orphanage? Tell Husband afterwards and bring it up quite openly in the family? Smother it, as poor Kwangsi villagers smothered unwanted girl-children (certainly not).

Mui was acquiescent enough now. It would be a different story, Lily knew, when she had the baby in her arms: within that short, plump person was a core of obstinacy that was as strong in its passive way as Lily's will. It almost vibrated, like a tuning-fork, setting up sympathetic stirrings in herself.

'We shall have to meet our difficulties one by one and surmount them,' Lily said aloud. Mui, Number One difficulty, nodded obediently.

'Mrs Law has become very ill,' Lily told Husband. 'Ah Jik is too old to look after her properly. Mui will have to be away for several weeks.' (Let him have the truth in instalments: he might not want to spare her from the deliveries for three months.) But Husband made no fuss, didn't even suggest Mui might come back for weekends or work a nursing rota with Lily.

'All right, all right, that's fine,' he said. 'Take the car, she shouldn't have to go on the bus or train.'

'Tomorrow I drive her, Husband.'

'Come straight back, though, Lily. Don't stop off anywhere yourself.'

Too bad: she had been going to treat him to nice sausages and smoked duck from Chinese Street. A shame – he deserved it for being so solicitous now. For a moment Lily wondered whether to take him totally into her confidence. Discretion won. And the hoodwinking of Husband was as easy as that.

Lily packed Mui's few belongings into her own Great Wall suitcase. She transferred the week's takings into a recently discovered cavity beneath a floorboard (no predecessor's hoard in it, much to Lily's disappointment). In a white envelope on top of Mui's second cardigan she placed ten £1 notes. Also a photograph of Son in *Toh No Ngaap* jersey. Mui would need new clothes as she got bigger and mustn't be a burden on kind Mrs Law. Lily planned the departure after she had got back from taking Son to school. She didn't want any last-minute weeping upsetting him.

Of course, Mui *was* crying when she got back.

'Did Husband see you?'

Mui shook her head and blew her nose.

Lily took the discreet allotments-gasworks route to the main road. As Husband had warned her, clever of him too, it was a slow, complicated journey in heavy traffic. At length they were crossing the Thames, at low tide, its steep, muddy banks exposed. Through smart Chelsea, Kensington, dingy Kilburn, they rolled. For the last two years they had clearly been living in another city altogether. Along Finchley Road and now they were coming into Golders Green. Left turn and they were in the quiet street where Mrs Law had her flat. Lily took them up the stairs, eschewing the lift in case they met anyone and getting jammed with the suitcase in two sets of interlocking flame-proof doors.

Mrs Law personally opened the door to them, a welcoming smile on her face. Although of course deeply in Mrs Law's debt, Lily was rather brusque with their kindly friend.

'Young ladies, please don't stand on ceremony,' Mrs Law urged them and was disconcerted to have Lily take her at her word as that very single-minded, modern young person swept into the spare bedroom, unzipped the Great Wall suitcase and tipped its contents onto the bed.

'Moon Lily, how charmingly impulsive you are!' Mrs Law exclaimed, recovering herself.

Lily wasn't being deliberately uncouth, though Mui, already embarrassed, was now wishing she was dead in a well. Lily was worried about the time. The drive had taken far longer than she had allowed. She saw Mrs Law's domed transparent clock in the hallway.

'Eiyah! It isn't half past twelve!'

'I am sure my clock is wrong,' said Mrs Law, unwilling to contradict her guest. 'I invite you to eat midday rice, dear Mrs Chen.'

'My face is turned away, Mrs Law. I can't. Son will be leaving school soon.'

'Ah! And how is Son? Still so handsome?'

Lily ignored her, wishing to allude to the real reason for the visit and offer formal gratitude again, as she had done on the telephone. 'Mrs Law ... it's a big nuisance. I must thank you ... '

Mrs Law held her hand up. 'Not necessary, not necessary to say. Mustn't talk like that,' and seeing Lily was genuinely anxious to leave she ushered her to the door. Lily found she was still holding the Great Wall suitcase. She decided she would take it with her – as was only sensible. What use would Mui have for it? She'd bring it with her when she came again.

'See again,' Mrs Law called, keeping the door open until Lily was out of sight down a flight of stairs.

Big nuisance! Lily thought as she sat in a line of jammed traffic in Finchley Road. By the time she crossed the Thames, discernibly higher, over another bridge (she had been forced to follow the other traffic) she was most worried. She would never arrive in time to meet Son. Involuntarily, her foot pressed on the accelerator and she just missed shooting a red light. Coolness makes for celerity, she reminded herself. But all the considerable icy self-possession she was able to muster couldn't get her outside the school gate before half past two. The street was quite empty; all the children had gone home. Not even the lollipop woman was there who guided them over the main road. Lily felt sick. Might the teacher, young and kindly faced, have kept Man Kee until she arrived? But the playground was empty.

Maybe teacher had telephoned Husband. Lily imagined Son wandering in some wilderness on bomb sites and boarded-up houses (faint hope: a kindly Indian person bus conductor might have given him a free ride), the prey of wicked kidnappers and devil deviants. Or run over by a lorry in the thundering main road. Would Husband ever forgive her? Could she ever forgive Mui?

All the way home she kept an eye on both sides of the road for a little walking figure. Vainly, she knew, for how could he find his way back? Logic, not instinct, told her to make sure he was not at the house before she embarked on an exhaustive street by street search of the neighbourhood. She wouldn't tell Husband yet. Lily slipped in quietly so as not to reveal she was back. And there, plainly seen through the kitchen window, was Son. He was in his red wellingtons and the wicked boy was pouring precious medicine from her big brown bottle *onto his plant!* Husband was hoeing his vegetables.

Lily rapped loudly on the window. Husband waved at her. Man Kee dropped the bottle in his barrow and wheeled it up to the door. Lily took the bottle from him, her anger melting into relief. 'Son, you mustn't do that.' (How had he reached the bottle? How had he got home?)

'Did Ah Par-par take you home?'

'Walked road.'

'Not all the way!'

'All the way.'

And only seven-*sui* next New Year! Lily marvelled; she had given birth to a genius of resourcefulness. 'Next time you must wait for me, Son.'

Man Kee nodded.

'All right, play your gardening.' She rinsed the medicine bottle out under the cold tap. Unfortunately she had none of the special ingredients for the elixir now but the big bottle could be useful. She had seen one with a ship in it at the seaside; a sailing ship, not the kind of ship Husband had said he had seen through his telescope. Maybe Husband could insert a model into it, or she could use it for rinsing his hair in the wash basin.

TWENTY-SIX

With Mui gone the work was even harder than Lily had feared. Mui had certainly pulled her weight; Lily was able to see that now. Husband just managed to supply all the orders from the kitchen again, though this meant that he had to leave the garden to grow by itself (Lily's words). The brunt of the extra work fell on Lily herself. At the counter things were only slightly more hectic, Saturday night seven days of the week. What sabotaged everything was having to go out to the aitchgevees. Lily would rapidly parcel the silver containers, take money, delicately but decisively operate the keys of the till with the tips of oily fingers; the customers would shift a place down the pews; the crowd would be slowly whittled away. Then the phone would ring with the orders relayed by Mr Constantinides. Lily would have to run out with the chop suey or egg fu yung and when she returned apprehensively through her own front door, she would find the walls lined with leaning customers. Feeling small and vulnerable in her sneakers on which someone might accidentally tread with their big boot, she would pick her way through the crowd. Coming in under the gaze of strangers, she felt like a usurper of her own business, a confidence trickster taking money under false pretences. After slipping as unobtrusively as she could behind the counter, she would begin to cope with the new orders. On the whole the customers were good-tempered about the delay but Lily couldn't help feeling harrassed. Her face felt stiff with all the charmingly apologetic smiles she was dispensing (without very much discrimination). She doubted she could keep it up for four months. Maybe she should have kept pregnant Mui behind the counter, told Husband, and done the deliveries herself.

At least Son was being a good boy. Mui might have been a disturbing influence on him. He was quite happy to sit with Ah Mar-Mar and watch television. 'Son, do you want to play gardening? You don't have to stay here.'

He wouldn't bother to answer or even shake the big head, and Lily's arm would tighten around his stomach, protuberant with the Eight Precious Grand Vegetarian Ensemble she had improvised for him.

'Handsome boy,' she would say, kissing the top of his head for the first time in a while. She felt more able to stroke, squeeze, sniff him when Mui wasn't there; less conscious of the need to bring him up within a proper framework of values. Why should she be cast in the role of disciplinarian all the time? The one who enforced the rules would be respected but never popular. It was Husband's job. Surely? When Mui was here all Husband wanted to do was poke his rows of vegetables with that long tool of his. Now he was too busy in the kitchen to look up for ten seconds at a time.

One Friday evening Mr Constantinides rang with an order when the room was particularly crowded. It was imperative to clear it. Already the walls were plastered with standing customers who were beginning to form a second row; soon there might be a crocodile's tail of them going out of the door, up the steps, and through the gate. Lily was getting flustered and snappish with poor Husband. (With her rational side, she knew it wasn't his fault he couldn't keep pace with the orders.) Five minutes later the phone rang again.

'Are you coming or not? I've got three lorries out here.'

'I coming.' (Strain eroding improving grammar.)

She was in the middle of taking cash from a woman customer. Her sweet and sour prawns and rice cost five and sixpence. 'Please give my son. No necessary give sixpence this time.' Picking up cartons which had just come through the hatch, Lily hurried to the forecourt but was not too flustered to joke: 'Lucky special discount!' which raised a surprising laugh from the customers.

She didn't know the three aitchgevees, unshaven men in shirt-sleeves, anonymous in the elevated brightness of their cabs, but her own silhouette was obviously distinctive despite the dark.

'Where's Mui?' two of them wanted to know and, really startling her, 'All right, Lily?' one of them greeted her. Clearly, a whole new social life had sprouted for Mui in the forecourt; probably a new personality to match. The drivers were loyal. Her tips were smaller than Mui's for which Lily, not a blinkered businesswoman, could respect them.

Mr Constantinides came from his bright glass office. 'Sorry about that, Mrs Chen,' he said (boomed, near-shouted). 'All of it was getting on top of me, too. Must be something in the weather. Everyone's getting the hump with everyone else, aren't they?'

Lily formed a vivid picture of Mr C. with a large mound of bone and flesh, somewhat like a Tibetan dromedary's, swelling out of his hairy back.

'Glad you can smile about it anyway. Your old man wasn't doing too much smiling last week; nor was your brother. Can't sponge off you for ever, can he? He wasn't getting too much change out of your old man.'

'Ah.'

'Still, you know what they say – what *we* say anyway – when family quarrels it's the worst of all. Bitter it can be. Like my bleeding mother-in-law, pardon the French ... '

Lily was far too busy to waste her time listening to this stream of inconsequential nonsense. 'Mr Constantinides, excusing me. Big hurry for customer. Sorry.' She rushed off, wondering what he had been talking about.

Back at the counter, Son had a ball of plasticine weighing down four ten shilling notes and was reaching for a foil box on the hatch, arms overhead in the manner of a porter fording rapids. He took another note, climbing on the high stool to accept it.

'Son!' Lily was amazed.

Chen smiled at his wife through the hatch, more delighted than Lily in that Man Kee was not merely providing convenient help, as he was for his mother, but fulfilling his father's deepest aspirations for him. At least putting his Jumping Jacks on the first rung of the ladder leading to multiple proprietorship of restaurants. His son's future had come to the forefront of Chen's concerns recently. He was surprised how much comfort thinking about Man Kee's life could afford him. Another decision had also surprised him by lifting a terrible tension from within him. It should have made him feel worse but it hadn't.

At this stage of things, of course, Man Kee could only receive the exact amount of money; he was unable to work out change or operate the till. (For that matter his father couldn't either.) There had to be a certain amount of trust reposed in the customers. The way to look at it, Lily told herself, was this: Number One priority – Son was learning the business; Number Two – under present circumstances any help she got was worth having. To maximise Son's usefulness, though, she decided it would be best to rationalise the menu. She would make all prices not only round figures but also simple fractions of a pound, and she would introduce a minimum charge of ten shillings for two dishes. Rice, prawn crackers, Whore Lock, would have to be increased to a larcenous four shillings; outrageous, she knew, but the prices of their main courses still under-cut the kebab counter. If anyone complained she could point to Man Kee as the reason; he would have provided them with cover twice now. But none of the customers objected; they might not even have noticed. She realised they had been too modest in their approach when they started. Clever Son had no difficulty working out the correct amounts. She explained, chanting: 'One item equals one brown cash, two items equals one green cash, three items equals one brown cash, add one green.' She thought of putting up a notice: HELP BOY. GIVE EXACT CHANGES ONLY, like the sign on the buses requesting the passengers to aid the conductor but decided it might be an incitement to defraud.

'Now, Son, how much brown cash equals one green cash?'

'Twice ten shillings is one pound.'

'Son!'

'Ah Mar-Mar, we play buying things at school in play-shop with plastic meat and pretend-money.'

'Clever boy.' Kiss. 'But bad to tell lies, Son.'

Man Kee was most useful at night when the room filled with customers. This was when she had to leave him for the forecourt most often. In the afternoons she allowed him to trundle his barrow round the garden. In the evening, when he was bored with TV, she would let him sleep on her knee. When she was called to the dark forecourt she would gently place him on the seat she had vacated; he was like a little dozing Buddha. She would rouse him by squeezing both his arms at the same time. He never cried or complained, even though through some unfortunate coincidence he had a trick of falling asleep when his mother needed him. Other times she would lean forward over his slumped head to check he was resting, only to find his eyes open, blank, looking at nothing in particular. To get a bearing on what he was gazing at, Lily would place her cheek next to his and follow the line but it was never anything significant: a Whore Lock bottle, a folded newspaper, empty space even.

School began again. Now Man Kee stayed an extra two hours, until half past three. This was highly inconvenient as at this time Lily would be in the thick of slivering meat and chopping vegetables for Chen to cook in the evening. For a week she continued to pick him up in the Infernal Carapace but at last it was simply not possible. Lily wondered whether Son was old enough to make the five mile journey unaided, regularly. He had done it once already, of course. 'Son,' she addressed him as she knelt in front of his stool, holding him at arm's length by his tiny biceps which were about the size of large whelks.

'Wake up, Son. No, I don't want you to sell things now. I want to ask you if you can come home by yourself.'

'Can.'

'Not walking road, Son. I mean taking bus.'

Man Kee looked doubtful.

'Ah Mar-Mar will show you tomorrow.'

Lily was as good as her word. Next afternoon she took the bus to school and showed Son the stop. She was a little late and Man Kee was on his own outside the school gate. She held his mittened hand, her own mottled and blue with cold. Five minutes later came the bus.

'See, Son, every day you can catch bus at this time if you miss first one.'

She waited for it to slow down.

'You must be very careful when you get on. Hold pole.'

The bus showed no sign of slowing.

It swept right past them. Lily's head swivelled indignantly to follow it as the big double-decker disappeared round the downhill bend in a gust of dried old leaves and two newspaper pages. 'Ah Mar-Mar, you must put hand out to stop bus.'

'Not necessary. No good bus-conductor.' Lily was rather put out.

'Son, make sure bus conductor is black person. Indian person even better. Understand or not?'

'Understand, Ah Mar-Mar.'

'Son.'

'What, Mar-Mar?'

'Bad to talk to strange man on bus. Understand or not?'

'Don't understand.'

'Never mind. Bad to do it.'

'Good.'

Another bus came round the top of the hill. Lily was relieved to see the service was frequent. Erratic, unreliable, and utterly arbitrary, but frequent. 'Son, stick hand out.' (Good practice with additional consideration that Lily would not have to lose face in front of Son by admitting her earlier mistake.) 'Clever boy. Hold pole now. Swing leg. Good!'

Man Kee, quite a normal little boy for his age, headed upstairs, stamping his Jumping Jacks on the steps. 'No, Son, sit downstairs. Upstairs dangerous for boy.' Lily was at pains to find out the exact half-fare to the stop at the end of their road, and also the name of the stop.

She drummed it into Man Kee at home. 'Repeat, Son. "*Four please, sir. Constantinides Cars*".'

'Four please, sir. Constantinides Cars.'

'Clever Son.'

She made him say it again before she put him to bed at ten o'clock that night and again in the morning in the van as she dropped him at school.

'Don't forget, Son. Also remember: bad talk to strange person.'

Some older boys going through the gate gesticulated at them. What could they be possibly laughing at? Lily wondered. She waved cheerfully back. Probably playmates of Son's. She called Man Kee back through the window. 'Show Mar-Mar your four pennies. Good. Now put in your pocket and put handkerchief on top like I showed.'

Full of misgivings she could not conquer, Lily was waiting for him at the stop at 3.45. She had only meant to go to their front gate at first but her emotional side got the better of her. Her face relaxed as she saw the small figure, well back on the open platform of the bus. There was a nice Indian bus conductor holding him so he wouldn't fall off the edge. (Should have thought of that beforehand, she rebuked herself.)

'Were you frightened because Ah Mar-Mar didn't come?'

Man Kee shook his head.

'Brave boy,' Lily congratulated him, not really believing Man Kee. Father would have been proud of him, she thought, her eyes misting slightly as the well-metalled alien suburban road became just for a moment a dustier, bumpier, more odorous track from the past. How

Father would have loved a grandson to carry on his tradition!

Man Kee had a good sleep on her knee between 8 and 10 p.m. A little after the hour Mr Constantinides relayed two orders and Lily woke Son. As she was coming back in the dark she thought of robbers hiding behind the petrol pumps and hedges. One could hardly have made the journey, even with the little money she had taken, unarmed in Kwangsi, home of brigands. Tiger forks and muskets would have been necessary. Perhaps she ought to start taking an iron bar in newspaper. She really couldn't defend herself without a weapon against determined men, wiry Cantonese, let alone westerners or huge black persons. Let them just try if she had something in her hand, though! And when she got old Man Kee could fend for his mother.

She was greeted by a thoroughly disagreeable sight when she got in. A group of young English girls had lifted Man Kee off his stool, on to the counter, and were petting him. There was a lot of giggling and exclaiming over the velvet skin of his cheeks which the English girls were stroking with the backs of their pink hands. Lily was chagrined to see Man Kee was rather enjoying himself. She snatched him off the counter. 'Not playing boy. Boy working,' she snapped. What were they doing out at this scandalous hour? They were really bad girls. She could hardly throw them off the premises – she wanted their money, after all – but Lily treated them to her frostiest manner. After they left, cheerful and completely unabashed to her annoyance, she chided Man Kee.

'Son, what did Mar-Mar say about not speaking to strange people?'

'Ah Mar-Mar, you said not talking to strange man on bus.'

'Bad to tell lie, Son.'

'Ah Mar-Mar, I don't tell lie.'

'Son!'

Lily raised her finger, indicating not another word was to be said on the subject. Man Kee looked distressed but was too tired to argue. A little later he fell asleep, giving sighing little snores, so that Lily had to put him to bed in his room, tucking him up with great tenderness.

She continued taking him to school in the mornings. Logically speaking, if he could make the trip in the return direction, he was quite competent to undertake the forward journey. Lily's motive related to herself rather than Man Kee. In the same way as she used to force soup on Chen, she felt she would have been failing in her maternal duty if she had not inconvenienced herself on Man Kee's behalf at least once every day on a routine basis.

Unfortunately here, as with the bad girls, Son was to betray her.

She was lovingly watching him suck up his piping hot breakfast bowl of rice congee (similar-looking to the porridge the glowing schoolchildren seemed to enjoy so much on the TV advertisements) when she felt a tremendous surge of affection for him. (So liberating with Mui gone!) 'Son, are you cold?' Despite his shake of the head, she turned on a gas ring. 'Don't fear, Mar-Mar is taking you to school.'

'No need.'

'What did you say, Son?'

'No need.'

She couldn't believe he was rejecting her like this. 'You don't *want* Ah Mar-Mar to take you to school?'

No response.

'Son, that is most unnatural.' Lily was more hurt than she had ever been. So hurt she couldn't even scold ungrateful Son.

'Big boys laugh at old car.'

Lily, hot with pain and indignation, stopped with her hand on the gas knob. So that was it! 'Son, don't listen to them. Our car is stronger than new car.'

Man Kee looked unconvinced. There were times when he was maddeningly like his father. 'Pack satchel now.'

Man Kee scrambled off the stool, eager to be away from unpredictable Mar-Mar whose changes of mood were confusing and not a little frightening.

Lily drove Man Kee to school in purse-lipped silence. Two hundred yards from the gate she flicked out the side-indicators and drew up to the kerb. Man Kee looked at her. She put a hand on top of his black thatch and stroked down a spiky tuft which sprang up again. She said softly: 'Son, nobody can see you here. Walk carefully on the pavement.' She watched him go inside the gate safely before executing a neat three-point turn and driving home.

TWENTY-SEVEN

After six weeks came Mui's letter. Lily knew what it was even before she saw the Golders Green postmark; the only mail *they* got was in the form of brown envelopes with those threatening transparent panes for the address. Mui's was addressed in English in her clear block capitals to a Mrs Chen. It had been stamped at the post office at 3.30 p.m. the previous day, at about the time (Lily estimated) that Man Kee must have been boarding his homeward bus and she had been dicing carrots. Mid-afternoon was an odd time, Lily thought, to post a letter. She tried to reconstruct the circumstances under which it had been written. Perhaps at night, Mui toiling away by lamplight until the early hours, rising later than she realised and rushing, so far as her condition allowed her, to the post-box, maybe office itself. Or perhaps she had risen early, shivering, a coat thrown over her pyjamas, worked on the letter till the afternoon and just managed to catch the van as it drew away from the pillar-box. Unlikely; anyway Mrs Law's house was well-heated, so she wouldn't have been wearing a coat. Lily put the envelope down, unopened, and stirred Man Kee's rice gruel in the pot just before it was going to burn.

'Ah Mui has written a letter to give us, Son.'

Man Kee tried the hot gruel.

'Blow on congee, Mar-Mar.'

Lily obliged. 'Good to eat?'

'Good.'

'Handsome boy.' Lily played with that recalcitrant tuft of hair. 'You have some peanuts and sweet things in your satchel, Son. Quickly now, you will miss bus.' She walked with him to the stop, saw him safely on and watched it round the corner. Did he stamp up to the top deck once round the corner?

Home again, she at last opened the letter which, naturally, was written in Chinese: *Younger sister: Mrs Law is very kind to me. I eat rice four times a day with dishes of meat, chicken, fish, and egg at every meal. Not to mention tea and savoury and sweetmeat snacks at odd times of the day as well as late at night, and plenty of fruit. I owe all this kindness to Mrs Law. I watch plenty of television. Mrs Law has a big TV but reception is poor in this part of London and the picture is not as good as on my little TV. I mean our TV, of course. Previously, I found the house hot but I am used to it now. Tell Man Kee he is often in my thoughts. Give my respect to Brother-in-law. Lily, please send my Ho Yeh calendar on the wall in my room. You forgot to pack. I pay extra stamp money when I see you again. Do this for me. In Mrs Law's house. Your elder sister, Moon Blossom.*

Lily's face had creased into a scowl while she read this insolent missive. She stamped her foot and crumpled the letter as soon as she had read the last line, then threw it into the waste-bin. Once again she asked herself: just who exactly did Mui think she was? Not a hint of contrition anywhere. Lily hadn't been expecting a formal apology for the inconvenience Mui had caused but this swanking about central heating and incessant snack-taking was insupportable. Then Mui had the gall to pass on a message to Son and criticise Lily for omitting to pack the calendar. No thanks, incidentally, for the £10 in the white envelope – which was hardly going to cover four luxurious meals a day for eight weeks or more.

Lily sat down at the counter and picked up one of Son's brown crayons, lying handily there. *Elder sister* (nobody could say she didn't observe etiquette) *have you no shame?* she began; then amended herself. *Elder Sister, you have no shame. Not only do you bring disgrace on our family but you show a proud and ungrateful spirit to those who have helped you . . .* The crayon fairly drilled through the paper as Lily viciously described the characters from right to left in a series of crude horizontal and vertical strokes and abrupt hooks and dots. The crayon felt sticky on the paper and gave little variation in thickness but it conveyed her anger better than the finest brush. After covering two sheets of brown wrapping-paper she ended: *I respectfully give you my letter, your younger sister, Moon Lily.* Let Mui put her head under a pillow for very shame when she got that, Lily thought with satisfaction as she read the letter through again. Fruit and savoury and sweetmeat snacks at all times of the day and night indeed! While she did all the work at home in the meantime. One might think kind Mrs Law was running a high-class inn for fallen women. As they were temporarily out of envelopes (the last having gone with a card of national insurance stamps inside) Lily put the letter for safe-keeping in the cash till. It was the last place Husband would stick his hand in. But she had written the rage out of herself, she found. Looking at the letter, when she emptied the till late that night she discovered she no longer wished to hurt Mui.

She found her tone a little excessive. What if Mui decided to take her own life when she read it and realised the extent of her misbehaviour? (as deranged, pregnant Mui was quite capable of doing). Lily tore the wrapping-paper into small pieces after thriftily hesitating whether to use it for a customer's foil boxes. You never knew, it might end up in the hands of a Cantonese.

Two weeks later another letter: *Lily: Our TV has broken down here. Yours may blink but at least it works. We rent one in the meantime. I forgot to thank you for your money in the case. It was not necessary but very kind. Your elder sister, Moon Blossom.*

Lily pretended to be grumpier than she really felt while she read the letter. At the end she gave a little gruff grunt. At least Mui was now showing some loyalty to the family, even if rental was reprehensible and un-Chinese. She might be missing them all now, for all the comforts at Mrs Law's.

Then came the postcard from Mrs Law herself, after a long silence. This informed them that Mui had given birth to a girl (five pounds).

Chen picked the card off the newspapers.

Lily had missed this communication in the second post as it merged so closely with the newsprint on the floor.

Husband handed it to her stolidly, without comment. He went to the kitchen and began washing vegetables. Lily flushed as she read the card. This was not how she had wanted him to find out. Would he think of it as a big betrayal? How *stupid* of Mrs Law to send a card; you might think she had actually wanted to publicise the fact.

She opened the kitchen door with uncharacteristic timidity.

'When is Ah Mui back?'

'Soon, Husband.'

'Good. We need her. Little niece can share Son's room.'

'Ah.' Lily occupied her fidgety hands with stripping leaves from a cabbage.

'No need, Lily. I do.'

'Husband, you are not angry she left home and we didn't tell you?' Chen shook his head. He was silent. His adam's apple worked.

The door-bell tinkled. 'Sell things now, Lily.'

'As you say, Husband.'

At the counter, she mis-keyed on the till, calculated the change wrongly on the corrected sum, and had to write down the error. When she juggled with the figures on the next customer's purchase, he accused her of trying to cheat him. Mui could have cleared the air with a few lucid, well-chosen sentences. Lily, already flustered and guilty about other things, had a job of it when her muddled explanation was so obviously at odds with the culprit's manner. After the muttering customer had gone, she had to have a good, strong glass of tea before she was herself again. She hoped he wasn't a regular customer she might now have lost.

TWENTY-EIGHT

But Mui didn't want to bring her daughter to live with them.

She was adamant.

Lily had been proud of Husband's kindness. 'He is a good man,' she informed Mui with faint condescension. 'You can bring Niece here.'

Mui said nothing but quietly unpacked her new case.

'Why didn't you tell me you were coming, Mui? I could have taken our car. Taxi is very expensive.'

'No need, Lily. Big nuisance.' Changing the subject, Mui asked: 'Is Man Kee well?'

'Well.'

'Taller?'

'No. Mui, Niece can share Son's room.'

Mui sighed, 'She stays with Mrs Law.'

'No, Mui. You don't understand. Husband says she can live with us.'

'Younger sister, it is you who does not understand. It is better for her to stay in Mrs Law's house.'

It was some time before Lily realised Mui was not just showing the proper humility of one in her position. Lily had just got over worrying about what 'people', meaning Mr Constantinides, garage-mechanics, aitchgevees, not to mention regular customers, were going to make of the new addition to the household. Now she was put out. There she was feeling sorry for Mui, only to be rebuffed. Her face showed bewilderment, annoyance, hurt pride. She didn't trouble to conceal it from Mui, as she would have done with a stranger.

Mui smiled at her crestfallen sister. 'Better for everyone.'

'Our house not good enough, I suppose?' Lily enquired,

aggressively. This was the easiest way to recover from her surprise, hurt, and embarrassment. 'Son not good enough to share room with Niece?'

Mui said: 'Don't talk like that, Lily. She is a girl. There is no place for a girl in this family. Do you understand what I am telling you? No place for a girl. I want the best life for her. I want the best life for Nephew. Do you understand what I am telling you, younger sister? Mrs Law is rich. She has plenty of money and she is kind.'

Lily was silenced. There was nothing strange about this kind of adoption in the China of their childhoods. Uncles might sponsor the education of a gifted nephew, granddaughters might go to live with their grandmothers. But then Mrs Law wasn't a relative.

'We owe much to Mrs Law. She is lonely.'

For Lily this was to look at the whole affair in a completely new light. So Mui actually thought she was doing her benefactress a favour; her values must have become seriously distorted. Lily tried another line. 'Ah Mui, won't you miss your baby?' She wished to insinuate that Mui was abandoning her daughter and also to hint at unhappiness to come. (A sense of fair play was notably lacking in Lily's own scale of values.) To this Mui said simply: 'Yes. I will miss the baby.'

Looking forward to a brisk argument, Lily was taken unprepared by Mui's admission and at this point she owned defeat. 'All right, Mui. Now come and drink tea with Husband.' She embraced her. 'I am glad you are home again, eldest sister.'

Mui was as hard-working as ever. There was no moping, no tears. Sales picked up again. Forecourt tips returned to their old level once Mui was delivering. 'Regular service resumed,' as the TV card said. Husband could potter about the garden weeding and watering to his heart's content with Son's assistance.

While Mui was away Son seemed to have forgotten about her. In the early weeks of her absence he had asked for her by name a few times, then stopped mentioning her. Now she was back he took hardly any notice of her. Lily was both gratified and alarmed. Obviously pleased because she had supplanted a serious rival; worried because Son seemed so fickle. Might someone replace her in his affections with equal ease? Surely not. Wasn't the bond between mother and son one of the most basic and natural of all relationships? Still, she watched him closely. Bored with spying on the gardening, not the most eventful of activities, she took to watching him as he slept. She would pay quick trips upstairs or abandon Chen at three in the morning for a quick reconnaissance. This could be inconvenient and draughty. It would have been much easier to steal glances at him as he took money at the counter or played with his toys on the pews when the room was empty but an important requirement of Lily's full satisfaction was that Son should be defenceless, unconscious, as she inspected his relaxed features for clues to incipient traits of character. Over the years she had gleaned much from the expressions that had passed over Husband's sleeping face but there was neither history nor as yet a future to be discerned on Man Kee's innocent little countenance. The big head was comfortably supported by the plump pillow; the shock of black hair spilled down on the embroidered linen case; and his mouth was turned down at the corners in the subtlest of happy smiles. Not a traitor's face, Lily would think with relief, only to feel need for re-confirmation hours later.

Man Kee hadn't forgotten Mui so quickly, though. Of course, he remembered her, the pleasant person who always had something nice for you to eat, whether it was a hot snack or just an orange jelly candy or liquorice plum; who was so much softer than hard, sharp Mar-Mar when she cuddled you; who made a friendly hissing when you tiddled instead of pushing your back in a rude and impatient way.

Through no fault of Mui's, Man Kee was soon to revise this charitable opinion of his aunt. Mui was very keen to take him to Mrs Law's and, of course, to her daughter. 'Please, Lily,' she begged Man Kee's mother.

Even before asking, Mui had known Lily would object without ever giving a specific reason. To argue would be to make her more obstinate. Mui carried on with her duties perhaps with a touch more cheerfulness than usual, and, in the end, as Mui expected, Lily relented. In fact, she even offered to drive them. Mui sensibly declined this piece of generosity.

'Just make sure he's back for school,' Lily warned at the bus stop.

But for Man Kee, the weekend was a disaster. Mrs Law was utterly engrossed in the baby – which no one had warned him about. She said 'Handsome boy!' in only the most perfunctory and absent-minded way and none of the attention Ah Jik lavished on him could make up for this first neglect of his pampered life.

He was *very* pleased to be going home on the bus on Sunday evening and got more and more boisterous as Mui became quiet. At home Mar-Mar had something nice for them to eat and after Mui had retired quietly upstairs to her room and, unusually, shut her door, Lily startled Man Kee.

'Did you like baby, Son?'

'Didn't like it.' Man Kee was surprised that his mother should know about the baby. If she knew so much already there was no point in withholding anything from her. 'Whose baby, Mar-Mar? Is it Mrs Law's baby?'

'Yes, Son, she found it.'

'Ah Mar-Mar, did you find me?'

'No.' Lily changed the subject. 'Did you have good play or not?'

'Bad. I didn't like it.'

'But Auntie Law gave you lucky money, Son. You showed me. You can use to buy pencil or study book.'

'Bad play,' Man Kee repeated obstinately. 'Nobody was my friend.'

Lily was pleased; he must have missed Mar-Mar then. She needed to be sure of one thing, though. 'Son, no one smacked your leg, did they?'

He shook his head.

Good. She wouldn't have liked that. 'Now help Mar-Mar count till money. Clever boy.'

From this time on Man Kee went once a month to spend the weekend at Mrs Law's. Mui would have liked to have taken him every time she went but she and Lily had compromised. At first, Lily had tried to restrict Mui to a fortnightly visit – it really was extremely hard work on Friday and Saturday, although Sunday didn't matter so much – but Mui had got quite upset about this. She had wanted to go every weekend – taking Man Kee, too. They had finally agreed she could go three times a month on her own and take Son on one of these trips. One weekend in every month would be spent at the counter; Mui would also stay on public holidays. And if Son had enjoyed himself more on his first visit Lily might not have released him at all. Knowing it only made him love her more, she was content to let him go regularly. And there was also need for a bridge between the two parts of the family. Mui must not become separated from them. Beneath all the everyday surface of irritation, recrimination, and squabbling, Lily acknowledged that this should be a rock-bed principle. Mui herself could not be the link in this human chain. It was fitting that Son should be the ambassador for his mother and father. It would be nice if he could become more of an elder brother than a cousin to his little relative. He could supply a little beneficial male influence as well. And if the two children knew and played with each other, saw each other grow up, then the link would be continued into the next generation. How could one fail to approve of this? Lily thought. Anyway Mrs Law might remember him in her will if she saw enough of him. Her handsome Son must be far more charming than any mere girl of Mui's. (Typical of Mui to produce a girl.) And typically too, Mui fell in with her sister's arrangements without fuss. Only Man Kee was unhappy. He didn't like the idea of regular weekends at Mrs Law's at all.

'Ah Mar-Mar, bad to send me,' he protested. 'I don't like it.' But 'Do what I say, Son,' she would command, with a strange smile on her face, half-pain, half-pleasure. In arguing with him it was as if she was overcoming the slacker side of herself, and she enjoyed the pang of sending him away all the more. She was quite self-righteous about it; she extracted every possible ounce of pathos and sacrifice from the situation. If Mui resented the parade of Lily washing Man Kee's ears, putting on his best clothes (unsuitable for playing on the floor with Ah Jik), and waving her handkerchief until the bus rounded the corner half a mile down the road, she never allowed herself to show it. And strangely enough, Man Kee began to reconcile himself to the visits as well, for Mrs Law had started to pay excessive attention to him again.

It was not just the baby which had caused her to ignore him. She had been, and was still, genuinely fond of him. But the events of the last few months had affected her kind heart greatly. Her commitment to Mui's welfare and the baby's was total and in the rawness of her feelings she had been unable to dissimulate with a surface of impersonal good manners; behaviour which was so ingrained that under normal circumstances she would not have failed to employ it, even in her dealings with an intelligent and sensitive five and a half year old boy.

Talking into the night with Mui, Mrs Law had learned a great deal about her family. She had felt both anger and pity. Her earlier worry that Chen might be maltreating the girls had finally been put to rest. But she had been chagrined to learn details of Lily's treatment of her sister, details which Mui had mentioned unwittingly. She began to develop a deep dislike of Lily: one which she would naturally never show. Several times she tried to persuade Mui to stay. 'There is a home here for you,' she urged.

But Mui had smiled a sad, determined little smile. 'No. Younger sister and Brother-in-law need me. And the business would not work without three people. Maybe when Man Kee is older or things change. Nothing stays the same for ever.' Mrs Law left matters there for the time being.

When Man Kee came, Mrs Law had been unable to see him as anything other than Lily's representative. After a struggle she forced herself to give him time and affection – more than she had given before. And before long she had seen that, after all, he was just a little boy and, later, that his aspirations were not his mother's, whatever she might think. In that might lie her punishment, Mrs Law thought without vindictiveness.

TWENTY-NINE

It was at this time that Chen's mother died. Her death took the family by surprise. She had always enjoyed robust good health. Unlike her husband whose health had been undermined over the years by tuberculosis, malaria, and a dose of typhoid, and who by now could only just move his skilled, arthritic old fingers, she had not suffered more than a few days' illness since she had married into the new village. She had dropped dead, just like that, from an initial stroke brought on by a lifetime's salt-rich diet of dried fish and soya sauce. She had just picked up her wooden bucket to return home from the communal tap when she collapsed.

There was now a big problem with the old man. None of the sons living in the village had the room to take him. His own ancient house, one of the oldest in the village, in the early row of habitations hard against the mountainside, was spectacularly dilapidated, with a leaking roof, cracked floor, crazy single window, and malodorous cess-pit. He had spent his son's remittance money on feasting and gambling, quite legitimately of course as was his right, instead of building the kind of two-storey concrete and corrugated iron pill-box that other sons and other remittances had constructed on the settlement's outskirts.

None of the sons wanted to move their families into the parental house, though the old man could not just be left there on his own. Already their children were sleeping a minimum of three, and in one case five, to tiny rooms. The contingency of their *father's* death had not been overlooked by his sons. One or other of them could have squeezed the old lady in. She could have slept in the same room as her daughter-in-law, her son moving to sleep with the children. Rotation of homes and sons would have ensured the continued propagation of the line and the satisfaction of other needs. But such an arrangement was not possible for the old man who, in any case, was entitled to some stability in his last days. The obvious solution – the *only* solution, the other sons agreed – was to send him to live with his son in England. There he would eat fat pork every day, be honoured by daughter-in-law and the as yet unseen grandson, and generally speaking live in the lap of luxury. Chen didn't so much receive a letter; he inherited a *fait accompli*.

Lily was not displeased. Having the old man live with them completed the structure of the new life she had made for herself. She found it fulfilling: wife, mother, and now dutiful daughter-in-law. In taking on these new and successively more demanding roles she had a sense of advance in her life. Respect for age had always been a fundamental moral principle with her. She looked forward to the chance of putting her ideals into practice, the more so in this alien country where such respect was notably lacking. She looked forward, too, to showing off to Husband's father her nice home, her flourishing business (it had been her idea and she did all the hard work, didn't she?) and, above all, the old man's grandson. He must love Son immediately, the boy was so good-looking.

Lily's assumption was that it was simply necessary to buy the old man a ticket and meet him at the airport, as with Mui. Mui disabused her of this illusion.

'Very difficult, Lily,' she told her.

'Why, Mui?' (Lily's tone was a little patronising.)

'English people don't want many foreign persons here. Laws are strict about who can come and cannot come. Don't forget he is an old man, a mouth to feed. I am a young woman. Authorities are much stricter than when I came.'

'So?'

'Maybe they won't allow him to join us. I think we can bring him in as our dependent but it may not be so easy as before.'

'No problem, Mui. Only a little tea money.'

'It's not like that, Lily. Really, it's not like that.'

Lily smiled. 'There are plenty of ways. Let him come as visitor and then disappear. Who could find him here?'

Mui said: 'Please, younger sister, nothing like that. Only let me arrange.'

'All right, Mui,' Lily said airily. 'But quick, hah?'

That afternoon Mui was away, playing the bureaucrat. If she feels it gives her face, let her do it, was Lily's thought.

In due course Mui announced she had official permission.

'I told you it was easy, didn't I?' Lily said.

Mui ignored her.

As she peeled plasticine off Son's floor and dragged his bed into Mui's room, Lily hummed a new pop-song to herself. She put the small bed in the centre of the floor and re-arranged Mui's bed so that it would be under the draughty window-frames and the feet of would-be burglars.

Much of Lily's zeal stemmed from her imagining old Mr Chen as her own father. Having met him, she knew this was far from the case. But she was unable to resist fantasising until she had deluded herself into thinking it *was* actually Father who was coming to visit them. She pulled herself back to reality with a strong sense of disappointment. She had swept and thoroughly scrubbed the floor of Son's room, hung a clean net curtain, put a single flower in her brown medicine bottle, now full of nothing more special than water, and placed beside it on the window-sill an unopened packet of best black incense (she wouldn't dream of giving Father those cheap yellow sticks). What a change! It was no longer Man Kee's chaotic little animal's lair, the den where her cub slept, but an elegant cell fit for the most redoubtable of monkish practitioners to mobilise his *chi*, his internal energy. There was a view of greenery, trees, water too, seen as in morning mist on a mountain top through the muslin. The old man could re-arrange the scanty furniture in the way he thought most auspicious but the external *fung shui* couldn't be faulted – not in spring anyway.

She showed Husband her handiwork, ushering him into the tranquil room, airing now to eliminate the smell of Dettol, with the muslin shimmering in the light breeze. She modestly awaited his discerning praise. What a good wife she was to him!

He was so unappreciative as to be insulting. 'Not suitable,' he commented. 'Too bare. We must put more things in.'

'What things, Husband?'

'How should I know? More things. Doesn't matter what.'

He stumped off downstairs, leaving Lily with her eyes prickling. She sniffed, thoroughly upset. The curtain lifted as a stronger breeze blew through. Could Husband be right? The room grew unclear through her misty eyes; she blinked rapidly several times and focussed on it again. Maybe he was right after all. It was the room she would have prepared to honour Father but it might be too austere for Husband's parent. From the kitchen she brought two chairs and a wooden crate which had held Whore Lock bottles. She placed the chairs touching each other, right up against the wall, so that they were there for ornament rather than use. The crate she turned upside down and covered with an embroidered pillow case, which looked as if it might have been expressly designed to be a smart little table-cloth. On it she put a pyramid of rosy apples in a clean saucer and the transistor radio. She lined the wall with calendars, never mind if they were out of date, the pictures were still pretty. She would also get a big picture of Son framed and hang it over the bed. It was quite cosy for the old man now, she thought. She squeezed her way out sideways; there was just room for her to get out; Mui would never have made it.

'Husband!'

She watched his face eagerly as he stood on the threshold.

'Better.'

She followed him downstairs, almost as disappointed as the first time but valiantly smothering the disappointment any wife might feel.

Chen was frightened and depressed by the turn things had taken in Hong Kong. The family had landed him in an impossible situation. It was out of the question to refuse to take his father. But this turned everything upside down; made his whereabouts quite obvious to his 'benefactors'. He had stopped his payments to one party, and nothing had happened. He had correctly judged that situation. But this ... as he had read the letter his pulse had quickened; his stomach had gone tight and hollow; he had actually wanted to vomit. He had gone to the bathroom, locked the door, bent over the basin, head slumped forward over the taps in despair. Then he walked round the garden. After a while he picked up a hoe and half-heartedly turned over some earth in his cabbage patch. When he saw Son watering his mango plant over at the compost heap, he turned his head away from the house in the direction of the gasworks and wept. Soon he mastered his emotions. He picked up the small hoe and went over to Son. He took the boy's warm, responsive hand, the hand of a grower, and led him away.

'Leave your plant, my Son. It's big enough to grow without help now. Ah Par-Par will teach you something.'

He showed him how to shorten his grip along the handle of the hoe and throw the tool out among the plants without hurting them. 'Good. Good.' The hoe was too heavy for Man Kee but he struggled manfully under his father's eye.

Chen patted his head. 'That's right, bring the stones in towards you; there's a weed there, get that out, it will kill the vegetables. Careful not to hit the cabbage. Never mind, then, Son, it's not important. Ah Par-Par isn't angry with you.'

Then Lily had called him. It was to see a room. He had been short. More weakness had threatened to manifest itself; he had had to leave quickly. It was difficult to think of Lily as just being all unwitting rather than deliberately unfeeling. He tried to make the obvious allowance but she had this unfortunate brisk manner, unbecoming in any woman and particularly unsuitable in a wife, which led you to think she might not care that much anyway. In his heart he knew this wasn't true. When she called him again, he complimented her. Then left with a choking in his throat.

Lily would go to the airport, they agreed, in the van. Chen was supported by Mui in this. The Underground would be frightening for the old man. He had never crossed the water to Hong Kong island and had been to Kowloon City only five times.

'Take car is best,' Mui agreed – the tunnels and stairways of the Underground were suggestive of some grimy, Buddhist hell, particularly upsetting after the recent bereavement.

'You will come, of course, Husband?' Lily asked.

Chen shook his head.

'Don't be frightened, Brother-in-law,' Mui said. 'I can manage for the few hours you are away. You must honour your parent.'

But Chen wouldn't hear of this.

'Doing business is *very* important, I suppose,' Lily agreed hesitantly. Since when had Husband been so keen on making every last halfpenny he could? Did he not trust Mui to put all the money honestly in the till? How hurtful if so! Mui wasn't perfect but she was never a thief. Husband's next words reassured her: 'Ah Mui, you sell in front while I cook as usual. It will be no longer than three hours. We have to lose some garage sales but that's unavoidable.'

As she was eager to acquire merit in the old man's eyes, Lily fell in with the arrangement. 'I shall take Son in the car,' she announced, and was surprised no one tried to prevent this. It was all working out as she wanted; she would much rather Son as a companion. This way the old man would be presented with his grandson first, and neither she nor Son would have to stand smiling sheepishly in the background while Husband bowed and pumped his hands in the old-fashioned style (as he was sure to do). She would also get a chance to explain their home situation her way; not to mention the fact that Son, at that enquiring stage, was livelier to talk to on a long journey than stolid old Husband. Might Husband's father not be shocked, too, to see his son being driven by his wife? Bearing all these excellent ideas in mind, Lily still felt slightly ashamed, as if she were absconding, when she drove away with Son in the cool, sunny morning.

It was lovely to be by themselves. While still observing the cardinal rules of the road (that was, so far as she was acquainted with any but the commonsensical), she took fond looks at him from time to time. 'Not ashamed to be in car, Son?' she teased him gently. Man Kee shook his head. Lily playfully pulled down the peak of his cap, the one with the earmuffs and chinstrap. He pushed it up again with an irritated grunt. Lily laughed. 'You are lucky you have no big sisters to make your life a misery.'

The journey was much nicer than either the trip to London or the sea. They passed along a series of minor roads and lanes, with little traffic in either direction. Man Kee was silent. There were no shops or buildings to stimulate him into those enquiries which once started never seemed to stop.

'Make horn noise, Mar-Mar.'

Lily checked in the mirror. They were rolling along on their own. She obliged.

'Having fun, Son?' ('Ho m'ho wan?')

'Fun.'

Lily began to sing him a Kwangsi cradle song, the one about the wicked pirate who steals children. He shook his head, the cap swinging from side to side, and in a clear, higher than treble voice, without an ounce of self-consciousness, began to sing in English a song about being a teapot. He mimed to the words with gestures: crooked arm on hip for the handle, other arm for spout.

'Again, Son.'

Man Kee repeated his performance:

'Here's my handle, here's my spout.
Tip me over, pour me out.'

Lily was delighted. She clapped her hands together, causing the Infernal Carapace to swerve violently onto the grassy road verge before she nonchalantly brought it on to the tarmac again with a twirl of the wheel. 'Show Mar-Mar how you do with your hand again.' How clever! Imagine the English having a tea song. This was really quite civilised of them – for a change. But what a peculiar, eccentric thing to teach children in school, she couldn't help thinking with misgiving.

Man Kee had been leaning to his left (to pour tea from his spout) as

Lily regained control of the van. She had over-compensated by bringing it well over the centre of the road into the other lane and as she brought it back to the left, Man Kee lurched into the door, banging his big head against the window-pillar. (Unfortunately not the one with coiled rope to buffer the impact.)

'Are you all right?' she enquired anxiously.

'All right, Mar-Mar.'

His headgear, though, was not all right. The peak had taken the brunt of the impact and had now been bent backwards over the top of the cap, leaving a large expanse of his wide forehead exposed. Man Kee looked like one of their dustbin-men. Lily tried to turn the wrecked brim down again but now there was traffic coming from the other direction and she had to concentrate fully with both hands. She mustn't run any risk of a collision with Son in the car. Almost drunk with exhilaration, though, she drove more erratically than she had ever done until as the roads grew bigger and the traffic thickened she became hemmed in and took her initiative from the vehicle ahead of her. Strange how one was safest braking and starting in unison in a crowd.

'Sure you are all right, Son?' (you didn't have to tell *her* how concussion felt in a child's skull). 'Why don't you turn your cap down? Must look smart for Grandpa.'

'I like it this way.'

'Do what Mar-Mar says.'

'Can't reach.'

'Arm clever enough to be teapot can fix hat.'

Man Kee made a few ineffectual passes as if he was trying to unscrew the dome of his head like a lid.

'Take cap off, Son.'

'Button too tight,' said Man Kee, reading his mother's relaxed mood correctly.

'All right, Son,' Lily sighed.

They were now on a big dual carriageway. There was a grass plateau to their right, wire-fenced for miles around. Huge jets thundered, dangerously low overhead, it seemed to Lily, occasionally making a disturbing, high-pitched whine. 'Airplane, Son!'

'Comet 4,' Man Kee said nonchalantly.

'Hah?'

But now they were rolling into a long tunnel and when they emerged were actually in the airport. Lily saw their building at once but only found the way to it with great difficulty through the roundabouts and one-way systems. Once she had parked conveniently outside it with a sigh of relief, a terrible honking rose from the taxis in a row behind her like horrible black crows waiting for scavengings. Lily considered sticking it out with the imperturbable smile – but perhaps better not today. It wouldn't be nice for Grandpa Chen to walk into an unpleasant scene in his first hour in the UK. Besides, there seemed a lot of policemen around. Lily eased the clutch out and moved the Infernal Carapace away as smoothly and unobtrusively as lay in her power, which was rather jerkily and noisily since it had been a demanding journey for the engine, if not for Lily. After searching vainly for a space, she entered a multi-storey car-park. She paid ten shillings and she grudged every penny of it.

Automatic doors flew open as they approached the terminal, shattering the reflections in the tinted glass of a slim, graceful woman and a tiny boy. Lily couldn't remember these when she arrived. She was taken aback by the way they flew apart just like that as if they were devils approaching on a straight line. Son, of course, was delighted and went outside again for another go.

Holding Man Kee's hand more to reassure herself than him, Lily went cautiously into the crowded, brightly lit hall. What a lot of people! What big, smart cases! She and Son stood in the middle of the loft building, drinking up the exciting sounds and sights and stimulated by the strange electrical stinging in their nostrils. Soothing music played, interrupted by a voice which seemed to speak nothing but numbers.

Gradually, under the influence of music and ozone, Lily became more confident. No one was taking any notice of them. She let Man Kee pull her ahead. She began to march purposefully in step with the music like the other people. She swung her shoulders; she became part of the scene herself. They stood on shiny steel and glass escalators which sped them smoothly up to the first floor with its shops, restaurants and bars. They looked down on the heads of the people milling below. Lily was enjoying herself; she hadn't had such fun for a long time; it was even more fun than the trip to the sea. And at the same time she was discovering things she hadn't known before. 'Ho wan?' she asked Man Kee in an interrogative pitch. He nodded.

It was eleven o'clock by the enormous dial on the other side of the terminal, still a good three-quarters of an hour before Grandpa (as Lily was now teaching herself to call him) arrived. She decided she would treat Man Kee to a drink at the long self-service counter. Down its prodigious length they went, Lily sliding the tray gaily along the rails –

to be met with a nasty shock. For a tiny, little-little glass, the size of a giant's thimble, the girl rang up on her big electric machine three shillings. Shockingly expensive! At Dah Ling they charged only slightly more for three times the amount. (And Lily had felt guilty enough about charging that much!) Unable to restrain herself, Lily exclaimed: 'Eiyah!' If she didn't actually reel back with a hand clapped to her forehead, she certainly felt like doing so. Still shaking her head, Lily took Man Kee to an empty table at the edge of the bar compound. Man Kee drank with both hands, looking around over the rim of the glass, anxious not to miss anything.

'Nice, is it, Son?'

He nodded without removing the glass from his mouth. Lily opened her frayed crocodile-skin purse to count what she had left: thirty-three shillings and sixpence halfpenny, mostly in florins and half-crowns. Lucky she had filled the tank before leaving. The way she was spending money, she and Son might have got stuck here otherwise.

Lily checked the clock: 'Let's go, Son.'

Downstairs at the arrivals barrier Lily pressed her way to the front with ruthlessness and aggression born of the fear that they might be late. Once at the cordon, Lily hissed in Man Kee's ear: 'Don't forget, Son. Hold hand in front of chest and bow head. Then say: "Grandfather, unworthy grandson presents respects." Understand?'

'What?'

Lily saw he still had his earflaps over his ears. She lifted one up to whisper in the little pink whorl underneath, then decided the whole thing was better off. She repeated her instructions.

'Good, Mar-mar.'

A man behind her was squashing something springy but hard against her bottom; something unmentionable against her vulnerable, warm bottom in its thin trousers. Could it be? Yes, it could. Lily flushed. Elbow ram into solar plexus; simultaneous stamp on metatarsals; followed by shin-hack, attacking surface: back of heel. She did it in a flash; she just stopped herself following the elbow up with its natural sequence in the combination: a same-arm claw attack on the Golden Target. There was a low moan behind her. Out of the corner of her eye she saw a man in the sort of long fawn raincoat Mr Constantinides wore on pump-duty on rainy days (today was sunny!) limping away. Serve you right, thought Lily without an ounce of remorse. Clearly, Father was watching over her. The automatic countermeasure had not been hers; had you asked her about it a moment earlier she wouldn't even have remembered the classic *Hung gar* response to rear-attack. She made Man Kee hold her hand, though goodness knew, it wasn't he who ran the risk of being outraged here.

All around them friends and long-lost relatives greeted and embraced each other. Forgetting her own little annoyance, Lily watched with a vicarious, happy smile as a grey-haired old lady wept in the arms of someone who was obviously her daughter. The old lady had a sheeny black fur coat on, so she must have come from somewhere hot, expecting bad weather when she got here. How nice for her that it was sunny! Don't forget to put a stove in her room tonight, Lily felt like shouting after them. And put the nicest things to eat nearest her on the table!

This particular load of arrivals was now finished. Another came. Then another. Forty-five minutes passed. Had they missed Grandpa? Had his plane crashed?

'Grandpa is where?' Man Kee asked in a shrill voice. 'He walks road by himself to meet us?'

Despite her anxiety, Lily smiled. 'No, Son if he is doing that, then we wait a long time.' She hesitated. Could she leave him here to keep a watch for Grandpa while she made enquiries? It would be awful if the old man arrived to find no one there. On the other hand . . . 'Man Kee, come with me.'

There were many, many counters sited (in the way of *some* restaurants) close together in a huddle. You would think one of them might have the enterprise to split away and see if they could sell more tickets that way – do like Dah Ling. Maybe people bought tickets before they got here. Must ask Husband. Lily had a scrap of paper, provided by Mui, with the time and number of Grandpa's flight. She showed this to a counter-girl. The counter-girl pointed her to another. They all looked the same; their uniforms might be different colours but they all had those silly round hats, with not a wisp of hair showing, and tight jackets constricting the bust. How uncomfortable. Also inches of crusted make-up; you could probably cook them like turkeys. Lily took an immediate dislike to the BOAC girl to whom she gave her paper. She had a shiny nose, and a superior manner. 'This flight,' said the young lady with the shiny nose in a superior way, 'is delayed five hours. We have been announcing it for the last hour.'

Lily took the paper back without showing her resentment. Her face was blank, her mouth slightly slack. As she turned away with Son, lines of anger tautened her cheeks, closed her mouth, narrowed her eyes, as if there were fine wires under her skin. How was she meant to know what they were speaking over the music, or listen to it and still concentrate on other things (like not losing Son, preventing thieves from stealing her purse, molesters from interfering with her person)? It was quite unreasonable.

'Mar-Mar, you hurt my hand.'

Lily stroked the injured part. 'Some more to drink, my Son?' She tried a vending machine this time, which was better value for money; after which Man Kee wanted to go to the lavatory. When she had found the place and taken him in it was half past twelve. They still had a very long time to wait. She could have driven home and back and still had a quick pot of tea. That was out of the question, though. She settled herself on an empty sofa and waited. And waited. She knew she could amuse herself by watching the people but what about Man Kee?

'Son, you can watch airplane land and take off.'

'Give money for telescope, Mar-Mar.'

'There, Son, buy comic and chocolate, too.' The purse was now distinctly flatter (it was her right to spoil him). 'And, Son, bad to talk to strange people.'

She watched him trot off to the telescope on the balcony. It really was a very comfortable sofa compared to what she had become used to at Dah Ling. The sun through the plate-glass window (nice, strong, clean window: how much did it cost?) was hotter than you would have thought. She lay back; the sun toasted her face pleasantly. She closed her eyes. Son still at telescope. She closed her eyes again; you had to because of the glare. She dozed a second or two. Was woken up by Son breathing chocolate breath on her. 'Mar-Mar, don't die,' and was off again before she could remonstrate with or just correct him. She shut her eyes. How much later she didn't know, someone put a knee between her thighs, a hand on her breast, and another over her mouth and nose. In time to catch herself, she realised it was Son. 'Bad to jump on people, son. Play things again now.' Her heavy eyelids drooped once more. And she slept in earnest.

There was no Son when she woke this time. Moreover, it was five o'clock. With growing panic, she went round the first floor. He was nowhere to be found: not in the shops, on the observation balcony, at a cafeteria table. In forty-five minutes Grandpa was due to arrive. This was a nightmare. Quicker than seemed possible it was 5.45. A dilemma: let Grandpa wait, she decided. Something was nagging at her on the fringes of her awareness. She frowned and halted. Now what could it be? She stared hard at a telephone as if it could provide the clue. Then she heard the voice: ' . . . should go to the lost children's centre on the first floor.' She was there, breathless, within the minute.

And, sure enough, Son was on a chair, licking a green lollipop with great composure. Lily thanked the uniformed girl hurriedly – not ungrateful, just in a rush – and set off for arrivals. She was far too much in a hurry to scold Son, even if he deserved it. For his part, Man Kee was highly indignant: he had been riding the escalators down and up, up and down, quite happily until whisked off to where Mar-Mar found him. He had known very well how to get back to her. Lily listened as she pulled him along by his sticky hand. They were nearly half an hour late.

Where was Grandpa? There was no crowd of arrivals. The others must have been met already. Lily looked around. Man Kee pulled her hand.

'There, Mar-Mar.'

'Where?'

'*There!*'

Lily dropped her eyes. Ah! She had been looking too high. Squatting on his hunkers by himself, under the rope, guarding two cases, three plastic carrier bags, and a cloth bundle tied with string, was a stick-thin old Chinese man with a stubbly grey head. Lily approached him.

THIRTY

Red Cudgel was in a rage. The eyes had become tiny; a tic on each side of the face, as if a section of bark on a dead log had quivered and shown itself to be the camouflage of some darting-tongued predator. For a moment the Swatownese's anger was so great he actually beamed with a flash of silver bridge-work. His subordinates looked down on the table. They were all intimidated, Grass Sandal and Night-brother included; all except White Paper Fan who shot the beads along the rails of his abacus with complete indifference. Red Cudgel said: 'I am going to wash faces, little friends. I don't break promises.'

Night-brother said: 'Such traitors deserve severest punishment.'

Red Cudgel ignored him; he said: 'Those who relaxed vigilance and allowed this to happen are also culpable.'

Night-brother bit his lip.

Red Cudgel said: 'This fool of a 49 who supervised the runner deserves punishment as well. I cannot conceive of such blindness and stupidity in a member of family Hung.'

White Paper Fan said evenly: 'When you recruit widely and indiscriminately you take such risks. Of course the quality of membership falls.'

The two senior officers stared at each other. Neither would look away. Red Cudgel continued without removing his gaze from the Deputy Leader's face: 'Cash loss is not in itself significant. The ten bottles, what consequence are they to us? It is the principle. That a runner, a son of a leper should dare cheat us ... '

White Paper Fan said: 'This is infuriating but surely far more disturbing if an actual society member tried to do this?'

Red Cudgel grimaced.

Night-brother said: 'So far as I have ascertained, the 49 himself has nothing to do with the theft. I am continuing my enquires along these lines, however. Not concluded yet. The runner seems to have absconded with the ten bottles or, in my opinion, the proceeds from them. The 49 tells me he has, of course, fled the restaurant.'

Red Cudgel said: 'He dies then. Do your work properly and find him.'

White Paper Fan said: 'We ought to make sure of everything first. I think you act incorrectly.' He spoke with a forthrightness alien to his usual mode of operation.

Red Cudgel reacted angrily; he was put in a position where he had to reassert his authority or lose face. 'Careful of what you say. I am the Leader. Do not forget this, any of you.'

White Paper Fan murmured only a perfunctory apology.

Red Cudgel said: 'I am unlucky in having incompetent subordinates. A leader should be able to rely on his lieutenants to carry out and oversee this kind of affair. When things are finished there will be some changes. This should never have reached the point where I was involved. 432 officers are badly at fault. There are many important businesses requiring my attention.'

Night-brother said: 'Elder Brother, my face is turned away. But at least I have worked hard to gather intelligence about 14-K. Both younger sister and myself have worked extremely hard on this. All indications are that they plan a large-scale attack some time early next year. No sooner.'

Red Cudgel said: 'They would find it hard if we are prepared.

Obviously they hope to catch us off guard.' He said to Iron Plank: 'Your fame has spread.'

There was polite laughter from all except Night-brother and White Paper Fan. Grass Sandal laughed loudest.

Red Cudgel turned to Night-brother with a face from which all trace of humour was expunged. 'Treat the affair of the absconding runner as most important for yourself. This is work I entrust to you. All you are fit to do.'

The new air-conditioner in White Paper Fan's office was exceptionally powerful. For Night-brother, leaving the heat and smell of the street, it was like coming into a furnished giant refrigerator. White Paper Fan served him a brandy and 7-Up from his ice-box.

After refreshing himself, Night-brother began with the matter of least consequence. 'Something rather curious at the Excellence. The man hasn't been working there for over two years, almost three. He left without serving notice. I spoke to its proprietor, not the 49.'

White Paper Fan looked interested. 'Very curious,' he agreed. 'But I think I can guess what has been going on, can't you?'

Night-brother raised an eyebrow.

'You will find that when you reach my age, things tend to repeat themselves. The imagination of the petty thief is strangely limited.'

'You mean our 49 has been marketing the bottles himself – despite the directive forbidding this?'

'I would imagine so. Then, perhaps, he got greedy and decided to make more money by stealing the bottles. This would end a regular source of income from selling the bottles but then this kind of person only ever looks to the short-term. Perhaps he has a debt to meet. I would not be surprised if he had been putting squeeze on the "runner" as well. The whole thing looked suspicious to me from the start.'

'Try telling that to our Leader.'

White Paper Fan diluted the brandy in the younger man's glass with more lemonade from the green bottle. 'Ice?' He dropped some in, using tissue-paper to hold the cube. 'Follow this matter up, Ah Ricky. It occurs to me, small though it is, that it can be turned to use for us in our big matter.'

'Is there any point in me finding out the former runner's whereabouts if he is free from involvement in the fraud?'

'There is point. Don't forget, you still act under Ma's instructions and should there be,' the Shanghainese chose his words, 'a miscarriage of justice, shall we say, then he is responsible. A trifling error but the effect of every mistake is cumulative. It could help sway things for the more traditionally minded.'

Night-brother said: 'In this case I follow up. Shouldn't be hard. Can be traced from Hong Kong if he has been in touch with his family. I can tell our Wo branch headquarters it's to do with welfare. If this fails, then I'll persuade the 49 to do some talking myself. I can be quite persuasive.'

'Good.' The Shanghainese opened another bottle of the carbonated beverage. 'Now the important business I mentioned to you, my young friend. But can I rely on you? We tread a dangerous path.'

'You can rely on me to the death. I speak for the other party as well.'

White Paper Fan was on the telephone, an instrument he usually abhorred. It was late; he was alone in the travel agency. He spoke in his beautiful mandarin: 'This is political not military. That is to say, it takes place within clearly defined limits and it does not exceed its objectives, even if the way lies open.'

He listened carefully to the Taiwanese voice at the other end. 'It is. It is. Correct. No. My attitude is that it is business. Personal feelings do not enter into it. Think of me as a chess-player. I take pieces of yours, you take mine. One makes sacrifices. Yes, no mistake. I give a time later; place I already have in mind. Clean and disciplined. Nothing excessive. You understand? He is worthy of respect. Do you understand that?'

THIRTY-ONE

'Do come out from underneath, Grandpa. There is no need to stay in that place.'

The speaker was Lily; it was seven o'clock on a July morning. 'Come on, Grandpa, three months is far too long to be living in there.'

She got a broom and poked him with the handle (in a gentle and respectful way) to make sure he was awake.

Grandpa Chen was already awake but in the darkness of his cubby-hole it was not possible to see that his eyes were open. He crawled out from under the take-away counter, where he had made his home shortly after arriving in the UK, stretched his old bones, and headed for the bathroom to relieve his weak bladder. He had perfectly logical reasons for wanting to live in the counter. Never a despot, even when his family had been young, he was disinclined to try and lord it in his son's house. He wished to make himself as useful and unobtrusive as possible. The most immediate way of doing this was to take up minimum physical living space. He had spent his first nights in his son's house in the chamber which had been prepared in his honour. He had found it draughty, alien, and unpropitious. He had never in his life slept anywhere except on a ground floor, near the earth, as man was meant to sleep. Animals lived in the cock-loft. Upstairs he had a sensation of vertigo; he feared he might float up into the clouds unless he stayed awake. The window was also frightening: the drifting white curtain, the colour of death, and filmy too, indicating the world was a dream, seen through a veil of illusion. (He had got morbidly imaginative since his wife's death.) In any case a window had no right to be at the back or front of a house, where devils and spirits might enter. In any sensibly planned home they were at the side. He left the top floor and established himself under the counter between four crates of Coca-cola which wedged him in snugly. He was deaf to all attempts to lure him upstairs again.

'Take no notice of me, take no notice of me,' he said in his quavering voice. 'Old man sleeps it doesn't matter where.'

Actually, the old man didn't do much sleeping at all, dozing lightly for not more than three or four hours a night. 'Old man has sharp ears, can hear burglar,' he would say, gesturing at the till. No matter he saw his daughter-in-law empty in every night. Lily couldn't help being put out by Grandpa's behaviour but short of trussing him up every night and flinging him on the upstairs bed, there was little she could do. Mui had been odd, too, for a long time. Maybe Grandpa felt protected in his little hideaway.

In the day he liked to squat on a pew. Literally on it: his feet on the sitting surface, buttocks an inch from the wood, his long knees (shiny black trousers rolled up just under those creaky old joints) grazing his ears. As he read his newspapers with elbows flung wide apart he looked for all the world like an elderly giant cricket. After the room filled with customers he would hop off his perch to squat in the corner under god, or retire altogether to his place under the counter. Occasionally he would emerge to play his part in enlarging the profits of his son's business. He was unable to understand that the prices were fixed. He had been to the lorries once with Mui and the sight of varying amounts of cash had been formative. Now, at the counter, he would approach ordinary customers as they paid, pulling insistently on their sleeve and remonstrating with them in his braying village Cantonese: 'Give her more, give her more. Don't be so tight-fisted.' Or if a blue £5 note changed hands he would try to usher the customer to the door as Lily got change from the till. 'That'll do nicely, that'll do nicely,' he would say, shooing them away.

'Please, Grandpa,' Lily would say, her bright blue eyes fairly sparkling with mischief and humour, 'don't trouble yourself. It only frightens our customer, you know. He might think you are a bandit.' Then she would call Mui and they would hug each other, almost weeping with laughter in the locked bathroom. The sight of Chen expressionlessly peeling potatoes in the kitchen would be enough to drive them back in with a slam of the door in further paroxysms.

There was nothing disloyal in the girls' giggling. Lily warmed to Grandpa for his endearing little eccentricities. She respected the idea of grandfathers and the piety owed them. Nothing could shake this belief. But how much easier to make obeisance to the idea if you felt affection for the human being who incarnated the principle.

'Grandpa, when you want anything you must tell me at once,' Lily exhorted him on his first night. At meals she sat next to him and made sure he got all the tastiest morsels by pincering them with her own chopsticks and depositing the tit-bits of chicken, pork, or chewy fish-eye (delicious: just like salty old chewing-gum) on the rice in his personal bowl. Old man Chen basked in the fuss that was being made of him. All the other daughters-in-law treated him as an Old Useless (would have been different if he'd had money to leave; they'd have been scraping round him then). Lily was a good girl to him. Not good-looking by any stretch of the imagination but she had a respectful way behind her brisk manner. She wasn't a typical modern girl by any means. For form's sake he tried to remove his bowl from the reach of Lily's nimble, ever-supplying chopsticks, which she had a knack of curving round the narrowest of gaps between porcelain and cheek. 'Unnecessary, unnecessary. Old man doesn't want.' But he ate with gusto all he got.

'We must put some flesh on your bones, Grandpa,' she chaffed him. 'We must make you plump as my husband.' Even Chen had to grin.

The old man had offered money to Lily which she refused to take.

He kept HK$950 in new tens in a black money-belt. 'Then it shall be your son's when I die,' he told her.

'No, no. Bad to talk like that,' she scolded him. (HK$950: that would buy uniforms and books for at least ten years. Alternatively: lay it down as a nest-egg and amass funds for a private education.) The old man's fundamental concern was already safe-guarded. He had also in his money-belt the unused half of an unlimited expiry return air-ticket to Hong Kong, subscribed to by his other sons in lieu of a coffin. How terrible to have one's lonely bones lie (as good as strewn) in alien soil and roam for ever as a Hungry Ghost far, far from the peaceful green hillside over the village. Now, he knew, he could depend on Lily, after the proper interval of interment, to air-freight his washed and purified bones to Hong Kong for his sons to place with reverence in a burial-jar and entomb with the bones of his fathers. He would not be able to have the lavish funeral with paid mourners and magnificent coffin it had always been his ambition to impress the village with. (How he would have liked to have seen the mortified, envious faces of his enemies Horse Face Hu and Addict Hing as they paraded his remains around the streets of the market town with brassy music and firecrackers!) But it was not given to one to have everything. He was happy to be assured of proper burial at least.

At seventy-one the old man had great curiosity and a lively sense of adventure. He had enjoyed the airplane flight. He was stimulated by the strange sights, sounds, smells of his new home. He was not at all home-sick for the New Territories; although he did miss feasting and smoking with his friends. But he had a way of being with them.

Soon after Grandpa arrived, Lily noticed he was wearing two watches, one above the other around his stringy left forearm, rather than the stick wrist. Politely, she hadn't commented. She supposed this was the safest way of carrying the extra watch on the journey. When she saw him still wearing them weeks after he had landed, she decided he might be using them to check each other or insure against the possibility of one breaking down. But then Grandpa didn't have the smallest reason to know the time to the nearest hour, let alone minute.

Lily approached the subject in a roundabout way. 'Very handsome watch, Grandpa. Must have cost a lot of money.'

'A *lot* of cash,' he chuckled. 'Grandson inherits when I die.'

This wasn't what Lily had been driving at, not at all; she didn't want Grandpa to think her avaricious. 'Grandpa, how clever to wear two watches! Must be more accurate than one.'

Now the old man really cackled. 'That's not why I wear two watches! Look!' He brandished his arm under Lily's eyes. 'See!' Lily saw the hands of the top watch were at eight o'clock. Those on the bottom gave the time correctly as midday. 'What a shame, Grandpa! Top watch is it too slow. Or is it too fast? Maybe you shouldn't wind it so hard.'

The old man hugged himself gleefully with his stick arms. 'Not so! Not so! Look, top watch tells Hong Kong time, bottom watch tells England time. Understand or not?'

'Understand,' Lily said doubtfully.

'Any time I want to know what my friends are doing, I just look at top watch. Ten o'clock they eat fried doughsticks and pink rice congee with boiled soft bone fragments. One o'clock they eat steamed pork buns and fried beef noodle. Four o'clock they start playing *mah jeuk*, drink tea, smoke cigarette, eat melon seed. Dinner with Snake and Tiger Bone wine (very good for old man!) at eight o'clock, ten o'clock gambling begins again . . .'

Lily interrupted this recitation (why was Tiger Bone wine good for old men?), which Grandpa seemed to be enjoying as much as if he were back in the village engaging in all these amusing activities. 'But, Grandpa, can't you just look at your watch and add eight hours to know Hong Kong time?'

Grandpa looked extremely put out. 'That's not the same thing at all. I'm surprised at you. That's not the same thing at all.'

Lily hastened to put herself among his good opinions again. 'Well, think of your friends when you play this nice Cantonese music. I ordered it from Chinese Street. It came in the post today. I remember you said you didn't like English music on the radio.'

Grandpa was delighted. 'So thoughtful! You shouldn't go to such trouble for this useless old fellow.'

He went at once to play the music at full volume on Lily's old turntable. A little later Chen came hurrying up from the bottom of the garden to see if Lily had spilt boiling oil on herself. Even to Lily the music was excruciatingly discordant, whether faulty equipment or simply the long time since she had heard Cantonese opera were responsible, but Grandpa was happy as anything. Plenty of tea, a little tobacco, and cheerful music, that was all he asked for. On top of two square meals a day, naturally.

The household became excessively familiar with the opera music which Grandpa had a fondness for playing early in the morning. Lily had tactfully hinted that the customers, uncultured outer barbarians that they were, might not find Cantonese opera played at maximum volume (as indeed it had to be for you to appreciate it fully) altogether congenial. It might make it difficult for them, for instance, to hear the TV which, unlike Mui, Grandpa showed not the slightest interest in watching. 'Filthy caterwaulings' someone had called Grandpa's music already, sending Mui to her dictionary with interest, as she had imagined it a slander on the fried meat with furry bean pods. After surprising Grandpa with the possibility of this point of view, neither Lily nor the others had the heart to ask him to stop playing his records when he woke up in the morning. This was at about 5 a.m., once he had got used to the time-shift. He liked to drag the turn-table under the counter, turning it into a giant echo-chamber and creating booming bass waves which lapped eerily at the floor-boards under Chen's and Lily's bed, though oddly enough the voices of the individual actors sounded even shriller.

Man Kee loved this. Up as early as the old man, he padded downstairs as soon as the sounds floated up the tunnel of the stairs to his room. He crawled under the counter, grinning all over his big face, to sit with Grandpa. When he emerged he was understandably slightly deaf and slow to respond to his mother at the breakfast table, which caused her a great deal of unnecessary worry.

His grandfather had taken a great fancy to Man Kee. With characteristic bluntness the old man had immediately remarked on the unusual development of his grandson's head compared to the rest of his body. What Lily found insulting and reprehensible in Husband was, issuing from Grandpa's lips, both acutely perceptive and extremely witty. 'This worthless boy *does* have a big head,' she agreed, as if struck by a highly original notion for the first time. Grandpa Chen patted Man Kee's head affectionately. 'Plenty of brains in there. Give plenty of fish, head particularly. Or chicken head would do,' he advised. 'He will be rich man, do much business.'

Lily shook her head. 'Worthless boy. Brings his parents to ruin.' She stroked his back proudly.

Chen kept shovelling rice into his mouth with an expressionless face, his eyes staring at the tin dishes over the side of his bowl. Without taking the bowl away from his mouth, he picked up a piece of blubbery pork with his chopsticks (Lily had given Grandpa all the best fat bits). Lily looked scornfully at him. 'What do you have to say, Man Kee's father?' Chen raised his eyebrows, bowl still clapped to mouth. 'Huh.' Lily gave a little contemptuous laugh which fooled nobody. 'Perhaps you'll find words when you see the sweet red beans I've cooked for you.' She made sure he had plenty. Grandpa, she knew, didn't have his son's sweet tooth.

Chen, while wishing to show as much respect as Lily, couldn't help feeling awkward with his father. It was so long since he had seen him, or really corresponded. He warmed to his wife for her efforts with his family both now and in the past. The regular remittances had all been her work and her forethought; she alone had maintained the connection. It hardly mattered that it was his money she sent. Hers was the love and the inconvenience. Without Lily's bustling and scolding now it would have been too embarrassing to sit opposite his father. He could hardly look him in the face as it was. When their eyes did meet accidentally over the emptying dishes, his slid uneasily away over the spiny skeleton of the fish floating in its oily sauce, the bright green vegetable, and brown-bloody meat, until he buried his face in the bowl and his eyes flickered sideways once more. The old man's steadier gaze would linger on his son, so that as Chen compulsively came round to meet the eyes again he would see a strange look in them. Was it reproach, love, or assurance that guilty Chen saw reflected in those pale-brown irises? He was never sure. But he knew that, slowly, Lily was building a bridge between them: it might be a bridge of complicity, of shared maleness between them against her female fussing, her bossiness; a bridge of humour and shared experience. And speaking for herself, Lily didn't mind if the cost of this was that they should laugh at her. For this she would happily make herself seem ridiculous. More often now, Chen and his father would find themselves laughing together, and when this happened a spark of recognition would leap between them.

'Ah Mui, give Grandpa more rice.'

'I have already given him, Lily.'

'Give more. And give Man Kee more bean-curd.'

'Well said, well said, younger sister.'

'Thank you, Ah Mui, old man doesn't want.'

Mui was as quiet as ever. She and Chen had been brought closer together by the recent changes. There was sympathy between them. There was nothing said; no open demonstration of feeling. Their growing regard could not be ritualised into empty forms of address or behaviour: Chen got no extra bowls of rice; Mui didn't wait on him at table. Her regard for brother-in-law was not necessarily stronger than Lily's conventional veneration of the old man, nor yet more genuine, but it was less looked for, more accidental and spontaneous and for that reason more vulnerable and therefore, perhaps, more precious. Chen was less stolid when he was with Mui. Once, Lily was almost certain, she heard him singing with Mui to the strains of the rejected transistor radio in the kitchen: either that or Mui had a frog in her throat, which was unlikely in high summer. Extraordinary! And sometimes she would go to the bathroom and find the two of them talking together – only god knew what about. Lily thought it might be *her*, for they veered away quickly to their chores when *she* came in.

Grandpa Chen's arrival also had the happy result of allowing Mui to go to Mrs Law's more often than she had been able so far. The old man's usefulness in the business was strictly limited; in fact he might be said to be useless. (Lily never allowed herself to think in these dangerous terms; just acted on them as if they were instinct.) However, Grandpa could at a pinch sit on Lily's tall stool (sit, not squat) and smile at the customers (for while Lily trusted Man Kee to take money, she was less sure of Grandpa) or he might just stack foil boxes neatly. Really, though, it was just the distraction and excitement of the old man's coming which gained Mui her release. Lily had more to occupy her. She was less interested in dominating her sister. That, and Chen's quiet readiness to support his sister-in-law, got Mui leave of absence every week.

If Grandpa noticed she was gone for the night, he never said anything. So, again, the household (that amoeba), presented with change and challenge, shuddered like jelly on impact with the obstacle but jelly-like suffered no damage, poured itself around the problem, dissolved what it was able to and absorbed what it could not. And went on its amoeba way.

THIRTY-TWO

Man Kee's education, English-style, continued on its eccentric way. Things, in Lily's view, were going from bad to much worse. She was quite resigned; had no intention of making a struggle. What could *she* do? It was a form of protest which was comparable, in order if not degree, to suicide. As Man Kee grew more communicative about his lessons her horror deepened. Basically, Lily's philosophy of education was simple: it didn't matter what Man Kee studied so long as he didn't like it. The main purpose of his lessons was to train his character, foster diligence, teach him discipline and obedience. Acquiring knowledge was almost secondary to this. That was what pupils learned at Ling Nan primary and middle school, Stubbs Road, Hong Kong – possibly the best school in the world. What did Man Kee learn here? Quite the reverse, it was now apparent. There was little or no discipline, minimal organisation in the classroom. They interrupted Teacher, walked around the room, chatted in little groups, went to do big business and little business whenever they felt like it. They even, if you could really believe Man Kee, decided what they were going to learn. It was perfectly disgraceful. There was hardly any difference between lessons and what was officially play of which, incidentally, there was a deal too much. In her humble opinion, homework, too, was a tremendous nuisance. Contrary to Mui's conventional wisdom on the subject, Son had, at this academy of misrule, just started receiving tasks to do at home at what his aunt regarded as an unusually precocious age for the foreign system. 'Perhaps head teacher is Indian person, hah, Mui?' Lily teased. How ridiculous Mui was. She remembered homework at age three or four. If it was unusual here Lily, always a pessimist now where school was concerned, suspected the teachers were simply too lazy to supervise the children properly. This was just shovelling *real* studies onto the parents when their offspring might be doing better things – like helping Mar-Mar earn a living. She wouldn't, of course, stop Man Kee doing his homework which was the only orthodox leg of the curriculum and without which he could fall seriously behind. But she had him doing it at the counter where he was available to give her help when absolutely necessary. It became *absolutely* necessary just before eight o'clock, which left him plenty of time for playing in the garden, bath, and supper as well. Every now and again she would catch him watching TV instead of attending to what was in front of him and then she would give him a little poke in the ribs with her forefinger.

Lily herself would have put him to bed at nine o'clock after the rush of customers was over but Husband insisted he should stay up to gain practical experience of the business. It was about time he started, he said. But the poor little thing kept dropping off and Lily hadn't the heart to wake him. Fortunately, Husband's quirk about keeping the hatch shut prevented him from seeing. When Mui did raise the shutter, Lily kept her back across the opening. Generally, Husband seemed to be much stricter with Son these days. Poor Man Kee had blisters on his hands after hoeing in the garden and she had caught

Husband poking around the accounts book with Son next to him on the tall stool. 'Is he teaching you or are you teaching him?' she joked. Husband hadn't denied it! She had rescued over-taxed Son.

'Really!' she scolded Husband. 'He is too young for things like that. You'll give him brain fever. There's plenty of time for him to learn before we are old and decrepit. Excuse unthinking words, Grandpa.'

Husband had looked unaccountably upset, making Lily wish she hadn't been born with such a hot chili's tongue.

Nowadays Man Kee finished school another half an hour later again, which meant he just missed his old bus. The next bus he could catch dropped him off at the garage exactly fifteen minutes later.

The week before half-term he didn't arrive on this bus. Grandpa had been waiting for him. The bus conductor, he said, had shrugged sympathetically at him, stopping the bus specially to say a few kind words to him. Probably that Man Kee was coming a bit later; naturally, Grandpa didn't speak a word of English.

Mui abandoned her chopping to return to the bus stop with him. Three, four, five buses went by, and still there was no Man Kee. Lily relieved Mui. Grandpa squatted on his hunkers back against the bus stop, and smoked one of his powerful countryman's cigarettes. The buses came less frequently. It became dusk. Grandpa's cigarette glowed at knee height like a paralysed firefly. Absent-mindedly, Lily passed near the bus stop, where she smelled burning. Suddenly there was a sharp pain in the side of her thigh. Eiyah! She slapped her leg. A vicious insect bite? No, Grandpa's cigarette. In some confusion she retired to the house where she discovered a relatively tiny hole in the thin floral material and a huge brown area of scorching: a curious sort of damage. Trousers were ruined but would make useful dusters. Changing hurriedly into an originally red and white patterned pair (blended into a pretty pink) she was soon back at the bus stop where there had been no further developments.

She wasn't in fact terribly worried. It had all happened before. Son could easily walk the distance if he had lost his money. He had done it when he was younger and every day he was developing.

Sure enough, at length a small figure trudged round the corner. As this was the first time Lily hadn't been seriously worried, it was also the first time she felt like scolding him. The sight of his tear-stained, dusty face drove all such thoughts out of her head.

'Son! Why are you crying? Mar-Mar isn't angry with you.'

Man Kee took her hand and held it tightly. He snuffled. 'What's the matter, Son? You can tell me.'

'Bad boys take bus money.'

So that was it! 'Son, did bad boys hurt you?'

'Hurt ear.'

Lily examined it. Even in the dark she could see it was heavily swollen. Under the kitchen light it was a bright angry red and purple, the colour of a baboon's backside. The helix was thickened and coarsened, giving Man Kee's delicate little auricle the look of an old man's ear. It seemed visibly to throb and swell before Lily's anguished eyes, though on his large head the size was less remarkable than it might have been. Apparently, bad boys had twisted it, lifting him off his feet, until he gave them his bus money. It didn't hurt now, he said (which was actually no more than the truth, though no one believed him and his courage and concern to spare them worry only upset his family more). Mui cried – all over the vegetables. Lily's eyes were misty too, while Chen's face became wooden in unhappiness. In the morning Man Kee's ear had taken on truly extraordinary hues of crimsons, purples, blues, greens, and the beginnings of the sickly yellow it would assume during the next eight days.

The sight of it infuriated Lily. Something had to be done; someone had to do something. No use complaining through official channels. That way you only drew attention to yourself, made trouble for the powers that be, and then they got at you indirectly. It would only bank up more trouble for Son. No, self-help was the way.

'Son,' she called to him as he was picking up his barrow, a primrose-coloured but now normal-sized ear turned to her. 'No garden-play today. Today Mar-Mar intends to teach you thing.'

She took him on to the concrete by the back door. 'Son, Mar-Mar is going to teach you fist.'

Man Kee stared at her with big, bewildered eyes. She spoke softly, lovingly. She would not be harsh with him. She remembered.

Father had given her a classical education in the way of the fist. It was the first stage in a long apprenticeship which would have led to a lifetime's study. It was not a system which had any place in the modern world. The five years she had spent studying were no more than the shallowest initiation. She had spent (her thighs twitched when she thought about it) the first months just bent into the horse stance for an hour. Son wouldn't have the time for this. Nor would she want to inflict it on him. Some practical abridgement was necessary. Moon Lily's Simplified First Method.

'Give me hand, Son.' She stroked the pretty, dimpled fingers and palm, ever so slightly roughened and, turning them over, gently pushed back a ragged cuticle she noticed. Never would she let anyone misshape or hurt this hand; she wouldn't even have allowed Father.

She curled his fingers against the palm and placed his thumb outside. 'Son, this is fist.' She unwrapped his hand. 'Now do yourself. No, Son. Thumb outside. Good boy. Other hand now. Clever boy.' She would not, she decided, confuse him with knife-edge hand, spear-tip fingers, or tiger claw, which could damage the hand. Even fist would be dangerous if he wasn't so young. 'Stand sideways to Mar-Mar. Feet there and there. Bend knees.' She pressed on his narrow shoulders. Maximum flexion and leverage now attained. Now give attacking weapon concealment and deceptive angle. 'Tuck fist under armpit.'

'Under where, Mar-Mar?'

'Just here. Thumb side on top. Now stick left arm out. No, leave that fist under arm. This is left arm: same arm as spout for teapot. Now stick it out here. Turn wrist over at same time as you give fist. Good. Now, Son, push right fist out slowly. "Handle" fist, Son, that's right. Again. Good. Now fast. Good. Now hit Mar-Mar's hand.'

'I don't want to hurt you, Mar-Mar.'

'Don't be frightened. Give fist.'

Man Kee missed wildly and fell over.

'Slowly, Son. Do three times slowly, then quick. All right. Now give fist fast.'

There was a smack as Man Kee's fist flew into his mother's palm. Lily was pleased.

'Now left fist, Son.' She expected it wilder and less hard than the right. It landed with exactly the same force. She was surprised.

'Which hand is stronger, Son?'

'Both same, Mar-Mar.'

Ambidextrous! What a gift! Even Father hadn't had that. Perhaps it was to do with her being left-handed. But she had to go on with the lesson without wasting time.

'Now Mar-Mar teaches how to give kick.' She showed him the cardinal kicks up to the waist, using the heel and edge of the foot (toe and instep were too fragile for a child's foot or untrained man's in a cloth shoe). The strikes were to shin, knee-cap, and groin. 'Clever boy!' This wasn't encouragement. Lily really meant it. Man Kee was a natural, a real natural, with his feet. Just like his mother had been.

'Same like football kick, Mar-Mar.'

Lily was startled. 'Is that so, Man Kee?' Either way Father wouldn't have been pleased: a puncher first and foremost he had been. He had used only his fists to beat the Northern champion. 'Now, Man Kee, give fist again.'

'Want to give kick, Mar-Mar.'

'Do what I say.'

Man Kee, nevertheless, lashed out a few more kicks before obeying his mother. 'Must do what Mar-Mar tells, Son. Mar-Mar did everything she was told when she was a little girl. This is study of fist, Man Kee. Very serious.' She put his feet in the correct alignment again. 'Give fist.' He missed her hand and punched her surprisingly hard on her left breast. Lily winced despite herself but turned the accident to instructive and profitable use. She mustn't get angry; it wasn't Son's fault. 'If someone hurts you, Son, you must never show on face. Understand or not? All right. Give fist. No, don't move feet. *Stupid boy!* Push out other hand, not handle one. *Never* lead with back hand.'

Chen, watering his plants with a sprinkling device which Grandpa had made for him from an old tin of ground-nut oil punctured in an ingenious pattern, turned round and smiled sympathetically at Man Kee. What was Lily doing with him? Something he wasn't enjoying for sure. She ought to let him help with gardening; that was what Son liked best.

Man Kee pawed at the ground sulkily with his Jumping Jack. Lily sighed. 'All right. Give kick if you think that's better.' She moved backwards while Man Kee dealt kicks at a cushion she held in front of her. Now that she had shown him, he put the different kinds of leg technique together in a way that could never be taught. Contrary to the conventional, self-interested wisdom of teachers of any kind, you either knew how to do things or you didn't.

'Ah Man Kee, this is good. Now listen: hold hand in front of face when you kick to stop Bad Person's fist. Never go backward. Always attack. Understand or not?' After a few more passes up and down the concrete, Lily decided this would be enough. He only needed the rudiments after all. 'Play with your father now. And, Man Kee, bad to hurt person with fist. Only use if person wants to hurt you.'

She was in a satisfied mood as she went indoors.

Mui, who was washing pots in the sink, had observed all this: those violent, choreographed motions, so fierce and mindless. She found it unpleasantly familiar, conjuring up childhood and her father's neglect again. She said angrily: 'No good will come of this. You do wrong, younger sister.'

Lily smiled contemptuously. Mui would never understand these things.

'He is *my* son,' she said.

But Mui would not be outfaced over this. 'You will regret what you have done, Lily.'

Lily said: 'You should never run away from your problems. Always

233

go to meet them. You are safest when you take the initiative.

Mui said: 'You will regret this.'

'We will wait and see.'

Nothing happened for a while. Always glad for a chance to prove Mui wrong, Lily still felt a bit disappointed. What she had taught Man Kee could stand him in stead for the rest of his life. He needn't even make a practical application of it; she was just happy she had passed secrets on to him which only they might share. Nevertheless, like any teacher, she was curious to see practical results from her instruction. She went to meet the bus herself for three days, from which Man Kee descended unscathed and somewhat absent-minded, too bound up in who knew what childish concerns to concentrate on his mother's hints and queries. 'School good today, Son? Teacher punish any bad boys? (I don't mean you, of course, Man Kee.)'

Trotting along at his mother's side, Man Kee just ignored her, his big head turning any direction but upwards. Stolid, Lily thought, like his father. Or like an Englishman! Phlegmatists all. Lily halted. She saw now the way things were going. Man Kee, keen to get home in time for the start of Blue Peter, tugged impatiently at his mother's hand. 'Quickly, Mar-Mar.' She allowed him to drag her along while her mind raced with schemes.

Some days later, while Lily's plans were still germinating, Mui came angrily into the shop. She had just collected her nephew from the stop. 'It's all your fault,' she shouted at her sister. 'I told you this would happen.' Man Kee was behind her, looking chastened.

'Hah?' Lily kept her face blank until she could find out what Mui was going on about.

'You and your stupid "Give fist, give fist".'

'What is this, Ah Mui?'

'Man Kee is in trouble with his teacher because of your foolish interference. Big nuisance you make for everyone.'

'What is this, Son? You hit bad boy and make his nose bleed?'

'*Bad Boy?* He strikes a girl as well, that's all. No, that is not all. Wicked things you teach him. Nobody should know these things.'

Lily pulled Man Kee protectively towards her. He shuffled his feet and would not look at her. 'Son, tell Mar-Mar.'

'Teacher says I do "*dirty*" fighting.'

'What "*dirty*" fighting, Son. I don't understand.'

'Teacher says only coward kicks other person in leg. Bad to hit with head and bite.'

'Hah?'

'Teacher says so.'

Lily turned to Mui. '"*Dirty*" fighting means what?'

Mui said curtly: 'Unfair.'

Lily was considerably taken aback. What was 'fair' about fighting, or 'unfair'? You fought to win and you won any way you could. You used every part of your body in its most effective way – just as in business you made use of all your assets, human and material, never mind how humble they were. Why wasn't it brave to attack someone in the leg? What an insult to reduce way of fist to this! It was all too confusing.

Mui had taken Man Kee to the bathroom where she was rubbing his hands with a yellow flannel. She started on his face. Man Kee resisted half-heartedly, twisting his head away and making an angry whimpering but refraining, for instance, from hacking at his aunt's shins or stamping on her slippered feet. Lily tore a cigarette to plaster tobacco from it over a graze on Son's forehead but her hand was pushed away by Mui. Son's eyes filled with tears as his aunt applied stinging iodine.

'Not your fault, Son,' Lily reassured him.

'No,' Mui snapped, 'it's all your fault.'

Lily shrugged her shoulders, giving Mui her coldest look. When Mui bent her head, she stuck her tongue out at her.

The whole extraordinary incident, the amazing perversity of the foreign view-point, could only confirm Lily in the decision she had been fumbling towards. Man Kee *must* go to supplementary Chinese classes straight away. Already it might be too late. She could either have a tough argument with Husband, remembering his previous strange obstinacy, which she would probably win if she set her mind to it, or she could just do it without telling him. Tempting as this last alternative sounded, Lily regretfully discarded it. Husband was bound to find out sometime, just as he had accidentally discovered about Mui. Man Kee would probably enjoy sharing a secret with Mar-Mar but at some stage he must inadvertently blurt it out, giving say an ancient New Territories term for one of Husband's odder vegetables. Anyway, she supposed, Husband really ought to have some say in Man Kee's upbringing.

Surprise of surprises when Husband said: 'Well spoken, Lily. I was going to suggest the same myself.' Lily wondered if this was a trick.

Husband seemed quite sincere, if rather miserable. 'You don't mind, then, Husband? You have changed your mind?'

'I want, Lily, I want.' He was unusually emphatic. 'Let the boy learn about the things which belong to him.'

'You want to make the arrangements, Husband?'

'You do them, Man Kee's mother.'

Lily's hand twitched at her side as she controlled a brief, over-powering impulse to pat Husband on the head and tell him he was a good boy.

It was Mui who was the awkward one.

Point-blank, she refused to take Man Kee to the Street school. It would have been so easy. Lily was deeply injured. All Mui had to do was drop him off on Saturday morning on the way to Mrs Law. One day a week was enough to start with; no need to go more than that to start with. Lily could pick him up at Morden car park while once a month Mui could take him back to Mrs Law's. A nice treat for Mrs Law and convenient for Lily. Lily had it all planned.

And Mui just said no.

'You are being most inconvenient.'

No reply.

'I intend to pay your train fare, if that's what's worrying you.'

'Don't insult me, Lily.'

'Doesn't it worry you that you could make Son grow into a foreign devil boy? You don't care about that?'

'Man Kee is very important to me, younger sister.'

'So take him to Chinese Person School.'

'No, sister.'

Lily stamped in anger. But she was unable to coerce Mui. Lily was at a loss to understand this awkwardness. Mui's eccentricity came close to crankiness sometimes. Was Mui jealous of the family, envious that her sister had a fine boy while she had only a girl? Lily doubted Mui would ever do anything to harm Son; in her peculiar way she had his best interests at heart. Which was why it was so difficult to manipulate her since she had an utter conviction of being in the right. Only a fortnight ago she had bought him a windcheater and new Jumping Jacks from her tips when she could have spent it on her own daughter.

Lily made fresh plans. It was a shame Grandpa wasn't knowledge-able enough to take Man Kee. He would have to do duty at the counter while she ferried Man Kee into Central London. 'Just call out to Ah Chen the number of the dish they point to,' she told him, 'and,

Grandpa, *please* just take the ordinary money from them. Don't try to get more than they owe.' Cackling, cracking his finger-joints, the old man promised with a crafty glint in his eye which did nothing at all to make Lily think he would keep his promise.

Son didn't appreciate the efforts made on his behalf. Lily didn't expect him to: he was play-mad like any youngster. But he obeyed like a good, dutiful Chinese boy should.

'This won't be like ordinary school,' Lily promised him grimly.

She was lucky to be able to get him accepted by the school, which was a large upstairs room and a smaller one. The premises were not prepossessing but who cared when the core of the curriculum, the great heritage of Chinese language and culture, was such a priceless acquisition. She took Son into the rooms, in which there must have been seventy or eighty little Chinese children, many smaller than Son (she knew she had been right to want to send him eighteen months ago). The size of the class reassured her: they meant business. None of your frivolous English-style groups of twenty or thirty. This was organised on the same traditional principles as a boxing class, with the children learning by example and repetition. A handful of older children were copying a complex character from a black-board. Lily had no idea what it was but she approved. A reassuring drone of young voices chanting, learning by rote, came from the other room as if from some forgotten chamber of Lily's own remembrance.

It was with a sense of immense satisfaction, of a deed well done, connections made and a circuit completed that she went to eat steamed pork buns and prawn dumplings and drink her favourite jasmine tea. She had time to see a Cantonese love story at a cinema club and buy Son a cheerful pink and brown striped pullover before picking him up. She had no need to ask prying questions about this school; she knew what he'd be doing *there*. And when they got home even the revelation that Husband had been forced to make refunds to irate customers over-charged by Grandpa could not impinge on her good humour.

Lily couldn't resist saying to Husband in a loud voice so that Mui could hear: 'I really enjoyed myself. It was quite a holiday. Buns and dumpling were delicious.' As Mui chopped away, showing no signs of rising to her bait, Lily shook out Son's new jumper from its tissue paper with more rustling than necessary. 'Beautiful jumper. More pretty than grey windcheater. Come here, Son.'

Man Kee approached reluctantly.

'Arms up.'

Man Kee made the gesture, incidentally one of surrender. Lily pulled the sleeves down but the neck of the woollen stuck on his head. Lily pulled down hard. The top of Man Kee's head appeared. Lily gave an even fiercer tug but at this point it seemed to have stuck for good. The neck was simply too tight for Man Kee's head. Persistent Lily tried again. There was a muffled, anguished protest from deep within the pullover.

'What's that, Son?'

'*Ear!* You hurt my ear. You make it fold in half.'

'Don't be silly.'

'Ow! Ow! Mar-Mar!' Lily gave up. With difficulty she got the pullover off Man Kee's head again. His tousled hair, big, reddened face appeared.

'You hurt my ear,' he accused her.

'Bad to say cheeky things, Son.'

But the ear, only recently back to normal flesh-tones, was bright red and Lily put cold water on it straight away.

A few days later she noticed Man Kee was wearing the pullover under the windcheater and was pleased. 'Did it yourself, hah? Clever boy.'

'Ah Mui cut with scissors and sewed up again with new elastic.'

Lily was cross for a while but then, really, what did it matter next to the overriding importance of the fact that Son was having those vital Chinese classes?

THIRTY-THREE

Hands thrust deep in the pockets of his overcoat, Red Cudgel had observed the late gambling until early morning. He saw large sums won, larger lost, heard the curses of losers, the exclamations of winners, but his face never showed the remotest flicker of interest. At 2 a.m. he retired to a curtained annexe and sucked up a bowl of soup noodles, lacing the *mien* with enough streaks of red chili sauce to burn the roof and lining out of an ordinary mouth. There were still twenty men gambling, despite the hour.

At the corner of Gerrard Street and Dansey Place a car parked. A tall young Chinese in a fawn raincoat stepped out of the back and limped stiffly to the other side of the road. A man waited for him in the staircase to a travel agency in Horse and Dolphin Place. The limping man, his senses already heightened, could smell cologne ten yards away. He greeted the man waiting for him: 'Your face is green.'

The other replied: 'It's a melon face: outside it's green but my heart is red.'

The limping man could see that the agent was, like himself, quite a young man. He had been expecting the older man.

The agent said: 'Act within the limits agreed. Don't kill. Otherwise we may be forced into full-scale war.'

The limping man ignored him. The agent touched him on the arm. 'My friend, you heard me? Easy for you to go in, perhaps harder to come out. You understand me?'

The man nodded.

The agent said: 'You know the signal. When I send four men out together.' He walked away slowly, lighting a cigarette on the corner. After he had gone the limping man pulled his raincoat tighter round himself.

Red Cudgel was having a second bowl of noodles, with even more chili sauce. The *foki* who had brought him the big bowl wondered if he had nerve endings in his mouth and throat like normal people. He ate with a rushing noise, sucking the noodles over the chopsticks. The oily chili had made scummy rings on the broth.

The domino game of Big and Small was finishing. A winner hawked and spat on the floor before pushing the notes into the back pocket of his black trousers. He was about to leave with three companions when Night-brother who had just returned from a routine check stopped one of the men. He had a £5 note in his hand. 'You dropped this,' he said.

'Not mine,' the gambler replied.

'I saw it fall,' Night-brother insisted. The gambler's friends had already left the basement in a group. Night-brother now allowed the man to go; he had been standing in his way.

He went behind the curtain into the annexe. 'Everything in order, Elder Brother. Guards still posted.'

Red Cudgel grunted. Night-brother poured tea for him. Then he went back into the room, where there was now only a handful of gamblers. He told the two pairs of fighter 49s seated at the door: 'Go to fetch Miss Lai from her flat. She has need of you.' The men left obediently.

Three minutes later a tall, deceptively slim young man entered the basement. He walked stiffly, arms straight by his side. When he reached the curtain to the little annexe, he threw apart his fawn raincoat and from under his right arm-pit, where the butt had been nestling, produced a doctored pump-action shotgun. Then he reached up and tore down the curtain.

Red Cudgel had a bowl of noodles to his face.

The man held his weapon by the single stumpy barrel. He hit Red Cudgel across the face with the butt. The noodle bowl shattered. Red Cudgel was knocked off his stool to the floor.

His assailant stepped round so that he had his back to the wall. He kicked the Swatownese in the face. Red Cudgel rolled from his hands and knees on to his back.

They were both out of the annexe.

The man in the raincoat released the safety-catch with his long thumb and jacked a round into the breech with a snick and rich rattle of oiled mechanism. He poked the barrel into the Swatownese's face.

'This is Black Dog,' he said.

Red Cudgel did not look into the wide barrel. He stared over the top into his enemy's eyes. There was no fear in his own eyes but anger and calculation. The armed man smiled. 'Why don't you try, Uncle?' he urged him. 'Leg sweep perhaps?' He stepped back nonetheless. The other occupants of the basement stood where they were. A man still had a domino in his hand.

The man with the gun kicked the Swatownese's shoe. 'What's this, Uncle? I think it might be *turtle*. Your young boys can't help you now, old man. All eggs gone. Old turtle on back can't defend himself.'

He dropped the gun barrel and fired at the Swatownese's left shoe. The report was tremendous. It seemed to go on for ever. The entire top of the shoe had disintegrated into a red pulp. The Swatownese was doubled up; he clutched his heel and shin. It was not possible to say whether he had shouted or not. The explosion had been deafening. Now he made a strange sucking noise, his eyes closed, the spittle in his mouth hissing and seeming to boil as he arched his tongue in agony.

'Can only shoot flippers of old turtle in his shell,' the man in the raincoat said. He worked the mechanism, sliding the ridged wood under the barrel back and forwards again.

A red and gold cartridge clinked on the floor.

He took aim and fired again at the right foot.

Again the blast. The Swatownese cried out, twisted to the side, and then rolled backwards and forwards, making his hissing noise. There was blood all over the floor. Most of the foot had been blown away. Red Cudgel began to vomit white noodles into a pool of blood. The sourness rose and mixed with the harsh, choking powder fumes. The man with the gun walked to the steps. At the top he thrust the gun under his coat again, then he stepped out into a waiting car.

Night-brother was first to Red Cudgel. Still in control of himself, the Swatownese was groaning. Night-brother ordered: 'Call an ambulance.'

As the man ran up the stairs to the telephone in the disused coffee-bar Red Cudgel said: 'No. No. Get Second Brother. White Fan arranges. Must be that way.'

Night-brother rose and waved the man up the steps. 'Give the call for an ambulance. Quickly now.'

He went back to the stricken man, whose suffering was increasing. Night-brother removed his own tangerine corduroy jacket and tucked it under the Swatownese's head, sweeping aside old cigarette butts.

'Help comes soon,' he soothed the 426 officer.

The shock was wearing off the Swatownese and as his pain increased he began to rock and cry out rhythmically.

Night-brother left him and went up the stairs. As he left, he said to the men in the basement: 'Big mouths may regret talking.'

He was already in Piccadilly when the ambulancemen arrived in the empty basement with a stretcher. One of the last men to go prepared a syringe and injected the wounded Swatownese with a dose of No 4.

Grass Sandal brought the tray in and served the two men deferentially. White Paper Fan said: 'Neat job. I'm sure much of the credit goes to you, my young friend. I would not like to try to control an enforcer at his own game.'

Night-brother smiled but said nothing.

Grass Sandal said: 'Why didn't you let him blow his head off? No good stopping at the leg. At least blow his *yang* off.'

The two men looked quickly at each other.

Night-brother said: 'It would have been unthinkable. I regard him as almost my father. I owe him much and so does our society. Besides we would be obliged to avenge his death and explain it to Hong Kong.'

Grass Sandal pouted, and for a moment her pretty face looked ugly. Then the conventional charm returned. 'So be it. I don't know these things like you men.'

Night-brother said: 'I traced the runner quite easily by the way.

241

Remittances had been arriving in Hong Kong stamped from a South London postal district. I merely searched the area for Chinese businesses started in the last three years. I assumed this would be how they earned a living. Quite a flourishing little business, too. They chose their place well. Do a lot of business with long-distance lorry-drivers on their way to the ports. Obviously had things well-organised from the start.'

Grass Sandal said sharply: 'Could be trafficking on their own account or with the 49 then.'

Night-brother shook his head. 'I am certain this is not the case. The women seem to carry on the business.' He joked: 'As always. His wife and sister-in-law in this case. The wife's is quite an interesting background. Runner's father recently came over when the mother died. One son. He goes to one of the schools off the Street.'

White Paper Fan said reflectively: 'Good. May be a useful lever. We want discretion. Keep his family ignorant. You think they know? Unfortunately he didn't take Hung oaths.'

Night-brother said: 'How can one say for certain? I would imagine not.'

White Paper Fan said: 'I wonder whether he ever did any running at all.'

Grass Sandal said: 'That's irrelevant. We are not concerned with guilt or innocence in the past but his usefulness now. His usefulness is, as I see it, quite limited but we should make what capital we can out of it.'

'Agreed.' White Paper Fan looked to Night-brother who nodded.

Grass Sandal said: 'Then he dies. Get him up here – threat or pretext, whatever serves. You must do the rest.'

THIRTY-FOUR

'Lily! Ah Lily! Save life! Save life!'

'Ah Mui, what is it? You've chopped your finger off, haven't you?'

'Not me, younger sister. Grandpa has hurt himself. Quickly.'

Lily took the stairs three at a time and, emerging from the tunnel with a great bound, found Grandpa lying half on the landing, half in

Son's room. The old man's face was grey with pain and he was holding his leg. He was breathing heavily but otherwise not making a sound.

'Mui, go to garage and get help. Then phone for an ambulance. Grandpa, how did this happen?'

'Scaring big grey bird away from window and lost balance.' He sucked in his breath and held it before continuing. 'Must have put foot on something. I felt it move.'

Lily saw that one of Man Kee's friction cars, from Mrs Law's latest addition to a growing collection of 'hard' toys which comprised far more now than outmoded, malleable plasticine, was upturned on the landing by her own bedroom door. She pushed it into a dark corner with her foot while she inspected Grandpa's leg. Father would have known what to do. He was an expert at poultices and setting.

'Where does it hurt, Grandpa?'

He pointed to his hip. Ah, now she knew that was bad for an old person.

'I hurt the other side in the village,' he told her.

'Once you break a bone it sets again stronger,' Lily tried to console him. 'This side will be stronger like that other when it mends.'

The old man said nothing.

There were heavy footsteps on the stairs, which turned out to be not ambulancemen but Mr Constantinides himself. He had told Mui not to bother with the ambulance. Together, he and Lily brought Grandpa down the stairs. The foot of his injured left side, Lily saw, was turned outwards and the leg hung an inch or so shorter than the right.

'Do you want to call your man?' Mr Constantinides asked Lily. She shook her head. He was surprised how strong she was. Mind you, there wasn't much on the fellow. He hesitated at that broken-down old van. Never get him in there. Look at those ropes. What were you meant to do? Stick him in through the window? Mr Constantinides left Lily to prop the old man against the Infernal Carapace and returned in his old Rover 3500.

They put Grandpa on his back across the comfortable rear seat. What a car! Lily couldn't help but admire it, even at this most unsuitable moment. How fast she could go in that!

'Mind you don't get the seat dirty, Grandpa,' she said, making sure his legs were adequately supported but with his shoes over the edge. Mr Constantinides put the old man's feet back on the seat. From the boot he got a rug which he put over Grandpa.

'Back to work, daughter-in-law,' Grandpa called. 'Don't lose money on account of this useless old man.'

Lily scolded him: 'How can you talk like that?'

Actually he had voiced her own thoughts, although she might have phrased it more sentimentally. It was unfair, though, that kind Mr Constantinides should lose time himself. Already he had been put to big trouble. More for Mr Constantinides' sake than Grandpa's, Lily went to hospital where Mr C dropped them.

After a much, much longer time than might have been expected from TV, a young woman doctor examined Grandpa. Even before X-rays, she was able to diagnose a broken neck of the femur. This required an operation.

'Daughter-in-law, bad to waste time and argue. You go home straight away and sell things.'

After the bare minimum of respectful demurring, Lily took a bus home.

It was evening two weeks later when Grandpa returned, already dark, so that the spinning blue light on the ambulance roof threw an exciting glare onto the pavement and even down into the shop where it proved stronger than the soft flickering of the bracketed TV set on the wall. No siren, which was disappointing, but Grandpa's entrance was dramatic, flanked by two uniformed ambulancemen, his plaster showing, and a strange shiny metal tripod in his hand. In fact the whole scene stimulated business considerably. As it was only the news on TV, the customers flocked to the window, some even standing on the pews. Lily locked the till and then wiped her hands on a towel. The sweeping blue light on god's crimson face made him look particularly grumpy and fearsome, as if he had the plague and was going hot and cold by turns.

'Grandpa!'

The customers respectfully stepped back on either side, creating a sort of avenue of welcome.

'Ah Mui, Grandpa returns!'

Mui helped Grandpa to a pew and thanked the ambulancemen as they left. The old man was beaming, pleased to be the centre of attention.

'Never mind this useless old man. Sell things to the foreign devils. Quickly now. Before they go.'

Lily manned the till again and Mui brought tea and special sesame seed cakes for Grandpa. The hiatus had enabled Chen to catch up on the chronic backlog of orders and now Lily did brisk business, dispensing the silver boxes in rapid succession with a cheerful ringing of the till bell. The sight of Grandpa might even have put some of the customers into such a good mood that they ordered more. Lily felt like an auctioneer who has successfully raised bids with a well-timed joke or two. There seemed more warmth in the usually impersonal process of taking the money. One or two older customers actually smiled at her, as if to say: 'You make sure you take care of the old man.' And Lily let them know she would with a little smiling downward curve of the lip which hid her mole and a toss of the head as she rang up that as good as said: 'Don't tell *me*. Of course, I'm going to wait on him hand and foot.' But, provoked, she went to attend Grandpa when the room emptied and found him smoking a cigarette with his tea. Normally she wouldn't have allowed this – it might be too strong for the customer – but instead said: 'Eaten all your cakes, Grandpa? I tell Ah Mui to get you more.'

'No need, no need,' the old man cackled. He cautiously opened his fist, showing Lily the glint of silver. 'Sold them to foreign devil. He was very curious. Much money. Use to buy books for Grandson and plenty of head for him to eat. Fish very good but chicken is all right.'

A little taken aback but basically impressed, Lily mentally classified the money as in the miscellaneous category of Whore Lock and ice-cream and put it into a tea tin. Chen was surprised. His father had been a notoriously bad businessman in the village. It was, after all, the reason why he had to come here. Now here he was turning out sharp as the girls.

After closing time it became clear that Grandpa couldn't sleep in his favourite place. He wanted the girls to prop him up against a case of drink which Lily refused to do. For his part Grandpa was equally obstinate in refusing to go upstairs. Lily had to admit this might be dangerous. In the end Lily pulled together two pews for him. She suspected he had wanted to sleep flat out on the counter, which she wouldn't have allowed: too much like a corpse being laid out for washing. She left a thermos flask of tea and her defunct brown medicine bottle which, knowing his weak bladder, could save him a walk in the night. She rose earlier than usual to check he was all right, but not as early as Son whom she found swinging on Grandpa's metal tripod.

Throughout the day the old man held court on his pew, listening to loud Cantonese opera (permitted an invalid) and making pungent but fortunately unintelligible remarks about the customers. In the afternoon Mr Constantinides dropped by. With smiles, nods, gestures, Grandpa expressed his gratitude – far more eloquently than in Mui's translation. Mr Constantinides spoke in his loud voice. He had already been told Grandpa spoke no English but thought if he spoke loudly and clearly enough there was a chance he could be understood. His eyes bulged with the effort; rather like god's. With rapid nods and little exclamations, Grandpa encouraged him. Mr Constantinides began to feel that Mui's translation was unnecessary and started to talk over her, his voice growing even louder. Grandpa sympathetically offered Mr Constantinides a cigarette – he looked as if he needed it.

'Got to be getting back,' Mr Constantinides said, and in a flurry of nods, winks (from Mr Constantinides) and hand-waving, the two men took leave of each other.

Grandpa had to rest a few days before beginning therapy on his hip in case it seized up for ever. Mui had felt faint at dinner the night before when Grandpa told them about the metal pin which had been inserted into his pelvis. Lily hadn't turned a hair, had offered to manipulate it herself or take Grandpa to Chinese Street for acupuncture. Needles would be stuck in his third toe and the ear-lobes, she told them. She could try herself right now with Mui's needle (the one she was so ready to use on the pullovers of other people's sons). Mui changed the subject quickly, although Grandpa, the potential guinea-pig, had gone on wolfing his rice with sublime unconcern.

A few days later a green bus-type ambulance came (no light, no siren). There were other old people inside. Ambulancemen helped Grandpa in and they all drove off. Perhaps for compulsory euthanasia, Lily mischievously hinted to Mui. Despite herself, Lily was impressed. Of course, help from the State couldn't be compared with the loving care of one's own family but the English had slightly redeemed themselves in her eyes. Grandpa looked a spry old fellow when you compared him with the other grey-haired, wrinkle-faced persons she had seen at the windows. (He was shaved bald which helped, mind you.) None of the others seemed alive at all; they could have been waxworks, staring straight in front, without bothering to take a single look through the windows. The last thing Lily saw was Grandpa's eager, inquisitive, rather naughty – if that was a respectful description – eyes and face as the ambulance braked at the main road and signalled a right turn.

Back in the late afternoon, Grandpa swung his way into the shop like an elderly, agile monkey.

'Did it hurt, Grandpa?' Mui asked solicitously.

'Not at all,' Grandpa said. 'I had a really good time.'

Ho wan! Lily thought, staggered. He certainly couldn't have said that about being turned into a human pin-cushion. Still, it gave him an interest. And, she had to admit, it was a relief not to be bombarded with opera all day. Not that she wouldn't have gone on loyally enduring.

Son's schooling, English-style, continued on its peculiar, bewildering way. Lily rested her faith in his once-weekly exposure to Chinese curriculum, as a measured dose of radiotherapy might burn out cancerous growth. Occasional alarms still shook her confidence – when Man Kee's physical well-being was concerned. Such was the case of Teacher's Terror Pin. Lily was horrified but not basically surprised. Typical of the English: their discipline was either lax to the point of non-existence or ferocious – like beating Hong Kong factory workers senseless with truncheons and then giving them free medical treatment. The Terror-Pin was kept in a glass box of its own. (Display of force often eliminated need for its exercise.) Occasionally, it was brought out *when as an additional refinement of torture the children were actually allowed to handle it!* She discovered about it when she saw Man Kee taking some winter greens in his satchel, obviously as some kind of propitiatory offering, similar to the symbolic offering of lettuce (money) to the New Year dragon. Concerned, as what mother wouldn't have been, Lily examined Son's adorable arms for tell-tale puncture marks but hadn't found any. Good boy. They wouldn't have need to punish him. Fortunately, there hadn't been any more fighting between himself and other boys. He was friendly with Indian boys now, he told Lily. They ate the same special lunch and went round in a group. 'Nice for you, Son,' she said, pleased it wasn't those monkey-looking black boys. They looked so primitive. Might have got him into trouble and pricked with the Terror-Pin.

Son was still a keen gardener, and he and his father had been reinforced at their work by Grandpa. At first the old man had been content to squat, smoke, and watch from the back doorstep. As a carpenter he was ignorant of the first principles of husbandry; although that didn't stop him shouting advice to the bottom of the garden. Chen tolerated this, as was no more than the old man's due. Now Grandpa stuck his injured leg out on a stool and enjoyed the spell of fine weather. He was sawing up wood to make plant frames which would protect the young vegetables from hail and greedy birds. There was a pleasant smell of wood-shavings and golden sawdust. Soon Grandpa was able to stand and work and get around with a light cane.

He still went to therapy – more for companionship than cure, he told Lily.

'But, Grandpa,' she objected incredulously, 'you can't speak any English!'

'No need, no need,' he said, not at all discomfited. 'We old ones know things. We have seen life.'

Later, there was a bigger shock. Grandpa wished to give a feast for his new friends, rather like the entertainments he had given in the village. The mind boggled. Lily didn't know whether to laugh or beat her head on the counter (it being totally out of the question to dash Grandpa's bristly old head against the blue plastic sheeting).

'Where can we get a pig to barbecue for you? How can you teach the Westerner to play *mah jeuk?*' (Do be sensible, Grandpa. We'll do anything *reasonable* to please you.)

'No need for all that,' the old man said cheerfully. 'Who needs pig or *mah jeuk?* Just little-little to eat and drink. I smoke cigarette, foreign devil friend smokes pipe. Everyone happy.'

Lily wavered. 'Let me speak to Mui, Grandpa. *I* think it's a good idea, of course, but perhaps she won't like it. I can't make her do things against her will, you know.'

Responsibility was not to be passed so easily. 'Good idea,' Mui said, thus foiling her sister's stratagem of shifting blame for a refusal onto her. This made Mui's ready falling in with Grandpa doubly vexing.

'Big nuisance,' Lily muttered to herself.

'What was that, younger sister?'

'Lots of rice, I said.'

'No, I don't think so, Lily.'

'What are you talking about, Mui? You rave like a madwoman sometimes.'

'I am wondering about a suitable menu for the old folk.'

'Ah yes, that's very important if we're really going to do this.'

There was silence for a while as Lily, committed now to the lunatic venture, thought hard. '"Sweet and sour pork" is too hard for old person's teeth, if these English people have any teeth left. Grandpa has gold teeth, of course, but they don't go in for that. Perhaps congee and minced salty pork would be suitable.'

'Mmm.' Mui was doubtful. 'Old people may not like Chinese food, Lily. Even *real* Chinese food. Do you notice how most of our customers are young? Old people often become stuck in their ways.'

More silence, broken this time by Mui: 'I know!'

'Chips and omelette?'

'No (but that's a good suggestion, younger sister). I rather thought *"mince, jam tart and custard"*.'

'Eiyah! Of course!' Lily shouted. Easy to cook, not difficult to chew, light on the digestion, and good for them. Even if you only had a set of knobbly old gums in your head you'd never choke to death on that. 'It's settled then,' said a delighted Lily. And then she realised she had solved an older problem: 'Mui, do you suppose the school give it to children for the same reason?' Mui only nodded absent-mindedly, without looking up from her newspaper, but this couldn't stop Lily being pleased with her own perspicacity. She wished Son was still eating it. Mind you, he wouldn't have got friendly with those Indian boys.

Grandpa was easy about the arrangements. 'Good, good. I leave it to you, daughter-in-law,' and he hurried away on his stick with the slightest of limps into the garden where he had been occupying himself with some new construction near the plant-frames Chen had barricaded around his cabbages. You could hear the old fellow hammering away from dawn when he would creep out from the shop with his son's bag of tools and scare away all the twittering birds. If Grandpa was happy, then Lily was happy, too – and it was an improvement as alarm call on Cantonese opera.

She arranged his party for 3 p.m. Monday fortnight when, despite Grandpa's assurances that no such measure was necessary, they would close the shop for an hour and a half. 'And, Grandpa, I hope you don't intend to charge prices for your English friends.' (Husband had told her Grandpa's feasting cronies quite often allowed him to win money off them at *mah jeuk*.)

'No, don't intend,' he said, crestfallen. Not now anyway, Lily thought, dimples flickering.

Now, mince would be easy: not so different from some Chinese dishes, and they had practice from preparing it for Son. Jam tarts and custard they would buy from the Co-op. She went to show her tin and packets to Grandpa in the garden in the same way a restaurateur showed a banquet card to the host. With only ten minutes before the bus-ambulance arrived to take him to therapy, Grandpa was still working furiously at whatever his new project was. There were pieces of wood of different lengths carefully propped against the fence. Good quality wood, better than the stuff Husband used for the benches and beds. Grandpa seemed to be making a large box of some kind. 'At where buy?' Lily enquired brightly, wishing to encourage the old fellow in his happy hobby. He looked up, mouth bristling with nails, pointed to the garage and tapped his money-belt.

'Own money, Grandpa? You bought from your friend the garage owner?'

He nodded.

'What is it, Grandpa?' (Perhaps they could sell it and recoup on the materials, make money even.)

The old man stood rigidly at attention, then put both his hands together under his right ear and inclined his head sideways.

'A bed for yourself, Grandpa? Better design than Ah Chen's? It isn't? A table for your banquet?'

He shook his head agitatedly. Fearful the old man might swallow some nails, Lily dropped her enquiries. She wasn't terribly interested anyway. 'Good, Grandpa, keep it a secret and you can give me a nice surprise. Quick now, bus comes soon.' And she hurried back to serve her customers.

Come Monday, she and Mui worked quickly and efficiently. While Mui hung the CLOSED sign outside the front door, Lily prised the top of the counter loose. Mui helped her balance it on top of two pews. Grandpa had the place of honour at the top of the table. The mince, cabbage, powdered mashed potatoes, custard, were done nearly as fast as real Chinese food. Tasting the grey mince, Lily hadn't been able to resist dashing in some piquant drops of soya sauce while Mui's back was turned. Delicious! Mui was far too busy to notice Lily's sly seasong of the tureen. She had taken over responsibility for the day which Lily, in this instance, was happy to abdicate. Mui bustled. She put paper napkins, cutlery (borrowed from Mr Constantinides) and sliced bread on the counter.

'Toothpicks, Mui, for those with teeth?'

Mui pushed them impatiently away. Lily didn't resent it: she knew when to take orders as well as how to give them.

At 3 p.m., with impressive punctuality, the bus-ambulance drew up and began to disgorge on to the pavement elderly *faan gwai* folk in various stages of advanced senility and decrepitude. Quite how frail and ill they all looked disconcerted Lily until she realised they weren't representative; they were all going to hospital for treatment, after all. Big question: were they up to the excitement of celebration, however small? Would some drop dead? That would be too inconvenient and might get them into trouble. Highly distressing for all concerned, Chens and relations of the deceased.

Lily wouldn't allow the ambulancemen, though, to help the old folk down the steps. That was the responsibility of the hosts. With great care she assisted each of Grandpa's guests into the garden, where Mui helped them into the shop with a friendly and respectful word. Mui then served milk tea in paper cups. At the sight of this, the old folk began to perk up much in the same way as jasmine tea would have cheered Chinese grandparents. But one old lady, ninety if she was a day, Lily thought uneasily, remained slumped over her stick.

Lily touched her gently on her shawled shoulder: 'Drink tea, old woman, drink tea,' she exhorted her in the same sort of voice as she might encourage Man Kee to expel the waste liquid from his system. The old lady's response was to lift her chin off her hands which were folded on the knob of her stick and sit in a slightly less hunched posture. She nodded to no one in particular, ceasing to do so not at once but in imperceptible, shaking stages. That one would need watching, Lily decided, as Mui shooed her younger sister away to the kitchen.

Grandpa hadn't been taking the slightest bit of notice of his guests. He was properly seated at the head of the table, basically looking rather uncomfortable and repressed on the chair but every now and then a great grin would break out on his naughty old face and his gold teeth would glint.

'What joke do you laugh at?' Lily asked as she brought in the heavy tureen of mince single-handed. 'Hah, Grandpa?'

He just wriggled on his chair and grinned all the more, his eyes darting around the room. 'Eat things, eat things,' he said aloud, gesturing to the smoking plates in front of everyone but only lighting a cigarette for himself.

'You don't eat things yourself, Grandpa?' This was Mui.

'I eat smoke,' he quipped, laughing immoderately at his own wit.

One of the elderly English gentlemen now clambered up on his stick and said a short grace, the import of which Lily found rather insulting, implying that divine intervention would be necessary before they could feel grateful for the food.

But now the old folk were actually starting to eat and giving every appearance of enjoying the food (as well they ought to). Sounds of sucking, an occasional click of dentures, the unfamiliar, brittle sound of metal on porcelain, filled the room. Mui brought Grandpa a bowl of white rice with some beef and pickles on top which he snuffled down. Some of the old people who had finished their meal were talking to each other. No one was even looking at Grandpa but he smiled benignly down the table in an unfocussed sort of way. Did he talk to his friends at hospital, at least look them in the eye? Lily pondered. This was most peculiar. She began to feel the old people were here under false pretences. Perhaps the bus-ambulance had delivered the wrong load.

'Do you know these people, Grandpa?' A foolish-sounding question even to her own ears but there was only one way of putting it. 'Know, know, of course.' Grandpa kept staring into the middle distance but was it her imagination that noticed a fractional hesitation before he replied? As if to dispel her doubts, the old gentleman who had said the rude grace came up on his stick to Grandpa and shook his hand warmly, probably more to apologise for earlier breaching the laws of hospitality than to tender thanks for a free meal. Grandpa allowed his clawed, veiny hand to be pumped in this unfamiliar way.

'Jam tart and custard coming,' said Lily, rescuing bemused Grandpa. She had some herself, very nice too.

Mui was feeding the old lady at the end of the bench. 'Don't make her eat too much,' Lily called quickly. Sweet too soon after salty could upset the balance of the system, disturb the whole relationship between *yin* and *yang*. The old lady was quite whiskery already, as opposed to Husband who was merely fuzzy like a peach because of the same reckless indulgence. Identical cause, different effect: another basic principle of life. Feeling quite philosophical, she picked up the mince plates and took them back to the kitchen. Husband had finished some chopping there and was cultivating his beloved garden. He was watering Son's mango plant. Strange, because he had up till now made a silly point of leaving Son to learn from his mistake by trial and error for himself instead of making him learn by example.

Two old gentlemen came into the kitchen and Lily gave them the necessary direction. Was this going to be a problem? Must tell Mui not to pour so much tea. Husband wouldn't like them going on his vegetables.

In the shop Lily found Mr Constantinides, there at Mui's invitation, sampling the sweet. And the old people were, indeed, as she had feared, having tea. Grandpa had made another cigarette. Unfortunately, it was making the old ladies cough. Tears were pouring down one old person's cheek; most distressing. Lily snatched the cigarette out of Grandpa's mouth and without a word of apology stubbed it out in a bowl of custard. No one was to get asphyxiated in *her* shop. Air was what old lungs needed now. Accordingly, she was pleased when Grandpa, not at all resentful about the brusque way his cigarette had been peeled off its damp home on his nether lip, suggested a trip to the garden.

'Speak for foreign devil friends to hear we go outside now,' he told Mui. 'Have something to show old people to make them happy.' Grandpa hopped out spryly, in his enthusiasm without a stick, while Mui marshalled the elderly folk (no mean task) for their breath of fresh air. It took her a good three minutes, during which Grandpa could be heard scraping, bumping, and tacking in a few short nails with quick rat-a-tat-tat blows of the hammer – as opposed to the boom he made when driving in six-inchers. Lily saw him ducking and scurrying in the yard below the kitchen window. 'Everyone ready, Mui? Good. Grandpa, we come!'

'Wait a bit! Wait a bit!'

Lily tutted. She and Mui shared a glance of exasperated affection. 'Now all right? We're coming anyway.'

Grandpa had just thrown a tarpaulin over whatever it was he had to show as Mui ushered his guests into the yard. Contrary to what Lily had earlier supposed, there were muttered complaints amongst the old people about being turned out into the open, especially at such short notice. Lily brought up the rear, shepherding two or three elderly malcontents who clutched their shawls or jackets meaningfully. She was gentle but firm with them. 'You go into garden, old people. Good and nice thing to see.' She was supporting the nodding old lady with the stick, more or less carrying her tiny weight in fact, while the old person cast bewildered, frightened looks around her with the big watery blue eyes of her race and age.

Grandpa was limping up and down, just about beside himself with glee, in front of three rows of murmuring people. Lily urged forward the old folk at the sides so that they made a rough semi-circle, a friendlier and more informal configuration. 'Ready, Grandpa,' she called.

Grandpa stepped forward. With as much of a flourish as his arthritic shoulder permitted him, he whipped off the tarpaulin. Lily blinked. She knew the shape of what she was looking at; it took just a moment to absorb and digest its significance. Propped against the wall at a 45 degree angle were a coffin and coffin-lid in smoothed but unvarnished wood.

Mui sucked in her breath. There were three seconds of silence before a swelling murmur of angry protest arose from the onlookers.

The old lady Lily was supporting plucked at her sleeve. 'What is it? What is it?' she demanded agitatedly, at last showing some interest in what was going on around her. Grandpa, beaming, oblivious to even the possibility of unfavourable reaction, wrung his gnarled carpenter's hands, bowing his head into hunched shoulders. Taking the grace-saying old gentleman by the arm, he dragged him forward. Grandpa pointed to him, then to the coffin, indicating it was long enough to accommodate his English height and trying to get him to step in and try it out for size.

The old gentleman pulled away, beating at Grandpa's hand. He backed off, banging into others in the row behind who were already trying to squeeze through the kitchen door all at once.

'Don't be shy!' Grandpa called. 'Don't fear. I'm making one for all of you. Not dear at all.' He tried to seize another retreating old gentleman who beat him off. 'Tell them, Mui.'

Lily's old lady, now able to see the coffin, began to sing in her trembling voice 'Abide with me'.

Mui forced her way against the general direction to the front and was scolding Grandpa. He brushed her aside, still with a big beam on his face, and tried to capture another fleeing pensioner. Instead he found Mr Constantinides who, presented with the exhibits by proud Grandpa, said something strange but appropriate-sounding like 'Far kin aid her.'

Attracted by the commotion, Husband came from the bottom of the garden, turned the colour of a snake's belly when he saw Grandpa's work, and hastily covered it with the tarpaulin.

In the shop there was chaos. The grace-saying gentleman shook a stick at Lily. Mui tried to soothe, brought yet more tea, but before it could be served the bus-ambulance arrived, as scheduled, at 4.30 p.m. The visitors lost no time in leaving, showing surprising agility in scaling the garden steps.

'It's been a lovely funeral,' said Lily's old lady, suddenly lucid, as Mui opened the gate for her.

Despite the girls' remonstrances, Grandpa refused to admit anything untoward had happened. He worked harder than ever at his carpentry. One and a half coffins were now propped against the wall. He made the lids first, he explained enthusiastically. Brass handles and varnish were what he really wanted now. Chinese coffins were rounder but he knew foreign devils were buried in rectangular ones. He had still made sure the grain of the end panels pointed upwards to withstand rot better.

'Let him do it if he's happy.' Lily sighed.

The banging and sawing continued. As did Grandpa's visits to hospital.

'They don't say thing to you, Grandpa? Attack-you things?'

'They don't say such things! Why should they? All friends.'
'You sure they *are* the ones who came?'
'Hmm.'

But now she had a more important worry. Son had just disgraced himself. It had been at dinner on Friday while Mui was away. Lily was serving a special meal of Chinese sausage, aniseed lacquered duck, chicken liver, salt-fish, and greens from the garden. Man Kee had his usual fried egg and rice with bean-curd. She was making sure he had enough, spoiling him quite outrageously she supposed, when, more to be able to congratulate him, spoil him further, than to get a serious answer, she said: 'What will you do when you grow up, Son of mine?'

Already she was fondling his neck where the hair met the collar of his towelling sleeping-suit.

'Want to be gardener.'

'Is that what you want to be, Son?' Chen asked with interest. He had been eating stolidly.

Now Lily flew into a rage. 'You want to be a gardener? A coolie? Is that what you want to be, stupid boy? Do you think that's what I send you to special school for? Do you think that's what we work for?'

Chen said: 'That's all right, Son. Be a gardener if it makes you happy.'

Lily cuffed Son on top of his head with the flat of her palm. A few seconds later a big tear rolled down Man Kee's cheek.

'Bad, Lily. Let him speak for himself.'

'He must do what his parent says.'

'Son, you want to be a gardener, don't you?'

Man Kee nodded as another fat tear rolled down the other cheek.

Lily stormed out of the room into the kitchen. That Husband should abet him in his disobedience and wilfulness! She looked into the dark garden, her own eyes blurring and a lump forming in her throat. As bitter tears began to come, she opened the back door and strode down to the end of the garden, guided by the smell of the compost-heap. She put her hands round Man Kee's mango plant and tugged at it. It would not come up. She bent her knees and pulled with her back as well as her arms. There was a subterranean tearing, the sound of small roots, tendrils, and delicate fibres shearing and snapping. Still it wouldn't come. Lily took a deep breath. She wiped cold sweat from her forehead. She strained, fighting the plant with her whole body. With louder vegetable groanings it began to come out of the earth. Another long pull and then the plant was uprooted with a single loud snap that seemed to come out of her own body, so that for a moment Lily wondered if she had cracked her own vertebrae. She didn't very much care. Her blood pounded in her ears; she was panting; there was a sharp, almondy smell high in her nostrils. Yes, it was the plant; she sniffed the roots and the earth. Juice, sap must be running out from its ruptured veins. She threw the plant on the compost heap and walked back up the garden slowly, the earth lumpy under the soles of her slippers. She had to slap them together quite hard indoors to get the grit out of the insides.

Husband had Son on his knees. Grandpa had hidden himself under the counter. Man Kee's father was singing something, probably unsuitable, to him. Chen ignored Lily while she cleared the plates off the table in an angry silence. She didn't deliberately bang the tin dishes together; they just clattered unnaturally loudly because no one was talking. After putting them in the sink, she removed Son from Husband and coldly put him to bed. She tucked him up; then pressed hard lips to his forehead.

Breakfast was more uncomfortable – it hardly seemed possible – than the evening meal. Man Kee and his father lost no time in escaping to the garden. When Lily looked through the kitchen window an hour later to get Man Kee ready for his Chinese class, they had vanished. She put the radio on to jolly herself up. A little later Grandpa came in. She smiled at him, her only ally, and was surprised at how stiff her cheek muscles felt.

'Some opera, Grandpa? That would be cheerful.'

Grandpa ignored her greeting. His old eyes were bewildered. 'My coffin: my beautiful coffin! Where have they taken it?'

Without being told, Lily knew who had taken it (*them*, if you were going to be precise about a coffin and two lids). Husband and Son apparently had gone up the side of the house and through to the road, probably more because the coffin and lids wouldn't fit into the house than to avoid Lily (she hoped).

'Did you see which direction, Grandpa?'

'Right-side. No, not right-side. Left-side, is it? No. I remember. Right-side, daughter-in-law.'

Lily ran up the road. Half way along she tripped and skinned a palm. She *would* be wearing her slippers. Too late to go back. She chugged on, hardly lifting her feet now. Husband must be terribly encumbered. She could have caught them by now if she had been wearing her black sneakers. There was no sign of them on the main road. Where could they have gone?

She decided to go back for the van. They couldn't have gone to London or the shops. Perhaps to the school? She went to the roundabout and back but there was no sign of them. She crossed the road and within minutes was passing down deserted streets and empty houses with sheet-metal over the windows. She drove aimlessly at first, then decided to quarter the blocks.

She arrived at a large square piece of waste ground. Somehow familiar. Buildings on two sides, flanked by huge buttresses – it was where they had come on their reconnoitring visit. Now, as then, a bonfire was blazing in the middle but there were no clouds of greasy smoke this time. A taller figure, surrounded by small ones, was throwing more fuel on. Lily parked the van and walked across the empty space. Wind sang in her ears. White ash deadened her light footfall, so that she might have been high on some lonely grassland.

Husband was chopping the remaining coffin-lid into large splinters. Son, helped by four other (coffee-coloured) little boys, was throwing wood on to an already brisk fire. He ran round her to the flames without looking up. Shrivelling in the heart of the blaze were glowing leaves on a black brand.

'What a shame, Son,' she exclaimed. 'Could have planted again.'

Man Kee ignored this overture.

'Are those Indian friends? I think so.' She tried to catch his hand, got his arm instead. Man Kee kept running on the spot, making the angry whimperings usually evoked by a stale-smelling flannel roughly rubbed over the face. Lily released him.

Chen finished breaking the long box and threw a whole side and then the bottom on to the licking flames. The wood, the dead and the sappy, began to crack and bang like a string of firecrackers. Big sparks sailed out.

'Step little-little back, Son. Tell friends to be careful.' One could be blinded. How terrible not to be able to see things for the rest of one's life; more terrible to be blinded from childhood.

Man Kee went to poke the fire with a stick but his father stopped him. He went to break bottles against a wall with his playmates. Lily watched unhappily. Chen jabbed a large piece of wood off the top of the bonfire, allowing more air to circulate. The flames whooshed. Lily said; 'All take car home?'

Chen shook his head.

'Can wait for fire to go out, Husband.'

'Don't fear, Lily. I can bring Son home myself.'

'Good then,' Lily said doubtfully. She walked slowly back over the ashes and, almost at the van, cried out with a sharp pain. Limping, hopping, she arrived at the running-board and found her left slipper soaked with blood, drenched. A jagged lump of green glass had pierced the thin sole and was still mounted in it. She wasn't simply cut in an accessible place on the ball of the foot or even between the toes but underneath, just under the curl of the toes. She drove home in second gear to favour the foot which was no longer stinging but throbbing. Grandpa, who already knew at heart the fate of his coffins, gave her tobacco to poultice the wound after she had held her foot under the cold bath tap.

'Now we're both limping,' she smiled bravely, through tears which had nothing to do with pain in a foot. She hid the injury from Son and Husband when they returned.

For a while things were awkward between them. Lily was all goodwill now; rather guilty, she wasn't sure why. Husband, Mui, Man Kee seemed part of a conspiracy against her, a family plot. Was it just her imagination getting the better of her in this isolated place? Perhaps it had made her a little mad. For there was no exchange between her and anyone else here, though Mui might have her drivers and Grandpa Mr Constantinides.

One evening when Husband sat, by accident, in her chair she found herself ranged on her own at the table, with the others huddled close together opposite her. She was startled by the way the arrangement mirrored the rift of feeling in the family. Her shocked glance bounced off Mui. No one else seemed to have noticed, so it couldn't have been deliberate. And yet, when Husband picked up a piece of bamboo shoot and placed it in Son's bowl, she wanted to find a lonely place to hide and never emerge from.

It was ten days after this that Husband went.

He took nothing with him: no Great Wall suitcase, no clothes, no money from the till or tin.

THIRTY-FIVE

Red Cudgel swung into the lower ground floor of the restaurant on his crutches. With his immense arm and upper body strength he handled himself easily and adroitly but because of the old knuckle-damage on his right hand he was slightly lop-sided in his balance. He spurned offers of help. He dropped into his chair and propped the crutches within easy reach against the screen.

'Hope you feel somewhat better, Elder Brother.' The speaker was White Paper Fan.

Red Cudgel did not look at him. The other officers shifted uneasily but Night-brother was smiling. He said to Red Cudgel: 'Shall I check there are no serpents with the dragons?'

Red Cudgel said: 'There are no *strangers* here. Let us begin.'

White Paper Fan summarised the accounts. He itemised in far more detail than usual. He spoke rapidly and soon succeeded in losing all but Grass Sandal in the complexities of his reckoning. Red Cudgel's eyes were closed; occasionally he opened them to glance round the assembled faces. White Paper Fan jabbed the buttons of a slim battery calculator with the retracted tip of his Parker ball-point to work out the percentages of loans made at interest (a new line of business). He showed how these sums could soon bring in more than restaurant squeeze. He had a sip of tea and went on for another ten minutes. At last he was silent.

'Finished, are you?' Red Cudgel enquired.

White Paper Fan didn't reply.

'Then – with Second Brother's approval, of course – let me bring us to the important business. Or do we not talk about the important thing? The attack on me is no secret. We now have open warfare between ourselves and 14-K, including use of firearms. It is war to the death, with the strongest surviving. We must prevail or be finished.'

White Paper Fan said: 'This is not how I interpret it.'

Red Cudgel seemed unable to believe what he had heard. The blood left his face, a lividness which normally occurred only before he fought.

Night-brother still smiled at no one in particular.

White Paper Fan said: 'As I originally understood it, this was a piece of strictly measured retribution. An analysis borne out by the communication a 14-K 432 delivered to me. The attack was purely focussed on an individual – yourself.'

Red Cudgel sent a spray of spittle over the table with his first words: 'So this was how you "analysed" it then? You "analyse" a situation, do you, instead of acting to change it? I knew nothing of this "communication" between you and 14-K agents which you now suddenly mention. Friend, this sounds like traitorous behaviour to me. You negotiated with the enemy behind closed doors.'

'This was not done behind closed doors.' White Paper Fan was calm. 'You were seriously injured. For some time you were either unconscious or not in control of yourself. Moreover, you were in hospital, a place where it was impossible for us to communicate with you without jeopardising our entire chain of command. Even now we take risks.'

Red Cudgel said: 'There is no distinction between an attack on me and an attack on the society. It is the same thing.'

'Allow me to differ. Family Hung is greater than any individual, however high-ranking he may be. The individual is of no importance in himself, only in his office. He can be replaced. This applies to an Incense Master, let alone an officer of 426 rank.'

'So this is the way things go, is it?' Red Cudgel was suddenly calm again. He smiled, revealing metal. 'In that case we had better count how many chickens we have here.'

White Paper Fan said: 'There are no traitors to be found here. Only true patriots with the best interests of family Hung at heart.'

'Ah, I see now. And you, I suppose, are the one who says just what those "interests" of family Hung are.'

'Interests of family Hung are not to become embroiled in a pointless war; war which could destroy all of us because of the folly of an individual. This is a path to suicide. It is insanity.'

'There are many paths to suicide, my friend.'

'Do you threaten me? Do you think physical force intimidates me?'

Red Cudgel made a movement as if to rise, gripped the edge of the table, then fell back into his chair.

White Paper Fan said: 'To speak bluntly, what use is a crippled enforcer? My friend, you no longer have the ability to manage the situations you create. Situations which are entirely unnecessary. Their only purpose was to confirm your position and usefulness as Leader.'

Grass Sandal said: 'Elder Brother deserves our respect. Family Hung owes much to him. You speak too harshly, Second Brother. We should repay this debt. Before he leaves the country for higher office, we must honour him.'

Red Cudgel took a moment to digest the significance of her remarks. 'What did you say? What goes on here?'

Grass Sandal cast her eyelashes down over her rounded eyes. 'We greatly fear bandit authorities may wish to expel you from here, Elder Brother. This is our greatest fear.'

White Paper Fan said: 'You have committed no crime, of course. Nothing can be ascribed to you which is unlawful. But they can deport you without any reason at all. I advise you now of this unfortunate fact.'

Red Cudgel said nothing.

Grass Sandal said: 'Most unfortunate we could not have arranged for Elder Brother to be treated more discreetly.'

Night-brother said quickly: 'Elder Brother's life was my priority. He could have bled to death had I not got immediate help. He was in great pain.'

Red Cudgel said: 'Should be possible for you to arrange something. I recall similar circumstances arising before for a 432.' He addressed himself to Grass Sandal and his tone had changed.

She shook her head. Now she looked him full in the eye. 'Not possible, I think, Elder Brother. Woman does not automatically have a right to assure her husband of residence here. She is not equal as in family Hung,' she joked, 'and yours is a bigger matter. Yours is a much more difficult business than the 432's.'

White Paper Fan said: 'You are marked for bandit attention now. Our whole operation is jeopardised. Meeting even now, with all the precautions we have taken, we still face an unacceptable risk. How can you continue to command when you are under their surveillance? If they let you stay, then it will only be to catch us more easily.' He paused then said with real anger: 'This affair was even reported in *newspapers*.'

Red Cudgel found nobody would look at him.

White Paper Fan continued: 'Bandit harassment was not a problem even a few years ago. It is becoming so. You bear part of the blame for bringing this about. I, too, through negligence. Chinese people here will not betray us. We are part of their heritage. It was well said: the officials have the law, the people the secret societies. And it is well the people should fear us because respect is always founded on fear. But this tolerance is a delicate thing. Once, family Hung was all-powerful. In Singapore nine-tenths of all Chinese were members of our association. In Hong Kong at least half. This was when the Ching still ruled at the beginning of the present century. Now that our influence is slightly less, the actions of family Hung must change to suit the altered times. Here, too, where things are different even from modern Hong Kong, Taiwan, or Singapore, plans of family Hung must change all the more. This is why recent incidents can only undermine our standing. Family Hung is a great tree with many branches but it draws its nourishment from the soil underground. This soil is our community. It is good soil, fit for Hung to flourish. But if you pour poison on it, then it can no longer sustain. Toleration cannot be indefinitely presumed on. We depend on silence and peace. You have almost destroyed that silence and that peace.'

There were murmurs around the table.

Red Cudgel said: 'You talk cleverly. Is what you do as clever as your words?'

White Paper Fan said: 'I would have to be a genius to undo the damage you have caused.'

'How can you defend yourself against attack? Who knows these things? You know 14-K as well as I do.'

White Paper Fan said: 'We have a redoubtable fighter in one of our 432 officers. He has only now, incidentally, served the requisite term to hold that rank.'

Iron Plank would not look at Red Cudgel.

White Paper Fan said: 'Of course, there is no promotion as such between the sub-branch ranks. 415, 432, 426 are not in themselves superior or inferior to each other. Grass Sandals, Red Cudgels, White Paper Fans, are all eligible for the post of leader or deputy leader. There is no reason why the society's leadership would be monopolised by the enforcer, rather than the planner or agent.'

Red Cudgel said: 'Fools, how do you think Wo headquarters will allow you to do this?'

White Paper Fan said: 'They have already accepted it. It is an accomplished fact.'

Red Cudgel stared hard at Grass Sandal, who, like Iron Plank, would not look at him.

White Paper Fan said: 'To speak truth: we would have seceded in any case. New societies rise and fall. There is nothing exceptional in this. All Wo headquarters wish to do is safeguard their fees and remittances.'

262

Red Cudgel said: 'What you do means you face a stronger enemy tomorrow. The only beneficiaries of this are 14-K.'

White Paper Fan said: 'I think not, my friend. I should say your errors were not confined to military spheres. The runner you ordered *washed* – this man was innocent of fraud, and had been set up as guilty party by the 49 who supervised him. The 49 who was initiated at your mass induction. This wretch had also been putting squeeze on the runner. The runner had never actually sold a bottle of No 3 at any time.'

Red Cudgel asked: 'This man has already been washed?'

'Already. Too late to do anything. The dead cannot be brought back to life. Your precipitate action is solely to blame. How can one even calculate the damage this could do us if word spread? Better to lose ten dead to 14-K than this.'

'Who washed him?'

Night-brother looked Red Cudgel in the eye.

'How?'

Night-brother knew what Red Cudgel meant. 'He suffered neither fear or pain. He did not know. If he did, then he was braver than a shop-keeper has a right to be.'

Red Cudgel said: 'That type can die well. It is my experience that this is so.' He was silent for a moment. 'The 49 must be punished in the same way. He has behaved with utmost disregard and contempt of the society. The affair of the innocent man is regrettable. I acknowledge this.'

Grass Sandal and White Paper Fan each caught the other's glance.

Night-brother said: 'The man's wife has interesting antecedents. Maiden name Tang. Father Tang Cheung Ching.' This meant nothing to the others. Iron Plank looked momentarily interested. Red Cudgel said: 'Tang Cheung Ching of Kwangsi?'

Night-brother nodded.

Red Cudgel was silent for a long while.

White Paper Fan broke this silence: 'The 49 will meet appropriate punishment. We can actually make use of him. 14-K want revenge for one of their officers killed at Twickenham. Although this 49 was not one of the raiding party on that night he can substitute. His denials will only be expected.'

Grass Sandal said: 'This occasion should be a celebration. We are giving Elder Brother Double Flower prefix. He assumes 438 status. Let us drink to that. *Yum sing!*'

There was a ragged chorus of toasts.

Grass Sandal produced the golden symbol of the Double Flower. Red Cudgel looked at the table, fists balled. He neither raised his glass or acknowledged the others. He seemed to be thinking of something other than himself altogether.

Ricky Lam said: 'He went more easily than I expected. Far more easily. I thought he had a harder core.'

'He *is* a hard man. That was why he was able to relinquish control under the circumstances.' Mao Sung sounded almost regretful.

Miranda Lai asked: 'Do you think he may betray us? Go to the bandits? Or volunteer information if they question him? He may wish to strike some bargain over deportation.'

Mao Sung pretended to look shocked. 'Of course not. That is a most extraordinary suggestion. You show little knowledge of him or of the nature of the society.'

Miranda Lai apologised.

Mao Sung said: 'His weaknesses were old-fashioned ones. He could not adjust. All that bluster and threatening. You should never threaten anyone but eliminate them quietly and without warning. His strengths, nevertheless, were also old-fashioned ones. Such a man could never divulge our secrets to outsiders. It would be unthinkable. He would suffer imprisonment, torture even. Allow me to correct you on this matter. I have no sympathy for the man but even I can see this.'

Ricky Lam said: 'He was most insistent that reparation should be made to the widow and family of the man I washed. Community of feeling between fighters, I suppose. It must have been a way of life for them in the old days.'

Mao Sung said: 'As I remarked, he is very much an old-style officer. They took the oaths seriously – as they are meant to be taken.'

Lai and Lam exchanged glances. For them, the oaths and all the rest of the absurd ritual were glosses on the real purpose of their activities. They knew White Paper Fan had more in common with Red Cudgel, in fact, than themselves. This might be a problem in future.

Miranda Lai said: 'This question of the cash for the widow. So much sentimental nonsense. *I* would not tolerate such waste. However, it occurs to me that it may be expedient to allow it to continue – not for the ridiculous reason given, though. In view of the recent publicity drawn by the fighting, a disappearance like this could create unwelcome interest. But much more serious: it would be disastrous if by any chance the circumstances of his death were made known to any other Chinese. I do not believe in taking the smallest risks. The cash is a small price to pay to keep this hidden. Personally speaking, I cannot conceive of the stupidity of coercing an outsider into undertaking the work in the first place. We no longer live in the nineteenth century!'

Ricky Lam's smile became a little fixed.

Miranda Lai spoke with an incisiveness that was not new but merely unconcealed: 'Our organisation and operation in this country need re-thinking. It is simply not possible for us to function here in the same way as Hong Kong or Singapore. Mass membership here is not to be equated with strength. In any case, that membership cannot be sustained here. Let us face the truth – we cannot offer passive members the kind of benefits which would draw them in Hong Kong. Nor do they need those services here. We should be a small cadre of active members, withdrawn from the community rather than part of it. We should run a small number of lucrative businesses, the drugs, gambling, squeeze, and we should do it ourselves and not contract to outsiders, whatever the risk for the 49s.'

Mao Sung said slowly: 'There is much truth in what you say. I don't agree with all of it. But certainly we should send a small regular remittance to the man's widow now. Size is not important, its regularity is. We could do it from Belgium or Holland. No difficulty as such but perhaps you could arrange through your contacts? Mine, I am afraid, are mostly sympathetic to our former leader.'

Miranda Lai made a note in her tooled engagements diary.

'Now important business. We need to elect officers on the fourth of next lunar month. 426 post is obvious, of course; none of us is qualified to fill it; none of us would wish to. I propose you, Miss Lai, for Deputy Leader; you, Ricky, for Leader.'

Miranda Lai coloured and laughed in her most appealing way. 'You mustn't joke like that, Elder Brother. Of course you must be leader, of course Ah Ricky must be deputy.'

Mao Sung waved his hand deprecatingly. 'Well then. If that is what you want. Now, gifts of food and drink and also cash must be sent to the 14-K leaders as part of the promotion ceremony. I can arrange this. I have already agreed with them to split the Chinese quarter in half for purposes of revenue. The north side will be theirs, the south ours.'

Ricky Lam said: 'I also recommend we feast our own members, the newest 49s included. They should know their loyalty is appreciated and recognised.'

'Quite correct. You are astute. It goes without saying.'

They began the pleasant task of making their new arrangements.

THIRTY-SIX

And at first Lily was heartbroken. Good, kind, dependable Husband, where had he gone to? It was so unlike him. To go without warning, vanish just like that – even now she could hardly believe it. She refused to believe it. This incredulity was her weapon against sorrow. It was as if by an effort of will she could alter what had already happened. She began to feel better; she sang as she dusted; flicked jauntily at high corners with her cloth; gave god's belly a friendly wipe. His bulb had just burnt out – no complaints, three years almost was a long time – but she didn't have the replacement size handy. She served the customers cheerfully, was about to call through the hatch to Husband for more bean-sprouts. And then her eyes clouded over and she had to duck her head hurriedly. She blew her nose in a *yang*-ish way on a handkerchief already sodden, shook her head, and tried to laugh.

It was bad, of course, at night. No reassuring, recumbent form lay beside her then in silent companionship. Husband had never been the liveliest of companions (by day or night) but she knew she had loved him for that strange, quiet doggedness of his, his ... Lily looked for the word which would encapsulate in essence all the qualities of Husband, his Husband-ness, and she could not find it, search as she might. It was easier to think in pictures, images of him doing things: gardening hour after hour; working in the kitchen; looking over the accounts with a blank face, empty of all understanding; failing with obstinacy to learn to drive automobiles. She said to Mui: 'Husband is ... is ... is ...'

'*Stolid*,' Mui said. 'He's stolid.'

'Hah?'

Now that there was no Husband next to her, Lily found it difficult to sleep. Strange, it should have made it more comfortable. She had often kicked him in her sleep. She would throw an arm out and it would find empty space and the emptiness would wake her. She could also hear Mui turn in her sleep, something she had never noticed even through the thin walls of their council flat. Often she woke in the morning to find herself on what had been Husband's side of the bed with her arms and knees around the pillow in a fierce embrace.

Little things could be distressing. Going through her pantry, she upset a jar at the back and out poured a rattling flood of the tiny red beans Husband had loved boiled in sugar. She picked up a handful, letting them run through her fingers one by one, as if they were the days of the life she had shared with Husband, until there were none left and she looked at an empty palm, still slim and shapely but now badly work-roughened. She looked at the beans again and they were red as blood, the bitter tears of blood she could shed, she thought. She had already gone through the pockets of the clothes he had left behind for clues to his mysterious disappearance. But there was nothing much: a packet of Fison's seed – she recognised the picture of English broccoli on it – his key to the front door, a packet of fruit gums he had bought for the Son he loved, a box of matches, a half-empty packet of the cigarettes she had been sorry to see he had started smoking again. These articles she swept into a strong manila envelope and on it she wrote in crayon in English: *Husband's things*. If it was a bigger envelope I could get into it and seal myself in, she thought. Instead – it was five o'clock in the afternoon – she got into bed, pulled the white sheet over her head as she sat cross-legged and had a little weep, since this was the only place where she didn't have to be brave for anyone's sake.

Earlier, the first night of his absence, she hadn't been at all worried when Husband was late coming back. After all, it wasn't like Son losing his way or being snatched by some wicked man. He could have fallen in with old associates; been pickpocketed of his fare back; might quite easily have got drunk since his tolerance where alcohol was concerned was famously low (she remembered that New Year). He was a grown man who could look after himself.

By five next evening her annoyance about doing a lot of extra work at lunchtime had turned into mild anxiety. This increased at a compound rate so that at six she was concerned, by half past deeply worried, at seven anguished, and by eight frantic with dread and anxiety. She could not interest herself at all in doing work. She dumped the boxes into the customers' hands, took less money than she should, and – Mui thought – quite probably let some of them get away without paying at all. Lily's composure was quite gone.

'Now let me do it, younger sister,' Mui said kindly. 'You sit down and drink some hot tea.'

Lily allowed herself to be led away.

Grandpa, too, did his best to cheer her up. 'No fear, daughter-in-law,' he reassured her. 'He comes back soon. Don't concern yourself.'

Lily was going to put Son to bed while Mui worked downstairs but she wouldn't hear of it. 'I do it, Lily, I do.'

'But, Mui, you are already working so hard all by yourself.'

'Never mind. You can only upset him, Lily. You're not in the right mood.'

So Lily stayed in the kitchen and heard the creaking over her head as Mui tucked Son up and then found him a comic to read. At ten Lily could bear it no longer. Ignoring the pleas of Mui and Grandpa, she got in the van and drove up to the city.

'Please, Lily. Don't be so rash. What if Brother-in-law comes home while you are gone or you have an accident?' She was worried Lily's concentration would be affected. 'It's so unnecessary. What can you do?'

But they couldn't stop her. It seemed no time at all to Lily before she was in the city centre. She hadn't driven recklessly, just without thinking at all. Angry honkings, twice the screech of tyres, indicated she had shot traffic lights when they were against her. What did she care? She left the van half on the pavement, half on the street, tilted at an awkward angle. She was about half a mile north of Chinese Street which, as always, was blocked with a myriad cars, over-spilling into the neighbouring streets. Down the dark, empty throughfares she went, passing a hospital and department stores. These were wide, grand roads. They spoke to her of wealth and elegance she knew now she would never have. In the illuminated shop windows were not just individual objects of crystal or furniture displayed in isolation but whole rooms: here was a mahogany dining-table and chairs, laid with porcelain plate, heavy silver cutlery, thin glasses, an embroidered table-cloth. It only needed guests. There, in the next section of window, was a child's room, luxuriously appointed (not just a question of a proper, though child-size bed and mattress – *that* went without saying – but yellow wallpaper with red ducks on it, a fluffy tartan blanket, plump quilt, and furry white rug for little feet to find on a winter morning). Then there was a kitchen. You could see it was a kitchen because of the steel cooking rings and glass oven door set into tiles. But this vast, glittering room was a palace compared to any of the rooms they had. How cramped, how mean was the life they lived. The light in the kitchen display was malfunctioning, on the blink, and as it came on and off with a threatening buzz and hum, Lily saw her reflection. Then the bright display – and finally her own dark image again. There was a look of bitterness and self-pity on her face. She was shocked. She moved on quickly.

Now she crossed a still bigger road, almost stepping under the wheels of a taxi. She hardly heard the driver's shouts. On the other side the streets were narrower, darker and poorer, although there were more people in them. Strange furtive-looking men in raincoats, of a type already familiar, looked into the windows of cramped shops, the entries to which were screened in the same way as their staircase at home. Down an alley a woman stood in a doorway which was dark except for the glow in a bell-push. Now she went through an arcade, music coming from the basements. There was a life-size cut-out of a scantily clad girl, her stomach not quite as flat as Lily's. Curiosity was still strong in Lily and she sneaked sidelong looks: men sitting at plush red velvet counters, a woman (fully clothed, heavily powdered) at one. Someone caught her glance as she went by and she heard him call 'All welcome in here! Don't be shy now.'

But at last she was coming into the Chinese part. Over another big well-lit road, and then she was going into Chinese Street.

Where could she start looking for Husband?

She was no longer used to such bright lights, to so very many people – Westerners as well – all milling and jostling you off the pavement when you stood still and tried to have a think. She stepped from the kerb onto something slippery, a burst tomato, and quickly mounted the crowded pavement again. Perhaps she should try Husband's old place of work. If he wasn't there, his former colleagues might have suggestions. As she proceeded south, she began to limp. The cut on the underneath of her foot was almost healed but the fast walking in her hard sneakers had rubbed it and now salt perspiration was making it sting. Lily decided to hurt herself and she put her full weight on the tender foot. She enjoyed the pain. She passed a place with photos of men in towels being (incorrectly) massaged by girls in red shorts – no sign of the Indian restaurant Husband used to mention. And there was the Excellence. Someone, not Uncle Lo of course, was working at the chopping board.

No, his old friends couldn't remember seeing Colleague Chen for over two years and certainly not in the last forty-eight hours. Lily smiled a false smile and lied as convincingly as she could. 'Ah, how strange. He was planning to visit you all today as we are in London. He must have gone to our *car* already.' There were still some curious faces. Then the boss arrived and, on discovering who Lily was, if he didn't exactly show her the door, certainly did nothing to encourage her to prolong the visit.

She walked further up the street to see if Husband might be in any of the other restaurants. He wasn't. There was a small alley at the street's end with an iron bollard at its mouth, without a function since anyone could see the alley terminated blankly in a blind brick wall.

Lily went back to Chinese Street proper. She peered into all the restaurants she could, bravely walked into the ones with awkward windows, and stared around. She crossed to the north side, and he wasn't there either. She turned up a side-street and there was an iron staircase going into a basement. There were many young men lounging against the railings, smoking and using a lot of swear words, *lan jai*, bad types. She veered away, took a grip on modest inclinations, and forced herself to go down the steps. There was the smallest of chances Husband might have fallen in with bad company and gambled away the roof over their heads. She'd forgive him at once. Maybe he was too frightened to come home and tell.

As she descended she heard comments. Tears Lily resented came to her eyes and, as she became angry and stopped feeling upset, they brimmed over and fell. But she was out of sight and could sweep them off her cheeks with the back of a hand. Cigarette smoke stung her eyes and she had to wipe them again. It was more crowded than she could have imagined possible and deafeningly noisy. Was that Husband over there? Her heart fluttered. He was a stocky man in a windcheater and black trousers (never mind that Husband had worn a brown padded jacket to leave the house), the back of his hair cut square across and gleaming with brilliantine the way Husband liked it. He turned from the table to speak and, with that slight movement of the head even before she glimpsed the unfamiliar face in semi-profile, she knew it wasn't him. But how similar Chinese people looked from behind! She pushed her way out of the smoky basement and its littered floor. The street air seemed pure after what she had been taking into her lungs down there.

On her right she saw a small opening going into a wider area; it was like a bottle. You'd hardly notice it unless you knew it was there. Silly to go in there; Husband wouldn't be there.

She stepped boldly in. It was like being in a cave or tunnel almost. There were no stars above. Might someone try to rob her? Just let them try. She was the only person there. There was a scurrying sound coming from one of the huge dustbins. She squeezed along the line of cars parked bumper to bumper. Opposite the other exit was a cinema showing that kind of film. She hoped this wasn't the place Husband used to go to with Uncle Lo.

With a heavy heart she retraced her route to the car and began the long journey back in the dark.

It was past two in the morning when she turned by the garage (how familiar, reassuring, and ... *clean* it looked for all its oil and grease), turned off the motor, and silently coasted the last hundred yards in fourth gear to avoid waking anyone.

Mui was slumped sideways on a pew, short, podgy legs straight in front of her, her pigeon chest rising and falling, eyes shut. Above, on the wall, the TV emitted a high-pitched whine and hiss and jagged black and white squiggles shot across the screen. Lily switched it off.

'Ah, younger sister, you're back. I was so worried.'

Lily knew then that Husband had not returned while she was out.

'Sure to be back in morning time, younger sister.'

Lily raised a weak smile.

There was a loud report from under the counter. Burglar? Whore Lock bottles exploding? Of course not. Grandpa hiccuping. His sheepish face appeared by the till. His shoulders twitched; they seemed to rise to his ears. Unamplified by the counter, his hiccup was sharper, more like a hiccup in fact than a convulsion in the bowels of the earth.

'Ah, it's only you, daughter-in-law. Thought maybe robber was coming in.' Grandpa shook his hammer and saw at them over the counter in the way he might give a puppet show for children.

'No, Grandpa,' Mui said firmly, removing the sharp and heavy tools from him before he did himself an accidental mischief. 'But I'm sure we're all safe here with you to protect us.'

Grandpa ducked under the counter again, from which after a few seconds' interval there was another booming eructation.

'Don't you know one of Father's remedies for this, younger sister? No? Come upstairs then. Try to sleep. In morning time things may change but not now, I think.'

Lily allowed herself to be shepherded up the stairs.

But Husband was not back in the morning, nor the next, nor the one after that, nor any of the succeeding mornings of a life which had been turned upside down. For a long time Lily was sad; and even when she thought she was over her heartbreak, accidents like the spilled red beans or an order for bamboo shoots would remind her, and the tears would fall.

She had now decided Husband had run away with another woman.

It was a bitter thought but better than imagining him wiped off the face of the earth in some mysterious flash of lightning.

'Mui! Mui! Look!'

'What is it?'

Lily couldn't speak she was so excited. Instead she passed the envelope with a hand that shook. 'I knew he wouldn't abandon us, Mui.'

Mui saw there was money wrapped in tissue paper. £10 in ones. There was no other enclosure. She turned the envelope over. There were foreign stamps.

'Not posted in England, Lily.'

'Hah?'

Mui opened the front door for more light and tried to decipher the smudged postmark. 'Must ask an aitchgevee.'

Later: 'From Holland, Lily. Amsterdam.'

'Husband must have a restaurant job there. Many Chinese people in Holland.'

'What makes you think Brother-in-law sends the money?'

Lily said quietly but scornfully: 'It can only be Husband.'

Later still: 'I know why Husband left.'

'Why?'

'He knew our business was not making enough money. Enough to live on. Not enough to look after Man Kee properly as he gets older.'

Mui still looked puzzled.

'He has gone to add extra money to our family. Same was done in our village. He knows we can keep making money ourselves in this business. A true father. He makes any sacrifice for his son.'

Mui opened her mouth, saw the happy smile playing around Lily's cheeks, and shut her mouth.

'You see, Mui. I told you it was a silly idea to tell police. What could they do? They could maybe have spoken to tax collectors. Now we don't have to pay tax on Husband's money. It's just like our drinks and ice-cream money.'

Mui didn't argue any more. If Lily was happy, so be it. She had already had that distressing scene with her about reporting Brother-in-law as an officially missing person. Lily, of course, had taken violent exception to this conventional proposal.

There were in any case other matters requiring Mui's full attention. Things had to be broken to Lily gently; better to surrender now on matters which were of little practical consequence. It would be easier to get her to agree to bigger things later.

Such as getting married.

'To Mr Lo? *Uncle* Lo,' Lily added pointedly. She didn't know whether to laugh or treat Mui with the due care you'd accord a madwoman, the suggestion was so preposterous.

But Mui showed no signs of sharing the joke; or of being mad for that matter.

'That's right, Lily,' she said, rather coolly.

Lily had an inkling, ridiculous though it might seem, that she could have hurt her sister's feelings.

'Good, Mui, good,' she said, without sincerity or feeling.

Then Mui went on her forecourt errand.

'So,' Lily said to Mui as they were clearing up after the last customer.

'So,' said Mui straight back, uncooperatively.

Lily counted the money in the till, then tried Mui again. 'Met Unc . . . *Mr* Lo First-Born at Mrs Law's house, I suppose?'

'Right.'

'Ah, how nice for you both. That is . . .' Lily coughed without finishing her sentence in case she might be being tactless again. As Mui didn't seem offended, she continued: 'Got wedding day set? Make sure it's a lucky day. Husband and I chose our day very carefully. Gave fortune-teller lots of money.'

'Nothing arranged yet, Lily. Very informal at the moment. We will do it quietly. Only small people. You must understand, younger sister.'

'Ah.'

'By the way, Lily: I want to bring Jik Mui here.'

'Jik Mui is who?'

'My daughter. Your niece.'

'Ah, she's got a name!'

'Of course!' Mui softened her tone. 'Lily' – she hesitated. 'No reason why she shouldn't live with us here?' She was going to add 'now' but was able to stop it tripping off her tongue.

Lily's face clouded. Then she said: 'No reason why not. Bring her.'

She put the till cash in her crocodile purse, which still contained ten crisp £1 notes, and went upstairs without another word. Mui saw her bending over Man Kee's bed as she went quietly into her own room.

Since Mui had started 'going to Mrs Law's', Lily had stopped being so possessive about Man Kee. With Husband gone from her, the earlier jealousy returned. She was even annoyed when Mui spoke to him. She had taken to helping her nephew with his homework at the counter. The two of them were absorbed in his spread-out books, and Lily felt angry and isolated to see this. The recent shocks had interrupted her deliveries of Man Kee to Chinese school. She intended to resume normal service as soon as possible. She was reluctant to tread again those streets she had wandered in a vain search. It was an aversion so strong it amounted to nausea. Silly, but there it was.

As if to make up to Husband her negligence in bringing his son up properly, the way she was sure he in his heart of hearts would want him brought up (never mind what he *seemed* to want on the surface), she repeatedly dinned into Son the example of his father. Overnight, Chen had become a secular saint, a household deity to rival god. Never so revered when physically available to his family, Chen was becoming a paragon of all the traditional *yang*-type virtues and not a few of those more usually thought to be under the influence of *yin*. He was far-sighted, strong, resolute, kind, magnanimous, and brave; he was also considerate, unselfish, sympathetic, tender, and gentle to his loved ones and especially his son, Man Kee.

'Why has he gone away and left us, Mar-Mar?'

For this piece of impertinence Man Kee got a slap, an open-handed cuff about the ear and side of the head which had *really* hurt (far more than Lily intended). His eyes began to fill. Lily said: 'Bad boy. Bad to talk like that.' A tear dropped on the counter. 'All right Son. Go and play in garden.'

'Want to look at book.'

'Do what Mar-Mar says. Your father likes to see you gardening.'

She dressed him in windcheater and wellingtons and sent him out. When she looked up from her chopping a little later he wasn't doing anything, just running a stick along the broken boards of the fence. She must get Grandpa to repair it; that would be something useful he could do.

A couple of days later Mui brought her daughter to the house. Lily was admiring the old man's handiwork at the time. She found Mui and Son upstairs by the cot. It was a shop-bought cot, which was a shame as Lily was sure Grandpa could have knocked one up in no time (certainly one good enough for a girl).

Jik Mui lay on her back sucking her thumb. She had enormous

brown eyes. Man Kee put an arm through the bars of the cot and pulled her leg. This was obviously a game they played because Jik Mui laughed. Mui smiled at Lily but didn't say anything.

Quite a pretty baby, Lily thought (not as pretty as Son at that age, it went without saying). What Lily really wanted to do was work out Jik Mui's paternity. Those big brown eyes ... Indian maybe? Indian babies had big brown eyes. They were also, she had noticed, rather hairy. However, Jik Mui was quite smooth. The hair on her head was black but there was something about her cheekbones which bespoke Western ancestry. Lily was positive about this; was on the point of sharing the discovery with the mother when she realised the information was redundant and very likely offensive.

'Down we go, Son,' she said, more to keep herself out of mischief than Man Kee.

It was Mui's turn to be careful at the end of the evening. 'Younger sister, I am getting married in two weeks' time from tomorrow. Hope this is convenient.'

Lily was not altogether unprepared but still waited before she replied so that her voice would be steady. 'Ah. Good, good. What a happy occasion.'

'Yes, Lily. We go to registry office. Then banquet in a big new restaurant.'

'Have no fear, Mui, I can look after business. You enjoy. It's your wedding.'

'No! Bad talk! Really bad talk! Younger sister, you are the most important person I invite.'

'No, I'm not. Surely Mrs Law must be. You mustn't be ungrateful, Mui.'

Mui put her foil box down and hugged Lily. She, of all people, knew how Lily felt. She kept her short arms round her. How bony and hard Lily was! At first Lily's body was stiff and resistant. Then it was as if a central cord had been cut in her back. She collapsed against Mui who held her tighter.

'Mui.'

'Lily.'

They wept together. Finally, Lily pulled away, blew her nose, laughed.

Mui smiled happily, too, in a blurred sort of way.

'By the way, Lily. Mr Lo ... Husband and I are opening our own business.'

'But Mui ...' Then Lily said: 'Where is it?'

'Just near here. Remember the big empty shop with workmen in it that we saw the first time we came to this area? Yes, that place. Mrs Law is lending us money. She is our "sleeping" partner.' Mui laughed. 'Otherwise I would have applied to the bank for a loan.'

As if banks lent money to people like us, Lily thought. How Husband would have laughed. Even he, silly Husband, had known better than that. But what was this about leaving!

'Mui,' – Lily hesitated – 'I thought perhaps you would like to continue our business here, it's doing so well. I could move into your room and you and Mr Lo could have ...'

Mui said nothing. She met Lily's eyes sympathetically but firmly.

Lily said: 'You must do what you want. But won't we be splitting business in half?'

'No. Younger sister, we don't open a business like here. It's a restaurant. We open a fish and chip restaurant.'

Lily sat down heavily on the nearest pew.

'Of course we'll take Grandpa, if you wish. Lily, are you feeling all right?'

'Yes, of course.'

Mui continued: 'I am taking out citizenship. Naturalisation. This is my home now.'

'Don't worry, Mui. I can lend you money for this if you don't have enough.'

'No need, Lily.' Mui smiled. 'This isn't the way it's done. My aitchgevees are signing for me. Only needs four to sign. All of them want to sign! I have to be careful not to offend any.'

Mui poured Lily tea from the thermos. 'Husband has already left his job, by the way.'

'Would he like to live with us? Until you get your place? He must need money for rent.' Lily was determined to be as helpful as possible.

'No need. He is getting unemployment benefit.'

Lily's mouth opened.

'It is his *right*. Who else would look after him? He has paid money to the government for it.'

Lily judged it better to say nothing. But she was already feeling better. Mui had plainly lost all her bearings.

Mui said: 'I want to ask you a thing, younger sister, the thing closest to my heart. Come to live with my family.' Her voice was thick; her eyes prickled.

Lily shook her head soundlessly. Mui meant well. She was touched. But what was she talking about? She was in Lily's family, not the other way around.

Mui said, softly now: 'There is a place for you in my house whenever you want it.'

She thought: 'Lily needs looking after.'

Lily thought: 'Mui needs careful watching. I must take care of her.'

Mui said: 'What will you do? Business may be hard.'

Lily said the first thing which came into her head: 'I'll drive a bus!'

'Get licence first.' Then Mui suggested slyly: 'Do "meals on wheels" for old people, hah?'

They both burst out laughing.

And this was the end of the old life, the life of the loving, closely knit family Mui and Lily knew they had been. Mui might be living only ten minutes' walk away (fifteen in slippers, three in an expertly driven van); Man Kee might make frequent visits to his fond aunt, often go there straight from school, even sleep the night there (only after Mui had phoned anxious Lily). But distance, physical distance anyway, had nothing to do with the change in the amorphous but tough-skinned organism their family had been. There had been parturition, the single cell had contracted, swelled, and through the wall had escaped matter from its very nucleus. Now there were two cells, sharing the same territory, happily co-existing but quite autonomous.

And, later, Lily discovered there was nothing much to regret about this, not too much to be wistful about; or only in so far as it gave her something in common with Mui. For there were now no longer any reasons why she should get angry or jealous with Mui, even when Man Kee stayed with her, because this was just a gloss on the real definition of his life which was lived with her. Mui could now become a friend, an equal. Lily hesitated to put it that way but it was true; she had looked on Mui as an inferior to be scolded and bossed about for her own good. Now there could be the beginnings of comradeship. She was surprised Mui didn't seem resentful. In her place she would have been; she knew that.

What a nice man Uncle Lo was, too. Brother-in-law, as she must get more in the habit of calling him. So warm and considerate; he always had a nice smile and made a big fuss of you. He would be a good influence on Son, give him the man's example he needed, because she didn't want him growing up in an unbalanced home. *Yin* must have its excessive tendencies corrected by *yang*, and vice versa too for that matter. Mind you, he had some strange theories; that is, if they weren't really Mui's. One evening she motored round to pick Son up and found him coughing with a pale-yellow face. 'Feel all right, Son?' she asked with concern.

'Don't worry, Man Kee's mother,' Uncle Lo, Brother-in-law, said cheerfully. 'I just gave him a cigarette to smoke.'

'Why give him cigarette to smoke? Only seven-*sui* old! Bad to encourage this!'

'No, no.' He grinned. 'He'll never smoke another cigarette in his life, I assure you of that. That's the whole point of letting him have it.'

Wretched Man Kee – it made you feel queasy just looking at him – certainly seemed none too keen to embark on the adventure again. But what an odd idea of Brother-in-law's. It smacked of Mui to her, the old Mui. Quite a diplomat these days, Lily said nothing.

The remittances kept coming, regular as the beginnings of the months themselves. You could have regulated an almanac by the day they arrived. It was £10 cash every time. We Chinese know how to look after our own, she thought – and it was with warmth and pride which nearly obliterated the ugly fact that Husband had left them. Some people might say he had abandoned them here on this foreign shore, made her an 'autumn fan'. Sometimes Lily tried to probe the wound which, now she knew Husband was safe, was mainly to her self-esteem, but it hurt less and less. She felt guilty about this, tried to torment herself with her own imaginings, which worked at first, but came the day when thinking about this spot in her life no longer caused pain. And, later still, walking in a garden where the grass reached a waist which still showed no sign of thickening, stumbling into weedy vegetable patches which were still recognisable for what they had been, she realised she was content with what her life had become. She had loved, still loved Husband. She looked forward to the day he would return to her, as she knew with a certainty that passed beyond faith he would one day return to her. But in the meantime how light-hearted she could feel! Surely Husband hadn't weighed on her like that? He was such a quiet, self-effacing man. But it was as if a stone had been taken off her and she had sprung to what her height should have been. She thought she had found a balance of things for the first time, *yin* cancelling *yang*; discovered it not by going to the centre at once – which was a prude's way and untypical of her – but by veering to the extremes and then finding the still point of equilibrium. Man Kee was too young to understand this yet, even with his mind, let alone his feelings. But she could wait patiently for the day she could pass this knowledge, and other things, on to him. She might have lost Husband for a while but she still had Son. Who could take him away from her?

Author's Note

The ritual verses in Chapter Thirteen are drawn from Gustave Schlegel's *Thian Thi Hui, the Hung League* (Batavia, 1866), a collection of society documents and insignia discovered in the aftermath of rioting in the Dutch East Indies which were subsequently translated by a Dutch scholar.

The useful works of reference on the Hung family were: *The Triad Society* (Hong Kong, 1900) by William Stanton, a cashiered detective officer in the Hong Kong police force, and W.P. Morgan's outstanding *Triad Societies in Hong Kong* (Hong Kong 1960). The plural title of the last work is significant.

T.P.M.